D0287773

Daughters of Englai

Also by Philippa Carr

WE'LL MEET AGAIN

THE GOSSAMER CORD

A TIME FOR SILENCE

THE BLACK SWAN

THE CHANGELING

THE POOL OF ST. BRANOK

MIDSUMMER'S EVE

THE RETURN OF THE GYPSY

VOICES IN A HAUNTED ROOM

KNAVE OF HEARTS

THE ADULTRESS

WILL YOU LOVE ME IN SEPTEMBER

THE SONG OF THE SIREN

THE LOVE CHILD

LAMENT FOR A LOST LOVER

SARABAND FOR TWO SISTERS

THE WITCH FROM THE SEA

THE LION TRIUMPHANT

THE MIRACLE AT ST. BRUNO'S

DAUGHTERS
OF
ENGLAND

Philippa Carr

G. P. PUTNAM'S SONS   NEW YORK

G. P. Putnam's Sons
Publishers Since 1838
200 Madison Avenue
New York, NY 10016

Copyright © 1995 by Mark Hamilton
as Literary Executor for the Estate of the late E. A. B. Hibbert
All rights reserved. This book, or parts thereof,
may not be reproduced in any form without permission.

ISBN 0-399-14023-9

Printed in the United States of America

Contents

SARAH
1660–1678

The Waif and the Flight 3
Plague 36
Lost Illusion 62
A Ceremony in Knightsbridge 79
At Whitehall Stairs 112
Christobel 136

KATE
1678–1689

The Dower House 159
The Spy 189
The Devil's Tower 213
Francine 226
A Question of Marriage 249
Rebellion 275
The Return 302

SARAH

1660–1678

The Waif and the Flight

I FIRST SAW Kitty Carslake from the schoolroom window at Willerton House. She was walking across the lawn in the company of several young men and women. They were all laughing merrily together. It was a scene similar to others I had witnessed from the window, but this was different. Kitty was there, and she stood out among them all because she herself was different in some subtle way, which at that time I could not define. She fascinated me from that first moment, though I did not know then what an effect she was going to have on my life.

I had often looked from that window down on a world which was very different from my own. To me it was like a peep show, a glimpse into a way of life that was colorful and glamorous, a way of life of which I should never be part, so I had to be grateful to Maria Willerton for making glimpses of it possible.

I had been born on the Wiltshire estate of Sir Henry Willerton, by whom my father was employed as managing agent, on the thirtieth day of January in the year 1649, that very day when the King's triumphant enemies had cut off his head outside the Palace in Whitehall, in the sight of those who had gathered to watch. A new way of life had begun then, for the nation discarded its frivolous ways and was subject to the rule of the Puritans.

My mother approved of this; my father less so, but he was not a man to assert himself: in any case, we had to follow the law laid down by our rulers. So, no more frivolity, no more riotous living, no more flaunting ourselves in silks and velvets. Clothes were usually a somber black, with perhaps a white collar here and there; one must be humble, sober and God-fearing. As for children, they must speak only when spoken to. In those days I was led to believe that all the angels in Heaven carried notebooks that they might record each single sin committed by the unwary. Sin lurked everywhere and it was not always easy to recognize. That was the Devil's way of luring people to commit it and thus condemn themselves to burn in Hell forevermore.

It was a dismal prospect, but that was the atmosphere in which I spent my early years.

We had a comfortable house on the estate. There was always good, if plain, food on the table, for which we gave lengthy thanks to the Almighty before partaking of it. We had prayers in the morning on rising, and in the evening before retiring, which my father conducted.

I was an only child and that could have meant a lonely existence in a Puritan household; but I was always interested in people and had made some friends on the estate.

Sir Henry and Lady Willerton, to whom everyone referred as "The Family," were good to us. They did not behave as though we were their servants. This may have been due to their kind hearts or to the fact that this was an age of simplicity. In any case, many of the nobility had supported the King against the Parliament, and The Family must have felt grateful to have come through the conflict with their estates and dignity intact, and had no wish to call attention to their previous importance.

My father was often at the house, discussing estate matters, but he always went as a guest and my mother sometimes accompanied him.

There was a daughter of the house, Maria; and I was invited to share her governess, which pleased my parents, as it gave me an opportunity to acquire a better education than they could otherwise have given me. Frequently I was called upon to thank God for this blessing.

It was more than lessons I learned at Willerton House. Maria was a lively companion and she liked to impress me with her wisdom, and as I was only too ready to listen, we became good friends.

Through her I learned a good deal of the world beyond Wiltshire: and the years were passing.

Oliver Cromwell had died and his son Richard had become

Protector. Change showed itself in a hundred little ways. Rules became less rigid; there was a certain absence of solemnity. One heard people laugh more often. It was said that Richard was not like his father, which meant that he was not the same stern disciplinarian: he was kindly and well-meaning, but he lacked his father's strength, and a very strong man was needed to keep a race like the English in somber submission.

Maria, who was two years older than I, and never failed to remind me of that fact, said: "Something is happening. People are getting excited. There will be change."

"What change?" I asked.

"Just change. Everywhere. That is what people are saying. They would never have got it without war while Oliver Cromwell was there. But he has gone, has he not? Do you know there is talk of bringing back the King?"

I listened round-eyed. "He would not come here . . . to this house," I said.

"He might. Kings go round visiting. They stay in people's houses. We should go to court, and my brother . . ."

She was smiling, thinking of her brother. I had heard of him. His name was Rufus, and he was on the Continent with the exiled King. Rufus's story was very romantic. He was six years older than Maria, and she was very proud of him. When he was a boy, he had wanted to join the King's army, and at the age of sixteen he had left home and gone to France to be with the King.

Maria often talked of him.

"I remember he was always talking about the King, how he was hoping to fight to bring him back. He was so disappointed because he was too young to join the King's army. He really believed that if he had been old enough, he would never have allowed the Roundheads to win and King Charles would still be on the throne."

"And what is he doing now?" I asked her.

"I do not know. We do not talk of him. It would not be wise for people to be reminded that one of the family is now in France with the King."

It was small wonder that she was excited. I sensed Lady Willerton was too at the prospect of her son's returning in the train of the King.

"We shall go to London, you see," went on Maria. "After all,

Rufus will surely be in favor after all his loyal service. Everything will be different."

"How different?" I wanted to know.

"Nanny Tilling likes to talk about the old days. She has no love for Oliver Cromwell, nor his son. She is all for the King. She says what right have they to say, 'Go to church every day and twice on Sundays, and never have a bit of fun.' She says this to me, of course. She is careful of the others. You never know who's listening. She says we're not free like we used to be. You have to think before you open your mouth."

She was right about change coming. It was more apparent every day.

Tired of Puritan rule, no longer held in check by the mighty Oliver, and taking advantage of the slacker rule of his son, the people had their way.

King Charles was invited to return, and on one glorious day in May of the year 1660, King Charles II landed at Dover, come to claim a kingdom which was readily given to him by a people weary of Puritan rule.

England was determined to be merry again, and without delay enthusiastically set about it.

At that time I was eleven years old.

There was a great deal of entertaining at Willerton. The family were naturally delighted by the change. So were a great many people.

We heard about the welcome which had been given to the King in London. The people had gone wild with joy, singing and dancing, drinking his health, expressing in every possible way their rejection of the old ways and rejoicing in the new ones they expected now would come.

My mother shook her head gravely. They would pay for this, if not on earth, in the life to come. Disaster had come to England. The Devil and his minions were rejoicing while God and the angels wept.

I commented that, if God was all-powerful, He would soon send the King back to France.

My mother looked reproachfully at my father, reminding him that she had always questioned the wisdom of letting me go to the House.

"We thought it was a heaven-sent opportunity," my father mildly reminded her.

I knew that was true, and for once my mother could not deny it.

"They're going right back to the old ways," she said. "It seems the war did nothing at all."

"That is the way with most wars," said my father sadly.

My mother ignored that.

"The King was executed," she said. "That was meant to be an example, and the Lord Protector brought the country to God. And now it is going back, back to what it was before . . . and by the look of it, it's even worse. They say the new King does not lead a good life."

"He is very popular," my father reminded her, "and the people without doubt want him back."

"The people do not know what is good for them. They do not understand."

What my father understood all too well was that it was not only unwise but useless to carry on such an argument with my mother, so he said nothing more.

As for me, I liked the change. It exhilarated me, gave me a feeling of expectation. I thought it was wonderful to see people happy and not afraid to laugh. As for The Family, they certainly lost no time in reverting to the old ways before the coming of the Protectorate.

Sir Henry and Lady Willerton went to London. Their son Rufus had returned with the King, and came back to the parental home for a brief visit. He was a very grand gentleman in long wide breeches trimmed with lace. His hat was adorned with magnificent feathers, and he wore a wig, the curls of which hung about his shoulders. I imagined he was with the court, for he did not stay long at Willerton.

Maria was very excited and loved to tell me all about it.

"Rufus is with the King," she said. "He is having the most wonderful time. He will find a place for me at court, he promises."

It was two years after the King had returned when we heard that he was to be married. His bride came from Portugal. She was Catherine of Braganza, and my mother thought it was not a good match, for the bride was a Catholic. It should not have been allowed, she said. She was really uneasy about the King.

"He is very popular," insisted my father.

"Popular! If all accounts are right, he seems to be . . . profligate."

"You cannot rely on gossip," said my father.

Maria had already told me that the gossip about the King's life was based on a firm foundation. He made little attempt to hide the fact that Lady Castlemaine was his mistress, and that lady made certain that there was no doubt of it.

"The poor little Queen is very sad about it," Maria told me, "and although the King tries to be kind to her, he is so bemused by my Lady Castlemaine that he insists on her being one of those ladies close to the Queen, which of course means that *he* is never far from the lady."

"That does not seem to me to be very kind," I commented.

"No, but everyone likes him and is on his side. People make excuses for him. He is so charming. Lady Castlemaine is very beautiful, and the Queen . . . well, no one could call her attractive. It's natural, they say, and Oliver Cromwell is no longer here to make us feel we must not enjoy life."

When Maria was seventeen, the governess left and there was no longer an excuse for my going to Willerton as I had in the past, but Maria and I remained friends and, like her parents, she paid little attention to the difference in our station, and I was always welcome there. She liked to talk to me about the life which would be hers when she went to court, and of the people who now visited the house. I used to slip into the schoolroom and wait for her, and if she did not come I would go home. No members of the household took any notice of me when they saw me going up and down the stairs which led to the schoolroom. Thus I had a window on to another world, and watching those people became one of the great pleasures of my life at that time. I was, in fact, rather pleased when Maria was not there and I could observe alone.

It was due to this state of affairs that I had my first encounter with Kitty Carslake.

I knew there were guests at the house, and that the early afternoon was a time when many of them would be resting. I would slip into the house, up the stairs to the schoolroom and my vantage point at the window, and watch any who came into the garden. Perhaps Maria would join me, but now that she was seventeen she was often with the guests and was finding less and less time for me.

In the shrubbery there was a spot which I called the Dell. I had been attracted to it from the first. It was a little square shut in by the bushes. A gap in them made an entrance and was not very noticeable unless one knew where it was. There was an aura of privacy which appealed to me. I often sat there, for there was a convenient overturned treetrunk which served well as a seat.

One day, when I was speeding past the Dell, to my surprise I heard someone there speaking. I could not hear what was said, so I paused. It must, I supposed, be some of the guests. I did not want to be seen, for I had a notion that if my presence was commented on I might be prevented from coming. I listened.

To my surprise, it seemed that there was only one voice . . . a very musical one. I could not hear exactly what was being said, but it sounded as though this voice was reciting poetry. I crept closer. I was very near to the entrance of the Dell.

It was one of the softest and most mellow voices that I had ever heard.

> *What's Montague? It is nor hand, nor foot,*
> *Nor arm, nor face, nor any other part*
> *Belonging to a man. O, be some other name!*
> *What's in a name? That which we call a rose*
> *By any other name would smell as sweet . . .*

The voice stopped suddenly.

"Who's there?" it asked.

I stood very still. My impulse was to run, to hide if I could, but the owner of the voice would see me sprinting across the lawn and there was no place to hide.

She came out of the Dell and saw me. I looked at her in

amazement. She was the woman I had gazed at from the house. She looked more beautiful than when I had first seen her. Her hair fell loose about her shoulders, and her face was flushed.

She said: "Who are you? You are not the daughter . . ."

"No," I said. "I am Sarah Standish. I was coming to see Maria."

She started to laugh. She said accusingly: "You were listening."

"It was lovely," I told her. "I knew it. We did *Romeo and Juliet* the year before Miss Grey went. It did not sound quite like that when *we* read it . . . though the words were the same."

That made her laugh again. She was very friendly and not in the least upset because I had eavesdropped.

"I was perusing my lines," she said. "I am an actress, Kitty Carslake. I shall be on the stage in three days' time."

"How very exciting that must be."

"Do you think so?"

"I think it must be one of the most wonderful things in the world to be an actress."

"Stagestruck, are you?"

I looked at her in puzzlement.

She went on: "You'd be surprised how many people are, especially now that the theaters are flourishing again and for the first time women are allowed to appear on the stage. It is not always easy, you know. But one has one's moments. I tell you, I'm in a state of panic already, and it will be worse when the time comes nearer."

"You mean about playing the part? You seemed to be doing it beautifully."

"Others might not be as kind as you are."

"I wasn't thinking of being kind. I was only saying what I thought."

She smiled at me, then she laughed again.

"You must have wondered what sort of person you would find talking to herself and hiding herself away to do it."

"I thought there was someone with you, and that I should have to be careful lest I was seen."

"Should you not have been seen?"

"Well, I suppose it does not matter very much, but I always wonder whether I should be here. I am not one of them, you know. My father manages the estate."

"I see. And you are a friend of Maria's?"

"Yes. We did share a governess, but now that Maria is seventeen the governess has gone. But we are still friends."

"Is she expecting you now?"

"No. I just go to the schoolroom when I like. And if she is there we talk, and if not I watch the people from the schoolroom window."

I found I was telling her a great deal about myself. It was so easy to talk to her. I explained how I liked to see the people and how it had all changed.

She listened gravely, then she said: "Have you ever been to the theater?"

"No. I should love to go . . . more than anything."

"Perhaps you will come and see me one day."

"How I should love to see you as Juliet!"

"I believe you fancy yourself as an actress."

"I hadn't thought of that."

"I'll tell you what we will do. I should be practicing my lines. It is not easy without your fellow actors." She took a paper from her pocket. "Can you read well?" she asked.

"Oh yes, I am better than Maria really. So Miss Grey said."

"I have no doubt Miss Grey was right. Now listen. Here is the scene." She waved the paper. "You are Romeo, understand?"

I nodded.

"You see where he comes in. We'll do it together. You read your part and I'll come in with mine. Do you see what I mean?"

"Oh, yes . . . yes," I cried excitedly as I took the paper.

It was a magical experience. She looked so beautiful and she spoke the words as I had never heard them spoken before. I was caught up in the scene. For me she was Juliet in her balcony and I was Romeo looking up at her from below.

> *With love's light wings did I o'erperch these walls;*
> *For stony limits cannot hold love out,*
> *And what love can do that dares love attempt;*
> *Therefore thy kinsmen are no stop to me.*

I was living in enchantment. I *was* Romeo. This was not the Willerton shrubbery. This was Juliet's balcony. I had never experienced anything like it.

I stood very still, looking up at Kitty Carslake. She was gazing at me with what seemed like amazement.

She said slowly: "You were good. You were very good."

"It was lovely," I replied.

"I believe you are that unfortunate creature—a born actress."

"Did you say unfortunate?"

"Yes, I did. Perhaps I went a little too far. Perhaps some people find life unfortunate. No matter. But Sarah Standish, I believe you were born to act upon a stage."

She put her arm round me and kissed me lightly.

"There," she said, "that was for Romeo."

We sat down on the fallen treetrunk and she told me how she had always wanted to act and, when the King came back and the theaters were opened again, she had had her chance.

Then suddenly she cried out: "I must go. They'll be looking for me. Au revoir, Romeo."

I watched her running across the lawn. The dream was over. I was almost amazed to see that the Dell was merely the Dell. The Capulet house no longer stood there, and Juliet's balcony was the branches of a sapling.

Now that she had departed, she had taken the magic with her.

I did not tell Maria what had happened. I wanted to keep it to myself, but I did try to find out more about Kitty Carslake.

"Kitty Carslake," said Maria. "She would not have been asked but for Lord Donnerton."

"Why should she be asked because of him?"

"Oh, he is pursuing her. My father wanted to see Lord Donnerton on some matter . . . of business, I'll swear. He thought the best way of making sure he came was to invite this actress. Why are you interested in her?"

"Well, she is an actress."

"Not one of the really well known ones."

"I expect she will be . . . soon."

"How do you know?" But she was not really interested in Mistress Kitty Carslake.

A month or so later she was very excited because she was going to London. It was the most exciting place in the world, she told me. Everything happened there. The King himself was often seen strolling in the parks, and there were carriages everywhere, carrying elegant ladies and gentlemen to the theaters or the court.

"And while we are there," she added, "we shall go to the Donnerton wedding."

"Donnerton!" I cried. "Does that mean he is marrying the actress?"

"That is so," replied Maria. "She gave way in the end. I suppose it was irresistible. Actresses have a wonderful time while the people like them . . . but it might not be the same when they get old. Nobody wants them then. I reckon Kitty Carslake was lucky. Not every one of them marries into the peerage—and that is what they are all hoping for."

After that I thought of her often. I would enact that scene in my mind. I knew the words off by heart now. I thought: If she came again I could do it without the paper.

As if she would! As if she would remember! She had just been kind and she had used me to play the part of Romeo because there was no one else available.

Perhaps that might have been the end of my dreams if Kitty Carslake had not come back to Willerton. And this time she came as Lady Donnerton.

The first intimation I had of her presence there was when one of the boys from the Willerton stables came over to our house. I was very relieved that my parents were not there at the time when I heard that the messenger wanted to see me.

"I've got a message from Lady Donnerton. It's for you, Mistress."

He handed me a note on which was written:

> *Could you be at the Capulet balcony at three of the clock this afternoon? If so, I will be there to meet you.*
>
> *Kitty Carslake*

My heart was beating with excitement and the boy was watching me closely.

"Please tell Lady Donnerton that I shall be there," I said.

He sped away, leaving me somewhat bemused and overcome with eagerness to know why her ladyship wished to see me.

I was there before the appointed time. I had been telling myself she wanted me to rehearse something with her. I was immensely flattered that she remembered me.

She came and I was delighted to see that she had changed not at all, in spite of her grand title.

"I knew you'd come," she said. "Much has happened since we last met. I have become a ladyship!"

"Yes, I heard. Maria went to your wedding."

"A very grand affair, worthy of a high and mighty lord. Though there was much shaking of heads at his choice of bride—meant to be discreetly hidden, of course, from that unworthy lady."

"I do not believe that you are in the least little bit unworthy."

"Nor do I," she said with a laugh. "I guessed we would be of one mind on that point. Do you still think fondly of the theater? Of a surety you do. I see it in your eyes. I understand. There is nothing like it. The noise . . . the color . . . the elegance . . . the girls selling their China oranges . . . the people thronging the place . . . the apprentices and the like quizzing the grand ladies and gentlemen in their boxes. And then, of course, the actors and the stage . . . and the company. No, there is nothing in the world to compare with it."

"Now that you are a grand lady, do you miss being an actress?" I said.

Her eyes were a little misty, and she replied: "You sensed that, did you not? Yes, you knew it. Then I will tell you why I wished to see you. Up at the house we are going to do a little piece . . . a play."

"You mean here?"

"I suggested we should. It was at the dinner table last night. We talked of the stage. I said we could do something here. There is a dais in the ballroom which would do very well as a stage. I will take you into a secret, Mistress Sarah. I intended it to be. I came prepared. I had this little piece with me. It is very sim-ple . . . easy for those who know nothing about the theater. Lis-ten, my child. There is a part in it which is of interest. It is that of a little waif. Not the main part, but a good one. She is taken into a lord's house and the play shows what a difference she makes to everyone's life. Now, who should play the part of this little waif?"

She was looking at me intently. Then she began to laugh.

"Who," she went on, "but Mistress Sarah Standish? I have a romantic fancy that it is the beginning of a brilliant career."

I was speechless. I could not believe what she was hinting. It was not possible. I was letting my imagination run away with my good sense.

"I . . . ?" I stammered.

"Why not? I have already spoken to Lady Willerton. She is not averse. They are all excited about the prospect of doing a play. These house visits often result in a certain ennui for some guests. They are so predictable. One is so very much like another, and that is tiresome when one goes to so many. People aim to be a little different. So . . . our little piece will at least enliven the scene. They are all excited and I have said that you are the one to play our little waif. I told them that you had once rehearsed lines with me, so I was sure you could do it. And there was no one who could play the part. Maria perhaps, but she had no heart for it and is happy to pass it on to you. So no difficulties there. Will you take the part, Mistress Standish?"

"I am overcome," I stammered. "I do not know whether . . ."

She gave that easy laugh of hers. "That means you will. Then it is settled. Now, there is little time to lose. The play is only three nights away. Tomorrow is a rehearsal. I have a copy here. You will read it through and learn your part, and tomorrow at four of the clock you will come for rehearsal. Take this copy, study it. I want you to show me that I have not been mistaken in you."

"But . . . I do not know . . . I have never . . ."

"That is all part of the life, my dear. It is not all listening to an audience shouting 'Bravo, Madam Sarah.' It is learning parts, suffering that indescribable terror when the moment to go on stage arrives . . . and sometimes the audiences are not kind. This will be different. This is not the King's Theatre in Drury Lane, or the Cockpit. This is the home of Sir Henry Willerton where, if you give the worst performance ever seen upon a stage, they will give you some applause. They will be polite . . . always. Do not fear. It is a tryout. It is to amuse the guests who are very ready to be amused; and it will show me—to a degree—whether

I was right in my feeling that Mistress Sarah Standish will be an actress."

"It is so . . . exciting."

"So, you will do it, Mistress Standish? You will play the part?"

"Oh, I will, I will!"

"I knew you would want to. You are myself when I was your age. Even your name is right. Sarah Standish. I hear it on people's lips. Well, we shall see . . . soon. Learn your lines. Practice them every moment you can. There will be someone to prompt you, so do not let the fear of forgetting affect you. On the night, you will be that little waif. Are you happy? Delighted and a little frightened? Is that not so? It is as it should be . . . a mingling of the two . . . then you will get right into that little waif's skin; and, Sarah Standish, you will decide your fate which, remember, none can do but yourself. I preach. I always do, you know. It is because of my enthusiasm for my profession . . . and when I see someone who feels as I do, I rant, as some would tell you. Sarah, Romeo, and little waif . . . Good luck on the night."

When she had left me I sat for some time clutching the paper she had given me, staring ahead of me at those shrubs which on another occasion she had converted into Juliet's balcony; and I had never known such exhilarating anticipation before in my life.

When my mother heard that I was to go to Willerton House to perform in a play, she was disconcerted, and I greatly feared that she would forbid me to do so.

"Play-acting!" she cried. "It is doing the work of the Devil. It is against God's laws."

"Oh, come," said my father. " 'Tis not really so. 'Tis nothing but a little diversion."

"Flaunting herself on a stage!"

" 'Tis not really a stage. 'Tis only the Willerton ballroom. Sir Henry approves of it. 'Tis merely a game."

"Game!" snorted my mother. "A game of the Devil."

"Oh, come, Mildred. That is a little strong, is it not?"

"*I* do not like it."

"I do not see how we can forbid Sarah's going. Sir Henry would take it amiss."

It was the right approach. My mother, practical in the extreme, was fully aware of the advantages which came to us from my father's benevolent employer, and the folly of offending him. She deplored the way of life which the Willertons had taken up since the Restoration of the Monarchy, but, as my father pointed out to her, that was no concern of ours. It was a fact that almost everyone in the country had changed their way of life since then.

So, shaking her head and grumbling that no good would come of this, my mother did not persist with her objections.

As for myself, I was in a haze of wonder. I quickly learned my lines and went about feeling that I was indeed that little waif.

I had stepped into another world. Always before I had gone to Willerton House as the daughter of the estate manager who was there because of the bounty of Sir Henry and Lady Willerton towards the humbler folk. Now I was a guest.

Kitty Carslake was in control. She seized me as soon as I arrived.

"Ha! Here is our little waif. Have you learned your lines? Yes? We shall see. Now we have no time to waste. There is a dress rehearsal first. You will get into your waif's dress at once. There may have to be alterations and what is most important is your gown when you turn to grandeur. I have rifled Maria's wardrobe and have taken one of her gowns which I hope will be a near fit. Get to it. In there, my child. We are starting almost immediately and you are in the first act."

There were several people present. Maria smiled at me and lifted her shoulders, as though to say, "What next?"

I was hastened into a room by Kitty, who showed me the waif's dress and the other which I should wear later. She gave me a special grin.

"Good luck," she whispered.

I had never known such exhilaration.

The performance itself was like a dream to me. I felt this was what I was meant to do. When I stepped on to the stage, I *was* that little waif. I had a basket which was supposed to contain herrings. I called my wares as one or two of the players strolled past. Then came the moment when the elegant gentleman accidentally knocked my basket from my hand and I had to express my dismay. I heard a faint giggle from the watchers, but it was all real to me. I was nearly starving, and the gentleman had destroyed my hope of eating for the next few days.

"Bravo!" cried a member of the audience—a gentleman sitting in the front row. I was immersed in my part, but I was delighted.

Then I was changing into my beautiful gown—such a contrast to my rags. No herring basket now. I was having an effect on all their lives: on Kitty, who had the main part, of course; on her father, who kept forgetting his lines; and on the young lord who was attracted to Kitty; and she and he might not have overcome their misunderstandings and have regretted it all their lives but for the actions of the little waif, now as splendidly attired as any of them.

It was all highly sentimental, scarcely suitable for the London stage, but it was just the thing for a group of amateurs, and when it was over we stood hand in hand at the front of the dais while the audience applauded. I was standing beside Kitty and she suddenly pushed me forward. The clapping was loud and again I heard that shout of "Bravo!," and I believed it came from the man who had said it before.

This time I was able to see him. He was sitting in the front row of chairs, his arms folded. He looked straight at me and smiled rather roguishly, as though this was all something of a joke—which I suppose it was to the rest of them, though it was very serious to me. He looked very distinguished, but far from young. He must have been in his mid-thirties, and from my fifteen-year-old stance he seemed quite old. There was an air of authority about him, and he was one who would be singled out in a crowd.

As we left the stage, Kitty said: "There is to be a supper. I have sent a message over to your parents to tell them that you will be staying for that, and that they are not to worry, for someone will escort you home."

I was in a haze of happiness. I had never dreamed that anything like this could happen to me. Tonight I had learned something about myself. I wanted to be an actress, to play on a real stage in a real theater.

Kitty was smiling at me. I think she knew exactly what I was feeling. She was amused and I think rather pleased.

In my beautiful dress—which Maria had worn when she was in London—I felt just like one of these people. The dress had had to be altered a little, but not much, so that it fitted me perfectly. It gave me confidence. I felt I was an honored member of the company, especially when people told me how they had enjoyed my performance.

Maria said: "You were good. You should have seen your face when you lost the herrings! You made us all feel very sorry for you. We were so glad when Lord Whatever-his-name-was took you home. My word! You showed them all, did you not?" She laughed. "It was fun, anyway. People will be talking about it for weeks. My mother is very pleased. Everyone will be wanting to do plays in their houses."

Kitty was with me when we went into the dining room where, in addition to the main table, several small ones had been set too.

"We help ourselves, I believe, from the long table," said Kitty, "where the food is laid out. I'm hungry. I always am after a show. That's because I am too overwrought to eat beforehand. Lady Willerton was a good prompter, did you not think? And she needed to be! Your benefactor kept getting lost, did he not? I noticed you helped him more than once. You learned his part as well as your own."

"It was necessary," I replied, "in that long scene we did together in the first act."

"Oh yes, when the clumsy oaf knocked your basket out of your hand and told you his life story. You lived it, did you not? You believed every word of it. That is why you came over so well. You were really deep in it. Now, food."

Somebody was beside us. It was the man who had been in the front row and who had applauded so vociferously.

"I shall join you," he said.

Kitty laughed. "That is just like my lord," she said to me. "Never a 'May I?,' always 'I shall.' "

"It is better that way, I do assure you," he replied. "So I repeat that I shall take the liberty of joining you two young ladies for supper." He turned to me. "I was entranced by the play."

Kitty gave him a supercilious look. She said to me: "He is going to tell us that we outclassed Mrs. Betterton, and Mrs. Anne Marshall would have been mad with envy if she had seen the play tonight, that Thomas Killigrew will be determined to put on our little masterpiece and he will, of course, realize that none could play it as we did tonight."

"You take the words out of my mouth, Lady Donnerton," he said, "and your wit is equal to your Thespian talents."

"This is the way they talk in the circles frequented by my lord," said Kitty to me. "In the words of another playwright, 'Full of sound and fury, signifying nothing.' "

"I assure you, sweet Mistress," he replied, turning to me, "the lady maligns me." Then to Kitty: "May I have the pleasure of an introduction to our charming waif, now transformed by the happy matter of an overturn of her basket of herrings into a young lady who would grace the King's court?"

"This is Mistress Sarah Standish," said Kitty.

He bowed to me, his eyes twinkling and an expression of what I could not fail to know was admiration.

"And this," went on Kitty, "is Lord Rosslyn."

"I am enchanted," he said, looking at me.

As for myself, I was still in a state of exultation. This was how people behaved in court circles, I imagined. One would have to remember that they did not really mean what they said, but such flattery was very pleasant to hear.

"Let us take this small table," he said. "It will be pleasant to sup *à trois.* Pray be seated, ladies, and I shall see that we receive the necessary attention."

Kitty and I obeyed and he went off.

She was smiling at me. "I can see why you find this evening's entertainment amusing."

"I have never before known anything like it," I told her.

"You must not think an actress's life is all gaiety and attention from charming lords. It has its darker side."

"It was the play that excited me," I said. "This is just amusing and everything is so new to me."

"Those who praise you to your face often have a very different tale to tell when you are absent. But tonight you have had a glimpse of a kind of theater." She leaned on the table and looked at me very seriously. "*You* will be the one to make up your mind what you will do. If you are born to be an actress and do not use your gifts, you could spend a lifetime frustrated and regretful."

A man came to the table. It was Lord Donnerton.

"There you are, my love," he said to Kitty. "I was looking for you." He sat down beside Kitty and smiled at me.

"No need to introduce the young lady," he said. "Your performance was wonderful, my dear."

So this was the man whom Kitty had married and, if I had read her aright, she was already regretting have done so.

He went on: "Rosslyn is getting something for you, he tells me. He'll get one of the men to bring it over."

He was right. Lord Rosslyn soon joined us and with him was one of the serving men, carrying a tray.

It was a merry evening, although I did not understand some of what was said. They came from a different world from the one I knew and I had to realize, I told myself, that after tonight I might never have another glimpse of it.

Lord Rosslyn paid a great deal of attention to me and I noticed that Kitty was a little uneasy about that. I wanted to tell her that, although I could not help being delighted by it, I did not take his flattery seriously.

But there was something more than that on her mind. Kitty was not a happy woman.

The supper was over and people were beginning to move out of the dining room.

Kitty said: "I think it is time you were taken home, Sarah. Although your parents agreed to your staying for supper, they would not want you to be too late home."

"I shall escort Mistress Sarah," said Lord Rosslyn, and, turning to me: "Are you ready?"

"It is a very short distance from the house," said Kitty.

"I dare say I shall be wishing it were longer," said Lord Rosslyn, smiling at me.

I said: "It is very gracious of Lord Rosslyn to offer, but it really is not necessary."

"It is necessary for my pleasure," he said. "Come, Mistress Sarah, I shall take you to your home."

"You see," said Kitty, "I am right, am I not? What did I tell you? Never 'May I?,' always 'I shall.' Methinks my lord is a very forceful gentleman."

"As ever, Mistress Kitty, you have assessed the situation accurately."

"Get your cloak," said Kitty to me.

"I shall await you here," added Lord Rosslyn.

So, he would escort me home, I thought. Well, it was gracious of him. After all, he was a noble lord and I but the agent's daughter. I believed such distinctions were very important in the world of which I had just had a glimpse.

I said goodbye to Sir Henry and Lady Willerton, thanked them for a most enjoyable evening and told them that someone was going to escort me home.

They nodded, relieved, I was sure, to be free of the need to concern themselves with me. Lady Willerton told me how pleased she was that I had come, for I had contributed a great deal to the success of the play.

Lord Rosslyn was waiting for me.

"Now you shall guide me," he said, "and together we will undertake this perilous journey across the fields to your home."

"It is not very far and it was not really necessary for you to come."

"It is very necessary and I would not be deprived of it for a king's ransom. Come."

Kitty was beside us. She was wearing a black velvet cloak and her eyes were sparkling with mischief.

"Lady Donnerton," said Lord Rosslyn, and it was the first time I had seen him taken aback.

"The fancy took me for a little walk," said Kitty, "so I have decided to accompany you."

As I had guessed, life returned to exactly what it had been before the summons had come to act in a play at Willerton House.

The world seemed a very drab place now. I had to help my mother in the kitchen and learn the duties of a housewife. I was no longer a child. She would like me to marry in a year or so. My mother had the very man in sight. He was Jacob Summers of Runacres Farm on the Willerton estate. My father said that Runacres was the most prosperous of all the farms on the estate and the reason was that William Summers—father of Jacob, Thomas, David, Rebecca and Esther—was the best farmer in the district.

My father approved of the Summers family because of their skill in tilling the land; my mother because, like herself, they deplored the turn to what they called Licentious Living and adhered as firmly to the Puritan way of life as she did.

So she had chosen the eldest son of that dismal household to be my husband.

As for me, I considered the possibility with acute distaste. It was not that Jacob was unpleasant; he was a very ordinary young man, but I had found him excessively dull, even before that wondrous night. Now I regarded the prospect of spending my life with him as something not to be taken seriously for a moment.

Weeks went by. I saw Maria occasionally, but since we had ceased to be in the schoolroom together, our friendship was gradually fading. The Willertons were away a great deal. In fact, it seemed that they were rarely at home. I had begun to believe that that glorious adventure was an isolated incident in my life and I should never know the like again.

It must have been three months after that occasion when I heard that the Willertons were back at the House and there was once more entertaining. Foolishly, I hoped that there would be another play and I should be asked to perform. Several days passed. The house party would soon be over, for they rarely lasted more than four or five days, and the Willertons would then go back to their London residence, and here we should settle down to the old dull routine. I told myself I was a fool to have believed that playing the waif had been a turning-point in my life.

And then, as had happened on another occasion, a serving man came to the house with a note for me. My heart leaped when I saw that it was from Kitty. She wanted to see me at the Capulet balcony as before, she said. We could talk there.

Another play, I thought! A part for me!

Eagerly I kept the tryst, and with what joy I greeted her. I saw at once that she was different. Her expression was strained; she had lost weight and her face seemed a little drawn. The hopes I had harbored that she had come to tell me there was to be another play vanished.

I said: "Something is wrong."

She nodded. "Yes, very wrong. I am very uncertain. I thought of you. I have thought of you a good deal. You remind me of what I was . . . once . . . when I was about your age. All the opposition I had to face. Now I have to face a decision."

"And you want to talk to me about it!"

She laughed. Then she said: "I want to talk to you about something else."

She was staring straight ahead.

"What?" I asked.

"It seems to me that my position is not unlike yours. We are both prisoners."

"Prisoners!"

She was silent for a few seconds, then she went on: "Yes, prisoners—held captive by circumstances. We have come to a point in our lives when we have to make a choice. This way . . . or that? To accept what fate has given us or break out and make our own way."

I had no idea what she meant, and I must have looked very puzzled.

"Oh," she cried, "how foolish of me. I talk in riddles and you think I am crazy. Perhaps I am. Let me tell you something. I want to go back to the stage, but I am married to Lord Donnerton. Lady Donnerton could not be an actress, could she? The wife of one of the foremost peers in the land! You see, it could not be."

"Could it not?"

She shook her head. "There are rules . . . obligations. I should never have married him, Sarah."

"Why did you?"

She looked at me and gave one of her laughs, but this one was without mirth.

"Why does one do these things? He was very eager. I thought it would be foolish to go on refusing. I considered all the advantages. I told myself that one day I should regret it if I did not take this chance of wealth and comfort. He is a kind man. He would have looked after me always. But I cannot endure this life, Sarah. I am bored . . . bored . . . so hideously bored."

"So you are going to leave him and go back to the theater."

"I have to, Sarah. I want the excitement . . . that feeling that comes to you when there is a sudden hush, and the play begins. You understand?"

"I think so."

She turned to me, smiling. "I knew you would. Perhaps that is why I came. That . . . and something else."

She was biting her lips and staring ahead.

"When are you going back to the stage?" I asked.

"Soon."

"What does Lord Donnerton say?"

"He does not know yet. He has been good to me, Sarah . . . but he does not understand. He never will."

"No, I suppose he could not."

"But you do."

"Yes, I think I do."

"All you have seen is an amateur attempt on an improvised stage and people pretending to act for fun. Most of them would have been booed off the London stage in five minutes. But we kept it going, you and I between us, Sarah, and I think some of them actually enjoyed our little piece for what it was. Well, Sarah, you are an actress. That is why I am telling you all this. You know what I am talking about. Few would. Not the people I am now surrounded with, that is. They would think I was crazy, giving up a life of luxury for one of uncertainty. But I have to do it. Sarah, I'd rather die than go on like this."

"Then you must do it," I said.

She seized me suddenly and kissed me. I saw tears in her eyes.

"I am going to, Sarah," she said. "I am going back where I belong. Do you think it strange that I should come and talk to you like this?"

"I . . . I am not sure."

"I have been thinking such a lot about you."

I looked at her in amazement.

"Yes," she went on, "I have. You would think I had troubles enough of my own, and in a way they are linked. In you I see myself. I was always acting when I was a little girl. It was born in me, as it is in you. Of course, when I was growing up, there were no theaters."

"No. In my childhood neither."

"But you were young when the King came back."

"I was eleven."

"And now you are fifteen. It has worked well for you. I remember the day. There was rejoicing throughout the land. Not

with everyone, of course. But there were many of us who were
tired of being Puritans. We wanted some life . . . some gaiety.
The theaters were opened and women were allowed to appear on
the stage. When I heard that I came to London. My family were
against it. They wanted me to settle down and marry. I could
have done. There was someone very eager to marry me, but I
knew what it would be like. Prayers morning and evening. A
sober life, regular churchgoing, gloom and so-called virtue I could
not endure. And in London the theaters were open. I ran away
from home, Sarah. I came to London. I had a good friend who
helped me. She had always wanted to be an actress and I was
fortunate to have her. I cannot explain to you the wondrous feeling
of stepping on to a stage for the first time."

"I know it," I cried. "I know it well. I do not have to experience
it to know."

"It is because of what happened to me that I think of you. I
can see myself in you. I see you staying here. There would be no
easy way out for you. I feel a responsibility towards you. Does
that seem crazy?"

"No . . . no," I cried excitedly. "It seems good and kind and
caring."

"I am not sure about that. But I think you will never truly be
happy if you do not try that way of life for which you were born."

"How?" I cried. "How?"

"I told you I was going back. What would you think of coming
with me?"

A tremendous excitement was overtaking me. I was trembling.

"It is something not to be decided hastily," she said. "You are
very young. Perhaps I am wrong to suggest it. Yes, I am. I take
too much upon myself. Forget I said it. I just came to tell you I
shall be going away. You will not see me at Willerton House
again."

"No, no," I cried. "Please do not forget it. I want to hear
more. I must hear more."

She turned to me and smiled quite radiantly. Her moods
changed from extremes in a very short time. She was so volatile.
She was an actress, of course. I supposed that, in truth, she acted
all the time. It was second nature to her. Perhaps I was a little
like that myself.

She said: "Yes, of course, you must have your chance . . . just as I did. I believe I should never forgive myself if I did not do all I could to help you. Sarah, are you going to live all your life here? Imagine it. You marry, you bring children into the world, you keep house, you give orders to your servants, life goes by, quickly, colorless, predictable, like the past when it was considered a sin to smile. Sarah, are you going to live your life . . . regretting?"

"No!" I said vehemently. "No!"

"Then you are going to try your luck on the stage?"

"Yes," I said fervently. "Yes!"

She was smiling again. "Then . . . how?"

"You are going to tell me."

"You could come to London with me."

I stared at her in disbelief.

"Your parents . . . they would have to be told," she said.

"They would never allow it. At least, my mother never would. And the theater! She would think I was walking straight into Hell."

"Ah, there's the rub. How then, Sarah?"

"I only know they will never allow me."

"So you will 'let "I dare not" wait upon "I would"?' Then you are right to give up. What you will need in life, dear child, is something more than the natural gifts with which fate has endowed you. If you are to be successful there must be the determination to succeed. If you are going to turn away at the first hurdle, then, my dear Sarah, the best thing is to give up before you start. You need all the courage, all the willpower, everything you have, if you are to succeed in life and, believe me, one of the most difficult professions in which to succeed is that of the theater."

"Tell me what I have to do."

She looked at me steadily and I saw alarm in her eyes.

"Dear God," she murmured. "What have I done? I have meddled too far. I should have said nothing. She must work out her own salvation. What am I doing? I am acting God."

"No . . . no . . . you are kind. You are helping me. I am frustrated. I do not know what I should do."

"You must be sure of what you want, Sarah. You must think . . . think seriously. Is this a passing fancy? I detect something special in you, or so I think, something that tells me you are not just a stage-struck girl seeking excitement, having an idea that perhaps you will make a grand marriage . . . tired of life on this estate, with its occasional glimpses into a different way of living."

"I know in my heart," I said. "Please. Please help me. You understand what it means to me."

"Then," she said, "we must consider deeply and there is little time. Ask yourself. Is this thing vital to you? That is the heart of the matter. If it is, and you are old enough to know . . . as I did at your age . . . you must do all in your power to bring it to pass. Do you understand what I am saying?"

"I do. I want this more than I have ever wanted anything. If I missed it I should be unhappy for the rest of my life."

"If you are sure . . . and only then we will plan."

"Please . . . please . . . let us plan."

"Then you must come to London."

"With you?"

"Of course. And I shall be leaving soon. I have to tell my husband. He will be sad, but he will recover. It is a task I do not relish, but it has to be done. He will understand, I think. He knows I fret for the stage. My dear Sarah, you must tell your parents."

"If I do they will never let me go."

"They should at least have a chance of denying you."

"They would most certainly do all in their power to stop me. I believe they might well do so."

"Then we shall have to make careful plans." She looked at me steadily. "It will be your first test," she went on. "You will have to be ready to tackle all the difficulties which will await you. Your career will have to come first with you. If it does not, there is little hope for you."

"You believe that I should tell them, I see. I know they will refuse to let me go."

"The decision is yours, not theirs."

"You mean I should run away from home?"

"We shall have to see. It depends on your determination. If they tell you they refuse to let you go and you accept that, you will have made a great discovery. You would never succeed in overcoming the difficulties which you would have to face. Therefore it is better that you do not attempt them and that would be an end of the matter. We are staying at Willerton only a few more days. Before I leave we must have made our plans. You must speak to your parents without delay. I shall be here at this time tomorrow. Come here and we will plan how we shall go on from there. Sarah, be absolutely sure in your mind. There must be no shadow of a doubt—then and only then shall we plan together. Only you can know how deep this determination is within you."

"I know my mother will be horrified."

"But she must have a chance to consider. I am sure it is right to tell her. If she persuades you or you are afraid to tell her, you must be glad that you have discovered the shallow depth of your desire in time."

There was no doubt in my mind. Life had suddenly become full of expectation and delight . . . apart from the terrible ordeal which lay before me.

I let the day pass. I spent a sleepless night rehearsing how I should approach the subject. In the morning I arose exultant, yet filled with apprehension.

I had to see Kitty that afternoon, I had to, as she put it, have passed my first test by then.

I was very nervous; the time seemed to pass very slowly. Surely we were on our knees longer than usual that morning at prayers. Then they were over. Our two maids went to their work and my parents and I sat down at the breakfast table.

My father noticed my mood.

"Is all well, Sarah?" he asked.

I hesitated. Now was the moment.

I stammered: "I have been thinking of my future."

They were both attentive now and I went on: "I want to be an actress."

My father looked alarmed; as for my mother, she was staring at me in horror.

"An actress!" she said. "Whatever put such nonsense into your head?"

"It is not nonsense," I replied. "I am serious. I have an opportunity which I should be foolish to miss."

"Opportunities! Actresses! What are you talking about?"

"Please listen," I begged. "I know I can act. It is something people are born with, and if they have it they feel they must do something about it. They must use their talents . . . as it says in the Bible," I put in triumphantly. "You remember the parable of the talents. People are never happy if they do not use them. And so, as I have a chance . . ."

My mother turned to my father. "Do you understand this gibberish? What is the girl talking about?"

"I do not know," said my father. "Pray let her explain."

"Kitty Carslake, the actress, has been talking to me. She says I have talent."

"Oh!" said my mother. She looked reproachfully at my father. "This is what comes of play-acting. Did I not say that the Devil watches for the unwary? We should never have allowed it. Did I not say so at the time?"

"Nay, wife, we could not have objected at the time. It would have seemed like a criticism of Sir Henry and her ladyship."

"We should have refused to allow it, nevertheless. I told you so. Now look what's happened."

"It is a childish dream," said my father. "Young people have them at times. Not to be taken seriously."

"I like not this talk of play-acting. It is sinful. Actress indeed!"

"It is just fancy," soothed my father. "I tell you, it is not to be taken seriously. Now let us hear no more of the matter."

"I was telling you that I have had an opportunity which I do not want to miss," I said. "I am going to London."

"Is it Maria Willerton who is involved in all this?"

"If Sir Henry and Lady Willerton approve of Maria's —" began my father.

I said quickly: "It is not Maria. It has nothing to do with her. Mistress Kitty Carslake will take me to London with her. I shall have an opportunity to do what I want. I have a compulsion . . ."

They were both looking at me in horror.

"I do not wish to hear another word," said my mother. "Go to London with an actress! London is no place for decent girls, and actresses are certainly no fit company for them. I am surprised that Sir Henry has such people in the house."

"Some of them are highly thought of," ventured my father, but my mother gave him a withering look.

"I never heard such nonsense, or such impertinence," she said. "Our daughter . . . going to London . . . with an actress!"

"It was not seriously meant." My father looked at me pleadingly. "Was it, Sarah?"

"But it was," I insisted.

"I think you must complain to Sir Henry," said my mother firmly. "I do indeed. Sarah should go no more to Willerton if she is expected to mix with actresses."

"She is Lady Donnerton, in fact," I said.

"But she is an actress, you say. I am really most distressed."

I realized that I could not go into explanations, for if I did I should betray the unsatisfactory nature of Kitty's marriage. I felt frustrated in the extreme. But what else had I hoped for? I had known from the start that I should never go to London with their permission.

I had done what Kitty had said I must; and the reaction was exactly what I had expected. I must take the matter no further with them and pretend to accept defeat.

My mother continued to talk of the wickedness of the theater. Satan's playground, she called it. The breeding ground of sin. I was sure she was wondering how much damage had already been done in the eyes of God, merely by my being concerned in it. There would be prayers for my wayward soul for days to come, I was sure.

My father looked miserable. He hated such contretemps while my mother seemed to revel in them. As for myself, I felt a mild exhilaration. I had passed the first test. I had steeled myself to tell them and the result was by no means unexpected.

They would never agree to my going to London, and I was more determined than ever to go.

I met Kitty in the Dell and told her what had happened.

"I did not proceed with it," I said. "My mother made it clear that she would never give her approval to my becoming an actress. She called the theater 'the breeding ground of sin.' " I gave a rather hysterical giggle. "I know more than ever that I can never reconcile myself to such an attitude. Even if you had not made the suggestion, I should have to get away."

"And your father?"

"He might have been persuaded, but he is easily overruled. My mother is so sure that she is right and that God and she are of one mind and everyone who does not agree with them is the Devil's own. You would have to know her to understand how it is."

"I understand full well. What did you tell her?"

"That you had offered to take me to London. Then I wondered whether I had said too much."

She shook her head. "Everyone will know that I am leaving my husband. As soon as this visit is ended, I shall be gone. What shall you do?"

"Tell me what I must do."

"If you have decided to take this chance, you will have to leave your parents' house soon. They will try to stop you and if they do I doubt if you will ever find it easy after that. You must let them believe that your desire to go was just a childish dream. Say no more about it to them. Listen carefully if they tell you how childish it was to have such notions and appear to accept what they say. That should be simple. You are an actress, remember. Then I shall make plans. Someone will come to take you to London. You must leave discreetly. You will bring a few clothes with you, but not much . . . just what you can easily carry. I will give you more details when I am ready. If at any time you change your mind, you must let me know. There is a serving man at Willerton. His name is James. He works in the stables. He brought my notes to you before. He will get a note through to me should you change your mind and by him I will send instructions to you. You will have a little time to think about it and all it means. You must consider very carefully, for this is a great step which will change your entire life. You must be absolutely sure that you want this more than anything else. You must reflect that you are giving up a life of comfort, if dull. You are not content with it, I know, but you have to realize the hazards of the life you are choosing."

"I have. Oh, I have."

"You must be sure."

"I am sure."

"There is this respite. Remember that, until you have left, there is time to change your mind."

Then followed one of the strangest periods I ever lived through. Kitty's seriousness had communicated itself to me. It was indeed a gigantic step for a girl of fifteen to take. I fancied there were times when Kitty was terrified of what she had set in motion. I was too. The thought of leaving my home and family was alarming. I was fond of my father, but I had always been a little impatient of the way he allowed himself to be governed by my mother. As for my feelings for her, I could not honestly say that I loved her. She was too censorious of almost everyone except God; and in her mind they were always in agreement. No, I could not say, in truth, that I should regret leaving her, but I could not help wondering what effect my departure would have on her. She would rage against my wickedness, of course, prophesy the evil which would befall me in this life, while the fires of Hell awaited me in the next. I might even say that, apart from everything else, I should be relieved to escape from her. My father, though, would be very saddened, I knew. He would reproach himself for not paying more attention to this obsession of mine. I believed he would be unhappy and that made me pause.

But I had to go. That was becoming more and more clear to me as the days passed.

I waited for news from Kitty. It came in a letter delivered to me by James. He waylaid me and caught me as I was coming out of the house.

"I have a note for you from Lady Donnerton," he told me. "I have to go up to London on business for Sir Henry and I can take a letter back. If you come to the place you know in the grounds tomorrow afternoon at three of the clock I shall be there."

The letter he handed me confirmed the arrangements. In it she wrote:

I have left Lord Donnerton. He is very sad, but he is old and it is not the same as an ardent young man. I am thankful for that. I now have a house in London which I share with a friend of long standing. You will join us for a start.

Now we have to plan carefully. I take great risk in writing thus to you, but I could see no other way. You must destroy this letter as soon as you have read it. Letters have a habit of going astray and James may have been seen handing it to you. You will be picked up and it will have to be at night. A carriage will be waiting for you at eight of the clock on Friday night of next week close by the copse in the road leading to the house. It will be partly hidden by the trees and bushes there. You must hurry to it and get in. Then it will set off for London. You must not be seen leaving the house. Only Heaven knows what trouble there could be if we are discovered. You can still change your mind. Write to me. James will bring a letter.

You must be sure that it is what you want to do.

Kitty

I read the letter several times before I destroyed it.

Then I wrote to Kitty and the next day gave the letter to James.

With the passing of each hour doubts came, but never for long. Was all this on account of one amateur performance, I asked myself. But Kitty knew there was a spark of talent in me. She must be right. She herself was a professional actress.

I wished I had someone to talk to. If only I could see Kitty! But there was no one. Maria was not a great friend. We had never been close, even at our most intimate. I wondered what her opinion would be of this project. She would think I was crazy. I supposed most people would—except Kitty and myself and those who understood.

I looked at all the familiar things: my bed, with the picture of Jesus over it . . . one of the sad ones with the crown of thorns on His head. It had always frightened me a little. It was a continual reminder of His suffering. I would rather have had Him walking on the water or having His feet washed by Mary Magdalene.

I saw it all afresh—the house with its plain necessities and no concession to the luxury which would be sinful in my mother's eyes. Our home had not changed with the times.

Yes, I was stifled here. If I failed to undertake this adventure I should be unhappy forever. I had to do this. It was the only way. That was something I was sure of.

The last day came.

I had to overcome my urge to talk to someone. If only I could see Kitty! But I should soon be with her. I *was* going to take this tremendous step. I knew it was right for me.

I had put a few things together in a small traveling bag. We had chosen the right time of the year. It was September and the nights were drawing in. It would be dark almost by seven of the clock. In a few weeks' time it would have been entirely so, but the weather might not have been so good for traveling if we had waited. Still, you cannot have everything in your favor.

The day seemed endless, but at last it was half past seven. At ten minutes to eight I would have to slip out of the house. I should be wearing my cloak and carrying my bag—and if I were seen everything would be ruined.

My heart was beating wildly as I cautiously came down the stairs and slipped out of the house. Now I made the perilous journey across the grass to the shelter of the trees.

I went along the road. I saw the outline of the coach. The two horses were pawing the ground, as though with impatience to be gone.

I ran to it. The door was flung open. I threw my bag in and stepped in after it.

I heard Kitty's laugh, and I fell into her arms.

Plague

AS THE COACH rattled through those country lanes, the enormity of what I had done dawned on me afresh. Now that the excitement of planning escape had passed, I was realizing that I had left the security of my home for a new life with someone I scarcely knew. I had allowed myself to believe that I could be a successful actress on the strength of one amateur performance in a country house. It was, I kept reminding myself, a belief shared by Kitty.

I glanced at her sitting beside me. She was quiet, immersed in her own thoughts, which must be running along the same lines as mine. She had left a husband who was kind to her, a life of ease and security. The thought that we had both faced a similar decision comforted me.

As we approached London, the excitement returned, dispelling uneasiness. New experiences would soon be crowding in on me.

London itself—waking to the morning. Already people were in the streets: stalls were being set up; wheelbarrows containing all sorts of produce were trundling along. People were shouting to each other in an accent unfamiliar to me. There was a stirring activity which I guessed would grow with the day.

Kitty pointed out streets and places which I had heard talked of. We passed through Long Acre which, before the reign of Charles I, had been a thoroughfare where people took their walks on Sundays and holidays. There was Covent Garden itself, of which I had heard so much. Who had not? I knew that it was so called because it had been the convent garden of the Abbots of Westminster and that they had buried their dead there.

And there was Drury Lane and the theater itself.

It had been newly built since the Restoration and was known as the Theatre Royal. That other theater, the Cockpit, had been in existence much longer. Kitty told me that once the Puritans had burst in when a play was in progress and broken up the stage and seats and taken the players prisoner, parading them through the streets before thrusting them into the Gatehouse Prison.

And here was my new home, in a small cobbled courtyard close to the Covent Garden Piazza. It was one of a row of six tall narrow houses.

Kitty jumped out of the coach and I followed.

"Maggie will be waiting for us," she said.

I had heard about Maggie Mead. She would have liked to be an actress, but since women then did not appear on the stage, she had married soon after she came to London. Her husband had died quite ten years ago, leaving her, as she said, "comfortable," so that she did not have to go on scratching a living and wondering where the next meal was coming from.

"Maggie was my friend in the early days," Kitty told me. "She is the best friend I ever had. She has this house near Drury Lane, and when I was out of luck I went in with her. We get on well, though you might not always think it. Don't be put out if she goes for you now and then. She may be somewhat bristly outside at times, but underneath there's a soft heart. She knows about you and she thinks you ought to have your chance. Martha has been with Maggie, looking after the house, for years. They fight sometimes too, but they think the world of each other. Little Rose is there too. She's a comparative newcomer. Starving on the streets she was when Maggie found her. She brought her in, fed her and put her to work. Rose thinks Maggie is the Angel Gabriel and the Pope—she's a Catholic—all rolled up in one. Well, that's the household."

So I was prepared.

The door had opened and I had no doubt that the woman who confronted us was Maggie. She was big and commanding-looking—some fifty years of age, I guessed, red-haired and strong-featured.

"So you're here," she said. "About time."

"It was a long journey, Mag."

"I know that. Come in. So this is Sarah. H'm. Little scrap of

a thing. Bless you, child, you're cold. Come to the fire. There's
a pot boiling and I reckon a dish of soup is what you need."

"We're tired out," said Kitty. "That coach! How it rattled! I
feel that all my bones are broken. Let us get in first."

"You need that soup," said Maggie; and I knew then that we
should have it before we were allowed to do anything else.

Martha came in with a tray and we sat down and took it without
further preamble. It tasted delicious and I felt better for it.

"Don't suppose you slept a great deal during the night," said
Maggie.

"Hardly at all," replied Kitty.

"Then it is bed. Rose has put in the warming pans so you'll
be comfortable. Next you'll get up there and have a good sleep.
Then we'll hear all about it."

"Don't rush us, Mag!" said Kitty.

"Who's rushing? You'll be fit for nothing till you have had a
good sleep. The girl needs it. Look! She's dropping with ex-
haustion."

Her eyes were on me and I smiled wanly.

"Come on," said Maggie. "Upstairs. Do not think about anything else. Do as I say."

I knew she expected immediate obedience and she had it. I
imagined she always would. She was right. I guessed she always
was that, too.

Those first weeks in London are like a hazy dream to me now.
The big city of which I had thought so often in the old days was
unlike anything I had ever imagined. The streets, which were full
of bustle and noise, amazed me. I was entranced by the tradesmen
and -women who paraded the streets, shouting of their wares,
from hot pies to pins, describing the latest executions and scandals
which were chronicled in the sheets of paper they flourished.
These tradespeople, the beggars, the fine gallants and those aping
them: they all jostled each other in those streets. I liked to see
the grand ladies and gentlemen riding in their carriages, elabo-
rately dressed, the men no less than the women, their wigs—

masses of luxuriant curls—showing under their feather-decked hats.

Maggie commented that it was better than it had been in the old days when, if a girl had a pretty face, she had to keep it out of sight as much as possible, though now they had all gone to the opposite extreme and wanted to show more than their faces.

"It's always the way," she added. "Push people back too far and they'll come prancing too far forward as soon as they get the chance."

I was fascinated, but most of all, of course, by the theater. As I sat in that wooden building, in the pit, which was far from comfortable and indeed rather draughty, for there was no heating save that which came from the press of people—and that could make it too hot—and as I looked up at the glazed cupola and watched the people around me shouting to each other, gazing up to the boxes filling with fine ladies and gentlemen who looked down with disdain on those in the cheap seats, I knew that I had been right to come. And when the play began, that was utter enchantment.

In the beginning, the prospect of how I was going to find my way on to the stage had not yet struck me, for in those first weeks of settling in, there were so many new experiences that I found it difficult to absorb them all.

Within a few weeks of our return, Kitty was offered a part in *Rule a Wife and Have a Wife*.

Maggie Mead, from the first, had treated me as though I was no stranger to her—just another member of her household to be kept in order.

She told me: "Small wonder Kit got the part. People come to see her, not the play. That's how it is, Sarah. You'll learn. Scandal of a sort. The girl who left a lord for the stage. See what I mean?"

"How do they know?"

"The Lord have mercy on you! Sarah, you're a babe in arms in this world of ours. They know everything that goes on every minute of the day, these people. They live in the big city, do they not? They're alive to it all. They would tell you whom the King slept with last night if you asked them."

"I would not dream of asking any such thing!" I said in horror, which made her laugh.

"You'll soon be just like the rest of us, dearie. It will not take much time, I'll swear. The fact is that Kitty got the part because Charles Hart knew that she would bring them in. And she has. I'll swear to you that half the people in the theater tonight have come to see Kitty, the girl who gave up a lord for the stage."

I realized she was right, as she always was.

During those first weeks, Maggie, having taken me under her wing, gave special attention to me. She was a woman to make quick decisions and she had taken a liking to me. This was how it must have been with Kitty. But she considered that my youth and innocence needed special care. I did not realize then how fortunate I was in this.

She introduced me to London. She took me shopping with her and I was able to listen to her bargaining with the stall-holders. She was expert at making a bargain and at the heart of this was a certain bantering belligerence.

"Never let people get the better of you," she advised. "Go in and fight them. But never go into battle if you think you are going to lose. That's no good. You'll falter and fail at the next one you undertake."

It was indeed like a battle, and I never saw her beaten, yet she always parted with her opponents on the best of terms. They clearly had a great respect for her.

She talked to me a great deal about the theater. She loved it, but she had the sense to know that she would never have been a great actress.

"I hadn't the figure nor the face for it," she said sadly. "It's no good having what is necessary in parts. You've got to have it all. Mind you, all actresses don't have to be beautiful. Some are so good at the game that they can make you think they are. Well, I'd never have been good enough for that and time was against me. I lived at the wrong time. All that down on your knees every few minutes, reminding yourself how humble you are . . . miserable sinner and so on . . . never daring to laugh, for that was something that was going to send you straight to Hell when your time came. I was in my prime when the Puritans closed the theaters and all that was going on, and that was not the life for me.

"Then the King came back, God bless him. But why in the name of all that is holy did he not come back ten years before . . . or better still, never go at all? That would have suited Mistress Maggie Mead very well, that would. But alas, the good times came too late for her."

One day Kitty came home from the theater and said: "The King is coming to the theater on Friday. Many from the court will be there. The Queen will be coming with him, they say, so it will be a really formal occasion."

"To see you!" cried Maggie.

"No. They are putting on *The Humorous Lieutenant* for him—a special performance. There's no part for me in that."

"That Beaumont and Fletcher piece!" said Maggie in disgust. "They could have chosen something better."

"The play will be of small account. The theater will be full to overflowing."

She exchanged glances with Maggie and they both looked at me.

"Then we should add to the overflow," said Maggie. "What think you? It will be an opportunity for our girl to see His Majesty."

"Do you really mean that we shall be there?" I gasped.

"You could scarcely see him if you were not," retorted Maggie.

"So you want to go, do you?" Kitty asked me.

"Of course she wants to go," Maggie said. "And if she didn't I'd make sure she went all the same."

We were all laughing, and Kitty asked Maggie if she remembered the occasion when they had seen the newly married Queen in the King's Theatre with the King, and Lady Castlemaine had been there, scowling at the royal pair all the time.

"It was something I shall not forget in a hurry," said Maggie. "Everyone was waiting for trouble to start. Lady Castlemaine was capable of anything, and she was furious that the King should pay more attention to the Queen than to herself . . . even though it was only done for form. And the poor little Queen did not know anything about it. That was before she discovered her ladyship's position in the royal household."

They went on recalling little incidents from that occasion, and laughing immoderately at what seemed to me far from a laughing matter . . . especially for the Queen.

It was something I shall always remember: my first glimpse of the King and Queen. Excitement was great in the theater that night. It was full. I sat tightly wedged between Maggie and Kitty. We had come early to make sure of our seats, and I was glad of that when I heard the angry shouting from outside from those who had been unable to get in.

Everyone kept glancing up at the royal box, as yet unoccupied.

Then the nobility started to arrive, and there was a buzz of excitement when some notable figure appeared.

Maggie nudged me. "That's my Lord Rochester. Just look at him! He's one to be wary of. The greatest rake at court, and that says a good deal." She put her head close to mine. "I'll tell you more of him at some time. And look who's with him. The Duke of Buckingham himself! And there's Sedley and Savile . . . the wildest fellows in the land. Any girl would be wise to keep clear of them, what say you, Kit?"

"I should say that, as usual, Mag, you are right."

Now a hush had fallen over the company, for the King was coming into the theater.

My eyes, in common with everyone else's, turned to the royal box. The King had entered. So tall was he that he dwarfed most of those near him: he was dark-skinned and his features were heavy; he might have looked almost saturnine but for the smile which lit up his face with an indescribable charm. There was an innate grace about him and a dignity which was so natural that it was almost disarming. I could see in that first glance why he had effortlessly won the people's affections.

"Long live the King!" cried someone; and there was a burst of applause.

Beside him was the Queen. She seemed very small and rather plain, though she smiled charmingly, and the King had taken her hand as though to remind her—and us—that the loyal greeting was for her as well as for himself.

He sat down and just at that moment there was a certain bustle in the theater. Someone else had arrived.

All eyes were on the newcomer. He was young; I imagine not much older than I was. With him was a man a few years older. He was most elegantly dressed and in a manner which called attention to his importance. He lifted his face to the royal box. The King was looking straight at him. The young man gave an elaborate bow and the King lifted his hand in acknowledgment and smiled.

"Who is he?" I asked.

"Mr. James Scott or Crofts or Fitzroy some short time since, and now if you please Baron Tyndale, Earl of Doncaster and Duke of Monmouth," Maggie said. "The airs and graces indeed! And His Majesty looks on and smiles. Well, he's a handsome boy and proclaims himself the King's own son. Nor does His Majesty deny the charge."

This was indeed an exciting night.

And then, among the crowd, I saw a face I recognized. The young Duke of Monmouth had turned and spoken to a tall, dark man. They laughed together. I was taken aback, for I had recognized the man at once. He was Lord Rosslyn.

I said to Kitty: "Did you see? Was that not Lord Rosslyn who was at Willerton when we did the play?"

"It was indeed," she said. "I believe his lordship spends a great deal of time at court."

The play had started. Few in the theater were much interested in it. All eyes kept straying to the royal box.

After that visit to the theater I was all eagerness to hear about the people I had seen. Kitty and I spent a great deal of time together; she was learning a new part and I was often called upon to rehearse with her. This I enjoyed. It brought back vividly my first experiences at Willerton. It was the next best thing to acting on a stage.

I was often Maggie's companion too.

I said to her one day: "Maggie, do you think I shall ever have a part? Please tell me the truth."

"You must not be so impatient," she said. "Parts do not lie like stones by the wayside to be picked up when needed. Kitty does her best. She watches for you all the time. It will come." She looked at me intently. "You want this with all your heart, do you not? You must be watchful. Some might offer you a part and want payment. There are such men. Indeed, they abound. No, my child, not that way."

"I do not know what you mean."

"Then you will understand. Many have climbed by way of the bed, my dear, but I would not have that for you. You have talent. There is some respect for those who do not resort to such ways. Kitty says you have enough talent without that. You shall not do it that way."

"Is there another way?" I asked anxiously.

She looked at me sharply. "Some have found it, and if some, why not others? It is the only way for you. All you need is one chance. It will come, I know."

"It seems so long."

"I tell you, you are impatient. It is luck you need, that is all. You must be there . . . ready to snatch it when it comes. That is the way to live. Be patient. You are young. There is time ahead. Kitty and I want you to proceed with dignity. Do you understand?"

"You have been good to me."

"And you do not wish you had not left your home that night?"

"I have never felt that."

"Then pray God you never will."

Then she started to tell me about her own life in that Puritan household where she had been brought up. I could share with her the sensation of stifling restrictions such as my mother had imposed on ours, and I knew that as I grew older I should have found them intolerable.

No. I had no regrets, even though my dreams of startling the theatrical world had considerably modified. I was growing more fond than ever of my new life; and Kitty and Maggie were closer to me than any people I had ever known.

The theater was my goal and although so far I had only glimpsed it from afar, one day it would dominate my life.

Maggie talked a great deal about the theater and the happiness which the return of the King had brought to her and many others.

"It was a glorious day," she said, "that twenty-ninth of May, his birthday. He was thirty years of age then, and think of all those years when he had been wandering about the Continent, a homeless exile and the King of England! What a welcome they gave him, and no wonder! There was the cavalry and soldiers on foot, their swords shining in the sunlight, and people shouting their joy; there were flowers on the path; they had cloth of gold hung from the windows and there was wine flowing from the fountains! It was a delight to see, I can tell you! There were the noble lords in their finery which had been hidden away all those years, bells ringing, people cheering. Oh, there never was such a day! I stood there watching, thanking God for it and knowing it had come too late for me."

"So he came back," I said, "and one of the first things he did was reopen the theaters."

"Ah yes, that's true. He hadn't been back more than two or three months when he called Thomas Killigrew and Sir William Davenant to tell them to set about creating two theaters. One was to be the King's and the other the Duke's—the Duke's being that under the patronage of the King's brother, the Duke of York. Not only did His Majesty command the theaters to be built, he assisted them in every way. I remember seeing the production of *Law Against Lovers*. It was the old *Measure for Measure* altered, with the characters of Beatrice and Benedick brought in from another play. It was a sight to see, because the King and his brother the Duke and the Earl of Oxford had given the actors their coronation suits which they were able to play in. That shows how the King feels about the theater. Oh, why did all this have to happen so late! If it had come even ten years before it might have been some use to poor old Maggie Mead."

"Maggie," I said, "I think you are happy as you are."

"One thing you learn in life—or should, for some never do—is to take what you can get and make the best of it. I've had Kitty to look after and Martha to keep happy and there is little Rose. I've got a lot to be thankful for and now I've got you, and we are going to see you get that fame and fortune which might have been mine if the King had come home earlier, or better still never gone away."

"You love being here, do you not?" I said. "Close to the theater, looking after Kitty. How did you feel when she went off to marry Lord Donnerton?"

"I thought it could have been good for her. It might have been. Donnerton was a steady sort, and I was glad he was not some young rackety Jack. He was fond of her, too. She'd have been settled for life, and a ladyship too."

"What did you think when she left him?"

"I thought she was being foolish, throwing all that away. But I understood. After all, she was one of us. She had to come back."

"Could she not have stayed with him and been on the stage?"

"She did not think so. Perhaps it was more than just coming back to the stage. Perhaps it was her noble husband from whom she wanted to escape. What shall I say? Kitty would know and I fancy she is not telling. I should have thought she was lucky to get a faithful husband. When I look round at some of these young bucks . . ."

"Like those men we saw in the theater?"

"That was a good assembly, was it not? And all because the King was there. A company of—"

"Rackety Jacks?" I suggested.

"There you have said it. Rochester, was it not? Sedley, Sav- ile . . . you could not find many to match that little bunch."

"Does the King not reprimand them?"

Maggie laughed. "He finds them amusing. Their wit forgives them a great deal in the eyes of the King. Rochester is a particular favorite and one of the King's closest associates, although he is about seventeen years younger than His Majesty and the King twice his age. That young man is continually up to some villainy. The King reproves him and the next day will be walking with him and they will be seen laughing together. Rochester is a very merry man, and witty in the extreme. But he is a poet of rare ability; he is devoted to literature and there is none that can pen a couplet with his skill. The King seems to find such men irre- sistible."

"I am glad I saw him. He is certainly a most distinguished- looking gentleman. And what of that other who was present— the Duke of Monmouth?"

"Ah, that's a different story. There could not be two men less alike than Rochester and Monmouth, and the King—for different reasons—dotes on them both. I doubt whether Monmouth would aspire to being the King's companion but for one thing. Monmouth is the King's son."

"But . . ."

"It is all very irregular, but thus is the life of His amorous Majesty. The King finds the society of ladies irresistible and always has done since he was a very young man traveling from court to court on the Continent of Europe—an exile from his country, waiting for the time when he could regain his throne. And of course there were women, and one of these was a Welsh woman, Lucy Walter. She was the same age as the King. Her home, which was said to be a castle, had been destroyed by Oliver Cromwell's men. She was about fourteen years of age at that time and she came to London to seek her fortune and to live the best way she could with what she had to offer. She was not noted for her intelligence, but she had a certain bold beauty which might attract some provider. London was not the best hunting ground at such a time, so she crossed to The Hague, where a number of the English nobility had taken refuge—among them the King. He was not her first lover, but he was very taken with her. It was said of her that, in addition to her exceptional good looks, she had a certain cunning, and Charles, being young and already showing signs of his intense need of female company, was entranced.

"The association lasted for some time. I have heard it said that she accompanied him to Jersey. Her son had been born and the King accepted him as his. None could doubt that now. Monmouth, though certainly far more good-looking than the King, undoubtedly has a look of the Stuarts. Well, when the King went to Scotland, he left Lucy at The Hague. I do not know much about Lucy's adventures after that, except that her association with the King was over and that she took other lovers, then returned to England. When she arrived, Cromwell had her arrested and sent to the Tower . . . but not for long. It was decided that she was too insignificant to be dangerous and her association with the King was in the past. She was freed, returned to the Continent and soon afterwards died. The King, aware of his obligations to his son, put the boy in the care of Lord Crofts and Monmouth was said to be related to him. He was educated as a gentleman of noble birth, and two years after the King was back in England. James Crofts, as he was then, was given apartments in the Palace."

"So everyone knew then that he was the King's son?"

"Yes. His looks betrayed that, if nothing else, but young James Crofts was determined to remind people who he was at every turn. This amused the King and only last year he was given the grand titles of Baron Tyndale, Earl of Doncaster and Duke of Monmouth. This son of Lucy Walter had become a Duke. You can understand why he cannot forget it and tries to make sure that no one else shall."

"And so he came late to the theater, when everyone else was seated."

"He must make his entrance, of a surety. This is characteristic of this young man. He wants everyone to know that he enjoys special privileges. So he comes late, bows to the King and receives a warm *paternal* smile. You understand?"

"I do."

"This is not such a simple matter as you might think. You see how it is. The King has no legitimate son. Well, of course, it is early yet. But the Queen has miscarried. There is this failing with royalty—an inability to get male heirs. Charles the Martyr was fortunate only in this one respect. Not so our present King. Strong, most certainly capable, he has several bastards, but no legitimate child. The heir to the throne is the Duke of York. And there are rumors about the Duke."

"I suppose there are rumors about all people in high places."

"Their relationships with women, you mean. That is light-hearted gossip and the people love those who provide it. And even those who are shocked enjoy their disgust. But I speak of a matter which could affect the whole country. The Duke of York is flirting with the Catholic faith and the people of England are determined never to have another Catholic monarch on the throne. They still talk of Bloody Mary and the fires of Smithfield. Three hundred people were burned at the stake in her reign. And although many more were tortured and put to death in Spain by the Inquisition, this is England. Never again, they said."

"But we have our Catholics."

"Therein lies the danger. But there are many here who would stand firm against a Catholic monarch, and if the King has no children by his wife—Heaven knows he has enough and to spare from others—the Duke of York would be King of England, and he is a Catholic. Now the Duke of Monmouth is the King's son, although born, as they say, on the wrong side of the blanket. Monmouth would dearly love to be King. That is why he appears at all Protestant ceremonies. He wants everyone to know how firmly he supports that faith. Now suppose the King should have no legitimate children, would not Monmouth be a better choice than the Duke of York?"

"But surely that could not be, since he is not the King's legitimate son?"

"What is to prevent some long-lost documents being found? Charles was a wandering exile. Suppose he really did marry Lucy Walter? He was not the crowned King then, was he? He was only an exile. He was young and the young are reckless and the relationship with Welsh Lucy was not of short duration."

I stared at her in amazement. "Maggie, can you be sure of this?"

She smiled. "Of one thing I am sure, and that is that no one can be sure of anything in this world."

That was the way she talked and for me brought to life so many of the people who had just been names before.

It gave an added interest to the life which was going on around me. It made intriguing and exciting listening while I waited to get a start in the theater.

At last it came. Charles Hart was arranging to put on *A Midsummer Night's Dream* at the Theatre Royal and Kitty had prevailed on him to give me a chance to see what I could do.

Maggie was able to tell me something about the great actor before I was summoned to his presence.

"You will find him a very grand gentleman," she told me. "He acts all the time. Sometimes I wonder whether he ever stops, even in his bedchamber when he is alone—as I suppose he sometimes is. But it is second nature to him. You will have to be careful all the time to treat him with the utmost respect. Kitty will be there to help you along. Mind you, he is a very good actor. He never forgets his relationship to Shakespeare. I can tell you what that relationship is, because he makes sure that everyone who comes in contact with him is aware of it. William Shakespeare had a sister named Joan, and Charles Hart's father was her eldest son. The great Master Hart is of the opinion that he has inherited his kinsman's genius, with a little more thrown in."

"It is small wonder that he 'struts and frets upon the stage,' " put in Kitty, who had come in while this conversation was taking place. "But he reckons his will not be a case of being heard no more."

"Well, he has done well. He has acting in his blood, and the theater means a great deal to him," said Maggie. "You must admit that he is one of our finest actors."

"I would not deny it," agreed Kitty. "I was merely pointing out that he may not be quite so good as he thinks he is—but then, that could apply to most of us."

Maggie told me that he had played some good parts in his time, and when the war broke out he had joined the King's army and fought under Prince Rupert. When the war was over, he was playing in Beaumont and Fletcher's *Blood Brother* when the Roundheads broke in and carried him off to prison. When he was released, he acted privately and secretly in the house of a nobleman.

"Yes, Charles Hart has acting in his blood. And God bless him for it."

When the time for my appointment came, I was filled with apprehension. Suppose he did not like me? I asked myself. What then? Suppose I did not get the part? Could I go on hoping? How would Kitty feel? She would think she had made a mistake and should never have brought me to London.

Maggie tried to cheer me. "You're nervous, that's what it is. It's like going on the stage to play a part. Most actresses feel then as you do now. If you don't feel nervous, you don't bring out everything you've got and you're not going to give of your best. It's natural, dearie. It means you'll be all right when the moment comes."

"Yes," said Kitty. "If he thinks you are right for the part, you'll get it. And if he does not think so? Well, it's not the only part in the world, is it? There are others in London besides Charles Hart, I can tell you."

How they cared for me, those two! How lucky I was to have

been "discovered" by Kitty and to have been brought through her to Maggie!

In due course, Kitty and I were ushered into the presence of the great man. The room was small and dark with a little window looking down on the street. He stood up at the window—tall, upright, his hands clasped behind his back, striking a dramatic pose, I guessed, from some role he had played. Before him was a desk on which some papers were scattered. He was an impressive figure, accustomed to dominate the scene, and I tried not to be overawed. I remembered Kitty's words. If I failed with him, there were others.

Maggie had said he acted all the time, and I knew he was playing a part now. At least, I thought, I cannot be so insignificant if he takes the trouble to act for me. I, too, was acting my part, that of the humble, inexperienced girl in the presence of genius— and acting so, I forgot my fear.

He was looking at Kitty. "So, dear girl, you think this child may be an actress?"

Kitty replied: "I am sure of it, Charles. You and I know talent when we see it."

"Oh, yes. And you, my dear child, you think you may be an actress?"

"Yes, sir," I said humbly.

"Do you know that every wench in every tavern . . . selling her wares in the streets . . . wherever she may be . . ." He was declaiming to an audience, his resonant and musical voice rising and falling as he listed the girls of London and analyzed the drama of every milkmaid churning her butter in some remote country village . . . all were sure that they were great actresses.

"You are right, Charles, as always," said Kitty. "But when they are found and proved, they should be given a chance."

"They are very few, dear lady. Talent is a rare gift."

"That again is true."

"I know I have it," I said boldly.

That seemed to startle him, but I could see that he was not displeased—indeed, he seemed faintly amused.

"Kitty, dear girl, I trust your judgment. What if we were to put this child to the test? It is a small part. The play is *A Midsummer Night's Dream*, written by my kinsman, William Shakespeare, who is reckoned to be a dramatist of some considerable ability. A small part, it is true, but small parts are for beginners. We must all perforce prove ourselves, as you will agree." He turned to me.

"Dear child, I shall require you to read the part. Where is the piece?"

He turned to the desk and turned over some of the papers. At length he found what he was looking for.

"Here," he said. "You will read this. Just a few lines, that is all. The part is of a Fairy. It is the beginning of Act II. A Wood near Athens. You come in on one side, Puck on the other. He will say to you . . ." He threw back his head and declaimed with dramatic emphasis:

> *How now, spirit, whither wander you?*

"Then . . . here are your lines:

> *Over hill, over dale,*
> *Thorough bush, thorough brier . . .*

"Read from there, my dear."

I took the paper and read until I came to the lines:

> *I must go seek some dewdrops here*
> *And hang a pearl in every cowslip's ear.*
> *Farewell, thou lob of spirits; I'll be gone:*
> *Our Queen and all her elves come here anon.*

I was there. I had forgotten him temporarily. The words enchanted me. It was indeed a small part, but how I wanted to do it! I longed for the opportunity to say those words on the stage and give them the rendering such poetry deserved.

Charles Hart was swaying on his heels. Kitty was smiling triumphantly.

I was not surprised to hear the great man say: "It would appear that you have the part of Fairy in my kinsman's piece. You must learn your lines with all speed."

For the next days before the great occasion I practiced my lines continually. Kitty and Maggie helped me. At odd moments one of them would start up with *"How now, spirit! Whither wander you?"* and I would start up with *"Over hill, over dale,"* and go through the lines. Even Martha and Rose took it up, and *"Whither wander you?"* became a phrase constantly heard throughout the house.

I think the lines are engraved upon my mind and will be until I die.

The great day came. I cannot say that my performance was received with wild enthusiasm, but neither was I booed off the stage. It seemed that no sooner had I stepped on stage than I was off and that was the end of my brief glory. But I had made a start. I was a professional actress.

Those were happy days. Kitty was still playing in *Rule a Wife and Have a Wife*, and there was I, a Fairy in *A Midsummer Night's Dream*. We were indeed a theatrical household, and I was a part of it all, as I had not been before.

Sometimes I would complain that mine was such a little part.

"There'll be others," Kitty assured me. "Charles is pleased with you, I can tell. He watches you. He'll have something else for you and each part will be a little better than the one before. We shall soon have you complaining of the number of lines you have to learn."

"If only that could be so!"

"It will, I promise you." And with the coming of the new year, there were other parts. They were still small, but with each one I felt myself creeping nearer to success. Mine was not to be a spectacular rise, such as are dreamed of.

"Meteors do not last," soothed Kitty. "They fly across the sky, brilliant, admired, and then they fall to earth and are forgotten. You are doing it the best way, the gradual rise, and with each part you are a little more experienced."

I often thought how fortunate I had been to have fallen in with those two wonderful and loving women.

Kitty was particularly careful that I should be guarded against what she called the pitfalls of life, which meant the ever-prowling male.

"They come to the theater. They select those they want and they then tell you they will die if you deny them. You are the most wonderful creature that ever lived—until they have what they want, and then it is goodbye and they've forgotten who you were in a week or so. That's not the way. Keep them at bay."

"Lord Donnerton was not like that."

"There are few like him, I do assure you."

"Are you regretting?"

She shook her head. "The soft life was not for me. This is where I belong and what's best suited to me."

So we were happy, and I believed that life would go on like that forever.

The spring had come. It was warm and pleasant. I felt I was now a seasoned actress. I had a small part in Killigrew's *Claracilla*, and one night, after the play, I was walking back to the house, which was but a short distance from the theater.

It was a warm and balmy night, and as I came through the cobbled alley which led to the square in which we lived I saw a woman lying on the pavement.

My first thought was that she had been robbed.

I went over to her to see if I could help.

"Are you all right?" I asked.

She did not answer.

Then she opened her eyes. I saw that she was flushed and she stared at me as though she did not understand what I said. She was obviously very ill.

As I stepped nearer to her, she shook her head at me violently, as though urging me not to approach.

"Go, lady," she murmured. "Do not stay near."

I did not move. I felt I must take some action, help her to her feet. If she could not walk, perhaps I could bring some friend or member of her family.

She was shaking her head, obviously frantically urging me not to come near.

Then suddenly she opened her blouse and on her breast I saw the ugly red spots.

I understood then why she did not want me to go near her.

I was aware that the plague had visited the villages near the city. There had been one or two outbreaks recently. Maggie and Kitty had talked of it.

I turned and left the woman, though I felt I should not have done so. However, she was so eager for me to keep away.

When I went home and told Maggie and Kitty of the incident they looked grave.

"There have been one or two cases this year," said Kitty.

"There always have been," added Maggie, but I continued to wonder what had happened to that woman.

June had come. The weather was exceptionally hot, and before the month was out there was no doubt that the plague had come to London.

Many people were leaving the city and our audiences were becoming smaller every day.

"If it goes on like this," said Kitty, "we shall be playing to empty houses."

We did not do that because the theaters closed down. It was no longer profitable to stay open, for people did not congregate in numbers, for fear that among them might be someone who carried the dreaded infection.

We were fortunate in being able to rely on Maggie. She was, as she had said, comfortably off, and insisted that we share that comfort. She had stored cases of ale and flour to make bread should we need it, she said.

By the time August had come, we knew that this epidemic of the dreaded plague was different from the others which had come to the city. During the first week of that August, four thousand people died, and the numbers were rising. The streets were quiet, for few people ventured out. London had lost that air of bustling activity which had been one of its main characteristics. It was strange to walk out into those quiet streets, which we did very rarely. Shops were closed, and only occasionally did one see another person, who would hurry past, glancing fearfully about, suspicious that anyone might soon be a plague victim who would pass on the infection to them—just as I was wondering the same about them.

Many of the houses were marked with a red cross on the door and with it the words "Lord have Mercy upon us." One avoided passing such houses, for the sign meant that within the house was someone suffering from the plague. The law was that if there was such a person in any house, that house must show the sign and none of the inmates could emerge for a month.

A terrible gloom hung over the city. At night the only sound was the bell of the pest cart as it came through the streets, followed by the dismal cry "Bring out your dead," and we knew that the dead body of some loved one would be put into the cart with others in the same state, to be taken outside the city, there to be thrown into a pit where many other victims of the dread disease already lay.

The King and the Parliament had moved to Oxford. London was a dead city and behind the walls of our house the five of us waited in fear for what would happen next.

It was the end of August. I heard later that during that week the death toll had risen to over seven thousand. I was glad I did not know it at the time. Even so, we were all aware of the horror of this fearsome plague. We had survived largely through Maggie's foresight. Food was not plentiful, but we managed on what she had got together in her wisdom. Shops were closed, and the stalls had long since disappeared. London was a city of gloom.

Kitty said to me: "Perhaps I should never have brought you here. You would be safer at this moment in the country."

"I wanted to come," I assured her, "and I have no regrets."

I could imagine my mother's reaction to what was happening. She would say it was God's vengeance for the wickedness of the great city. Then I thought of the poor woman I had seen dying in the cobbled alley, and the sound of the death cart trundling through the streets, and I knew that I would not wish to be there and to hear her continual condemnation. Indeed, I knew there would have been a certain gratification in what she would perceive as God's vengeance on the unrighteous.

"No," I went on, "I have had my little triumph, and I would not have been without that, whatever happens now."

"That comforts me a little," said Kitty. "You have always been on my conscience."

"When you see me as a great actress you will be pleased, Kitty, for one day it will happen."

"Oh, bless you," she said. "It is true that that will make me a very happy woman."

The next day, when she arose in the morning, she felt unwell.

As the morning progressed she said her head was aching and she felt hot although she was shivering with cold.

Maggie and I looked at each other and dared not say or even

consider the thoughts which came to us. When anyone felt faintly unwell, we kept telling ourselves, we always had these uneasy feelings. It was nothing at all to be concerned about.

By the evening Kitty was worse.

Yesterday she had gone into the streets. She could not stay in any longer, she had said. She needed some fresh air and she would see if it were possible to buy food somewhere. Could it have been that she had picked up the dreaded infection somehow?

I scarcely slept that night and I knew it was the same with Maggie.

First thing in the morning, I went to Kitty's room. She was lying in bed. Terror beset me when she looked at me rather vaguely and said: "Oh . . . it's Sarah, is it not?"

"Kitty!" I cried. "How are you? Are you better?" I was beseeching her to say yes.

She said: "It was cruel of me to leave you. I had made my vows. But I could not endure it."

Then the awful truth dawned on me. She was delirious. It was one of the symptoms . . . headache, shivering, nausea, delirium.

She seemed herself suddenly. "Oh, I am better this morning, Sarah. I am a little tired. I think I'll rest awhile."

I drew the sheets about her. I felt sick with fear.

I went to Maggie and told her.

Maggie stared ahead, her face tense with anxiety which she was obviously trying to thrust aside, rather than accept what she feared.

"She's a strong girl," she said. "She went out yesterday. I wonder . . ." She looked at me steadily. "If it is . . ."

She was silent for a while.

"We get fearful sometimes without cause," she went on. "It cannot be. But if it is, Sarah, we must needs face it."

There was silence throughout the house. Kitty remained in her bed.

That afternoon I went to her. She was lying very still, her eyes wide open.

"Sarah," she said. "It has come. I fear I have brought it into the house. I must go while there is time."

"Go . . . where would you go?"

"I would go into the streets, as so many have. They go there to die because they do not want to take the plague to their families.

It is what I must do. Give me my clothes. Help me to dress. I know I must go . . . before it is too late."

"You shall go nowhere, Kitty. You shall stay here in your bed."

"Oh, God help me, no. I am afflicted, I know. Soon the dreaded signs will show themselves on my breast. I must go before that."

"We shall never let you do that, not I, nor Maggie. This is your home. You will stay here and we shall care for you."

"And die for it."

"It may be that it is not the plague. It is just a rheum."

She laughed, without mirth. "I know it. I stopped in the street and talked with a woman. I know her slightly. She was one of the orange girls at Drury Lane. She was looking for food to buy. That was it. I could have caught it from her, or perhaps it is in the very air we breathe. I don't know, but I am stricken, Sarah. Go away from me. I would go myself, only I am so tired, so feeble. But I cannot bear to think that you or Maggie or Martha or Rose should suffer through me."

"Kitty, listen to me. If you have this terrible thing, there is nothing to be done about it now. We have both been out. So let us not talk of your going out. Do not dare move from your bed. I know Maggie feels as I do. We are going to look after you."

"You don't understand what this means . . ."

"I understand well. We are together, you, Maggie and I. Nothing shall part us, not even this terrible plague."

Her eyes were filled with tears. She said: "Yes . . . we are together. It would be too late. If it is as I fear, it is already too late. I can never forgive myself. I should not have gone out. I should not have stopped to talk. It was folly. Oh why, why? All our dreams . . . where have they led us? To a house in a desolate city with a red cross painted on the door."

"Not yet, Kitty. No, it is nothing. You are going to be better tomorrow. You will laugh at this."

"Shall I, Sarah? Oh yes, let us say that . . . even though in our hearts we do not believe it."

When I told Maggie of this she was sober.

"It must not be," she said. "Not Kitty. She has her life before her. Oh no . . . this terrible plague. The misery . . . not Kitty. We will nurse her back to health, you and I, and we have Martha and Rose. People do recover. I heard of a man years ago. That was not as bad as this time . . . but he took the plague and he returned to robust health. Just go on as though we are not unduly concerned, Sarah. If it is the plague—and I fear it is—let us fight it. We'll keep our Kitty alive, in spite of it."

"Yes, Maggie," I said, "we will."

That night I saw the dreaded macula upon her breast.

Our door now bore that tragic sign: the red cross and "Lord have Mercy upon us."

She wanted me with her and that was where I wanted to be.

I was with her throughout the night.

She wanted to talk. I believed at times she was not sure where she was. It seemed as though she were talking to someone I did not know, and then suddenly she would be lucid and fully aware of what was happening.

In one of those moments she said to me: "Sarah, I am dying. I know it. I never thought it would be like this. I thought I would come back to the stage and prove to myself and them all that I had done was right for me. And now . . . it seems so worthless. We strut and fret our hour upon the stage and then are heard no more. I played in *Macbeth* once. I loved those words so much. I never forgot them, though I did not have the honor of saying them. Charles Hart's grandmother's brother was a great poet, Sarah . . . Sarah, I think of you so often and in particular now . . . when I shall not be there."

"Kitty, you will get well."

"No. It has claimed me, Sarah. There's no hiding from the truth. My time has come. I blame myself. I should have gone away to die. Sarah, listen to me. You are very young. There is so much you do not understand. I fear for you. I always thought I should be there to look after you. You would be as a daughter to me. From the first moment I saw you I felt something for you . . . something strange and sweet and strong."

"I was drawn to you, Kitty," I said. "We were drawn to each other. Do not talk of dying. It is more than I can bear."

"I was to be your guardian. You will be an actress, I know it. This terrible plague will pass and everything will be as it was before. There have been other epidemics . . . it just happens that this is bigger than those others. Life will go back to what it was. The theaters will be open. There will be the triumphs, the failures and the dangers. I was going to protect you from them. I was going to make you into a great actress. Oh, Sarah, did I think I was God, to mold your destiny? And who was I, to think I could do that? Now I see how feeble I am. Look at me now. Where are my plans? I married because I thought it was best for me. I left my husband to return to the profession I loved. You see, I thought of myself all the time."

I tried to speak lightly. "Kitty, we all do . . . every one of us."

"You make excuses for me, Sarah. I can see that I was brazen in my belief in myself, and God has struck me down to show me what a feeble person I am in truth. What am I now? What use to anyone? Use indeed! What have I done? I have brought the plague to this house. The red cross is on the door. This house is unclean. Do not enter."

"Kitty, you are acting as though on a stage. Thousands of people have this sickness. It could happen to any one of us. Stop talking nonsense about God's punishing you. All you did was try to help. I should have left my home sooner or later, I am sure. It was you who found a way for me. You have done more than I can say for me, Kitty. Thank you."

"My dear child, I do want all to go well for you. My last words to you . . . for there will be few more, I am so weak . . . I know I am failing fast, Sarah. Guard your virtue. Do not be deceived by fine promises. Maggie will be a good friend to you, but promise me you will be careful. If a man loves you enough to want to spend the rest of his life with you . . . if he wants to make you his wife and you love him, that is well. But only then, Sarah. Promise." She laughed. "Ah, here I am, guiding you again. It is because I love you, Sarah, and I wanted to see everything good for you. Everything that went wrong for me must go right for you, everything I did not have myself you must have."

"I promise you, I shall remember your words forever."

She seemed satisfied. She lay back exhausted, and I realized that talking like this had sapped what little energy she had.

I bent over her. Her lips moved slightly.

"Remember," she whispered. "Remember, Sarah."

I stood by her bed, watching her. All the life seemed to have left her now.

I went to Maggie. I said: "She is very ill, I think."

Before the day was out, Kitty was dead.

It was growing dark. We sat together, myself, Maggie, Martha and Rose. We were listening for the sound of the pest cart. We knew that soon we should hear the tinkling of the bell and the sound of the wheels on the cobbles.

It came. We sat there tense, not looking at each other.

"Bring out your dead."

It was close now. We opened the door. Maggie and I carried her out and there she was, our dear Kitty, once beautiful and merry, who had dreamed of becoming a great actress, and yet . . . one blow, perhaps a chance encounter with an old acquaintance, and that was the end of her dreams. Life was cruel. This was happening in thousands of homes in London. Ours was a common tragedy. But this was Kitty—our Kitty—and she was no more.

Lost Illusion

WE HAD TO REMAIN in the house. A month had to elapse before we emerged, and during that time the dreaded sign of the red cross would remain on our door.

Ours was a house of mourning, a silent house. I know Kitty was in all our minds; we did not speak of her, but she was with us every moment.

In the evenings we sat together, Maggie and I with Martha and Rose. How silent everything was. I longed to hear the old sounds of those pestilence-free days: the street-sellers shouting of the excellence of what they had to sell, the rattle of a passing vehicle . . . people laughing, quarreling . . . fighting sometimes . . . perpetual noise. But now there was only this unnerving quiet.

Kitty was always in my thoughts. She lay buried in a pit with many others. Never again should I hear her voice, never see her . . . there was nothing left but to mourn her. I could see that Maggie's thoughts were similar to mine, Martha's and Rose's too. And the silence seemed unbearable.

If we went to our beds we could not sleep. We were imprisoned in this house for another month and if, by that time, none of us had contracted the disease, we would be considered free of infection and free to go out.

Where to, I wondered? To closed theaters and empty streets and more memories of Kitty.

Martha had warned that the flour would run out soon and there would be no bread, but no one seemed very excited about that.

We were too deeply sunk in gloom to think about such a trivial matter.

One evening, as we sat there, there was a knocking on the door.

Startled, we looked at each other. Who could be there? Had whoever it was not seen the dreaded notice on the door warning all to stay away from a contaminated house?

"Someone has failed to see the sign," said Martha. "They will, and then they will run as though the Devil were at their heels."

We sat still, and the knocking started again.

"Who in the world can it be knocking at a door like that?" said Martha.

"There is one way to find out," I said. I went to the door and opened it.

A man stood there. Tall and thin, he wore no wig on his fine fair hair. He was somberly dressed like a Puritan.

I said: "Go at once. Have you not seen the sign?"

I was preparing to shut the door when he said: "It is because of the sign that I have come."

I stared at him. He must be mad, I was sure. Did he not know the law? Did he think anyone would put up such a sign without good reason for doing so?

"I am Rupert Lawson, a priest. I visit such as you in the hope that I can be of some help. I could bring you food. Would you allow me to come in?"

Startled, I stood back and he entered the house.

Maggie had come out. I saw Martha and Rose behind her.

I said: "This is the Reverend Rupert Lawson. He visits those in our position in order to help them."

"I thought you might be in need of comfort, and perhaps food."

"Let him come in," said Martha.

Maggie said: "Do you realize, sir . . ."

Martha interjected: "We're running short of flour . . ."

"We have had a death in this house," I explained. "It is less than a week since . . ."

"I am aware. I have visited houses such as this since this terrible epidemic came to us. Yet I have never caught the sickness. I believe that God protects me so that I might do His work of mercy."

It might have been hard to believe such a statement, but there was an air about him of what I think of now as saintliness. In any case, unlikely as his story seemed, I believed him and I think we all did.

"If I might come in, and hear your particular needs . . ." he said with a smile.

Maggie was silent for a moment, then said: "As long as you realize what risk you are running. I must repeat, it is a very short time ago that a victim of the plague was carried from this house."

"We have already told him that," I said.

"It is of no consequence to me. I am here to help."

He sat there among us. The promise of food had interested Martha; Rose was round-eyed with wonder. Maggie was inclined to be a little suspicious, but even she was beginning to believe his story with every passing minute. As for myself, I immediately felt a great trust in him.

He said: "Your grief must have been intense."

We were all too moved for speech.

He went on: "God will help you. I will pray for you. You must speak to Him too. Just little simple prayers as you go about your daily tasks . . . just naturally, as you might speak to each other. He will understand. Tell me about the friend you have lost."

Strangely enough, it was easy to talk to him. In a little while I was telling how I had come to London with Kitty and had just been getting a few small parts when the theaters had been closed down.

I had expected him to say that it was good to close the theaters and that God was punishing the wicked city by making it impossible to continue with its licentious ways; but nothing of the sort. He said that the theaters would doubtless open when the plague had passed. We had only to wait for the end of the summer, for the plague thrived in the heat, and the cold would kill it as it had before.

He talked to us of the people he had visited. He had been doing this since the beginning of June. He was a priest of God and he believed that in what he was doing he was serving Him far more effectively than he could by preaching to a congregation.

"Do the work that is at hand," he said. "That is a good law to follow. People cannot get to church, so I visit them. It is true that in the beginning, when people were aware that the sickness was about to come upon them, the churches were filled with people who had never thought to visit them before. It is often only in times of terror that some people remember God. I have found a great satisfaction in this work . . . such as I never had before."

Martha said: "We are getting short of flour, and we're living mainly on bread and ale. It suffices, but I can't think what we will do when it's gone. We can't get out and none will come to us. I do not know how we shall live."

"I shall bring you flour," he said. "There is no fresh food I can bring, but flour I am sure I can procure."

"While I have flour I can bake bread," said Martha.

"You still have a little?"

"I'm using the winter's store. It won't last the month, and then what, I say? Who knows . . . ?"

"The winter will soon be with us. When the cold weather comes this must pass."

Martha was looking at him superciliously. I could see then that she did not believe he would bring us flour.

He sat down with us and talked. He told us there were signs that the plague was abating. We could only wait and hope. He asked if he might say a prayer, and we sat with our eyes downcast.

"Lord," he said, "give us courage to bear this cross; give us hope that it may soon pass from us, and the fortitude to rebuild the lives which are left to us."

Then he left us, promising to return the next day with flour.

"He's a madman," said Maggie when he had gone. "Stop thinking of that flour, Martha, we've seen the end of him."

I did not believe that. He had made a deep impression on me. There was an aura of saintliness about him, of absolute selflessness. It was sincerity. He seemed to have no thought for his own safety. I was aware that he believed that God would spare him to do the work he had chosen. His faith was absolute.

I was right. The next day he returned with the flour. He stayed and talked with us for a while, then he said a short prayer as before.

His visit had a marked effect on me. I felt different. I was certain that we should pass out of this, that in spite of our sorrow I should have, as he said, the fortitude to lift myself out of my melancholy and be able to face whatever lay in front of me.

With the coming of the cold weather the plague gradually abated. What a relief it was to see no more red crosses on the doors of the houses, no longer to hear the pest carts roaming the streets at night.

Those who had fled the capital were now returning. There were stalls in the streets, the shops were beginning to open, and the theaters followed. Life was rapidly returning to normal.

I was on the spot and an actress of some experience, and one or two parts came my way. It was the best thing that could happen. My work absorbed me and helped to subdue my unhappiness at the loss of Kitty.

We were trying hard to accept the fact that she had gone. Rupert Lawson was a help to us all at that time. He continued to visit us, and Martha, who would be grateful to him for the rest of her life because of the flour he had given her during our great need, liked to give him a good meal.

"What we should have done without him, I do not know," she declared. "There was I, down to my last bag of flour, and no end in sight. I reckon he saved us from starvation, that I do. And I don't think he knows what a good meal is at that place of his. Well, I'll show him."

I was sure she was right, but Rupert was not much concerned with food, nor the domestic comforts of any kind. He had a room in a kind of lodging-house and was looked after by a landlady.

I heard that one or two others of his calling had acted as he had done during those months of the plague, visiting those who were dying, and bringing comfort to them. People said that it was a miracle, for not one of these men, and there were several of them, had been smitten by the disease, in spite of the risks they had taken. And considering how virulent the sickness was, and how it could be caught merely through speaking with one who was afflicted, as must have been the case with Kitty, it did indeed seem miraculous.

Time was passing. A new year had come, and then the winter was passing into spring. When I walked through the streets it seemed that the plague might never have visited us, bringing the desolation it had. I could almost delude myself into thinking that when I returned to the house Kitty would be waiting for me.

I was seventeen years old, and very different from the child who had run away from home that night. I had known deep sorrow since then, perhaps the greatest sorrow anyone can know—suddenly to lose a loved one, one who was at that time the most important person in my life. So much had happened to me since then. I had achieved a little success. Nothing spectacular, of course, but I could say that I had taken a few steps up the ladder to a career in the theater.

Since the plague had subsided, I had been employed almost regularly. I suppose some actresses had left London, some may have been victims of the sickness; perhaps it was because there were not many to choose from that I was given this chance. I had played in Beaumont and Fletcher's *Scornful Lady* and Dryden's *Indian Emperor* with some success. My acting absorbed me, and Maggie, Martha and Rose enthusiastically followed what I did, and came to the theater to see me act. What a boon the theater was to us all during that difficult time of mourning. It helped the others no less than me. They listened to me rehearsing my parts. Often I would think: If only Kitty were here, how delighted she would be.

Moreover, I was earning money—not a great deal, but enough to give me a feeling of independence, which meant a great deal to me. Oh, if only Kitty were here! I thought that a hundred times a day.

Summer had come. We were very apprehensive, fearful that the plague might come again. When the sun was hot we were particularly fearful. It was during such weather in the previous year that we had become aware of the scourge which had taken possession of London.

People were alert. If anyone was mildly ill, that person was regarded with suspicion and contact would be avoided.

But the summer was passing and there was no sign of the trouble. July was hot and sultry. Fear grew. But it would not be long before the cold winds started to blow, and we had come through so far.

One day, when I was leaving the theater, a man came to me. He bowed deeply, lifting his hat from the luxuriant light brown curls of his wig as he did so.

"Mistress Standish," he said. "Do you remember me?"

I looked at him and I vividly recalled that night he had wanted to escort me home and Kitty had emerged suddenly to accompany us.

He said: "Congratulations, Mistress Standish. No longer the little waif with her herring basket, but an actress of fame on the stage of the King's Theatre. Well, it had to be, had it not, for such a talent could not remain hidden for long."

I laughed. "You are Lord Rosslyn," I said.

"I am honored that you remember me. I must speak to you. I want to tell you how much I enjoyed your performance. Did you hear my cheers at the end? They were all for you. In fact, I scarcely noticed the rest of the cast."

"This," I said, "is blatant flattery."

He lifted his shoulders and looked at me a trifle whimsically.

"Much has happened since we last met," he said. "It would please me greatly if we might talk together. Would you come to one of these new coffee houses? We could sit and talk with ease. What say you? There is one at Covent Garden right here. I was at Tom's in Change Alley a little while ago. I am mightily impressed with these places. I think they will become very popular. Well, what say you to the Covent Garden?"

"It would be a pleasure."

I had not yet visited one of the coffee houses. When the first one, the Rainbow, was opened in Fleet Street, there was a great deal of speculation about it. People wanted to visit it and that accounted for its initial success, but when that had faded and Dick's in the City was opened and others followed, it seemed as though they had come to stay and were popular with the people of London, and almost immediately they were supplying customers with something stronger than the coffee which had been the first intention.

When we were seated in the Covent Garden Coffee House, my companion urged me to take a little wine. But I wanted to try the coffee. I reminded him that this was a coffee house and therefore it was appropriate to drink that beverage.

He drank the coffee with me. I found it good, and I was aware of a very special stimulation in his company.

He was an extremely attractive man, years older than I. He

must have been in his mid-thirties, which would make him twice my age. I thought he was more interesting than any man I had ever met. There was an air of the "man of the world" about him which appealed to my youthful innocence. Perhaps I was flattered that such a distinguished man should concern himself with me.

He leaned towards me and said: "You have grown up, Mistress Standish, since that day I took you home after you gave that wonderful performance at the house of your friends."

"He was my father's employer. My father was agent for Sir Henry Willerton's estates."

"I know. In fact, Mistress Standish, I know a great deal about you. So you came to London."

"Yes, Kitty thought I might do something in the theater." I could not say her name without emotion. He saw this and stretched out his hand and took mine. He looked into my face as he held it, and I tried to hold back the tears which came into my eyes.

"It was such a tragedy," he said. "I was desolate when I heard. She was so young, so vital . . . and you were with her, were you?"

I told him how she had died and how the Reverend Rupert Lawson had assisted us by bringing food, of which we were in desperate need.

"A good man," he said. "Many have suffered, I fear."

"You were not in London?"

"No. I was in the country. There were one or two cases there. It was not a time to come to the capital if one could avoid it. My poor Mistress Standish. It was very, very sad indeed for you."

"As for so many."

"A punishment on the unrighteous, as the Puritans tell us. Alas, it was not they who suffered. Most of them had their country houses to which they could return, while those who could not get away suffered for the sins of the unrighteous, which would seem a little unfair—if one believed in this theory, which I do not."

"Nor I," I said.

He was smiling a little ruefully.

"Enough of this sadness. 'Tis a time for rejoicing, for we have met after all this time. I have thought of you often. The little waif with her herring basket. She touched me mightily, and then when I heard that Mistress Standish was playing at Drury Lane . . . well, nothing would hold me back, and then I gathered together my courage and spoke to her."

"Did it need so much courage?"

"A great deal, for if you had refused to talk to me I should have been desolate."

"I cannot see why I should refuse. I shall always remember how kindly you walked home with me."

"With you and Mistress Kitty. She took great care of you, did dear Kitty. But enough, I do not want to make you sad again. She would be pleased to see your success in your profession. You are happy about that. So let us forget all sadness. That is the best way. Tell me, where do you live? Tell me all about yourself."

"Kitty took me in to her home with Maggie Mead. We lived there and I live there still."

"I have heard of her. A lady of great character."

"That would describe her well."

"And she has taken on the role of guardian angel to the young lady recently come to the wicked city."

I laughed. "That could be so. And what of you, my lord?"

"My name is Adair. Jack Adair. Could I prevail upon you to call me Jack?"

"It seems a little . . ."

He smiled. "Familiar?"

"Well, perhaps."

"Shall I tell you that nothing would please me more than such familiarity? I shall call you Sarah. May I? And I hope you will forget our brief acquaintance and call me Jack. After all, we did meet at Willerton and it is not the duration of a friendship which is so important, but its depth. I am going to be very bold and suggest that this meeting tonight is going to be the beginning of many for us. What would you say to that?"

"What could I say until I know what follows?"

"How wise. How cautious. The more I know you, the more you delight me."

We talked in this light bantering way until suddenly I realized that the time was passing and Maggie would be wondering where I was.

I said I must go. He looked a little disappointed but he did not seek to detain me and said instead he would walk home with me.

As we walked the short distance to Maggie's house, I realized that I had not felt so happy since Kitty died. I found this man's company exhilarating and I was delighted because of his insistence that we must meet again.

When I said goodbye to him he once more took my hand and held it for a few seconds before he raised it to his lips.

"It has been so wonderful to find you," he said. Then he smiled and added: "Rest assured that, having done so, I shall not let you elude me again."

I laughed, pretending to believe that it was merely gallant words, not to be taken too seriously.

But how I hoped this was not so.

I was eager to tell Maggie of my meeting with this gentleman, but as soon as I entered I knew that something had happened. Before I saw Maggie, Martha came to me. She had that eager and excited look people have when they have some surprising news. Whether good or bad, it makes no difference. They know something you do not and they cannot wait to tell you.

"Martha," I began, "is Mistress Maggie all right?"

She lowered her voice. "She's in a bit of a state, Miss Sarah. It's that nephew of hers."

Nephew? I remembered vaguely that Maggie's sister lived in the country somewhere and she had a son. This would be the nephew.

"What . . . ?" I began.

"He's here." She pointed towards the parlor door which was shut.

"With Mistress Maggie?"

"Shut in together. It's talk, talk. He's come all the way from Dorsetshire. What it means, only the Lord knows."

"I am sure Mistress Maggie will know as well by now, Martha," I said. "Has she said anything to you?"

"No. He's had a bit to eat and he's to stay the night. I'll have to make him up a bed in the parlor. What I do know is that Mistress Maggie is all in a daze, which is not like her."

"She's in the parlor, is she?"

"Yes, with him."

"I'll go and see what is wrong."

I knocked at the door of the parlor and was bidden to enter. Maggie was seated on a chair and beside her sat a man who must have been in his twenties, not unlike Maggie in appearance.

"Oh, Sarah," she said, and I fancied it was with relief. Had she been uneasy because I was late? No, I realized this crisis had driven everything else from her mind.

"Come along in, Sarah. This is my nephew, Master Abel Bagley." She turned to the young man. "Mistress Standish is a great friend of mine. She lives here."

The young man stood up and bowed.

"Sit down, Sarah," said Maggie. "I must tell you what has happened. My sister Rachel is very ill . . . not expected to live. She is eager to see me. It is years since we have seen each other. Not since I first came to London. But now there is little time left to her she is most anxious that we should be together."

"I see," I said.

"Abel wants me to go back with him to Dorset."

"That is a very long way."

"It is so indeed, but Abel has made the journey. I shall go back with him."

"When do you suggest you go?"

"Abel will go back tomorrow. I shall go with him."

"But how?"

"By stage wagon."

I looked at her in horror. I had heard of the stage wagons. It was not very long ago that they had come into being. I guessed the journey to Dorset would take a week or more and, of course, it would be far from comfortable. But there was an air of determination about Maggie. I knew her well and I knew that she had made up her mind.

She came to me in my room that night. Neither of us could sleep. The effect of Maggie's news had put from my mind temporarily the excitement of the meeting with Lord Rosslyn.

She wanted to tell me what was on her mind, so she sat on the bed and we talked. She told me more about her life in that Puritan household where she had been brought up. Her sister Rachel had been her parents' favorite.

"Rachel was made in their pattern," she said. "I never was. She was a good little Puritan. I was a rebel. And she married

Jacob Bagley, another such as our father. A righteous man, my father called him, which meant that he hardly ever smiled and thought it was a sin to be happy. I did not know how Rachel could have married him, but she did and with our parents' blessing, so she was proclaimed a good and dutiful daughter. I could not endure it. I left and came to London. I wanted so much to be an actress, but there was no opportunity in those days. That was when Kitty and I became friends. When I married Tom Mead I went back to see my family. It was not very successful. I knew that I could never be as they were. Rachel and I were quite different. Rachel tried to be friends but it was not easy. I could not endure that way of life. I left in a temper and I did not hear any more of her after that . . . until now. She is asking for me, Sarah. She is dying. I cannot refuse to go.''

"But it is such a long way, Maggie. It is a very trying journey by stage wagon.''

"How otherwise should I go? I should never forgive myself if I did not give her her dying wish. I know how she is. Abel tells me she has this on her mind. We parted on ill terms. Mind you, she will have convinced herself that the fault was mine, but on the other hand, does it not say somewhere in the Bible that one should not let the sun go down on one's anger? Love one another, forgive us our trespasses as we forgive others? And although I am the unrighteous one—already in the angels' black books for my desire to appear upon the stage—there is just the possibility that someone up there may have a distorted way of passing judgment . . . and her place in Heaven may be in jeopardy.''

I could not help smiling. Maggie always made me smile.

"As for me," she went on, "well, she is my sister. She was all right when we were very young, before she was caught up with Jacob Bagley and learned to see sin everywhere she looked. Mind you, she had had a fairly good apprenticeship with our parents and it suited her nature better than mine—it's the truth, Sarah. But I could not be at peace with myself if I did not do all I could to bring us together. We are sisters. There is a bond between us which nothing can change . . . the same flesh and blood. Do you understand, or am I ranting on?''

"I do understand, Maggie, and I see that you will not be happy if you do not go. But come back soon.''

"You can be sure of that," she said.

The next day she left on the stage wagon for Dorset.

I had not mentioned my meeting with Lord Rosslyn. I had thought of it on the previous evening but Maggie was, of course, too immersed in her own problem to want to listen to a little light gossip. So I had refrained from mentioning it.

I thought much later of what a big part chance plays in our lives.

But for the arrival of Abel Bagley, my life might have turned out quite differently from the way it did.

My relationship with Jack Adair—as I thought of him now— progressed rapidly. I knew that he was a most impatient man and when he had made up his mind he wanted something, he pursued it relentlessly.

He was charming and gallant. He was the most interesting person I had ever met. In a few weeks he had shown me that without a doubt he cared a good deal for me.

I lived in a blissful dream. I had scarcely given a thought to Kitty for days at a time.

I was happy. He would be waiting for me after the theater. Because we had first gone to the Covent Garden Coffee House, coffee houses would always mean something special to him, he told me. So we visited others. We went to the Rainbow in Fleet Street—the first of them all—and Tom's in Change Alley, but we came back to the Covent Garden, which had now become Will's.

How I wished I could tell Maggie about this wonderful friendship of mine. I expected her home at any time now. She would have seen her sister, had a reconciliation and have eased her conscience. That was all she had to do. Every day I expected that she would be back. But the days went by and I had to admit that I did not miss Maggie quite as much as I should have done if Jack Adair had not been there to beguile me. Also, I hardly ever thought of Kitty during those days. I was completely absorbed by this friendship with what was surely the most fascinating man in the world.

He was always so courtly, so tender, and he paid me such

delightful compliments. In fact, had he been younger, I should have thought he was in love with me.

I told myself that he regarded himself as a father to me. He had never married. At least, he did not actually say he had not, but I assumed it was so and he did not say anything to the contrary. He had lodgings in London, and he referred sometimes to a place in the country, but he did not talk much about himself.

It was the beginning of September when a man who had traveled from Dorsetshire on the stage wagon called at the house. Martha was full of excitement when I came in that evening.

"He comes from Dorchester, and lives not far from Maggie's sister, and she gave him this letter to bring to you."

"Oh," I cried. "That is wonderful! It means she is coming home."

I opened it eagerly and while Martha and Rose looked on I read it.

> *Dear Sarah,*
>
> *I dare say you think I am a long time coming home. Well, when I saw how things were here, I could not leave.*
>
> *Rachel is very ill. The apothecary says she cannot live long. There is no one here to look after her as she should be looked after. Abel does his best, but he has to work and you know what men are . . . so I must needs stay a while. I could not leave her thus. She is my sister. She rejoices that I am here.*
>
> *I do not think it will be long. My poor sister is very sick indeed, and all I know is that I could not leave her now.*
>
> *I shall be back as soon as I can get there.*
>
> *I miss you all.*

I read the letter aloud to Martha and Rose. We were all bitterly disappointed.

In Will's, the Covent Garden coffee house, I told Jack of the letter I had received from Maggie.

"You miss her?" he asked.

"Indeed I do."

"She was your watchdog?"

"That is not a good way of describing her. She likes to look after me. She thinks a young girl needs someone to look after her in a city like this."

"And now she is away . . . do you enjoy your freedom?"

"I miss her very much. I was so disappointed to hear she was not coming back yet."

"Do you not find it a little . . . irksome?"

"Irksome?"

"To have someone restricting your freedom."

"I have never thought of it that way. I have always been grateful to Maggie. She has been a wonderful friend to me."

He took my hand and said: "I would be a wonderful friend to you . . . if you would permit it."

I said: "I have your friendship now. I treasure it."

He gave me a rather wistful smile. Then he talked about the lodgings he had in London.

"A pleasant enough place," he said. "I take these rooms in this house. Below me live the good woman and her husband who look after my needs. I should like to show them to you."

"I should like to see them."

"Then you shall. Then you can picture me in my rooms, as I can picture you in the house of the good Maggie Mead. Why not this evening?"

We left the coffee house, and he took me to those rooms. When I look back I can smile at my innocence, but it must be remembered that I had not been very long in London. I had never met anyone like this man before. His courtly charm, his good manners, made him seem like a knight of old, chivalrous, a defender of the weak, the perfect gentleman.

He unlocked the door of his apartment and led me in.

There were a sitting room and a bedroom, and some other rooms, all tastefully furnished.

"I am well looked after here," he told me. "I come and go much as I please. I have friends to stay when I wish."

"You have charming lodgings," I told him.

And then everything changed. He took my cloak from me and threw it on to the bed.

"Sarah," he said, and his voice sounded hoarse and different. "I love you. I've been very patient, but at last you have come to me."

I felt alarmed suddenly. It was almost as though Kitty were in the room. I could hear her voice . . . and the words she had said the last time I saw her alive. She was warning me . . . and with a sudden flash I understood, and suddenly I knew that this was what Jack Adair had been leading up to ever since he spoke to me that first time outside the theater.

"I think," I said, "I ought to go."

He stared at me.

"Why, in the name of God and all His angels?"

"It seems that I have not understood."

"Oh come, Sarah, you are not as innocent as all that. You must have known I wanted you from the first moment I saw you."

"I thought . . ."

He took my chin in his hands and pressed his lips down hard on mine. His arms were tight around me . . . possessive and strong. He was different from the man whom I had built up in my imagination. I was really frightened now. I felt I was alone . . . helpless . . . with a stranger. I knew now that this was just what Kitty had warned me of . . . Maggie too. Oh, if only she were here!

I heard myself saying in a shrill, almost hysterical voice: "No . . . no!"

"But you are fond of me, Sarah. Of course you are. You have shown it in a hundred ways."

"Yes . . . yes. But let me go. Let us talk about this."

"Talk! I have done with talk. We have talked enough in those dreadful coffee houses. I have finished with talking, Sarah, and so will you."

"Please," I said. "Please!"

He did release me, and looked at me with a hint of annoyance in his eyes which I had never seen before in him.

"I just did not realize," I began.

"Oddsfish," he said. "You are not such a simpleton as all that. Of course you knew . . . you thought you would have a little game with me. You would lure me on . . . I know the game. Then . . . no, no, no, I am too innocent." His anger seemed to pass as quickly as it had come. He was almost pleading now. "You like me, Sarah. You know you do. Why . . . why?"

"I don't think I should be here . . . like this."

He laughed.

"What a little Puritan you are! Come, little Roundhead, that went out of fashion some time ago."

"I don't think we see things in the same light."

"We will, Sarah. I know you are young . . . and innocent. It is what I like so much about you."

"I think you are suggesting that we behave as though we were married."

He laughed. "So, if we were, you would be willing enough?"

"It would be different if that were the case. It would be right . . ."

"So it was marriage you had in mind?"

I was silent.

He said: "I am old enough to be your father."

"I did not think of that."

I was afraid that the other mood I had glimpsed would return. I felt sick and foolish, and terribly afraid.

He put his hand to his forehead in a gesture of frustration, and I seized that moment. I snatched up my cloak from the bed and ran. I went down the stairs and out through the door. The cool air of the street enveloped me and I had no thoughts in my mind.

I ran and ran all the way home.

I was safe.

Martha was in the parlor.

I said to her: "I am going to bed. I am so tired."

I shut my door and sank on to the bed. I do not think I had ever been so wretched in the whole of my life.

A Ceremony in Knightsbridge

I LAY SLEEPLESS all through that night.

What a fool I had been! I should have known that from the beginning he had had but one thought in his mind: to make me his mistress. Men such as he was did not marry unknown actresses. But they often made them their mistresses. Some of my fellow actresses had their noblemen lovers. I should have understood that very well.

I remembered how Kitty had insisted on walking home with me that night at Willerton. Kitty had summed up the situation right from the first. She had warned me.

And what had I done? I admitted it now. I had allowed myself to fall in love with a man whose plans for me were dishonorable.

I had to look at this clearly. I had been warned, and yet I had refused to see what was obvious. What had I thought were his intentions? I had to be frank. I had thought he would marry me. Lord Donnington had married Kitty. He was much older than she was, and she was an actress and he a lord like Lord Rosslyn. The position seemed familiar, but I had deluded myself. Really, he was not to blame for assuming what he had. He had thought I was light, ready to allow him to seduce me. That I was just acting the innocent, so young and pure, and letting him wait a while before he achieved his goal. He had grown impatient and the result was that I had become scared and run away.

I had deluded myself. I had allowed myself to fall in love with him. He had brightened my life. He had made me forget my loss. I had been really happy when I was with him. If I were really truthful, I should admit that, in spite of my fear, my sudden awakening, I had wanted to stay with him.

If it had not been for Kitty, I believed I should have done so. But then, if it had not been for Kitty, I should never have known him.

He would not come near me again and I had lost him. I was bereft, lonely and wretched.

I spent a sleepless night and it was early morning before I dozed a little.

I wondered how I was going to get through the day.

I was at the theater that night, but I could hardly concentrate on the play. I was scanning the audience, hoping for a sight of him. He was not there. I was praying that he would be waiting for me when the play was over. What should I say to him if he were? "I will do anything to please you"? I felt that if he had been there, I might have done just that.

I need not have concerned myself. He was not there, and I feared I should not see him again. I had disappointed him. He was thinking I had led him to believe I would be willing to play the part he had prepared for me. He was frustrated and angry, and that anger was directed against me.

I had lost him. I had disappointed him. I should never see him again.

Yet every morning I arose with the hope that I should see him that day. But time was passing and he did not come.

I was invited with another of the actresses to go to Will's Coffee House with her and two gentlemen. I went. The company was merry enough, but it could not lift my spirits. All the time I was thinking of those occasions when I had been there with Jack Adair.

Several weeks passed. The weather had grown very hot. I was finding it difficult to sleep and when I did my dreams were haunted by memories of Jack Adair. I dreamed that he was my friend again. I was very happy. Then I would wake to the unhappiness of disappointment. Once I dreamed that I saw him in the theater while I was playing and I walked off the stage, calling to him. He looked at me with contempt and hatred and he cried, "Roundhead!" and all the people in the theater took up the cry. I woke with the word ringing in my ears.

It was the first day of September—a hot and sticky night, not conducive to sleep. I awoke in the early hours of the morning. I felt something was happening. I have been dreaming again, I told myself. But then I saw that there was a dull red glow in the sky. I sat up in my bed. I heard a cracking sound and a loud explosion, as though something heavy had been thrown to the ground.

It's a fire, I thought, a very big fire.

I got out of bed and went to the window. I put my head out. The wind was blowing fiercely. A fire on a night like this! I thought. This wind will make it difficult to control.

The household was stirring. I opened my door. Martha was descending the stairs.

"It woke me," she said. " 'Tis a mighty big fire somewhere."

We watched it. The flames seemed to grow greater rather than diminish.

"What can you expect in a wind like this?" said Martha.

People were coming out into the street. We put on a few clothes and went out.

"Big fire somewhere," said Martha to a man who was watching the blaze.

He said: "I heard it started in Pudding Lane . . . a baker's shop."

"Baking bread, I suppose. I'll swear it is the last time he'll bake it in that shop."

"By the look of it, the whole street is ablaze," said the man.

"And the wind's not helping. It'll spread like wildfire. Come to think of it, that's what it is."

We went into the house. It was a hot night and the fire was making it hotter. We could hear the crackling of the flames.

"It must be near," said Martha.

"Or it is so big that we can hear it from some way off. The wind would carry the sound."

"I'd be looking out for my property if I was anywhere near there," said Martha.

We did not go back to bed. Sleep would be impossible. We had to all wait until the morning, but we were also eager to hear more news of the fire.

It was very disturbing when we did hear. It was true that it had started in Pudding Lane, but by morning it had traveled far. The streets near the Thames were caught in the fire, which had spread right down to London Bridge.

The Great Fire of London had started.

No one who lived through those four days could ever forget them. It was something which had never been experienced before, and I trust will never happen again.

London was a blazing inferno. There was a reddish glow in the sky, the sound of crackling wood and falling masonry was constant and the air was full of the acrid smell of burning thatch and timber.

This was no ordinary fire.

There was pandemonium in the streets. People stood in knots, fearful and bemused. They watched the fire's voracious appetite as in a very short space of time it consumed one building and, with the help of the wind, leaped to devour the next. Everywhere houses were burning, homes were destroyed. The ancient Cathedral of St. Paul's lay in ruins and other churches throughout the city were burning.

The river was full of small craft into which the more fortunate had been able to load some of their possessions. They stood among them, staring bewildered from the safety of the river at the flames as they destroyed their homes.

The fire was triumphant. There seemed no way of halting its progress as it leaped from street to steet. The narrow byways, the wooden houses had made its task the easier. There was much to give fuel to the flames when the fire reached the City's warehouses, in which were stored all kinds of goods, among them pitch, tar and oil, and as the victorious blaze went its way, the hearts of the people were clearly sinking in despair and despondency.

No one had ever seen such a fire before. Something must be done.

At last, when more than half of the city had been destroyed, the idea was put forward that there was only one way to call a halt to it. Gaps must be made in the buildings, so that the fire could not spread so easily. This entailed blowing up buildings and so halting the progress of the flames. People gathered in small groups to watch this.

It was indeed a sight not to be missed. The King and his brother, the Duke of York, cast aside their royalty and joined the workers in the streets. It was necessary, when buildings had been blown up, to clear away the rubble so that when the fire reached a certain spot there was nothing combustible for it to burn, and so was halted in its progress. Fires were isolated in this way and could be more easily dealt with.

It was strange to see our elegant King and his brother wigless, sleeves rolled up, sweating and working with the rest.

It was a new image of him, but he was more lovable in such a role than he was in that of the elegant, witty King sauntering through the parks.

And the strategy worked. The fire, though still raging in some parts of the city, was subsiding. It had inflicted a terrible disaster on our city, for, in addition to St. Paul's, which had always been regarded as one of the landmarks of the city, it had destroyed eighty-nine churches and thirteen thousand dwellings.

When there could be no doubt that the fire was really under control, people thronged into the streets to watch the flickering flames as they died away. Everyone seemed eager to relate his or her adventures, mostly dire misfortunes. How had it started? What could it mean? Had the Papists started it? There were always those ready to attribute every disaster to the Papists. Of course, there were others to declare it was another example of the vengeance of the Lord on the wicked city. Had He not already shown His anger with the visitation of the plague? All this was talked of.

I was standing in the Piazza at Covent Garden watching the distant dying fire, which I was able to see easily because of the missing houses in between, when I became aware of someone standing close to me.

A voice said: "What a disaster! Has there ever been such a one?"

I swung round sharply. Lord Rosslyn was standing very close and he was smiling at me.

I felt dizzy with emotions I could not describe. I suppose the chief of them was delight because he was here again.

"Sarah!" he said, with a wonderful tenderness which filled me with great happiness. "Oh, Sarah, I could not live without you."

I was silent from sheer joy. He was back, and it seemed in that moment that nothing else mattered.

"I have come back to ask you to marry me."

It could not really be happening. It was something I had longed for in my wildest dreams. It was all too fanstastic to be real. The fire, which seemed like a foretaste of Hell, and now here was . . . Heaven itself.

"I want you to forgive me," he was saying. "What I did . . . was quite unforgivable. But it has taught me what I should have known before. You see, I am no longer young . . . I did not think to marry. But why should I not? And who but Sarah, whom I love so deeply that my life is empty and devoid of all happiness without her? You do not answer?"

"I am wondering," I said, "if I am dreaming."

He had taken my arm. His face was close to mine.

"We must go somewhere where we can talk."

I said on impulse: "You could come to Maggie's house."

"Maggie is still away?" he said with some concern.

"Oh yes. She is in Dorsetshire with her sister. There are only Martha and Rose at the house. We could talk in the parlor undisturbed."

He took my arm and we walked back to the house. I was still refusing to let myself believe I was not dreaming, for if I should awake I felt I should not be able to bear the disappointment that this was only a dream.

Martha appeared.

I said: "Martha, I have a friend with me. I have something to discuss with him. Would you bring some refreshments to the parlor?"

It all sounded natural enough.

Martha eyed Jack with approval and she went to get some of her homemade wine, on which she set great store.

As soon as we were alone, he took me in his arms and held me very tightly.

I withdrew myself. "Martha will be coming back," I said.

"Yes, and there is much to arrange."

We sat down. He was looking at me with great tenderness and the love was shining in his eyes. I was very happy.

"I have arranged for the ceremony to take place next Saturday."

"How could it be so soon? Is it really possible?"

"I will make it possible," he said. "Let me explain. I have a friend. In his house in Knightsbridge he has his chapel. He has a resident priest, who will marry us next Saturday."

"I thought that there had to be more time for arrangements."

"I will have no delay. I know ways of fixing these matters. Leave it to me."

"Who is this friend?"

"Charles Torrens. He has done this for others of our friends."

"Shall I meet him?"

"In due course. But for the time being I am only concerned with one thing. I want you to be my wife."

"You have changed so suddenly," I said. "It all seems rather like a dream to me."

"Understand me. I will be frank. I had no intention of marrying. Why should I . . . after so many years? I have cherished my freedom. But now, since I met you, I have discovered something about myself, dearest Sarah; I am in love."

"Oh, Jack. Are you sure?"

"I was never more sure of anything in my life. I love you. I want to marry you. Everything has changed. I was foolish. Will you ever forgive me for what I tried to do? I thought I was so worldly . . . I thought I knew how to live and keep myself free to live my own life. And then, suddenly, I knew. There was no happiness that way. Forgive me, my darling, forget what I tried to do. Now I see everything in its true light. I just hope that you will forgive me, for I find it hard to forgive myself. All I ask you to do is to be ready next Saturday. I shall come here for you and we will go to the priest. Will you do that?"

"Oh, yes . . . yes."

He kissed me then and said: "There is one thing. Tell no one of this. It is our secret."

"Why should I not tell? Martha will have to know."

"The servants? Oh, you may tell them you are going to be married. They are Maggie's servants, are they not? She is still away."

"She will get a letter to us, I am sure, when she plans to return. She promised to let me know when she was coming."

"Well, she is not here and there is no time to tell her. You will see her when she comes and by that time you and I will be married."

"Why must it be a secret?"

"I will tell you. It is only for a while. Charles Torrens asks it. He is doing this as a great favor to me. If it becomes known others will be asking for it. It is so easy to be married in his chapel by his priest."

"But he is allowing you this . . . er . . . privilege."

"Charles is a good friend of mine. I pleaded with him. I really did. I said I wanted a speedy marriage. I wanted no fuss. For me he is doing this favor."

"And so . . . we shall be married next Saturday. I shall need a gown . . . a wedding dress."

Martha had come in with the wine.

He gave her a very charming smile, and I saw that he had enchanted her. He put the glass to his lips as though he drank to her.

"Nectar," he said.

She bridled a little. " 'Tis a poor thing to what I'll warrant your lordship is accustomed."

"Would that I were accustomed to such a brew as this! It is indeed nectar, good lady. I swear I never tasted better in the whole of my life."

"You are teasing me, sir."

"I swear not."

She went out of the room, slightly pink of skin and with her eyes shining.

"You won her heart by praising her wine."

"An easy conquest," he said lightly. "Oh, my dearest Sarah, I long for Saturday. Promise, promise me you will be there."

"Of course."

"And you want this as much as I do? You will not run away from me again?"

"How could I run away from my husband? But I was saying that I should have had more time. I may not have a wedding dress that is suitable."

"Who cares for dresses? I shall not marry a dress. Oh, Sarah, are you as happy as I?"

"I do not know how happy you are, but if it is only one half of the happiness I feel it is a great deal."

"Sarah, my beloved Sarah! Together . . . just a few more days. Now, let us plan. I shall come for you at six of the clock on Saturday. We shall go to Torrens's house in Knightsbridge. A little way out, but not too far. And then the ceremony. It will not be long, and I shall take you back to my lodgings and then we shall go away to the country . . . where we can be alone for a while. London is not the best of places to be in at this time. What say you, Sarah? Are you as eager as I am?"

"I believe myself to be."

He would have taken me into his arms there and then, but I was aware of the close proximity of Martha and Rose. He might have charmed Martha with his compliments on her wine, but I could not imagine what she would have thought had she come in and found a man whom she had not seen until this day embracing me.

I warned him of this. I said: "This is a small house. The servants are our friends. There is little ceremony."

He nodded. "And you will tell them?"

"I must give them an explanation as to why I shall not be coming back here."

"Why not tell them now? Call them. Introduce me as your husband-to-be."

"I think that would be the best way of breaking the news."

I called them in.

They looked startled. "Martha, Rose," I said. "I have something to tell you. I am going to be married."

Martha gasped. "What . . . ? You can't . . ."

"She can," said Jack. "And I insist on it."

"I want to introduce Lord Rosslyn, who is to be my husband."

They both stared wide-eyed and, in Rose's case, open-mouthed.

"We have known each other for some time," I said. "I met Lord Rosslyn at the theater. The wedding is on Saturday."

I heard Martha murmur: "Lord have mercy on us."

Jack smiled on. "He has certainly had mercy on me. I am the happiest man alive."

"Who'd a thought it!" said Martha. "Sarah . . . marrying Lord Rosslyn!"

"I think," said Jack, smiling at her, "this is an occasion when we might all drink to the happiness of the bride and groom. Do you have any more of that most excellent wine?"

"Well, my lord, bless you! I've got a dozen or more bottles stowed away in the cellar."

"Then to it," he said.

"Come on you, Rose, you give me a hand," said Martha.

He looked at me and smiled when they had gone.

"How was that?" he said.

I was laughing. "You managed them perfectly. Martha is ready to worship you from now on."

"And the little speechless one—what effect did it have on her?"

"She was too bewildered—as well as she might be—to take it all in, but she will think what Martha thinks. Martha will see to that, so you have made a double conquest in this house."

"And of all who live in it?" he asked.

"All," I assured him.

It was so wonderful and very amusing. Martha brought in the wine bottle and goblets which were lifted to our health and happiness. Martha declared afterwards that she had never known the like—and I am sure Rose agreed with her.

So, I was to marry Jack Adair on the following Saturday and the ceremony would take place in the home of a certain Charles Torrens in the village of Knightsbridge, just outside London.

It was an exciting week. I could not believe it was really happening. Jack called at the house several times and Martha could not contain her pleasure.

"To think of it," she said to me. "You . . . marrying a lord. That's what comes of being on the stage. Actresses do marry into the aristocracy. And, bless me, he's a real charmer, that one. I could fancy him myself. Lord Rosslyn, eh? I expect he knows the King. Sarah, I reckon you'll go to court. Does he really know the King? You know what I mean . . . talk to him, just as we're talking now?"

"I suppose so," I said. And I thought: How little I know about him. But that was not important. I was going to marry him and his life would be mine.

"There's only one thing that's missing," said Martha. "Mistress Maggie's not here. I reckon she'd be so pleased to see you well settled. I used to hear her and Mistress Kitty talking about it . . . how they wanted the best for you. Well, wouldn't they like this Lord Rosslyn? You only have to look at him to see what he is. Some of them go round pretending. But you can see what he is . . . the right article. It's in every bit of him. Oh yes, he's a real lord all right."

They wanted to know a great deal and sometimes I was rather disconcerted to find I could not answer the simplest of questions. I consoled myself that this would soon be remedied.

I had told them at the theater that I was leaving to go away, and I was glad that most people were too interested in their own affairs to want to probe too deeply into those of others. I would play for the last time on Friday and the next day . . . well, I could hardly wait for it to come. I could not tell them at the theater that I was going to marry Lord Rosslyn since he had particularly asked that it should be kept secret, and to mention it there would, I was sure, arouse some interest.

It seemed a very long week. I made some preparation. I did get a new, rather simple, dress made in time. It had a bodice pointed at the front and rounded behind, a full skirt but slit down the front to show a petticoat of a lighter shade of blue than the dress, with silver thread making a finely traced pattern on it.

I felt sure that it was to be a simple ceremony, so the dress should not be too elaborate.

I came home from the theater on that last night. I had never been so excited in my life. Tomorrow was my wedding day. I was in turn exultant and apprehensive.

Lady Rosslyn. I murmured it to myself. Could it really be me? What would my mother say? And my father and Maria Willerton? Could this really be happening to me?

He was so distinguished, so handsome, so clearly of another world than that in which I had lived thus far. I began to wonder about my inadequacies. But he loved me. He would look after me. He would help me. And he wanted this marriage. He was so eager. I remembered how, so recently, he had had to satisfy his desires without it. It was only when he failed to do so that he had realized that he wanted to marry me.

All would be well. How I wished Kitty were here. She would have come to the chapel as a witness. One had to have witnesses, of course, but Jack would arrange that.

It was wonderful. If only, as Martha had said, Maggie were home. How excited she would be.

I was waiting long before he arrived in the carriage to take me to Knightsbridge. I went through agonies of fear and doubt as I waited. What if he did not come? What if he never intended to? Was it a huge joke? A revenge on me for refusing him? Terror seized me. He was not coming. I knew that Martha was peering out through the parlor window. Rose was beside her, all agog with excitement.

"O God," I prayed, "let him come."

I was being foolish. There were five minutes to go.

And there he was. Martha was at the door.

I went down and he said: "Sarah . . . my bride," and I was happier than I had ever been in my life.

He kept his arm round me as we rattled on our way out of devastated London to Knightsbridge.

I had never been there before, but I knew from now on it would always be preserved in my memory.

" 'Tis not a long journey," said Jack. "We shall soon be there. What a joy that will be. And the ceremony is not of long duration."

"There must be witnesses, I am told," I said.

"Do not worry your head about that. I have arranged it all. It will be over very soon. We are now crossing the old bridge over the Westbourne, the bridge from which this place gets its name. Now we are almost there. What a desolate place to have built a mansion! But I suppose it was done long ago. Charles was saying the old place goes back some two hundred years. The ancestral home, you know. And that is World's End . . . a rather notorious drinking house. Yes, my love. Indeed, we are there."

The carriage was drawing up.

It was certainly an ancient house. We had stopped before the gatehouse with a broad low arch flanked on either side by battlemented towers. It was very imposing with its gables and turrets built in red brick. Indeed, it had the appearance of having stood there for all of two hundred years.

Jack almost lifted me out of the coach and, as he did so, an old man appeared, evidently some retainer.

"My lord," he cried, "my master is waiting for you. All is prepared."

We followed him to a large hall with a high vaulted ceiling and many windows. Weapons hung on the walls.

A young man hurried forward.

"Charles!" cried Jack. "This is good of you."

"It is my pleasure," said Charles. He was looking at me and smiling warmly.

"Come along, my dear fellow," he said. "Introduce me. Are you afraid to let anyone else see her? I must say, that would not surprise me."

"Sarah," said Jack, "this is my good friend Charles Torrens. Charles, you know all about Sarah."

"He has not stopped speaking of you for weeks," said Sir Charles. "You are the luckiest of men, Jack."

"I know it well," said Jack. "Shouldn't we get along to the chapel?"

"Impatient bridegroom, we understand your need for haste now that we have seen the beautiful bride for ourselves."

"Is the priest here?"

"Ready and waiting."

"And you have the witness?"

"I have. Blakeman and Jefferson were ready enough to step into the breach and give their services. All is as it should be."

"Then let us get to it," said Jack.

We were taken from the hall to a room in which two young men were waiting. Jack greeted them warmly and they were introduced to me. They were our two witnesses, James Jefferson, who was about Jack's age, and Thomas Blakeman, who was much younger.

"It is good of you to come along," Jack told them.

"But of course we came," said James Jefferson. "We know you'd do the same for us."

They were all laughing and merry, but Jack was impatient to have the ceremony performed, and Sir Charles Torrens said we would proceed without delay.

"I'll go ahead," he said, "and tell Reverend Martin that we are ready. He is doubtless deep in prayer. He regards this as a very solemn occasion."

Thomas Blakeman said, "Not too solemn, I pray. I am sure Jack will introduce a little gaiety into the proceedings."

Jack frowned and Charles Torrens said, "Listen, Blakeman, our friend Jack is about to make his solemn vows. It is not a matter to speak of lightly."

"Forgive me," said Blakeman. "I am sure you are going to be very happy."

Reverend Martin was waiting for us in the chapel. He was a man of medium height and was rather unusual-looking. His hair was of a reddish tint of fair and was thin and curly. His pale eyebrows and eyelashes gave him a startled look, and he had a short nose and long upper lip which added to his rather strange appearance. Freckles were visible on his forehead and across his nose. He did not appear somehow to suit his clerical garb and pious demeanor.

He took my hands and looked into my face.

"So, this is the bride," he said. "Mistress, you will have studied the marriage service. You understand the seriousness of this undertaking?"

"Yes," I said. "I understand."

"That is well." He glanced at the others. "I should like a few moments alone with the bride."

Jack suppressed an impatient protest and Sir Charles laid a hand on his arm.

"Reverend Martin knows what is meet at such a time, I'm sure."

"We shall say a prayer together," said the priest.

And they left us.

"You are very young, Mistress," he said. "But I believe you are aware of the gravity of this step you are taking."

"Oh, yes," I said.

"Marriage is a very serious undertaking."

"Yes," I said. "I know."

"You have given this deep consideration, I hope?" he went on.

"I have indeed."

"Very well. Let us now pray together."

We both knelt and he asked God to watch over me, to guide me in my marriage, and he went on in this vein for some minutes.

Then he rose and said: "I will call them in now, and then we will proceed."

I stood beside Jack at the altar and we went through the marriage service.

When it was over Jack kissed me tenderly. And Charles insisted that we leave the chapel so that our health could be drunk.

I said goodbye to the priest and gave him my thanks, which he received very graciously, before telling me that God would guide me through my new life. He then said goodbye to me.

In another room we partook of the wine which Charles Torrens insisted was appropriate on such occasions. Jack thanked him for allowing his house and servants to be used for our benefit and the two witnesses for coming to help us.

"It was nothing," said Charles Torrens, "only what one must do for one's friends if it is in one's power. Martin has very little to do when the family is not in residence. He was glad to be occupied and there is nothing he likes more than officiating at a wedding."

Then we drove back to London to Jack's lodgings. How different it was on this occasion!

Jack was laughing.

"The deed is done," he cried. "Oh, Sarah, my love. There is not a happier man in the whole of this city."

"Nor woman," I said.

He took my cloak as he had before. He threw it on to the bed. The new life had begun.

Life was wonderful. We were together all the time. I was deliriously happy. He was all that I had believed him to be. He might have been impatient with me, for I was very ignorant, indeed completely unworldly; but he initiated me into the pleasures of loving in the gentlest and most tender way.

Indeed, my innocence delighted him.

We were in his lodgings for a week. His servants below were very unobtrusive. They would come at a certain time to ask our wishes and apart from that we saw little of them.

We only made one excursion into the streets during that week. And that was to visit the coffee house—not in Covent Garden, for Jack had a fancy to go to Tom's in Change Alley. If we went to Will's, it would be too close to the theater and we should see some of my old acquaintances. He wanted no intruders, he said. He wanted us to be entirely alone.

For a week we lived in this state of bliss and then he said he was going to take me away. He had told me he had a little place not far from Oxford Town. He would take me there. There we should not be disturbed by acquaintances and could continue this blissful existence. London was a dreary place just now, but soon they would be making it habitable again. Jack had heard that the King and the Duke were most interested in the matter. They had called in that fine architect Christopher Wren and were putting their heads together. Later we would come back and enjoy a fine city with wide streets, with most of those plague-infested houses gone forever.

So, to the country we went.

It was a wonderful life, living in a pleasant country house, not exactly large nor yet small. There were a few servants—as unobtrusive as those in his London lodgings—and we settled down to the idyllic life.

We rode into the countryside, and went and ate in inns. We lay in the meadows and it was all rather like a dream.

It could not go on like this. We would have a home soon. That was what I wanted. I knew so little about him. When I questioned him he would answer briefly and quickly change the subject.

"Sometimes I think you are a man of mystery," I said.

"Men of mystery are very attractive, I have heard."

"That may be, but a wife should know something of her husband."

"My Lord Rochester would tell you that the less a wife knows of her husband—or he of her—the happier they are likely to be."

"These clever comments do not apply to ordinary people."

"But we are not ordinary, my darling."

"I want to be. I do not want to be smart like my Lord Rochester. Is he a friend of yours?"

"An acquaintance."

"He is very cynical, I gather from his verses."

"He is extremely clever. That is why the King suffers the young rogue. The King will forgive a man a great deal if he has wit."

It was always like that. Whenever I wanted to talk about him, I would find the subject changed to something else. Only occasionally, when I awoke in the night, I would think how little I knew of my husband and ask myself why it should be so. He knew of my home on the Willerton estate, that I had come to London with Kitty and what had happened to me ever since . . . but with the coming of the day, there he was, laughing, merrily thinking of some new ways of making me happy.

The days passed quickly. We had been at the house in the country for nearly three weeks when I noticed that he had become a little preoccupied. And then, one afternoon, when we had ridden off and had tethered our horses near a stream and had gone to its edge to sit awhile, he put his arm round me and said: "Sweetheart, I have to go away for a little while."

"Go away?" I echoed.

"It is a matter of business."

"Business. I did not know . . ."

"That I had business? My dearest, why should I burden you? It's a matter of my estate."

"What estate? Your estate?"

"My place in the country."

It was the first I had heard of it.

"I did not know . . ."

"Most of us have such places. They are managed by . . ."

"People like my father."

"A good manager takes over most things, but there are times when one's presence is needed."

I knew of such things. Had it not been so at Willerton House?

"When shall we leave? I long to see the estate."

He was silent for a while, and then he said: "It will be easier for me to go alone."

I was amazed. I said nothing. He drew me closer to him.

"I can get up there quickly, settle things and then come back." He hurried on, as though fearful that I might ask questions. "I have to go back to London first. We'll leave tomorrow. You will stay in the lodgings while I'm gone. It will not take more than a week or so to settle the matter."

I felt a terrible alarm. He was going to his home . . . his estate . . . and he was not taking me with him. There seemed no reason why he should not. Was I not his wife? I wanted to know his family. It was my family now. I had the sudden feeling that I was being shut out.

"Why cannot I come with you?" I insisted. "I want to see the estate. I want to meet your family. You have not told me anything about them. What family have you?"

"Oh . . . only brothers."

"What do they say about our marriage?"

He shrugged his shoulders. "They are concerned mostly with their own affairs. Look here, Sarah. I shall only be away a short time, then I shall be back and we will talk over everything. We'll make plans. I did not want to think of anything else during this wonderful time except that we are together. Do you understand?"

"Oh yes, but . . ."

"Let's forget all this. We must be happy together. Now, no more of my parting. I shall be back before you know I have gone. I tell you what I intend to do. Early tomorrow morning, we will start for London. I'll take you to my lodgings. You will be well looked after there. You think of what we shall do. I shall expect well-laid plans by the time I return. It's going to be wonderful, darling. Don't look sad. Everything is in order, I tell you. Think about it. Where shall we live? You love the old city, do you not? Life is going to be better than you have ever dreamed of, I promise you."

"I wish you did not have to go."

"So do I. But these things happen, you know. Being away from you will be torture, but think what it will be like when we are together again."

"But . . ."

He put his finger on my lips in a playful gesture. "Do not let us talk of miserable parting. I forbid you to talk of it. There! Husbandly authority. You promised to obey me, you know. I insist. We are not going to spoil this night by thinking of to-morrow."

A week had passed. I felt desperately lonely without him. The days seemed unendurable. I saw little of the servants who were in their quarters below. One of them came up as before in the morning to take my orders. Often I compared them with Martha and Rose and I thought how I should like to see them.

I was so delighted when the week came to its end and I was expecting Jack to return at any moment. I thought it would be like him to want to surprise me and I expected to hear his voice calling me.

Instead there was a letter from him.

My dearest,
    This is a sad, sad disappointment for me. I cannot return to you for another week. I miss you so much. But never mind, we'll make up for it when we do meet. I cannot wait for that.
    God bless you, my darling.
    Your ever loving,

Jack

My disappointment was intense. I felt wretched and uneasy.

I had not gone far from the house as yet, but now I decided that I would go to Drury Lane. I would go and see Martha and Rose. I should enjoy telling them about my wonderful marriage and how happy I was and how my husband had had to leave for a little while on important and urgent business. When he came back we were going to find a house in London. He had a place in the country but he had insisted that we should also have a residence in London.

I felt a great emotion when I saw the house. I remembered so vividly the day when Kitty had brought me there.

Martha and Rose cried out with delight at the sight of me.

I flung myself into their arms.

"Ooh!" said Rose. "You're a ladyship now, aren't you, my lady?"

Martha said: "You didn't bring his lordship, then?"

I told them he had had to go away on business.

"We have been in the country and just returned," I said. "As I am staying not far away in his London lodgings, I thought I would come and see you."

They were excited.

"And you a real lady," said Martha. "It's more than I can take in. Our little Sarah. Wouldn't Mistress Carslake have been proud?"

I felt the tears in my eyes then.

I sat in the parlor with them. Martha brought out her home-made wine.

They wanted to hear so much—where had the wedding taken place?

"I'll swear it was a great affair," said Martha.

"No, Martha. We did not want to wait for that. It was in a chapel in the house of one of my husband's friends. It was very simple."

"And then he took you to his grand home, I reckon."

"No. We wanted to be alone."

"Ah yes," said Martha, smiling knowledgeably. "I'll swear Mistress Maggie will be as proud as a peacock at your rise in society, that I do. You becoming a little ladyship and all that. That is something I never thought to see. Oh, and I'd forgot. In all this excitement, it slipped out of my mind. It's the letter. Go and get it, Rose."

"A letter?" I said.

"It came by the same one as brought it here before. He was traveling down on the coach and he'd promised Mistress Maggie to bring it. It's for you, he told us, so we kept it and we've been wondering how we were going to get it to you. It only came two or three days ago."

Rose went off and came back with the letter. I seized it eagerly. It was in Maggie's writing and it had my name on it.

I opened it and they all looked at me in anticipation as I read it.

> Dear Sarah,
>   I shall be coming home in a week or so. My sister died. It was the best thing. She would never have been well again. There are several matters that have to be dealt with here, and I shall just stay to clear them up. My poor nephew has no idea how to manage. But I shall be starting back, I reckon, in say a couple of weeks from writing this. I am not looking forward to the journey, but I am to being home with you all.
>   Tell Martha and Rose I'll be glad to see them, and you don't have to have me tell you that it is the same with you. The truth is I am just longing to be home.
>   Your loving Maggie

When I told them she was coming home their pleasure was intense.

"What a day!" said Martha. "A ladyship comes to see us and the mistress is coming home."

We decided that she might be in London by the end of the week, considering when the letter must have been written.

They were too excited for talk of anything else, which relieved me, for I was finding some of the questions they had been asking rather difficult to answer, and now that I was no longer under the spell of Jack's presence, I was beginning to realize that there was something unusual about our marriage.

After that, I could not resist calling at the house each day to discover whether Maggie had come home.

There might be another letter, I thought. And, as she did not know what had been happening during her absence, she would expect me to be at the house and so would write to me there.

I marveled that I had not attempted to communicate with her. I had been so completely absorbed by Jack, and he had somehow insisted that I give no thought to anyone but himself, while implying that he preferred our marriage to remain a secret for a while.

When I looked back, it seemed that I had acted very strangely. Indeed, from the moment I had gone to that house in Knightsbridge and there had followed that most unusual marriage ceremony, I felt that I had been living in a dream.

I could never resist taking the way past the theater. Then I would think with some nostalgia of the excitement I had experienced—that feeling of mingling fear and triumph when I stepped on to the stage. There was nothing quite like it. Kitty had known exactly what I wanted. Dear Kitty. Now that I was alone I thought of her constantly, of her grand marriage and her inability to give up the theater. Her story was like mine in a way, for I was now realizing how much I missed my growing knowledge of the theater people and I wondered whether there would come a time in my life, as there had in Kitty's, when I should have regrets.

But I was deliriously happy with Jack. I wanted nothing more. It was only because he was not with me that my thoughts were following this line.

I paused for a moment to look up at the theater, and as I did so I heard someone call my name. A young woman was coming out of the building, and I recognized her as Joan Field, an actress with whom I had played on one occasion.

"Sarah!" she was saying. "If it isn't Sarah Standish! How fare you? And what do you here? Where have you been? You just disappeared mysteriously."

I was on the point of telling her of my marriage when I remembered that Jack had been rather anxious that it should not be announced just yet. In that moment I wondered why, although previously it had seemed such a trivial matter that I had not given too much thought to it. I felt he probably had his reasons and I naturally wished to do what he wanted me to, so I did not tell her of our marriage. She would learn about it in due course.

"I wanted a rest from the theater," I said.

"And now you are back?"

"Well, not exactly. I was just passing."

Fortunately Joan was absorbed by her own good fortune and wanted to talk of that, so she was not very interested in my affairs.

"I have the most wonderful part," she said. "You know it was decided to change *Measure for Measure*. They altered it a bit, and they brought in some of the characters from the other plays. They wanted Benedick and Beatrice in it and, well, I'm Beatrice."

"A good part, I'll swear," I said.

"Oh indeed, yes. Why, I think it is the best part, and I do believe the audience were of that mind. There's been such a to-do. Well, bringing Beatrice into *Measure for Measure*! You can imagine."

"I can indeed," I said.

"Let's go along. I'm meeting someone at Will's Coffee House. Have you been there?"

"Yes," I said.

"These coffee houses, they are so fashionable now. We can talk there. Do come."

I hesitated only for a moment. The days were so long. It would be pleasant to pass an hour or so in Joan's company.

We sat in the coffee house, where we talked—at least she did. She was so excited, first by the new part and even more so by a new admirer.

"He liked my Beatrice," she said. "He was there every night I played. Then . . . well, you know how it happens. He was waiting after the play. He is very distinguished. Sir Harry Fresham, that's his name . . . a very noble gentleman. He has breeding. Oh, you can always tell. He gave me a diamond brooch."

"Does he . . . want to marry you?"

She looked at me in amazement. "Well . . . there's been nothing said. He's talked of giving me a nice little place near the theater."

"Oh, I see," I said.

"As a matter of fact," she went on, "you may be meeting him. These coffee houses are good places to meet your friends."

She went on talking and I noticed how her eyes kept straying to the door. I said I thought I should go, but she prevailed on me to stay for a while. I had the notion that she was certain that her new friend would come into the coffee house sooner or later and she was eager for me to meet him so that I might admire and perhaps envy her.

And so it happened.

She was alert suddenly; a look of great delight spread across her features as a man came towards our table.

"Oh, Harry," she cried, as if in surprise. "I wondered whether . . . Oh, this is Sarah Standish."

He took off his hat and bowed and a deep shock ran through me. It was only the wig which might have deceived me for a moment. It was light brown, with luxuriant curls reaching to his shoulders. I saw the freckles across the bridge of his short pert nose and the long upper lip. It was a face I had seen before in the chapel in the house in Knightsbridge.

I was stunned. I could only stare at him in amazement.

"Sir Harry Fresham," Joan was saying proudly.

"I am delighted to make your acquaintance," he said.

It was the same voice which had said "We shall pray together" in the chapel.

I stammered: "I thought we had met before."

Both he and Joan were looking at me in surprise. I had been so taken aback that I feared I was behaving oddly.

"Mistress," Sir Harry was saying, "I think there must be some mistake. If we had met before, I am sure I should never have forgotten the occasion."

"They say we all have doubles," said Joan lightly. "I am glad you were able to meet Sarah. She is an actress, you know."

He was smiling at me and the likeness seemed more pronounced than ever. His was an unusual face, and the more I saw him the more like Reverend Martin he seemed to become. Mannerisms . . . voice, and that long upper lip. It was quite uncanny.

"What are you ladies drinking?" he said, and it was the voice of Reverend Martin.

"Coffee," said Joan.

"Coffee," he said, faintly contemptuously, and then smiling at us both. "You must use a little wine for the stomach's sake. That is a command from the Bible," he added, looking at me with an expression which might have held some mischief in it.

I was too shaken to listen to their conversation. The resemblance was too strong and I could not rid myself of the conviction that the man who was sitting opposite me in Will's Coffee House was Reverend Martin.

I quickly took my leave of them and hurried back to the lodgings.

That night I had strange dreams. They were incoherent and muddled. Jack was in them, and he was laughing at me as though he was enjoying some joke at my expense, and then he was Reverend Martin sitting in the coffee house in his clerical garb and calling himself Sir Harry Fresham. It was all nonsense, yet when I awoke I could not dismiss it. I had been mistaken, of course. Why shouldn't there be two people so much alike that they could be mistaken for each other?

If I saw them together I should see the difference.

But my uneasiness had increased. I began to think that from the moment Jack had taken me to that house in Knightsbridge I had stepped out of reality. When I looked back, nothing seemed quite normal.

Why had Jack disappeared like this? I asked myself. Why had he not taken me to his home? I did not even know where it was. Was that not very strange? Why? Why? There were so many questions to be answered. I had brushed them aside, but now I needed to know the answers.

I should demand to know, I assured myself, as soon as he came back. Was he not coming at the end of the week? I was being foolish to allow myself to fall into such a state of uncertainty, merely because I had met a man who looked like that strange Reverend Martin.

The next day I arose early. It was Wednesday. On Saturday the week of Jack's absence should be over. It was not long to wait.

I stayed in the next day, waiting, hoping that he would come. All I needed was to see him, to tell him of my meeting with Sir Harry Fresham, and how it had startled me.

All would be well. I was just fanciful because he was not here. When he came back, he would reassure me.

On Friday I could not rest, so I decided I would call at the house to see Martha and Rose.

When I arrived I knew something had happened and I was overcome with relief when Maggie rushed out to greet me.

We fell into each other's arms and then I saw the consternation in her face.

"Sarah!" she cried. "Where have you been? I'm sure they have not told me aright. Tell me it is not true."

I said: "I don't understand . . ."

"Martha and Rose . . . they said you had married Lord Rosslyn."

"It's true, Maggie. I am so happy. It is wonderful."

She did not speak. Her lips were trembling. Then she was fierce and angry.

"Oh, Sarah, Sarah, what have you done? What *have* you done?"

"Maggie . . ." I began.

She was staring at me in utter dismay.

"You cannot have married Lord Rosslyn. He is already married. He has been married for the last ten years or more."

I sat in the parlor with Maggie. I was numb, bewildered, and I asked myself whether of late in the depths of my mind I had guessed that something was not as it should be.

She made me tell her all about it. How he had taken me to his lodgings and there had tried to make me his mistress.

"And when I refused . . . he thought up this plan."

"And you were deceived by it."

"Kitty had always talked to me about men and how I must never be taken in . . . I was in love with him. He is very charming, Maggie."

"Charming!" she snorted. "Yes. I'll warrant he can lay on the charm thick and fast when it's about ruining some innocent young girl."

"Oh, Maggie, Maggie, what have I done?"

"Nothing that can't be mended in time."

"But I . . . it's not the same. Kitty . . ."

"Kitty would have been the first to understand, and you're not the only one, I might tell you, to be deceived in this way. I've heard for some time that it's been a habit of these young town dandies, and some not so young either, old enough to have a bit more decency. Mock Marriage, they call it . . . the game they go in for when they can't get their way without. They look on it as a sort of sport."

"Oh no, no, Maggie." And I took refuge from my shame in disbelief. "It could not be true." I could not believe it.

"If you take my advice, you'll never see him again," Maggie said. "That is, if you can help it."

I was silent. I thought of him returning to the lodgings, calling my name, waiting to catch me up in his arms.

Never to see him again. When I loved him, wanted to be with him. I wanted to hear him deny this charge against him.

Yet in my heart I believed it. I had the evidence of my own

eyes, had I not? From the moment Sir Harry Fresham looked at me in the coffee house, I had felt this suspicion. I had known that the man sitting opposite me, calling himself Sir Harry Fresham, was the same Reverend Martin who had conducted a bogus form of marriage in the chapel in Knightsbridge.

I knew Maggie was right, yet I was fighting hard to prove her wrong. I was bewildered and miserable, and very much afraid.

Maggie was brisk and practical.

"It's not the first time this has happened to a girl . . . not by a long way, I can tell you. You're lucky. Some might have left home, romantically eloped . . . Romantic! I'd give these villains romantic! Poor things, what can they do? Deceived just to satisfy the lust of these rakes and give themselves up to be joked about. What can the poor girl do when she learns the truth? But it is not so with you, Sarah. You have a home. I thank the Lord that I came back in time."

"Oh, Maggie, I'm so miserable . . . But it's not true. I am sure you are mistaken. I'm sure it's not true."

She held me against her and stroked my hair. "You've got a home. Always remember that. I'm back now and if he comes here I'll know what to say to him."

"He is coming back. He will be at the lodgings in a few days."

"That is, if he gets there. Like as not Master Rosslyn will find he has more pressing business to keep him occupied."

"I am staying in his lodgings."

"No more, you're not. This is your home, and if he wants to see you, he can come here."

"Maggie, I have to see him. I have to hear what he has to say."

"Some well-thought-out tale, I shouldn't wonder. Yes, he had a wife . . . but your charms so blinded him that you caused a lapse of memory and he forgot all about her."

"Oh, Maggie, this is very important to me. I would never be satisfied unless I saw him . . . unless I heard from his own lips . . ."

"Oh yes, I know. And when he tells you he was a naughty man who loved you so much that he resorted to this trickery and he'll die of a broken heart if you leave him, what are you going to say, eh?"

"You are wrong, Maggie. If this is true, I shall not stay with him. I shall always remember what Kitty said to me. If I knowingly did anything that was wrong, I should feel she was reproaching me. She was so anxious that nothing . . . nothing like this . . . should happen to me."

Maggie put her arms round me.

"When this sort of thing happens," she said, "or any misfortune, for that matter, it helps not to sit down and mourn. You get up, my girl. You start from there. What's done is done. You'll come back here. Who knows about this so-called marriage? Only those who took a part in it, and they won't tell. They might not be all that proud of it, and, more to the point, too much talk about something like this and their part in it spoils the next little game they might want to play. Listen to me. I have been around a good deal. You'll come back here. You have been away for a little while, visiting perhaps relations in the country—that's the tale if the need arises. When you've calmed down a little, you'll see it my way."

"Maggie, I am sure you are right . . . if this is true. I've heard it more than once."

"It is true, I tell you he's married. And did you not see the rogue who played the part of the priest? I've heard of Sir Harry Fresham . . . they're a wild band. Friends of my Lord Rochester, as wild as any. Why the King does not forbid them the court, I do not know. Yes, I do, because he is as much a rake as any of them. There. You have to be watchful. This is a different world we live in now. The times have changed and these little adventures of merry young men are not frowned on and treated with severity as they would have been in the days of Oliver Cromwell."

"I must hear of it from his own lips."

She looked at me in exasperation.

"Take my advice. Don't go near him. He'll get round you with some tale."

"I shall demand an explanation."

"No need for what's clear as daylight. If you take my advice, you'll forget you ever set eyes on him."

"If only it were as easy!"

"Listen. Don't you go back to that place. This was your home before all this started, and it still is. You stay here. Try and forget all about this grand marriage to a not-so-noble lord."

I did not know what to do. Good sense told me that Maggie was right. There was Harry Fresham to prove it.

I was very unhappy and very undecided.

Maggie took me up to my old room.

"There," she said. "This is where you'll be safe."

I stayed that night and what a restless night it was. I did not sleep at all. My mind changed continuously.

I would go back to him the next day. I had to wait for his return: and when I thought of how he had deceived me, I was bitterly angry and in despair at the enormity of what I had done.

I could see Kitty's reproachful eyes. Sarah, Sarah, how often did I warn you? Would you go back and be his mistress? And when he tires of you . . . what then? Have you not seen the fate of others?

How could I have been so foolish, I asked myself one moment; and the next: But I do not believe it. Am I not judging him because of what Maggie has heard? How could she be sure? It might be that his wife had died . . . that he did not like to tell. Naturally he would not call attention to the difference in our ages. That was it. And then in my mind I saw the cynical smile of Sir Harry Fresham across the coffee room table, and I knew that Maggie was right.

So passed that tragic night.

By the light of day I felt sure that Maggie was right, and my wretchedness returned. Before the morning was out I was finding all sorts of reasons why she could be wrong. So the mood of uncertainty continued.

I had to go back to the lodgings. He would return and find me gone. What if he were so angry that he went away back to his estate? How should I know?

I had to see him.

I went to the lodgings. It was Saturday and still he had not come back. I waited for a while and then left. I went back to Maggie. I could find some solace there. Maggie cared for me. Maggie would look after me.

She found me weeping quietly and she stayed beside me.

She said: "Life is hard at times, dear child. When we fall we must perforce pick ourselves up and start walking again. It will mend itself. And we should rejoice that we have become wiser and will not fall into the same trap again. Sarah, my dear Sarah, trust me. We will show this man that his attempts to ruin you have not succeeded, for they can only do so if you allow them to."

I listened to her words and thought how wise she was. She was a great comfort to me.

I did not go back to the lodgings again. The days passed. I thought of him continually. Had he returned, found me gone and then shrugged his shoulders and gone away again? Had he laughed at the simplicity of the stupid unworldly girl who had been so easily duped by a false ceremony and a false priest?

Perhaps I had made it easy for him. He had had the amusement he sought, played out his little charade, and now I had conveniently gone away so that he did not have the trouble of deserting me.

It was Tuesday of the following week at five of the afternoon when there was a loud knocking on the door.

We both started up. I thought: He has come; and my heart leaped with sudden joy, for if he had come it would be to take me back with him and to explain all that I had not understood until now.

As we went into the hall we saw him brush Martha aside and come in.

"Sarah!" he cried, seeing me. "Why have you not been at the lodgings these last days?"

He seemed angry, and I managed to say: "There is much to explain."

"Explain?" he said. He had come into the parlor. Maggie was standing there militantly, as though waiting for him.

He gave her a look of dislike and turned to me, his expression softening.

"I told you I was coming back. Why were you not there? Why should you come back here?"

I was dumbfounded and dismayed and then, in spite of everything, wildly happy. He had come for me. He was going to take me away with him. It had been a foolish mistake.

Maggie was angry. She said: "How dare you come here?"

"This is no matter for you!" he replied shortly. "I must ask you to keep out of it. I should be glad if I might be allowed to talk to Sarah alone."

"She may not wish to," said Maggie. "She has learned a great deal which you have kept from her. Sarah, tell him to go."

I looked at him and, after those days of melancholy misery and uncertainty, I felt my heart filled with hope. I was convincing myself that he would explain everything and then it would be as it had been before.

Maggie said: "Tell him to go, Sarah. You must have nothing to say to his sort."

"A little late in the day for such talk to my wife . . ."

Maggie laughed derisively, and he turned to me, and said in an authoritative voice: "Sarah, please tell her to go."

"Maggie," I said, "I have to talk . . ."

Maggie's attitude changed suddenly. "Talk . . . talk from now to Kingdom Come. Ask him to explain his little tricks. Talk . . . Sarah, you shall have your talk in my house, which is your home while you want it. Don't let go of your good sense, that's all I ask. Talk and then do the only thing you can reasonably do. Say goodbye to this villain here and send him on his way forever."

She went out and left us and, as she did so, he came towards me and would have embraced me.

I felt lost and frightened without Maggie. I knew that there was nothing he could say to reassure me, for my good sense told me that Maggie's interpretation of what had happened was the correct one.

"How could you have left my lodgings?" he demanded. "When I came back, I found you gone."

"You were a long time gone, my lord," I said, and was surprised at the coolness of my voice. There was something in his face and perhaps even in his demeanor which told me that he was not finding it so easy to deceive me as he had previously. There was a subtle change in his manner and, while it made me very unhappy, or perhaps because of this, it aroused my anger and indignation and gave me the courage I needed to face him.

"It was business. Did I not tell you?"

"Business on that mysterious estate of yours?"

"What do you mean? Have done with this. What has happened to change you? My darling . . ."

"I cannot have done before I have started," I said. "While you have been away I have been learning much. I have met your false priest. Sir Harry Fresham was very good in the part . . . but not quite good enough."

For a moment the expression which crossed his face betrayed him and he muttered something beneath his breath.

He recovered himself and asked, almost plaintively: "What are you saying, Sarah? Come, enough of this. I know you are angry because I had to be away from you. It was necessary. Do you think I should have taken myself away if it were not?"

"Oh, yes," I said. "I think you might very well have done so. It is no use hiding the truth now, is it? I have learned it all. That ceremony was no ceremony. It was what you wicked men indulge in. It was a mock marriage, with a mock priest and a mock bridegroom. I have discovered all about it. Do you wonder that I have left your roof and come to my real friends?"

He seemed to come to a decision that further pretense was useless. I believed in that moment that he thought I had not only seen Sir Harry Fresham but had made him admit that he had played the part of the priest at the mock wedding.

"Listen, Sarah," he said. "I will look after you, I promise. You shall have a fine house. It will be as we planned it. I shall be with you . . . whenever possible. It will be just as though . . ."

Every hope I had had then was gone. Up till that moment I was praying that he would deny the accusation, that he would explain to me why these suspicions had come into being and disprove them in every way.

As I was silent he went on: "Come, Sarah, admit it. Did you not know it was something like this? Did you think that a man in my position could marry like that?"

"Someone so far beneath your station?" I asked.

"Well, you must know something of how these things are arranged."

"I understand now. Good enough to be taken to sport with awhile, but not to marry. That is it, is it not?"

I was humiliated beyond endurance. I hated myself as much as I did him for allowing myself to be so easily deceived.

What a fool I had been! A silly, innocent girl, meek, trusting, overawed by the first man who had noticed me. No wonder Kitty had thought fit to impress on me the danger of life in London.

I hated him as he stood there, smiling cajolingly, trying to deceive me again.

"Please leave this house," I said, "and never, ever come near it again."

"Sarah, don't be so dramatic."

"It is probably a familiar situation with you. How many trusting women have you betrayed? Did you boast of it with those friends who helped you plan your villainous deeds? I wish to God that I had never seen you. I loathe you, I despise you for the miserable rogue you are. I never wish to see you again. The least you can do after having done so much to ruin my life is to get out of it."

"You do not mean this, Sarah. It is a blow, I am aware of that. But really, you should have realized."

"Go!"

"You will see sense in a day or so."

"I have already seen sense. That is why I ask you to go."

He lifted his shoulders and looked at me regretfully, bowed and said: "This is not the end, you know."

Then he was gone.

I slipped into a chair and stared blankly before me.

Maggie came in and knelt beside me.

"So, he has gone," she said.

I nodded.

"It is for the best," she said. "Sarah, my dear Sarah, we will turn our back on it. We shall do our best to forget it has happened. And we shall go on from here."

At Whitehall Stairs

I DO NOT KNOW how I should have lived through the weeks that followed but for Maggie. She was there all the time when I needed her. I had not realized until I had sent Jack away that it was all over, and I rejoiced that only a few people knew what had happened.

Maggie had talked seriously to Martha and Rose. She had told them the truth because she felt it was better for them to know the full story, of which they already knew a great deal, and then they would draw their own conclusions. They were part of the family, she told them, and this was our secret.

I scarcely went out during those days. I was afraid of meeting someone. I had the feeling that I wanted to crawl away and hide.

Maggie understood. She helped me in every possible way and in the midst of my unhappiness I thanked God for this good friend.

A few weeks passed in this state. I began to think of the theater and the thought excited me. Maggie brought in news of what was happening and who was playing in what. I knew some of the plays and would imagine myself in them. I went over the parts I had played; I felt the old excitement creeping back, and I wanted to be there, a part of it all again.

I tried not to think of Jack. That was not possible, of course. I had wild fantasies in which he returned and proved it was all a mistake. We were truly married and he was begging me to go back with him.

How foolish I was!

"Forget it," said Maggie.

There were times when I felt the need to be alone. Then I would go outside sometimes at dusk in my hooded cloak so that I could not be easily recognized, walk past the theater and watch the people going in.

I felt that if I could go back to work I might begin to be happy again.

Sometimes I would talk to Maggie about it. She was in agreement with me. "You'll make a fresh start," she said. "If you were back on the stage you'd grow away from all this as time passes."

"Some will know what happened. They will laugh at me for a simpleton who was an easy victim."

"It has happened to others before you."

"I could not bear the sly looks."

"You cannot think Rosslyn has talked."

"No. I do not think so. Harry Fresham . . ."

"They will not wish to expose themselves as such heartless villains."

"They might think they are very clever to have arranged such a farce."

"I think not. You will have to have courage. We will construct a story and keep to it. You have been away visiting your family in the country. Your mother was ill, perforce you had to stay and nurse her."

"As you did your sister."

"Exactly so."

"Perhaps one day, Maggie . . ."

"When you are ready," she said.

So I took my evening jaunts past the theater and when I came back Maggie would be waiting for me. She was convinced that one day I should be ready to face anything that would take me back and she believed that the theater could be my salvation.

There were times when I felt deeply depressed, when I lured myself into thinking that Jack would come for me and would explain everything. It was the old theme that there had been a terrible mistake. I found it becoming harder to convince myself, but I still went on dreaming.

Maggie would quite rightly dismiss my fancies, but on one particular night I did not want to hear her do this. I wanted to go on deluding myself.

It started to rain but I had no wish to return to the house. The gray dark skies and the rain on my face fitted my mood. I wanted to go on walking.

The rain was falling fast but I was hardly aware of my damp cloak. There were few people in the streets. Who wanted to walk on a night such as this one? Only those like me who were deeply sunk in a life of never-ending regrets, of lost hopes and with a view of only the dismal future.

At length I was cold and tired and I turned my steps homewards.

Maggie shrieked when she saw me. They had been worried about me.

She cried: "You are wet to the skin!"

Martha and Rose were fussing round me.

"Get those wet things off. Do you want to kill yourself? What have you been doing?"

My teeth were chattering. Martha came up brandishing the warming pan and soon they had me in bed, still shivering—chilled, as Maggie said, to the bone.

The next morning I was very ill.

I believe that during the week that followed I came near to death. The shock of my discovery had had a deep effect on me, and I was vulnerable. I must have walked in the rain for more than an hour. There was a cold wind and I had already been suffering from a cold.

To have walked through the rain in wet clothes as I had done was asking for trouble, Maggie pointed out. But I had not been aware of my wet clothes or the weather. I had been thinking of that last scene with Jack and that moment when, knowing it was useless, he had made no attempt to deny how he had deceived me.

I was delirious on occasions that first day and, when I returned to reality, Maggie told me she had been very frightened.

She brought a doctor to me. I was only vaguely conscious of what was going on around me. Maggie gave orders which Martha and Rose obeyed.

I do remember Maggie's sitting by my bed, holding my hand, talking to me. I was half aware of what she said. We would all be together, all of us. We had a great deal to look forward to.

Had we, I wondered, and in my half-conscious state I thought I was with Jack and he was talking of the future. I was listening to him avidly but all the time a black shadow was hanging over me.

The doctor came to see me several times. I had emerged from my hazy dream. I knew that I was very ill and I was in my bed in Maggie's house, that I had gone through a mock marriage ceremony with Lord Rosslyn who had now gone away forever.

Then I began to get better. Maggie looked happy; so did Martha and Rose, and I kept telling myself how lucky I was to have such friends. What should I have done without them? I tried to think, where should I have gone? I had very little money. What should I have done? Perhaps of necessity I should have had to accept Jack's offer . . . the fine house . . . the life of a mistress whose lover came to see her when it was convenient for him to do so. I should not have been happy thus. I saw now that my upbringing had not fitted me for that kind of life. Although I had deplored the strict rules of my childhood home, and indeed had escaped from them, they had had some effect upon me. I could never be happy in the sort of life I should have had with Jack Adair.

How grateful I was to Maggie.

I will repay her, I thought. I will go back to the stage. As soon as I am strong enough, I will go to the theater and ask for a part. The thought cheered me considerably.

I wanted to talk to Maggie about it.

I did, and she listened.

"Yes," she said. "When you are well enough. It would be good for you. There is something I have to tell you, Sarah. It may be something of a surprise . . . but I think you will be pleased . . . when you really get used to it."

"Maggie, what is it?"

She seemed reluctant to say, which was unlike her. If she had news—particularly if it were good news—she could scarcely wait to impart it.

She cleared her throat and looked at me anxiously.

"When the doctor was here . . . well, he examined you, of course . . . and he thought that you showed signs of . . . well, the fact is, he thought, and now he is sure, that you are going to have a baby."

I stared at her in amazement.

"He did not think he was wrong, but, of course . . ."

"Maggie," I gasped, "it can't be true."

"Why not? It's likely enough. It's a long way off yet . . . and, er, there's time to plan."

I was speechless. A baby? Jack's child. I had said this was an end, and it was really a beginning.

The shock had passed. A baby, I thought, my own child. At first I was terrified and I began to think of all the difficulties. And then a sense of wonder overcame me. A child to contemplate . . . my very own child.

I could see that Maggie was excited.

"A child in the house," she said. "That'll liven us up a bit. I haven't told Martha yet. I wonder what she'll say. Fuss around, I'll swear, but once the little one's here . . . Sarah, you're afraid. Don't be. We will manage."

As we grew accustomed to the idea the excitement grew and Maggie and I could talk of little but the child.

"We'll have to change our ideas a little, I fear," she said. "You had been home to your family, remember? That accounted for your absence. We'll have to have a husband now. What of this? You went home and married a long-time sweetheart whom you had known from childhood. Soon after the wedding he was recalled to the army. He is a soldier. He's serving with the army in Holland. When there comes a suitable time we shall have to kill him off. Yes, that's the story. We don't want our little one to be called bastard."

"And Martha and Rose . . ."

"Oh, they know too much. So it will have to be the truth for them. We can trust them. They like to share the family secrets. It makes them feel at home. Leave it to me. All you have to do is get well. You'll have to take double care of yourself now. Our baby has to have a good welcome when he or she arrives. Which do you want, Sarah, a boy or a girl?"

"I had not thought of that. It does not seem of any importance. All I want is the baby."

Maggie nodded, contented.

She knew, and I knew, that I had taken the first steps away from that disastrous farce of a marriage. Difficulties might lie ahead, but we could face them. The future would hold my child and that was more important to me—and to Maggie—than anything.

Now that I was well, there was so much to do, announced Maggie.

She had called Martha and Rose to her and talked to them very seriously, telling them that she expected their absolute loyalty. This was their home and they should not forget it. Then she explained about the baby. Their reaction was much as she had predicted. I knew that my baby would have a good welcome from all in this house.

Martha's comment was: "We shall need good fresh milk. I've always said that's the best food to give a baby."

Maggie explained about the imaginary soldier who was in Holland in the King's army. Martha nodded wisely. It would not be good for the baby if the truth were known. Maggie had settled that matter and now the whole household was eagerly awaiting the coming of the child.

Maggie had said that I must give up all thoughts of acting until after the baby was born.

"You'll have to cosset yourself, especially after that illness you had. That could have weakened you a little. Mind you, you're a strong girl. It'll be all right. But we'll take no risks."

I thought of Jack only rarely now. If he saw me now he would certainly not want me and I was sure he would not welcome the encumbrance of a child. Well, I could do without him. I had my very good friends whom I could trust completely. I need never think of him again.

The story of my fictitious husband had been accepted by the few to whom it had been necessary to tell it. Life was going peacefully along. I was getting larger every day and they all regarded me with delight. I was pampered by everyone in the house. There was little talk of anything but the coming baby.

The midwife whom Maggie had procured pronounced herself pleased with my condition.

"I reckon it will be an easy birth," she said.

And so, on a warm June afternoon in the year 1667, my child was born.

They held her up for me to see her as I lay exhausted after my ordeal.

She appeared to have been well equipped with everything that a child should bring into the world.

I held out my arms and they laid her in them. At that moment I could forget everything but that I had my child.

I had said I wanted her named after Kitty, who had been Katherine.

We called her Kate.

She was indeed a lovely child. She was of good temper, more given to smiles than tears. She was bright and very soon knew each one of us. We adored her and wondered how we had managed to live without her. As for myself, I could not be unhappy since I had Kate and could not entirely regret anything that had given her to me. She dominated the household, and if Martha or Rose were missing one could be sure to find them with the baby, even if she were sleeping.

Those first months after her birth were completely absorbed by her, but one day Maggie asked me if I had ever thought of returning to the theater.

The idea had entered my mind. I wanted to earn money to pay Maggie for all she had given us, although she was always impatient when I talked of this. It was certainly not for that reason she suggested it. She knew what it had meant to me, and I think she felt that now Kate was not exactly a baby and there were three other people in the house whose greatest pleasure it was to care for her, there was no reason why I should not have a career in the theater as well as a daughter.

"It is always well," she said, "not to stay away too long. If you are building up a name you do it gradually and it does not help to have people forget you. You have had a year or so away. That could easily be remedied. It's when it gets too long that it begins to be difficult to return. As Kate grows up she'd be proud of her famous actress mother, you know."

"There's something on your mind, Maggie," I replied. "I know you."

"Well, what do you think? I ran into Jenny Crowther yesterday. Have I ever mentioned Jenny Crowther?"

"Was she not one of your old theatrical friends?"

"Those were the days! She married and went to live in the country somewhere. Her niece is Rose Dawson. You've heard of her."

"Yes, of course. She's playing at the Duke's now."

"That's right. Well, Jenny had it from her that Killigrew is putting on *The Siege of Rhodes,* and he's looking for someone to play Iantha."

"That's a good part."

"Well, why not go for the good ones? If I asked Jenny to get Rose to put in a word for you, I reckon Killigrew would see you. And you'd soon convince him that Iantha is the part for you."

I felt a tremendous excitement creep over me.

"Rose is in high favor at the moment. She did well in *The Rivals* . . . you know, it was *The Two Noble Kinsmen* but Davenant and Pryde added some songs and dancing. You remember 'My Lodging Is on the Cold Ground,' the song Moll Davis was singing when the King noticed her. And Nell Gwynne used to make a parody of it in her part over at the King's. That sort of thing does something for a play . . . But what I'm telling you is that Rose's recommendation would count for something."

"Maggie, it sounds exciting."

"Well, there is no harm in trying. I'll speak to Jenny."

She did, with the result that I was interviewed and given the part.

So I was back again. My tragedy had faded far into the past. I had an enchanting baby. True, I was an unmarried mother, which gave me considerable qualms, in spite of the fact that Maggie had endowed me with a husband who had been fighting in Holland and who had now been conveniently killed off by Maggie's fertile imagination, and the past was safely buried. One cannot mourn forever, and Maggie, eternally optimistic, pointed out that as we learn a great deal from our mistakes, they are often blessings in disguise.

Iantha was quite a success. Davenant was pleased with my performance, and I knew there would be other parts.

Then one evening, to my dismay, when I was coming out of the theater I saw Jack.

I stopped short. I wanted to run. I could not, of course. There was only one course to take. I must face him.

"Well met, Sarah," he said.

"No," I heard myself say, as coolly as I could. "I would say ill met."

"Sarah, try to understand."

"I have understood too well and I am in a hurry."

"You can give me a moment."

"I have no time at all to give you."

I was feeling calmer. It was the sight of his handsome face that brought the memories rushing back. I had loved him. I had been so happy with him—until I had discovered him for what he really was: a rake, a libertine, a man who would lie and cheat and not care what he did to other people merely to gain his own ends.

"I just want a little of your time. You are not happy without me."

"You ever had a too high opinion of yourself. I am very happy to be away from you, thank you."

"I do not believe that."

"Believe what you will."

I turned, but he was beside me, laying a hand on my arm.

"I have been hearing news of you."

"I will say goodbye."

"Not yet." There was a note of authority in his voice and he was holding my arm. "I have heard that you have a child."

I forgot my cool dignity for a moment. "Who told you that?" I demanded.

"My dear, it is not difficult to get news of the rising star actress Sarah Standish."

"Yes, it's true," I said.

"A little girl, Kate. She is mine, of course."

"She is nothing to do with you."

I saw a smile touch his mouth. "So, it was some other. You left me to go to a lover."

"I will hear no more of this nonsense."

"I know that child is mine as well as yours."

I was afraid. He could not take Kate from me. That could not be. Besides, what would he do with a child? Still, I was trembling.

"You forfeited all rights," I said.

"It was you who left me, remember?"

"You deceived me. You ruined my life for a whim. The kindest thing I could ask you to do to repay me in some small way is to go away and never attempt to see me again."

He looked stunned. He was looking at me with a certain sadness in his eyes. I felt myself relenting a little. Then I thought: He is but playing a part. He is only trying to discomfort me. He has no right whatsoever to see Kate. I should not allow myself to be persuaded by him. I should have learned my lesson by now.

I turned and left him standing there.

The encounter had shaken me. I went straight home and told Maggie about it.

Maggie was perturbed. She did not like his bringing Kate into the matter.

Then she soothed herself. "Such as he are not concerned with children. He was just trying to trick you into taking him back," she said.

I noticed that she was very watchful with Kate. Martha and Rose were not allowed to take her out. Only Maggie and I were allowed to do that.

But after a while, when there were no further developments, we forgot about my encounter with Jack Adair.

We had slipped into a peaceful routine. Kate had made such a difference to our lives. Maggie said what we had missed before was a child in the house.

Kate was growing up fast. She was no longer a baby but a sturdy little girl, amusing us all with her quaint observations on life. Kate liked to learn about everything and Maggie and I were teaching her to read and to write, to which she took with great enthusiasm.

She liked to hear about the parts I played. I would rehearse with Maggie while she looked on. She would clap her hands and mouth the words as I said them, for she quickly had them by heart. Meanwhile Maggie would watch her with delight.

In due course Rose left to get married. She said she wanted "little 'uns" of her own. She was married to one of the traders in the market and would live close by so that we should not lose touch. In her place came Jane, a thin little creature of about thirteen years, the youngest of a family of ten who needed work and a good home. Greatly appreciating Maggie's bounty, she was very eager to please and soon became a worthy successor to Rose.

During those years I was progressing with my career. I had done well in several parts and was now quite well known in theatrical circles. There was a certain amount of gossip about me, as there was about most actors and actresses. Those such as Moll Davis and Nell Gwynne had made the profession somewhat notorious, though I have no doubt that some of these rumors were exaggerated and many of them were not so wild as they were made out to be. At the other extreme were Mrs. Betterton and later Mrs. Bracegirdle, who had a great reputation for virtue, with one or two others, including myself. Mrs. Betterton was married to Thomas Betterton and they played a good deal together; as for me, I had had a husband who had died in Holland and I had never looked at another man since. I had my child and that was enough for me. They sentimentalized about me, as they did about the Bettertons; but it was certainly true that I wanted no amatory adventures and was content to come home after the show to my daughter and friends.

Maggie had thought everything out so that there should be no embarrassments. I had kept my name. "Actresses often do," she said. "If you are making a name, you do not want to be known as Mrs. Campbell." Campbell was the name she had chosen for my fictitious husband. It was there if the need arose, said Maggie practically, "but Sarah Standish is the name for you. And so it shall be for Kate, for it is indeed her true name, and it is as well to keep to the truth if it is possible to do so." And no one thought to question why I should retain my maiden name.

Everything ran smoothly under Maggie's management and I never forgot that, had she not been called away to look after her sister, there would never have been that mock marriage with Jack Adair—but then no Kate either.

So the years passed. There was always something of interest happening.

We used to linger over meals at the table in the dining room and talk of things. Kate, at this time four years old, would listen avidly. Perhaps in a more conventional household she would have been in her bed. But she would have hated that. She loved to sit up and watch our lips as we talked and join in our laughter.

What happy days they were! Sometimes I would look round the table and tell myself I wished for nothing more. But I did, of course. I wished that I had been truly married, for whatever father we produced for Kate, her real father would always be Jack Adair, who was not married to her mother who had borne his illegitimate daughter. That saddened me. Everything should have been perfect for Kate.

Maggie tossed such nonsense aside when I told her.

"Kate will always fight her way through. She'll be all right. Her father is Frederick Campbell, lying on a battlefield, having given his life for his country. He's Kate's father until someone proves him not. And who could? My lord Rosslyn? Not a chance. He's quite content to take what he wants and leave the consequences to others. Nothing to fear, my dear Sarah. We've tidied it all up . . . And if by chance something should come out, do not forget, we stick by Frederick Campbell."

Maggie had a way of making everything seem simple.

There was great excitement when Captain Blood attempted to steal the jewels from the Tower of London. I remember the occasion. It was May and we were already planning the celebrations for Kate's birthday next month. She would be five years old, but she was more like a girl of seven or eight.

I remembered how we sat at table, talking of this wild adventure of the daring Captain Blood. All London was talking of it, so we were no exception.

"Tell me about Captain Blood," cried Kate, and naturally Maggie obeyed.

"He tried to steal the King's jewels. They are in the Tower of London, all locked up, ready for the King when he wants to put them on."

"Yes," said Kate. "Yes."

"Well, Captain Blood came to the Tower. Mr. Edwards was the man who had charge of the jewels. He had the keys to the place where they were kept. Captain Blood was dressed as a priest, so they thought he was a good man."

"But he was only *dressed* as a priest," said Kate. "He wasn't a real one."

It was at moments like that that I had a twinge of fear. My thoughts were naturally taken back to that other occasion when a man had dressed up as a priest in order to deceive his dupe.

Maggie went on describing the friendship which the Captain struck up with the keeper of the jewels, and how he brought presents for Mrs. Edwards.

"What presents?" asked Kate, her eyes sparkling.

"There was wine for the gentleman and white gloves for Mrs. Edwards."

Kate repeated, "Wine and white gloves," while Maggie went on with the story of how Captain Blood wormed his way into the family's confidence by promises that his nephew—a young man of substance—might make a match with the Edwardses' daughter.

"So," went on Maggie, with dramatic effect, "the stage was set. Then the wily Captain asked Mr. Edwards, as a special favor, to show him the Crown Jewels. No one was supposed to go near the jewels unless there was a guard there too, but Mr. Edwards could not refuse this generous friend, particularly as his daughter was going to marry the Captain's nephew. Well, then it started. Mr. Edwards took him into the room in which the jewels were kept. The Captain had three friends with him and as soon as they were in the room he and his cronies overpowered poor Mr. Edwards and took the jewels. One of them put the orb into the pocket of his breeches. The Captain took the crown under his cloak, leaving poor Mr. Edwards groaning on the floor."

Kate's eyes were wide with excitement.

"Ah," went on Maggie, "but that was not the end of the story, was it?"

"Was it not?" asked Kate.

Maggie shook her head.

"Who had just come home from Flanders, where he had been fighting for his King and country? Why, Mr Edwards's young son. And poor old Mr. Edwards had not been hurt as much as the robbers thought. He was able to shout for help."

"What did he shout?" demanded Kate.

Maggie shouted: " 'Treason! The crown is stolen!' And young Edwards came and saw his father lying on the floor. Now, the jewels were very heavy and not easy to carry, and the young soldier had time to rouse the guards, and they caught the villains before they could leave the Tower."

"And what was done to them?" Kate wanted to know.

"Now, this is the odd part of the story. It is not a moral tale for the ears of little ones."

Kate hunched her shoulders and looked appealing.

"Only," Maggie cautioned, "for very special ones."

Kate laughed joyously, and Maggie went on: "Well, he was a very merry gentleman, this Captain, and His Majesty the King is a very merry gentleman too. The King is clever with words, and he likes people who are like that too. When the Captain was brought to the King, he expected this would be the end of him. There he was, caught with the crown under his cloak. There could not be greater proof than that, could there?"

Kate shook her head vigorously and continued to gaze expectantly at Maggie.

" 'Well,' said the Captain. 'It was a very bold thing to do, I admit. But do not forget, Your Majesty, I did it for a crown.' Well, the King himself had done bold things for his crown, and it was like saying, 'You did the same, Your Majesty.' This made the King laugh instead of being angry. And there is nothing the King likes more than to laugh. Well, thought the King, he hasn't got the jewels . . . and it's all over and it made me laugh. So what do you think? The Captain was pardoned. Not only that, he was given estates to the value of £500 every year and the King became his friend."

"And what happened then?" asked Kate.

"For that," added Maggie, "we shall have to wait and see."

That was a typical scene during that time.

It seemed then that there was always some dramatic happening going on to give us exciting topics to discuss.

Maggie certainly had dramatic talents and there was nothing she enjoyed more than using them for Kate. She told her stories with the dramatic skills of an actress and her reward was Kate's obvious enjoyment. But the gossip we heard was not always as lighthearted as the affair of Captain Blood.

A few months before, there had been a notorious brawl in the streets, of which Kate had been told nothing. It was an ugly scene and concerned the Duke of Monmouth.

We heard a great deal about Monmouth during those days.

The Queen had not so far produced an heir and that meant of course that, if the King should die, the Duke of York, his brother, would be the next King.

The Duke was charming—though not as charming as the King; he was a good sailor whose love affairs were as numerous as those of his brother, but although he was a good and kindly man, he was not noted for his wisdom.

An instance of this was his frank and open admission of Catholicism. That would not have been so important but for his position. There was a tremendous aversion to the Catholic faith throughout the country, and it had been so ever since the reign of Mary Tudor, who had sent so many of her subjects to the stake because they did not share her beliefs. Never again, the majority of the people said; and here was the man who could well inherit the throne publicly announcing his adherence to the Catholic faith.

It was a foolish thing to do. But it seemed that, to a man of James's faith and honesty, it was necessary to make this known. This might be laudable from some points of view, but it was causing a great deal of disquiet in the country.

And because of this, the King's son, the Duke of Monmouth, was showing himself more and more to the people. He was stressing his devotion to the Protestant faith, and implying that they need have no fear, for if the King died without leaving a legitimate son or daughter to follow him, there was always his natural son— the Duke of Monmouth. Indeed, there were many who wanted to believe that there had been a marriage between Charles and Lucy Walter, the Duke's mother, in which case was he not the true heir to the throne?

Sometimes I was aware of the uneasiness in the streets of London. The people did not want another civil war—it was not so very long since the Cavaliers and Roundheads had destroyed the peace of the countryside and brought death to many Englishmen with their battles.

I had never forgotten my first, and at that time only, glimpse of the Duke of Monmouth when he had visited the theater. It seemed years ago now. He had staged his entrance, and had arrived immediately after the King so that all might be aware of him, for he had glanced familiarly up at the royal box and the King had smiled on him.

Now he had been involved in a vicious brawl, about which Maggie felt terribly indignant. She could not have made a light-hearted charade of this as she had of Captain Blood's escapade.

It was a custom among some of the young men of the court to roam the streets after dark in search of adventure and there was a great deal of gossip at this time concerning the King's interest in actresses—in particular Moll Davis and Nell Gwynne. The government was proposing to levy a tax on playhouses and the theaters had come under discussion in Parliament. During the debate, Sir John Coventry, Member for Weymouth, commented that he wondered where the King's pleasure in the playhouse lay—was it in the plays or in the women who acted in them?

Although everyone was aware of the King's delight in these ladies—and others—Sir John's remark was considered an insult to the King and many thought Coventry should not be allowed to talk in such a manner. Monmouth was among them, but he did not confine his indignation to words. Like so many whose claim to royalty was somewhat flimsy, he was particularly assiduous in his desire to defend it.

One night, with a party of young men, including the Duke of Albemarle, the Duke of Monmouth waylaid Sir John's carriage, set upon Sir John, dragged him from his carriage and slit his nose to the bone.

It might have been the end of the Member for Weymouth, had not a beadle heard the commotion and hurried over to see what was happening. It was his duty to keep order and, shocked and horrified by what he saw, he attempted to do his duty. In the scuffle that followed, he was killed.

Sir John had escaped with a mutilated face, but the poor beadle was murdered, a grave matter.

However, the perpetrators of the crime were never brought to justice, although everyone knew that the Duke of Monmouth was concerned. It was said that it was an example of the King's great love for his bastard son, and there was an undercurrent of speculation whether, if the Duke of York persisted in his determination to practice the Catholic faith and the Queen failed to produce a child, Monmouth, with his allegiance to the Protestant faith, which he never failed to show, might inherit the throne.

However, that was far in the future. The King was radiantly happy, stronger than most men. It was one of the sights of the town to see him sauntering in the park with his friends, such as the Duke of Buckingham and the Earl of Rochester, his little dogs at his heels. People used to say that all was well while King Charles reigned over them. He liked people to be happy; he was not concerned with forcing them this way and that. Let them worship God in whatever way they wished, so long as they caused him no trouble. All he wanted was a pleasant existence and the peace to enjoy it. Most of his subjects agreed with him, and they were very satisfied with their King.

But the Duke of York was causing more concern. His wife had died and he was seeking a new bride.

The people loved a royal wedding. It meant ceremony, holidays and revelry in the streets. But they did not want a Catholic wedding. There was something ominous about that. And it was typical of James that he should choose a Catholic bride; he was to marry Mary of Modena, a girl of thirteen. Negotiations had been satisfactorily concluded and she was shortly coming to England.

"A royal wedding," murmured the people. "But a Catholic."

However, the King was lusty and hearty. He would get an heir soon. Moreover, a wedding was a wedding, and as it was the Duke of York's, there would be celebrations. They were determined to enjoy them.

Kate was very excited about the royal wedding. She wanted to hear all about it and why some people did not seem to think it was right.

"Oh," said Maggie. "There'll always be some to find fault. Poor child. Fourteen, they say. It's too young. And him . . . why, he must be forty. Well, it is not for us to judge, I will say that. But poor child."

Kate was now six years old, more eager than ever to know what was going on around her. I was noticing more and more that Maggie was aging. She was far from young, but she had always been so full of health and energy. She complained, though not very much, more to explain her slowness of movement rather than anything else. There were creaks in her knees, she said, and sometimes I could see that she was in pain. I tried to make sure that she did not carry heavy loads or do too much about the house; but this had to be achieved with the utmost care. The last thing Maggie wanted was that we should be aware of her ailments.

We heard that the Duke of York was at Dover with his bride and that he was coming overland to Gravesend. Mary of Modena was very beautiful, it seemed, and if she were not pleased with her aging bridegroom, he was with her. He was bringing her personally to Gravesend. The King would go there in his royal barge to meet her, and they would all travel back to Whitehall where the new Duchess would be presented to the Queen.

There would be crowds on the banks of the river to watch the royal party, and Kate was eager to be among them.

I was a little anxious about Maggie. Standing for long periods, which was inevitable on such occasions, tired her very much. I wondered if I should dare suggest she stay behind. But I soon realized that that was out of the question, hearing her talking excitedly to Kate. Maggie would be there.

It was hardly the time of year for such ceremonies. November can be a dark and dreary month and this was no exception.

The crowds had assembled along the bank close to Whitehall Stairs, and everyone tried to see the royal barge arrive.

It was indeed a sight. The barge itself, the King immediately recognizable among the company, his tall stature, his magnificent wig of black curls, his feathered hat. He was indeed a King. I watched Kate's dear face suffused with pleasure and excitement.

"There is the Duke of York beside the King," cried Maggie. They were a handsome pair, I thought, and the bride was beautiful. But she looked frightened, as though she were not sure of what was going on.

The people cheered her for her youth and beauty. They forgot, but only temporarily, that she was a Catholic.

And then, among those elegant courtiers in the King's immediate circle, I saw him. He was chatting and laughing and I felt that mingling of pain and excitement which he would always arouse in me. I gripped Kate's hand firmly. She was unaware of this. I looked at Maggie. Had she seen him?

The people were cheering wildly. The cheers, I think, were for the King. He never failed to generate this applause wherever he went. There must be some among that crowd who remembered the days of Puritanism and delighted that they were gone and that life was merry under King Charles.

The King had stepped ashore. He had helped the little bride to do the same. He kept her beside him, holding her hand, smiling at her reassuringly, and she seemed to cling to him. And there was the Duke of York, smiling . . . looking happy. He had the Stuart charm, but not to the same extent as his brother. I thought in that moment that the people would have liked him well enough if he had not openly become a Catholic.

In spite of the august company, it was Jack of whom I was most aware. He had stepped ashore. He would pass very close by us.

There was a sudden surge forward and I was almost thrown off my feet. Kate fell and went down forward.

"Kate!" I called in alarm.

I saw Maggie's white face beside me. Kate was on the ground. Maggie was desperately trying to hold off the crowd. I murmured, "Oh, God, help," as I tried to reach Kate. A hundred terrifying thoughts passed through my mind in that split second. I had heard of people being trampled to death at times like this. Now it was my turn to try and hold back the crowd. Kate had disappeared from view. Maggie was trying to push forward, but her limbs were stiff and she had lost her agility.

Then I heard a familiar voice.

"Stand back! Stand back!"

It was Jack Adair.

The crowd immediately gave way to such a fine gentleman. He was forcing his way through. I saw Kate lying on the ground. He was beside her and picked her up. He was smiling his charming smile.

"All's well," he said. "No bones broken." Then: "Stand back, I say! Cannot you see that a child has fallen?"

His voice was authoritative. He was obviously a gentleman of the court. Some of the people might have seen him leave the King's party.

He stood with Kate in his arms and turned to look at Maggie and me for a moment. Then he said: "Come, follow me. Keep close."

He had moved down to the river's edge and there he knelt down and laid Kate on the grass.

She said: "It's all right, Mama . . . Maggie. I was frightened, though."

"Of a surety you were," said Jack. "Who would not be? Now, let us see if any harm has been done. Can you stand up?"

She did so.

"That is wonderful. Any bruises? No, I think we arrived in time. Crowds like that can be ugly."

He was watching Kate all the time he was speaking. I could not help noticing that she was charmed by him. He must appear to her to be a gallant gentleman, and one of the King's party, too.

"Thank you, sir," she said. "You saved me."

"Right glad I am to have done so."

Neither Maggie nor I had spoken. We were too shocked, and overcome with relief to know that Kate was safe, though deeply concerned because of who was her savior.

I knew that Jack was aware of our feelings and I guessed rather amused by them.

He said: "Now, I shall conduct you to your home. You will have finished with sightseeing this day, I'll warrant."

"Oh," began Kate, "I am all right."

"My dear little girl, you have been shocked. But I am going to be a dictator and tell you that you are to go home, and I know you will not like this, but you should have a little rest." His eyes surveyed me. I could see that he was enjoying this adventure. He had seen his daughter, spoken to her, shown himself to her—in the best possible light—and, of course, he was amused by my discomfiture.

"Are you a doctor?" asked Kate.

He shook his head. "Alas, no. At this moment I wish I were. But I know my advice is sound. So I shall get a carriage and take you home."

"It is not necessary," I began.

"I beg your pardon, madam, but I think it is, and I shall not allow you and my good friend Mistress . . ."

"Kate," cried Kate. "I'm Kate. Well, Katherine really."

"But Kate to friends," he said. "Well, Mistress Kate, I am

going to take you home in a carriage because I believe it to be very necessary."

"Where is the carriage?" asked Kate.

"I will send for it."

There were several soldiers standing on guard near the river stairs and he called to one of them.

"Bring me a carriage. There's been an accident."

To the delight of Kate, the man obeyed immediately.

I looked at Maggie. She had not spoken at all, which was unlike her.

I could sense the tremendous relief she felt. I believe neither of us just yet could think of anything else. When we had seen Kate fall down before that press of people such fear had overtaken all other emotions and we had not yet rid ourselves of it.

We had to keep staring at her to remind ourselves that she was unharmed.

And our joy was all due to him . . . Jack Adair, Lord Rosslyn, the court dandy who had betrayed me so callously.

Maggie's face was pale and I saw the lines of fatigue on it. She should not have come. She was no longer fit for these strenuous excursions.

I felt completely bewildered. He was going to take us home, after which we would thank him, as though he were a stranger who had come to our help. We must not let Kate know that he was her father. He must take us home—after all, Maggie needed a carriage and we could not be sure what effect the accident had had on Kate. Surely he must then say goodbye and go away. Which might well be what he would wish. This was just an isolated adventure to him.

He was evidently a man whose orders were obeyed, for the carriage appeared very quickly.

He helped us in. Kate could not contain her enjoyment.

"A carriage!" she cried. "Are you the King's friend?"

"We are all friends of the King, I hope."

"I mean a real friend . . . do you *talk* to him?"

"I have done so . . . on occasion."

"It must be wonderful to be at court. How did you get to us so quickly?"

"I saw you in the crowd and I realized what was about to

happen. Crowds will do that. Something of interest happens and they all want to go in a new direction to get a better view. They rush forward . . . people get swept off their feet, and if they fall, well, that can be dangerous. The crowd does not care . . . it goes forward . . ."

"Walking over you," said Kate, her eyes round.

He nodded. "But I was here just in time, was I not?"

Kate laughed. "I liked the way you made them stand back. You told them to and they did."

"It's what is called the voice of authority."

I knew that she was charming him as he was her, and my uneasiness increased.

I said: "It was a good thing you did, sir. We both thank you, and so does my daughter."

"It has been a great pleasure," he said, looking intently at me. "I am so delighted to have been of assistance to your charming daughter, madam."

I wondered what Maggie was thinking.

At last she spoke, but all she said was: "This is the house."

We alighted. He seemed as though he were expecting to be asked in. I saw Maggie's lips set firmly together.

"We thank you, sir," she said.

He took her hand and kissed it. She drew it away very quickly.

"It was a good deed you did . . . *today*." She emphasized the last word. She meant it was a good deed but it did not exonerate him for the cruel trick he had played on me.

"I thank you too," I said.

He then took my hand. "I must perforce be allowed to kiss it," which he did lingeringly, and in such a manner as to bring back memories.

"I thank you too, sir," said Kate. "You saved me from being trodden on by all those people."

She held out her hand. He took both of her hands and held them while he smiled at her.

"How glad I am that I was there. I have rarely been so happy about anything in all my life. It is a great pleasure to me to have made the acquaintance of Mistress Kate."

I took Kate's hand and drew her to the door. He bowed and turned back to the carriage.

Kate had suffered no hurt from her adventure; indeed, she was greatly stimulated by it. She could talk of nothing but her interesting and charming rescuer.

When she was in bed that night, Maggie and I talked.

"What do you make of it?" said Maggie. "It almost seemed as though he arranged it."

"He couldn't have arranged for the people to have surged forward just when he was on the spot."

"I thank God that he was," said Maggie. "But I would rather it had been anyone else who had rescued Kate."

"It may be that it was not entirely coincidental, Maggie. I have a notion that he has had some sort of watch on Kate for some time."

"What do you mean?"

"He knows she is his daughter and I suppose a father would be interested in his own child."

"Mayhap in a passing fashion. These men of the town—libertines, all of them—they want to amuse themselves with a woman and then be off. I never heard of them being overeager to share in the consequences."

"Perhaps he is not like the rest."

"You are trying to excuse yourself for having been so foolish as to have been deceived by him, perhaps," said Maggie with her customary frankness.

"That may be. But I have now and then caught a glimpse of him . . . sometimes when I have been out with Kate. I have avoided looking closely and tried to pretend I was mistaken. He was there this day in the crowd. I saw him before it happened. He saw us too. That was why he was on the spot and saw the crowd pressing forward. He could have been watching Kate at that moment."

"Let us thank God that he was. I must say, it was good to have him close then. She could have been trampled underfoot. And you had to admire the way he did it. 'Stand back!' he said. And then he had them all doing his bidding, and that is not easy with a crowd like that."

"He was very interested in her."

"She's a very interesting child."

"Maggie, I am worried about him. He . . . I think he liked her very much . . . and she liked him."

Christobel

HE DID NOT, as I had feared he might, attempt to renew his acquaintance with Kate, and as the weeks passed into months, I began to think that Maggie was right. His interest in her was only fleeting.

Then Christobel Carew came into our lives.

It happened about two months after that encounter with Jack, and Kate had ceased to talk about him. I hoped that she had forgotten the incident.

Maggie had kept in touch with Jenny Crowther, and Jenny often called. Often I returned home to find her in the parlor and she and Maggie would be exchanging reminiscences of their early days.

One day, when I came in, I knew at once that something had happened—Maggie, who could never hide her feelings, was excited about something and was eager to tell me what it was.

Jenny Crowther was there, and obviously shared Maggie's knowledge.

"Well," I said, "what is the news?"

"Come and sit down," said Maggie, "and I'll tell you all about it."

"Don't tell me that Charles Hart or Thomas Killigrew is begging you both to play the leads in some magnificent production."

"Pigs do not fly," said Maggie.

"That means that it is not your news."

"Something far more interesting."

"I should have thought nothing could be."

"Stop teasing and listen. Jenny has been telling me about a young lady. She comes from Somerset and of a very good family. Lord of the manor and that sort."

"She has been brought up to be the perfect lady," said Jenny. "The Carews of Somerset have been an important family for the last three hundred years."

"Very commendable, but what of this young lady?"

Maggie continued: "They have recently lost their money. A disastrous fire and debts and so on. This young girl is without means and a home. She has to work."

"It must be hard for her. I dare say it is not the first time something like this has happened."

"Kate is a very bright child," said Maggie. "I have often thought that she needs to be educated by someone who really knows how to do it . . . someone of good family who can teach her that little more than we are able to."

"You are suggesting that we employ a governess, and it should be this gentleman's daughter who suddenly has become impoverished?"

"That's the notion."

"Maggie, we are not in a position . . ."

Maggie said: "This girl . . . her name is Christobel Carew. Jenny thinks she would be delighted to come. Well, not Jenny so much, it's Rose—Rose Dawson—who knows about it all. You see, now that Rose has become so friendly with Lord Hazeldown, she moves in very high circles and that is how she has heard of this young lady. Rose knows a great deal about her. She had met her before disaster overtook the family and in fact she has spoken to her on this matter. Mistress Carew has told her that she would be glad to get a suitable post. She does not want some grand mansion. That would be too painful for her. What she wants is a home, where the people would be kind to her, treat her as an equal and there would be a roof over her head. She does not ask a large salary. I like what I hear. I think it is a big chance for Kate. Just think. She will learn gracious manners, as well as reading and writing. It's a chance in a million, Sarah."

I hesitated. I had often thought that Kate should have a governess. I was earning a fair salary at the theater, but an actress's work was not regular. Although I was by now fairly successful, I was not working all the time. I had encroached on Maggie's bounty enough.

Maggie knew what I was thinking.

"Christobel will only take a small wage. What she needs is to find the right place. When Rose told her, Jenny thought of us right away. They were certain that this is exactly the place which would suit Christobel." Maggie looked at me defiantly. "I am going to ask her to come to see us."

"Maggie, we have to think of the expense."

"It's not great. Jenny has told Christobel about Kate, and she is just the age Christobel feels she can manage. She is looking for a home like this. It can do no harm to see her."

So Christobel came.

I liked her from the beginning. It was obvious that she was of good breeding. Everything about her pointed to that. Moreover, she was modest and clearly anxious to please.

She told us much of what Jenny had and how she was eager to have some employment.

I said we could only pay a small salary and she assured me that that was not the most important thing to her. She had a very small income, which meant she need not be deeply concerned about the money. What she needed was a place where she could be with friendly people. I gathered it was her feeling that to be in a house similar to the one she had just left and in which she would now be relegated to the position of a servant—even a higher one—would have been intolerable. She was being very frank with us and she hoped we understood.

As she talked I was becoming more and more pleased with the idea. I was often at the theater. Maggie adored Kate, and Kate was certainly very fond of her, but Maggie was old and I knew that nowadays she was often in pain. It would be good for Maggie as well as Kate to have a young person in the house.

Christobel was bright and intelligent; and something told me that she was very anxious to come to us.

I looked at Maggie. "If you think we really can afford . . ."

"Of course we can," said Maggie.

"I do have my small income," said Christobel. "And it is very important to me to find a place where I can be happy. I was very excited when I heard that you were the famous actress."

"Well, perhaps a little known in theatrical circles."

"She is over-modest," said Maggie happily, for she knew I was won over.

"I should very much like you to come," I said. "Shall we ask Kate how she feels?"

"I was just about to suggest it," replied Maggie.

Kate and Christobel took a liking to each other at once.

The matter was settled and Christobel joined our household.

Christobel quickly became one of us. She was natural and had no airs and graces, as Maggie called them. I could see that she was happy with her new home. Martha liked her and she and Jane were clearly pleased to have such an interesting addition to the household.

Very soon Kate and she became inseparable and it was comforting for us to know that Kate had such a companion. Always at the back of my mind, and particularly since that encounter at the time of the Duke of York's wedding, I was afraid that Jack Adair might approach Kate at some time, and I had been afraid to allow Kate out alone. That was reasonable enough when she was very young; but it was not so easy to keep a constant watch on a girl of seven or eight—particularly as our house was run on rather informal lines. Christobel supplied what we needed perfectly.

We noticed the difference in Kate. Not only could she read fluently and write well but she was developing a certain poise and confidence.

In the evenings, when I returned from the theater and Kate was in bed, Christobel would join Maggie and me and we would talk. I would tell them of how the play had gone and who had been in the audience, to which they both listened avidly, and Christobel would talk of what she and Kate had done that day. She would tell me what they were learning. Kate was very interested in literature and they went through the plays of Shakespeare and Marlowe and occasionally some of the more modern ones such as Dryden and Beaumont and Fletcher.

"Do you think she will follow her mother in her profession?" asked Maggie.

"It may be. But she seems more interested in the words than the players. She is a very practical girl. She says she does not believe that a girl would only have to put on boy's clothes to be mistaken for one, so she cannot believe in the play. But the words, she says, they are magic, they excite her and sometimes they make her weep. She is bright and she is a pleasure to teach."

I said to Maggie what a good day it was for us all when Christobel came.

Maggie said slyly: "You will remember how reluctant you were to take her."

"I do, and I remember how you saw the virtue of the project right from the start."

One day she said to me: "I often think how lucky it was for me that Kitty brought you here, and I wonder what my life would have been like without you and Kate. When Kitty went you were there. Now that I am getting old and unable to get about as I did once, I should have been a very lonely woman."

Life had settled into a pattern. The days were peaceful and time was slipping past with a speed which startled me. Another month had passed—then a year. Kate was growing up. She was now nine years old. Christobel had become one of us and Maggie and I often asked ourselves how we could have got along without her.

With the passing of time Maggie grew perceptibly more crippled and often I was working, but we had the satisfaction of knowing that Christobel was there, so I had no qualms about leaving Kate when I was working.

We lived in a little world of our own. The scandals of the theatrical circles passed lightly over me. I was now and then pursued by some amorous gallant, but I was aloof and did not wish to be embroiled in further adventures. I had had my fill. I had a reputation for being cold and virtuous, which I shared with a few—very few—other actresses. I was glad of it. It was what I wished. My life was centered on the little household of Kate and Maggie and now Christobel, not forgetting Martha and Jane. A world of women—a safe world, it seemed to me.

In any case, I was very tired after the performances and had no wish to go anywhere but home. Ever since I had had that illness before Kate was born, I had tired more easily and I had a greater tendency than before to catch a cold.

This made me doubly glad of Christobel's presence.

We used to enjoy—Maggie and I—seeing Kate come in with Christobel. Kate, rosy-cheeked, glowing with health, eager to tell us what they had done, and Christobel looking very happy and contented.

"We were exploring London," Kate told me. "It is a sort of lesson, isn't it, Christobel?" she added.

"Well," replied Christobel, "it is knowledge and all knowledge is good."

"That sounds just like a governess, does it not, Mama?" said Kate.

"It is what I strive to be," replied Christobel. "I myself am learning too. I did not realize what a fascinating place London is until Kate reminded me."

"We have been to the Haymarket," cried Kate. "Do you know how long it has been there? It has only been there twelve years, so it is not much older than I am. Everything else seems to be so old. It is all hay and straw and horses. There is more to be seen in St. James's Fields."

They would laugh over the people they had seen bargaining and everything seemed very funny when they told it, although on contemplation one might wonder why it had seemed so hilarious. I came to the conclusion that when one was happy things seemed amusing when they might not have otherwise done so.

So Maggie and I would sit and wait for them to return to tell us what they had seen along by the river at Chelsea or near Rosamond's Pond in St. James's Park. When they saw the King sauntering in the park they were most excited and once they saw him along Pall Mall.

Maggie's gratified look of triumph often reminded me that I had almost missed this great opportunity.

Then one winter's day I became ill and was unable to go to the theater.

The doctor was brought to me and he said it was a return of the illness I had had before. I expected it to pass and that I would gradually recover, but it was not quite like that. I did get better, but my cough remained and I was very tired, and even when the spring came, I was not really well.

Often I saw Maggie watching me gravely.

She said: "You are not fit to go back to the theater." I protested but in my heart I knew that she was right.

"I shall be better when the summer comes," I said.

But my cough persisted.

For so long I had been shut in with my comfortable life that I had not thought of change. Christobel had solved several problems for us; we had gone on blithely. The country might be at war with the Dutch, but that was far away and did not concern us. There was constant talk about the possibility of the King's having no heir and the Duke of York's coming to the throne and whether the country would tolerate a Catholic monarch.

We gave little thought to that either. I was deeply concerned with my poor health. I had saved a little money, but that would not last forever and if I were not well enough to work during the summer, could I expect to in winter? I felt I had already taken more from Maggie than I could possibly repay. When I broached the subject to her she was indignant. I must not talk about money. We could manage. Christobel was undemanding and, as she was perceptive, she was already aware of my anxiety and its cause. She had secretly told Maggie that she would accept a lower salary, for this was her life now and she could not bear to be parted from Kate or any of us.

I was very fortunate, I knew, to be surrounded by such good people whom I loved; but I continued to worry.

It was September. Kate had been ten years old in June. The weather had been sunny and mellow and very pleasant, as it often was at that time of year, and I had been taking a short walk every day. I did not want anyone to go with me because I was apt to get a little breathless and needed to pause for a few moments before proceeding. But my spirits had risen of late, for I had been feeling a little better and my walks became a little longer every day.

I told myself this illness was passing. I had been ill before, when I was going to have Kate, and I had recovered then. I was going to be all right.

I still thought about Jack and I often wondered what he was doing now. Although I had been relieved that he had made no more efforts to see Kate, I was a little disappointed that he had not. How perverse one can be where one's emotions are concerned! Although I told myself that he was a black-hearted villain, somewhere in the depths of my emotions I was always hoping that I should see him.

So, during these little walks of mine, I often found my steps leading me to those lodgings of his where I had spent those blissful ignorant weeks when I had believed myself to be his wife. I supposed in my heart I could not really regret them, for I had never been—nor ever would be—so happy again, and during that time Kate had been conceived. So I had this desire to see the place and my steps invariably led me there.

I made a habit of remaining some distance from the house. I was afraid that Jack might suddenly appear, and how embarrassed I should be if he found me gazing up at it. I should have been utterly betrayed.

I would stand on the corner of the street. I would be hidden from view and, if by some chance he should appear, I could make a hasty retreat.

I felt exhilarated by the very sight of the building. I felt sure now that I should soon be well. It was only a pity that it was not the spring that was on its way instead of the autumn. But I would be well, I was certain of it. Meanwhile there was so much to remember. That first time he had taken me there. My shocked horror. And then, when I returned, how different! Although it was not really. It was just that he was deceiving me.

I stepped back against the wall. Someone was coming out of the house.

I stared. It was not Jack. It was Kate and Christobel.

For a moment I thought I was dreaming. Kate and Christobel in Jack's lodgings! It could not be.

They had turned and were walking back along the street the way they would take back to Maggie's house.

I stared after them. There was no doubt. It *was* Kate and Christobel, and they *had* come out of Jack's lodgings. What could it mean?

For some seconds I felt too numbed to move. I watched their retreating figures and told myself that I had imagined this. It was someone else.

But how could I mistake my own child? And there was Christobel with her.

What could it mean? I would soon know. They would have to explain to me.

I walked slowly back to the house. My breath was short and a little painful. Every now and then I had to pause.

When I returned to the house they were not there.

Maggie was in the parlor.

"Something has happened, Sarah!" she cried. "You look white as a sheet. You've overdone it. I knew you would. You go too quickly. You've got to take it more easily. Just because you feel a little better, you've got to dash around like a madwoman."

I let her scold on. I wanted to tell her . . . but I did not know where to begin. It would seem to her as incredible as it seemed to me.

She led me to a chair and said she would get something for me.

When she had left me, I asked myself if I should tell her. No, I thought. Not yet. I must think what to do. She will think I am foolish . . . imagining things. I could hear her saying, "And what, may I ask, were *you* doing outside his lodgings?"

I had made a mistake, I kept telling myself. Of course, the two I had seen emerging from the lodgings were not Kate and Christobel. They had merely looked like them.

That was the answer. I was not well. I was letting my foolish imagination take possession of my common sense.

I would ask them and they would stare at me in bewilderment.

Of course, they could not have been in that place.

But I had *seen* them.

Maggie came back with a glass of wine.

"This will warm you," she said. "Then I am going to say you should go to bed. You've overtired yourself, that's what it is. I'll bring you up something later on. First you must rest for a while."

I almost told her. But I could not bring myself to. I was clinging to the belief that I had been mistaken.

It had to be. What other answer was there?

I lay in my bed. I should have to speak to them first, to Kate, or perhaps to Christobel. I had to hear from their lips that I could not have seen them emerge from Lord Rosslyn's lodgings.

They were down there now. I could hear them laughing. They would be telling Maggie about their adventures. They would not tell her that they had been to those lodgings. Maggie would not be laughing if they had. She would have been as horrified as I was.

Kate would have been sad when she heard I was unwell. She would have wanted to come up and see me. I could hear Maggie telling her that it would be better for me to rest. I had been doing too much too quickly and I had tired myself.

The suspense was becoming too much for me. I could hear their steps on the stairs. They were going to their beds now. I saw the light of a candle through a crack in the door.

I heard their voices, whispering so as not to disturb me as they said goodnight to each other, then all was silent. But, as I expected, I could not sleep. I would speak to them in the morning. To Kate? Why had Kate not mentioned the fact that she had seen Lord Rosslyn? She would have been excited by the encounter. When he had saved her from being trampled underfoot by the crowd, she had clearly been impressed by him and would not, I was sure, forget him easily. But I had been in bed when she came back with Christobel. There had been no opportunity to tell me. But I had presumed that it had been the first time they had visited his lodgings.

How foolish I was! I seemed to have lost my grip on common sense. There was one way of finding out . . . I had made up my mind.

I slipped out of bed and put on a dressing gown.

I left my bedroom and knocked lightly on Christobel's door.

After a pause she said: "Come in."

I went in. She started up from her bed. "Sarah?" she said in a startled voice. "Are you ill?"

"No," I said. I sat on the bed close to her. "Only puzzled . . . and anxious."

"Why? What has happened?"

I came straight to the point. I had delayed too long. I said: "I saw you today . . . I saw you and Kate coming out of Lord Rosslyn's lodgings."

The color suffused her face. She was staring at me in horror.

I knew at once that, although I had been trying to convince myself that what I feared was not true, I had been right. Of course I had. I had never really had any doubt of it.

As she said nothing, I went on: "I was shocked. I could not imagine why you should be taking Kate to visit that man. I should like an explanation."

She was staring into space. I saw the fear in her face. She was biting her lips nervously. She looked as though she were trying to come to a decision.

I said coldly: "You had better tell me. Was it your first visit . . . or do you make a habit of calling there? Is he a friend of yours . . . of Kate's?"

Still she said nothing.

"Christobel, I insist that you tell me what is going on."

She murmured very quietly: "Perhaps . . . perhaps you should ask him."

I stared at her. "Ask him? I do not see him. I have no wish to see him. Listen, Christobel, you live here . . . you work for us. I have a right to know where you are taking my daughter. I insist you tell me without delay. I demand to know what you were doing in Lord Rosslyn's lodgings with my daughter this afternoon."

She said, after a pause, speaking very slowly: "I suppose I must tell you. There is nothing else I can do."

"Indeed there is not," I said. "So pray begin."

"It . . . it was Lord Rosslyn who wished me to come here."

"What? You are supposed to be the impoverished daughter of gentlefolk seeking a home in exchange for her services as a governess."

"That *is* true. I did need that. It is true, I tell you. And I have been happy here."

"So happy that you spent your time tricking us."

"It was not like that."

"Was it not? When you slyly take my daughter to visit this man and tell me nothing about it."

"He arranged for me to come here so that I could look after Kate, give her the education he thought she should have and tell him of her progress."

"He has no right."

"He thinks he has."

"So you are his spy. I cannot believe it. I thought you were so good in every way, and all the time you were spying for him."

"No, no, no. That is not so." She went on: "He cares for Kate. He wants the best for her. He told me that he did not want her to be brought up without a proper education. It was for her he did it."

"Go on," I said.

"My family were in difficulties. His estate is not far from ours. He is a friend of my parents. He said he knew of a suitable post for me. He knew that I must earn some money and was contemplating becoming a governess. He then had this plan. He knew the actress who brought me to your notice."

"Rose Dawson," I said.

"He would pay me a good salary, because he said you would not be able to give me what I should need. You were not to know of this arrangement, but in return I should tell him about Kate's progress."

I thought to myself: There is no escape from him. I was angry, but on the other hand I felt a faint glow of gratification. He *did* care about Kate and, after all, she was his child too. He had thought up this elaborate scheme. But then he was a practiced schemer. This was typical of a man who could plan a mock marriage.

"And you took her to visit him?"

"This was the third occasion."

"And what does Kate think of that?"

"She is becoming very fond of him. She admires him immensely. She never forgets how he rescued her from that menacing crowd."

"And what do you do when you visit his lodgings?"

"He talks to Kate most of the time."

"And all this has been kept secret from me. You have warned Kate not to tell me?"

She looked uncomfortable. "We thought that if you knew you might stop these visits."

"We?"

"Lord Rosslyn and I."

"And Kate? How did you pledge her to secrecy?"

"We simply both told her that if you knew you might stop the visits, so we would not tell you . . . just yet."

"So you prevailed on her to deceive me?"

"It is so difficult to explain."

"I can believe that. When you are caught spying and deceiving, it is not easy to convince people that what you have done is for the good of everyone concerned."

"I wish I could make you understand."

"You would have to try a little harder," I said.

"I wish I could make you see. Lord Rosslyn wants the best for Kate. That is why he thought of this plan. You were saying only the other day that Kate had changed since I came here. Please, Sarah, try to understand that all this was done for Kate's sake."

I was silent. I had to believe that. He had gone to these lengths to give her a better education . . . one which would equip her for his kind of world. But to have her taken secretly to his lodgings! That was what I could not forgive. I was deeply hurt because Kate had been persuaded to keep those visits a secret from me.

Christobel said: "I can see this has shocked you deeply."

"Would you have expected it to do anything else? Obviously not, as you took such great pains to keep it from me."

"I am so sorry. But I love Kate. I wanted the best for her . . . and so does he. I know you do too. How I wish that you had not been there this afternoon."

"So that you could have continued to deceive me?"

"It was all for the best. That was what I told myself."

"And so you reported to your employer what we are doing in this household?"

She was silent.

"Oh, Christobel, we were so fond of you. We thought you were one of us."

"I am, I am! I too am fond of you all. I have been so happy here."

"You were a good spy, and I dare say your employer is very pleased with you."

"Please, please, Sarah, do not say that. It is not like that at all. If you knew . . . Lord Rosslyn . . ."

"I think I did know him rather well."

"That was long ago. I was a neighbor. Our families have been friendly for years. He is not really a happy man. Oh, but that is his story. He is very fond of Kate. He thinks of her good only . . ."

"So he teaches deceit to match his own."

"Kate wanted so much to tell you. She hated having a secret from you."

"I know she would, but you persuaded her. I understand that."

"Sarah . . . what are you going to do? Are you going to send me away?"

I was silent.

I said: "You are as much Maggie's concern as mine. I will talk to her. I feel too shaken myself to think clearly."

"You should not be walking about in a cold house in your nightclothes," said Christobel practically. "Let me take you back to your room."

"I do not need to be taken."

She took my hands. "They are cold," she said. "Come, I will make sure that you have extra bedclothes. You must not get a chill."

I laughed. I said: "You talk as though I have not made this discovery and you your confession."

"That does not prevent me being concerned about your health. You know how important it is that you do not catch another chill."

She had taken my arm and led me back to my room.

I got into my bed and she tucked in the bedclothes. She said: "You are shivering. I shall find something more to put on you."

I lay in bed thinking what a strange day this was and of all the revelations it had brought.

I felt that exhilaration which the thought of Jack Adair never failed to bring to me.

Christobel came back with more bedclothes. She put them over me, then stood for a few moments looking at me. There was an expression of regret and deep affection on her face.

I said: "Good night, Christobel."

"Good night," she said and went out.

I felt bewildered and deeply shocked, and I did not know what I should do.

I thought: Maggie will have to know. I shall tell her in the morning.

I felt very weak the next morning; I had scarcely slept through the night, and my cough, which often troubled me, was now worse.

I was very anxious to talk to Maggie. But not when Kate was around. I decided that I would stay in my room and Maggie and I would talk there at the first opportunity.

Kate came in to see me, a look of concern on her face.

"Oh, Mama, you are not so well this morning."

She came and kissed me, and I held her close to me. I was thinking: She has been deceiving me, my own Kate. I would never have thought it of her. But she was young and Christobel, who had great influence with her, would have convinced her that there was no harm in what she did.

"Shall I sit with you, Mama? Shall I read to you?"

"No," I said. "I shall sleep a little. Then I will feel better. Perhaps Maggie will come and sit with me. You must get to your lessons."

It was not long before Maggie came up. She looked anxious.

"You overdid it yesterday," she said. "It's too soon to walk so far. You should take it slowly. Now, what's wrong?"

"Maggie," I said, "I must talk to you. I have made an alarming discovery."

I told her what had happened.

She listened incredulously.

"Christobel," she murmured.

"She has been his spy. Oh, Maggie, what are we going to do?"

Maggie was silent. Then a faint smile spread across her face.

"I was wrong," she said. "I thought he would have his way and shrug his shoulders at the consequences. But he really cares about our girl. He really cares."

"You find that amusing?"

"I find it revealing."

"We must ask Christobel to go."

"That would be a pity. She's excellent for Kate."

"But to take her visiting him . . . secretly . . . behind our backs."

"He is her father, Sarah."

"But he forfeited all rights to her when he cheated me . . ."

"Did he forfeit his rights? I am not sure. He may well have saved Kate's life at Whitehall Stairs, and now he is giving her a good education . . . equipping her for the world."

"Maggie . . . you are defending him!"

"In truth, I am thinking of what is best for Kate."

"She is being brought up to be deceitful."

"Sometimes a little deceit makes life run more easily."

"Maggie!"

"I'm trying to look at this sensibly. I'm thinking of what he can give her . . . what he can do for her. We have to consider Kate. That is more important than your hurt pride. Already his interest in her may have saved her life. Christobel has given her a great deal. We could not have educated her in the same way. Lord Rosslyn could do a great deal for his daughter."

"But . . ."

"Forget your grievances, Sarah. Let us think of Kate."

"You don't seem very shocked about his sly way of actually paying for a governess and then arranging these clandestine meetings."

"No, I think it is just enterprising and I am relieved . . . considerably so. Sarah, I'll be frank. I'm thinking of Kate's future. What could we give her? Consider that. Whereas he . . ."

"He would not acknowledge her as his daughter. He is married. He has his family."

"He still seems to have some regard for her, and he has gone to a great deal of trouble over her. Listen to me, Sarah. I am getting old. What could I do for Kate? You have not been in good health for some time. What is going to happen to Kate in the years to come? No, I welcome this. He cares for her. He keeps an eye on her. Kate needs that. Who knows? She may need help desperately. This is not an easy world, Sarah, for the poor. I could not bear that Kate should not have a chance to lead a happy life."

I was staring at her in horror. I noticed afresh those lines that pain had etched on her face. She was referring not only to herself, but to my long and lingering weakness and the fact that I had not been fit to take a part for some months now.

I thought of Kate . . . left alone in the world.

Maggie was right. If he had not really cared for her—and he

must, for this was more than a whim—he would not have gone to such trouble. If we were unable to look after Kate, what then? To think of him in the background was suddenly a comforting thought after all.

We were both silent for a few moments.

Then I said: "What of Christobel? Can we keep her after this?"

"What if we sent her away? How would we explain it to Kate? Kate loves her. They are the greatest of friends. Think what Christobel has done for her. She is making Kate into a young lady who will be at ease in any society. Is that not worth a little . . . er . . . loss of pride? Jack Adair is her father. There is no denying that. Why should he not take an interest in her? Why should he not contribute to her needs? Look at it from a practical point of view. There is such a thing as cutting off one's nose to spite one's face."

"You mean, we let everything stay as it is? Do nothing?"

Maggie nodded slowly. "It is always a good plan when in doubt."

So Christobel remained. And there was a tacit agreement between us that everything should go on as before.

And I had to admit to a certain relief. I had been secretly worried about Kate's future if anything should happen to Maggie or myself.

I had another bout of illness soon after that. I coughed a great deal, which weakened me considerably.

I had not been out for some time and the prospect of working seemed very remote. The winter was harsh and I could only promise myself that with the coming of spring my health would improve.

Nothing more had been said to Christobel and it seemed to be taken for granted that Maggie and I accepted the situation and that, since Jack was paying for Kate's education, he had a right to see her now and then and to take an interest in her welfare.

I guessed that he was very well aware of my frail health. He would know, of course, that I had not played on the stage for many months. He might even be amused at the manner in which

we had accepted the situation which he had thrust upon us because we were wise enough to see that there was no help for it.

So the new year was with us. I longed for the cold, dark days
to pass. I kept telling myself that I would feel better in the spring.
But it was a harsh January and I suffered another spell of ill
health.

I recovered in time, but was still very weak and spent most of
the time in bed in my room. Maggie, with Martha and Jane,
cosseted me a great deal. Kate would spend a great deal of time
reading to me. She used to read plays to me by Dryden, Shakespeare, Beaumont and Fletcher. I would listen and we would play
the parts together. Kate delivered the lines beautifully but I did
not think she was eager for a career on the stage. I was rather
glad of that. I was thinking a great deal about her future. Maggie
and I often talked of it. As yet, she was only ten years old.

"A great deal can happen in one year," said Maggie, "let alone
five or six." And there was a faint anxiety in her voice.

As the winter progressed, I believed I knew that I was never
going to be strong enough to act again. My cough persisted. My
weakness lingered too long. I would sit at the window of my
bedroom and look down on the cobbles below. I heard the cries
of the street traders and the sound of the carriages rolling by on
the way to the theater. I was no longer part of it. I thought often
of the days when I had first come here and how exciting I had
found it all. I often dreamed of those days when I was happiest
of all and when Jack had taken me from that house in Knightsbridge to his lodgings.

I would relive it all again, giving it my own ending. He was
my true husband and we lived together in harmony in his splendid
country house with Kate, our eldest daughter, and her brothers
and sisters.

A foolish dream, remote from reality. But when the future is
a little frightening, it is comforting to dwell in fantasy rather than
face stark reality.

Then a strange thing happened. We had a visitor.

Maggie came to my room.

She said: "He wants to speak to you. He is below."

"You mean . . . ?"

She nodded. "Yes. Jack Adair. He asked to see you."

"Oh, Maggie."

"I think you should. If you refuse, he will go away. He says he does not wish to disturb you. I'll bring him up, shall I?"

I nodded, and a few minutes later she brought him to my room.

He looked at me with great tenderness and I felt that lifting of my spirits which he could always bring about.

"You will have much to say to each other," said Maggie. "I shall leave you together."

When we were alone, he came to the bed and sat on it, facing me, and then took my hands in his.

"Sarah," he said, "I am so sorry it was the way it was."

I said ruefully: "How could it have been otherwise?"

"I thought we should go on being happy together, even though . . ."

"No," I said. "That was impossible."

"I have come to ask you to forgive me."

I was silent.

"I knew you would find it hard to do that. I did not realize that it would have meant so much to you. I thought we could have come to some arrangement. You see, I was not free . . . and I wanted you so much. Can you understand that?"

I nodded.

"I acted . . ." He paused and I finished it for him.

"You acted as so many men of your acquaintance would have done in such circumstances. I know that. It was a prank . . . an amusement. You would have set me up in a house, I know, and you would have been my lover for as long as it amused you to be so. But it was not the life I could live."

"I should have known that, and I am asking you now to forgive me."

"Well," I said, "it is a long time ago. And now I understand why you did it, so perhaps I do forgive you."

He kissed my hands.

"I love you, you know, Sarah. I always did."

"If one truly loves, does one trick and deceive?"

He was silent, but he looked very penitent.

"Then there is Kate," he said.

"I know. You have paid for her education. You have seen her. You are trying to win her affection. Have you told her that you are her father?"

"No," he said. "I would not do that without consulting you."

"Is that what you have come here to do?" I asked.

"No. I have come because Christobel has told me of your illness. You know that she has been seeing me."

"I was very shocked when I saw them coming out of your lodgings."

"Yes, I know. Oh, I am sorry it has gone this way, Sarah. Kate is an enchanting child. I am proud to claim her. What I wanted you to know was that if . . . if there came a time when you needed me . . . when Kate needed me . . . I shall be there."

"You mean you would care for her?"

"I do."

And in that moment I realized that which I had not accepted until this moment. I was more ill than I had allowed myself to believe.

Christobel knew this. She had imparted it to him. He wanted to reassure me that I need not fear for Kate if I were no longer there to care for her.

I thought of Kate . . . without me. Maggie was aging. Christobel was young and energetic. But Christobel was employed by Jack, not us. And I thought: If I were gone, he would be there to care for her.

I looked at him steadily and he said: "You can trust me, Sarah, this time."

KATE

1678–1689

The Dower House

My mother died on the first day of spring in the year 1678. I suppose it should not have been unexpected, for she had been ill for some time, but it was a great shock to us all nevertheless, and we were a bewildered and desolate household when the blow fell.

We had been so close, all of us, my mother, Maggie, Christobel and myself. Even the servants had been like members of the family. I had grown up in that happy atmosphere and, with the thoughtlessness of the young, expected it to go on forever.

The other day, when I was sorting out my mother's possessions—a task which I found heartrending, with its perpetual reminders of the past, and which I could not attempt until some little time had elapsed after her death—I found her notebooks in which she had recorded the events of her life from the time when she was living on the estate which her father managed, and her coming to London with Kitty Carslake and becoming an actress. I read, too, of her meeting with my father and how she went through a mock marriage with him. I was glad that I had already heard of this, for he had told me of it.

And later the urge came to me to continue with the story, and when I am old I shall read it and I shall be able to recall her as clearly as she was to me all those years before.

Perhaps, though, I shall not carry this out. But at the moment, I tell myself, I will at least attempt it.

I can never think back to the time of her death without experiencing a deep emotion. I recall so clearly that terrible realization that I should see her no more and that a life which had gone on smoothly for years could suddenly change so tragically.

Poor Maggie was completely devastated. For a time she lost that bold and rather domineering attitude toward the world. She was just bewildered and utterly miserable. I understood her feelings, for I shared them.

Christobel was a great comfort to us both at that time.

She was practical and made us eat when we had no desire to do so. She made us consider the everyday life around us which must continue, whatever tragedy we had to face. We were indeed a house of mourning.

About two weeks after my mother's death Lord Rosslyn called. He was shut in the parlor with Maggie and was there for over an hour. I was very disappointed when he left without seeing me. I stood at my window, watching him go, feeling deflated and hurt.

Almost immediately there was a tap on my door and Martha came in. She said Maggie wanted to see me at once.

I ran down to the parlor. Maggie was sitting there, looking very solemn.

"Come and sit down, Kate," she said. "I have something to say to you."

I did so and she looked at me very sadly, and went on: "You have known for some little time that Lord Rosslyn is your father. You will also know that he lives in a very different manner from the way we do."

"Yes," I said.

"I suppose, too, you have some idea of the nature of his . . . er . . . relationship with your mother. You are very young as yet."

"I shall be eleven in June."

She smiled at me rather wanly. "Still young, Kate. But you are grown up for your years."

"I do understand what happened, Maggie."

"Well, it has created this unusual situation. If your mother had lived . . ." Her voice quivered and she was unable to go on for a moment or so, but she quickly recovered her calmness and resumed. "It would have been a different matter then. But she is no longer with us. There is only myself."

I went to her and put my arms about her.

"Oh, Maggie, dearest Maggie, do not say *only*. While I have you I shall be all right . . . and I have Christobel too."

"My dear child, life does not stand still. I am getting old and more feeble every week. That brings me to what I have to say. Lord Rosslyn, your father, wants to take you into his care."

I stared at her in amazement. "Leave here!" I said. "Oh, Maggie!" And I clung to her.

"He will not snatch you away against your will. Do not be afraid. He knows what we mean to each other. He will not come here and carry you off forcibly. He would want you to go to him willingly."

"But how? When?"

"We have to think about this, Kate. We have to be sensible. You know how I care for you."

"Oh, Maggie, dear Maggie, and I for you."

"I know that, my dear. But look at me." She held out her hand. The fingers were enlarged and misshapen. "We cannot defy time, dear child. You see, it is catching up with me. I shall not be here forever."

I was staring at her in horror. What did she mean? I had just lost my mother. Was she going to die too? A feeling of intense loneliness came over me.

She went on: "There would be a home for you. It would be different from this. You know how careful we have been, and you have seen how quickly life can change. It is doing that all the time. This is your home. It always has been and it is dear to you. You are young to have to face such reality, but it is there nonetheless. We do not know from one day to another what will happen. Your father cares for you. He is a rich man and can do a great deal for you. He is willing to do this. But he does not want to force you to leave here if you do not wish it."

I hugged her. "Maggie, dearest Maggie, I am going to stay here with you. I shall look after you. I will care for you."

"Dear child, that would not please me at all. What I want more than anything—what your mother would have wanted—is to see you settled, your future secure. Your father can do far more for you than any of us here could ever have done. He understands how you feel about this, your home, but you must think of what he offers. He will take you away from here. Oh, it does not mean that we shall never see each other again. He will bring you on visits to London and then you will come to see me. You will live a different sort of life—a life which is more suited to his daughter. It will be better for you. Far, far better than anything you could know here."

"To leave you and Christobel?"

"No, not Christobel. Christobel would go with you. She would remain your governess and companion."

"But, Maggie, I could not leave you."

"Dear child, I am getting old, you know."

"That is all the more reason why I should not leave you."

"It is what your mother would have wanted for you."

"She would never have left you."

"Before your mother came here with Kitty I was alone, Kate."

"You cannot be alone now."

"Your father does not ask you to decide immediately. He wants you to think about it. He knows that you are sensible; he also knows that you are affectionate. But he wants you to look at this clearly. He wants you to have something of the life you would have as his daughter."

"But it is not quite the same, is it? Not like being his real daughter."

"You are his daughter, whichever way it is considered," said Maggie. "He is fully aware of that and he is fond of you. You might decide not to go to him now, but in the future I am sure you would come to regret that."

"Why did he not see me? Why did he go away like that?"

"He wanted you to make the decision yourself. He wants you to go to him freely."

"Perhaps he is hoping I will not and he will then be released from the responsibility."

"Kate! You say you will be eleven in June. You talk like a cynical woman of twenty-five."

"But if he wanted me badly he would have told me himself. He would have persuaded me."

"He may do that. But what he very much wants is for you to go to him of your own accord."

"He forgets that that means leaving you."

"He does not forget it at all. That is why he wants you to decide."

"I never thought of this. I thought . . ."

Maggie took my hand and looked into my eyes.

She said: "Listen, Kate. I am old. I grow older with every month. I shall not be here forever. You have lost your mother. She was not old, but she has left us now. Life changes all the time."

"Maggie, you don't want me to go?"

"Oh, my love, you know how much you mean to me. But what I want most is what is best for you. I think of the life that will be yours here when I am gone, and I think of what might be yours if you go to your father."

"Maggie, Maggie," I cried. "I cannot leave you."

She stroked my hair.

"We will think about it, Kate. There is no need for a hasty decision."

Christobel talked of it. I thought about it a great deal. Part of me wanted to go to my father. The prospect excited me. He had attracted me from the first time I was aware of him, when he had saved me from being trampled to death. He had seemed so noble and all-powerful then; and he made me feel that I was important to him. I could not explain why I had felt so excited, but there was no denying I was. I knew that my mother had not been very pleased, but I put that down to the fact that she had been so worried because I had nearly had a very bad accident.

Then, of course, there had been those visits to his lodgings.

Christobel had said: "I want to take you to see someone who is eager to meet you."

I had been excited, of course.

She had gone on: "It is rather secret. It's hard to explain. I'll tell you about it later."

Then we went into that house which was called his lodgings. It was much grander than our house and there I met the man who had saved me from the surging crowd.

It was like a fairy story. I could not believe that it was true. I did not know he was my father then. I learned that later. He talked to me a great deal, and I suppose I was flattered by his attention. Then when we left Christobel said it was a secret visit really. She thought I would like to see the man who had rescued me. But it would be better if I said nothing to my mother or to Maggie, or, for that matter, to anyone at home.

I was puzzled. I said my mother would be very grateful to my rescuer. She would be pleased that we had met again. She herself would want to say thank you to him.

Christobel said there were some things people of my age did not understand, and she would know when the time was right to tell my mother, but would I trust her when she said it was not yet that time.

I was very mystified, but I knew that Christobel was very clever, so I supposed she was right. In any case, it seemed to add something to the excitement of those visits that they must remain secret.

Now I understand. I have read my mother's notebooks. It was something very bad that he did to her. But I believed that he was very sorry for it and we are taught that we must forgive those who trespass against us when they are truly contrite. And I knew my father was that.

Christobel talked to me about my going to my father.

She said: "You have this big decision to make, Kate. It would not be wise to miss such an opportunity."

"What of Maggie?" I said. "How could I leave her now? She was so fond of my mother, and she has now lost her. If we went too, she would have no one."

"Martha and Jane will look after her."

"But she would be so lonely."

Christobel looked at me sadly. "You are very young, Kate," she said.

"I could not leave Maggie now."

So I stayed on, but even Maggie said I should go.

My eleventh birthday came and went.

Christobel said: "Do you know, Maggie worries a great deal? I think she would be happier if she knew you were to have a life suitable for your father's daughter."

"I am chiefly my mother's daughter," I said, "and this was her home."

My father visited the house.

He said: "Kate, when are you coming to me?"

"I cannot leave Maggie," I said.

He smiled at me rather sadly. "You are a good child," he said. "And I rejoice in that. But this is no place for you. It was different when your mother was alive."

"But there is still Maggie."

"She is anxious about you. I think she would be happier if you came to me."

I stared at him in amazed horror.

He said: "She would miss you, of course. But she is worrying about you all the time. If you came to me, you could visit her. I come to London. I would bring you to see her. She would know that your future was assured and that you were living in a manner suitable for my daughter. Christobel would come with you. Talk to Maggie about it. You will see that I am right."

I did talk to Maggie. I said: "My father and Christobel are saying that you are anxious about me. Maggie, I will not leave you unless you do not want me to stay."

"Dear Kate," she said, "indeed I want you to stay. But you see how it is with me. I find it more and more difficult to get about. Martha is so good to me. But as the days pass I grow more and more feeble. It would be a relief to know that you are in a good home."

"This is my home," I said.

"And always will be. Your father says that if you go to him, when he comes to London he will bring you here and your old room will be ready for you."

"Is that what you want, Maggie?"

"Yes. Because it is what is best for us all."

"But we have always been together, you and I."

"And I shall always be there. You can always come to me. But sometimes in life we have to make decisions and, when it is an important one, it is very necessary to make the right one. Think about it."

I did think about it. Every day Christobel warned me of what I was missing. She had educated me beyond most girls of my age, but I needed to be in different surroundings. "Background," she called it. It was very necessary to a girl's upbringing. I was undecided. I wavered continually. The prospect of going to entirely new surroundings excited me. There were days when I said to myself: I will go. It is what they all think is best, even Maggie. But is that more for my sake than hers? They all thought I should go. Even Martha. She said to me: "You know, Mistress Maggie frets about you. She'd miss you something terrible, but in her heart she'd be relieved. Jane and me, we'll see she's all right, and you could get word to her how you're getting on."

Then I would think of Maggie, alone, sitting in her chair, thinking of that Kitty of whom I had heard so much, and Mother . . . both gone. And now I, too, was thinking of leaving her.

There was a great deal of talk at that time. It appeared that one August day, when the King was walking in St. James's Park with his spaniels and a few companions, a man named Christopher Kirby presented him with a paper stating that a Popish plot was afoot. The Jesuits were offering ten thousand pounds to anyone who would kill the King. His assassination was to be followed by a massacre of Protestants so that Catholic rule could be reestablished in England.

The King might shrug this aside, but within a few weeks the Popish Plot was being discussed everywhere and the names of Titus Oates and Israel Tonge, who claimed to have discovered this plot, were on everyone's lips.

There was a great fuss about all this. People stood about in the streets, but I was too concerned with my own affair to pay much attention to it.

Autumn would soon be with us. The days were growing shorter. The streets were full of protesters against the Papists, and, as Martha said, there were many villainous people about, taking advantage of the unrest generated by the Popish Plot.

Maggie said to me one day at the end of September. "Kate, I think it would be best if you delayed no longer your going to your father."

"Maggie, is that what you really want?"

"You know I love to have you here, but I am anxious about you. Your father deceived your mother, but I think he wishes to make up for what he did. We all make mistakes in life. I think he is fond of you, Kate. He can look after you as I cannot. He can do so much more for you."

"I can look after myself and you, Maggie."

"I know, my dear child, and I shall never forget how you have clung to me since . . . since we lost your mother. But it is an anxiety to me, Kate. I think I should be happier knowing that you were having the sort of life that is due to you."

I was silent.

I tried to suppress a certain exultation which insisted on rising within me. Maggie was helping me to convince myself that I must go.

And I knew it was what I wanted.

And so I came to the Rosslyn Dower House.

Christobel could not conceal her pleasure as we traveled westwards on our way to Somerset. It was, after all, her home. This was what she had always thought would be right for me.

I had been very sad to leave Maggie, and the house where I had lived all my life. But it was now full of sad memories and, as Christobel said, I had to grow away from that. I must not go on grieving forever. It was the last thing my mother would have wanted.

My father had sent a coach in which we were to make the journey. It was drawn by four horses and there was the driver and another whose place was at the back of the coach. There was an outrider too, who rode on ahead, to make sure that the road was adequate for the coach and to spot any lurking highwaymen. The outrider carried a blunderbuss and sword. These men were not only our protectors but our servants. We stayed at inns every night and they made sure that there was cheese and cake, wine and beer in the coach, in case we should have some mishap and be unable to reach an inn by nightfall.

It took us more than a week to reach our destination, a week of new adventures and excitement for me. It stopped my brooding constantly on having left Maggie, which I would otherwise have done. It was my first experience of the hazards and adventures of traveling.

In due course we arrived at the Dower House. It was some hundred years old—a red brick building with creeper-covered walls. It was close to the gate leading to the Rosslyn estate, of which the Dower House was only a very small part, but to my eyes it was very grand.

Stiff and fatigued after long hours in the coach, we alighted.

The door was opened by a plump lady dressed in a blue and white wool gown.

"Welcome, welcome to Rosslyn Dower," she said. "I am Isabel Longton. I look after everything in the Dower House. We have been expecting you for the last two days. Ah, these journeys . . . I trust that yours was not too exhausting. And no need to ask if it was a safe journey, for here you are. So, you are Kate and, of a surety, I know Christobel. Come along in. I have ordered mulled wine to be sent down for you when you arrived. First of all you will need a warming drink . . . and something to eat, I'll swear. The others will be down to greet you as soon as they hear you have arrived. Bring in the baggage, Jim. You must be chilled . . . they will have something for you in the kitchens."

She went on: "Christobel, I have put you in the room next to Kate's since you will be staying here and you two will be working together."

"Thank you, Mistress Longton," said Christobel. "That will be very pleasant."

"I dare say you will be wanting to ride over to Featherston to see your family very soon."

"I thought of going tomorrow."

"Oh, yes. They will be expecting you soon, as they know you are on your way. You will want to introduce Kate to them, I dare swear."

"I think that would be a good idea. Do you not, Kate?"

"Oh yes, indeed," I said. "I am longing to meet them."

At that moment two men came into the room—one about seventeen, the other I imagined in his mid-thirties.

"Ah," said Mistress Longton, "here are Luke and Master Roger Camden. Master Camden is Luke's tutor. They are the best of friends, are you not, you two? And this is Mistress Kate Standish, who is coming to live here. You know Christobel, of course."

They bowed and regarded me with interest—as I expect I did them. I thought I should have asked Christobel more questions about this household, for she seemed to know them all very well, as I suppose she would, having lived so close.

I had expected to be greeted by my father. Where was he, I wondered? This was not even the house where he lived. It seemed that it was the Dower House which was to be my home.

The promised mulled wine arrived.

"I thought," said Mistress Longton, "that you would want to go to your rooms as soon as you arrived and I would have something sent up for you to eat there as it is rather late. Then you could have a good rest and we could introduce you to the house and everything tomorrow. I know what these journeys are. You long for nothing but your bed."

The young man Luke said to me: "I shall be your guide."

"Thank you," I replied. "It is very kind of you."

"Indeed, it will be a pleasure," was his comment.

"Christobel and Kate are already good friends of long standing," said Mistress Longton. "Christobel has been acting as Kate's governess in London."

"I am sure that was a very satisfactory arrangement," said the tutor.

Christobel yawned.

"Oh dear," said Mistress Longton. "You are tired. Would you like another glass of wine? No? Well, I am going to take you off to your rooms now. I know you gentlemen are very disappointed, but the hour is late and the young ladies are very, very tired. You both know what a jolting poor travelers have to suffer, especially on these country roads. Come, then. You will have a great deal of time after tonight to get acquainted with each other."

Christobel said: "I must say I am ready for bed."

"They will have taken your baggage up. But you won't want to unpack tonight, I know. I hope you can lay your hands on what you need. If not, perhaps I can help."

"I shall just take out a few night things. I believe I can manage that. Can you, Kate?"

"Oh yes, I am sure I can."

"Then," said Mistress Longton, "let me light you to bed."

I felt mildly bewildered. There was so much I wanted to discover about Luke and Master Roger Camden, and I was too excited for sleep, but it was true I was physically exhausted, and I was sure Mistress Longton was right to send us off to bed. I had an idea that she was usually right.

There was a ewer and basin in the room, so I was able to wash away a little of the grime of the journey. I found the few things I should need and put on my nightgown and got into bed.

Through the latticed window the light of a half moon penetrated the room. The oak beams of the ceiling were thick and the ceiling sloped a little, as did the floor. The bed was a four-poster, and I imagined it had stood there for all of a hundred years. There were a few chairs and a big oak chest, and the table on which stood the basin and ewer.

So this was my home. How different from Maggie's house! I felt a twinge of nostalgia. It was different also from what I had expected, and to be confronted with strangers when I had been expecting my father was a little disconcerting.

There was a light tap on my door.

"Come in," I said, and as I had expected Christobel entered.

"Not asleep?" she said. "I thought you would not be. I'm very tired, but I can't sleep either. I keep feeling as though I'm jolting along in that coach. Kate, you seemed a bit bewildered. I should have told you what I knew about this place we are coming to."

"Did you know the young man would be here?"

"Oh yes, Luke has been here for several years."

"Who is he?"

She was silent for a while. Then she said: "Perhaps you are too young to know of these matters. But you know something, do you not, so you should know the rest. A little knowledge can be more confusing than no knowledge at all."

"Please tell me, Christobel."

"It is late tonight. You need to sleep."

"I do not think I can. It is all so strange . . . so different. I thought I was going to my father's house."

"Well, you have. The Dower House belongs to him."

"But he is not here."

"No, of course not. He will be at Rosslyn Manor."

"Where is that?"

"On this estate. It is a large property in this neighborhood and the Manor is about a mile away."

"And my father lives there, and I am to live in the Dower House?"

"It seems a reasonable plan. It might be that it would not be quite *de rigueur* to have you living in the house with Lady Rosslyn."

"Lady Rosslyn?"

"There is naturally a Lady Rosslyn."

"His wife. Of course. I . . . see."

"There is much that you do not see. They have been married for about twenty years, I believe."

"And Luke? Who is Luke?"

"Another such as you are. He is Lord Rosslyn's son, as you are his daughter."

"So he is my brother?"

"Half-brother, I believe it is called."

"And he lives in the Dower House?"

She nodded. "Lord Rosslyn is what is known as a somewhat eccentric gentleman, and eccentric gentlemen do strange things."

"What strange things?"

"Like bringing a family, which society would say he should never have had, to live at the Dower House."

"You mean me . . ."

"You and Luke. I suppose one might have been brought into a family in such a way, but two . . . and openly . . . well, that is Lord Rosslyn."

"So you think I should not have come?"

"Indeed I do not. I think you should be here. It is due to you. I am merely saying that it takes an eccentric gentleman to act in such a way. Shall we talk in the morning?"

"I shall not sleep. Shall you? More than anything I want to know about the people here."

"I understand. It is to be your home. So it is natural that you will want to know, and you will sleep the better for knowing. I think you have been very fortunate to come here and live as your father's daughter should. Mind you, it is not as though Lady Rosslyn was your mother, but it is the next best thing. The Rosslyns are a proud family. They have been in possession of Rosslyn Manor since the days of the first Henry, the son of the Conqueror,

and that is a very long time ago. There have been Rosslyns at the
Manor for five hundred years and the line is unbroken . . . until
now. This is regarded as a great tragedy. Kate, you have lived in
London, close to the theatrical world. I think that has made you
old for your years. One forgets how young you are. But there are
times when I feel I should not be speaking of these matters to
you."

"Oh, please, do not say that, Christobel. I want to know. I
have to know."

"You are right. It is best for you to understand these things,
even if . . . oh well, no matter. The truth is that the Rosslyn heirs
have always, through the centuries, had their wives and husbands
chosen for them. They are proud of their family. They must be
of the right kind, you understand. Many men and women marry
for love. Not the Rosslyns. They have their lovers, but not perhaps
in marriage. The right stock is necessary and they will tell you
it has worked well through the ages, until now. The Rosslyns
have prospered because they are such perfect beings." She
laughed aloud. "It was different with the Carews, my family. We
have had some disreputable characters in our family. And it has
not lasted in the same way as the Rosslyns. Other names have
crept in. Cousins have inherited. And now this fate has fallen on
the Rosslyns."

She laughed. "You will say, 'What does it matter?' But it does
matter to them. I cannot help it, Kate, it amuses me, but it is
not amusing to Lord Rosslyn—nor to Lady Rosslyn. She is the
one at fault. She has betrayed the Rosslyns. And in what way?
Because she cannot bear a child."

"It is not her fault."

"Indeed not, poor lady. I'll warrant she has prayed till she is
hoarse, and perverse Heaven has turned its back on her. The
fault can only lie in her, for look, there is Master Luke, a proof
of Rosslyn manhood—and little Mistress Kate, another—and no
doubt others of whom we have not yet heard."

"What are you telling me, Christobel?"

"I am half asleep. I talk without thinking. I shall see my family
tomorrow and I am envious, I suppose. Why should everything
have gone wrong for us and the Rosslyns have so much?"

"You were telling me of a tragedy which has befallen them."

"Kate, my family has lost a large part of our estate . . . it is tottering to ruin and there are the Rosslyns, established in what must be one of the most flourishing estates in the country, bemoaning their sad fate because there is no legitimate heir to leave the place to. My lord will have to be dead before that happens, in any case."

"So this tragedy is simply that Lord Rosslyn's wife cannot have any children to leave the estate to."

"That is so. This wonderful, prosperous place will have to go to someone—well, not exactly outside the family, but on the distant edge of it, a distant relative, a remote cousin, usually a poor relation. Rosslyn, despairing of getting a family through the conventional channels, is bringing those obtained in others to live close to his home. Now, is that for his own satisfaction, because he loves his illegitimate offspring, or is it to bring home to his wife how much she has failed him?"

I was silent. I looked at Christobel. Her eyes looked a little glazed. I thought: She is very, very tired.

"Christobel, you ought to go back to your bed."

"So I should," she said, but she did not move from her position on mine.

She went on, as though to herself: "Of course, he might have a conscience. He might think he should care for these children of his. I'll swear these are not the only ones. Perhaps we shall have a little colony of them here. He and Lady R. are scarcely on speaking terms, so they say. She is very angry about this Dower House family."

"But I have only just come."

"That will not please her. I was talking of Luke. He has been here for a number of years. He must be about seventeen or eighteen years old now. He came here when he was ten. Of course, he is a boy . . . a double reproach." She yawned. "Well, you will learn all about it, very soon. I have just given you a little insight."

"You are so tired, Christobel. We both are."

She stood up rather unsteadily. She leaned forward and, taking my face in her hands, kissed me.

"You are a dear girl, Kate," she said. "I am very fond of you. You will adjust yourself, I know. There will be difficulties, but I am sure it is the best way for you. Good night."

She left me less prepared for sleep than I had been before her coming.

She was very unlike herself. I was sure she had drunk too much
of that mulled wine. It had been so warm and comforting, and
we were both very, very tired.

When I was dressed next morning and knocked at her door she
called "Come in," in quite a brisk voice.

She was up and looked comparatively fresh.

"It seems you have slept well after all," I said.

"After a while. I was so exhausted. I am afraid I drank a little
too much of that wine last night. It was so soothing and warming.
I think I talked a great deal." She frowned and looked at me
questioningly.

"It was just about the people here . . . all that I had to know."

She grimaced. "Well, it is rather an unusual arrangement. But
quite rational, when you come to think of it."

"What shall we do today?"

"Settle in. When your father appears he will no doubt give his
instructions. We shall certainly continue with lessons, for you are
young yet, my dear. But today I want to see my family. They will
have heard we have arrived, I am sure. You would be surprised
how fast news travels here. Of course Luke will want to get to
know you and he'll show you round—he loves this place. But I
do want you to meet my family. They will be very eager to meet
you. I've told them about you, of course."

"You have not told me about them."

"It will be better for you to make your own judgments."

"Judgments?"

"Oh, just a manner of speaking. Well, I shall go over to Featherston Manor this morning. It is not very far—on the edge of
the Rosslyn estate, but that is very big. I should like to take you
with me."

"And I should love to come."

"Well, why not? As long as you have not had a summons to
await the coming of his lordship, I think it would be an excellent
idea. Come along, let us go down and spy out the land."

In the dining room Mistress Longton was seated at the table.

She greeted us warmly and trusted we had slept well. We assured her that we had after a while, and we sat down to partake of meat pie and ale which a servant put before us.

"I dare swear you will not be at your lessons this morning," said Mistress Longton. "You will need to recover from your journey and to see something of this place."

"I was planning to see my family this morning," said Christobel.

"But of course. It is long since they have seen you and they have doubtless heard you are here, so will be expecting you. One of the men was on some business near there. He is bound to have seen someone from the Manor and he would have passed on the news."

"I was telling Kate how fast news travels even here."

"It's true. You must certainly go and see them."

"They want to meet Kate."

"Well, why not take her with you? I am sure you will find suitable mounts in the stables."

Christobel looked at me and nodded. "That will be pleasant, will it not, Kate?"

"I should enjoy it very much."

Christobel said: "They will know at Rosslyn Manor that we are here."

"I believe that Lord Rosslyn is not there at this time," Mistress Longton said.

Christobel looked relieved. "Well then," she said, "we will go and visit my home this morning, Kate."

One of the grooms found what he thought to be suitable horses for us and we set out. I was something of a novice and a very mild-mannered steed had been found for me. She was not so young, we were told, but was good for hacking round the lanes, too lazy to get up to tricks . . . just the sort to suit a beginner at the game. The fact was, it was only since my mother had died that I had been given riding lessons. Christobel and I had gone off to stables in the village of Kensington where I had taken some lessons, so although I was not a stranger to horses, I was by no means a practiced horsewoman. Christobel said that would soon change now we were in the country.

"We'll take it very slowly," she went on, "and trust your Lively

Lady will not live up to her name, which is hardly likely. I think it must have been given to her in her extreme youth and that was quite a number of years ago."

Rosslyn Manor lay before us. It was most impressive, with that look of rock-like endurance which was a feature of its period. Its round arches and cylindrical columns looked as though they could stand another five hundred years without strain.

I said: "It is very grand. I am not surprised the Rosslyns are proud of it and want to keep it."

"Some people set great store by such things, and the Rosslyns apparently do."

I thought how strange it was to belong—even in a furtive sort of way—to such a family. I was reminded of cozy evenings in Maggie's parlor, sitting round the fire with my mother and Maggie, and Martha's coming in with Jane. I felt another of those sudden waves of nostalgia which pierced the excitement of my new experiences and would not be dismissed.

"You will find Featherston Manor far less grand," Christobel said. "Rosslyn Manor is *the* big house round here. Featherston would have been considered very pleasant if Rosslyn were not there to remind us how insignificant we really are."

We rode on for some way. "This is our land now," Christobel informed me.

We came out into a lane. There was an almost derelict house before us and I heard a voice and realized that men were working there.

They glanced at us and one of them separated himself from the rest and cried out: "Chris!"

Then he ran towards us and, putting his hands on Christobel's horse, laughed up at her.

He was not exactly handsome, but I thought he had one of the pleasantest faces I had ever seen.

He was laughing, showing good strong teeth, and his thick hair was in disorder. There was a smudge of dirt on his forehead; his eyes were light blue, and I think it was the expression of sheer delight which made him so attractive. The sleeves of his shirt were rolled up to his elbows.

"Kirk!" cried Christobel. "Oh, it is so good to see you."

"I heard you were coming but did not know you had arrived."

"This is my brother, Kirkwell," Christobel told me. "And this is Kate, Mistress Kate Standish."

He had turned his smile on me. "Ah, so at last we meet. I must tell you that I have heard a great deal about you."

I felt at a disadvantage. Christobel had never told me about him.

"And so you have come to the Dower House. Well then, we shall be neighbors. I hope you will be very happy here. My sister is a good governess—so she tells me."

"Kirk, I have told you nothing of the sort! It is Kate who is the good pupil."

"No, no," I said. "It is really Christobel who is the good governess."

"It seems to me a very happy state of affairs when you can both speak so highly of each other. Let us say you are both very good. Are you going to the house, Chris?"

"Yes. I did not know I would meet you here."

"I am working on this cottage. It's been neglected too long."

"Is our father well?"

There was a faint pause. "He is as ever," said Kirkwell. "He will be overjoyed to see you . . . and Mistress Kate. We were not sure when you would arrive."

"It's good to be here, Kirk."

"It seems odd. You here . . . and not with the family."

"Yes . . . but I nearly am. I am home, really."

"You were so far away in London." He looked at me. "Are you going to enjoy the country, do you think, Mistress Kate?"

"It has all been very pleasant so far."

"Are you going home now?" said Kirk, turning to his sister. "I'll come with you. Wait just a moment."

He left us and went back to the cottage where he had been working.

"You did not tell me you have a brother," I said to Christobel.

"Did I not?" she said.

In fact, I thought, she told me very little. I believe now it was because she had come to us through my father and one of the conditions of her employment was that my mother should not know this. So it must have seemed wise to say as little as possible about herself. And now I was learning a great deal in a very short time.

Kirkwell had rejoined us. He was riding a strong-looking black horse.

"This is my home, Kate," said Christobel as a house came into sight.

I thought it was charming—more cozy than the great Norman fortress which was Rosslyn Manor. Featherston Manor was of red brick. There was a gatehouse and I was enchanted by the gables and turrets.

We alighted. Kirkwell said: "I'll take the horses. There's only old Tom in the stables nowadays with young Arthur to help him."

"Of course," said Christobel. "We'll go in. Father will be in his study, I suppose."

"I dare say."

We went into the hall. I was aware that it was rather shabby. Perhaps I noticed that after the perfection of the Dower House; and Martha had scrupulously attended to household chores in Maggie's house.

The walls were paneled from floor to ceiling with narrow oak planks carved in the pattern known as linenfold. I noticed that it was broken away in one or two places. The fireplace was high and open and there was a coat of arms as an overmantel.

It was beautiful, but in need of attention; even I could see that. I thought of the brother in the fields as a workman, and Christobel who had had to go into the world as a governess.

There was no doubt about it: the Carews were poor and this once-fine mansion must be a drain on their income.

"Miss Chris!" A woman had come into the hall. She was middle-aged and plump, with rather wispy hair straying from under the cap she wore.

With a cry of "Carrie!" Christobel threw herself into her arms. They stood holding each other for some minutes. They were laughing and nearly crying too. I stood still, watching them, sharing in the joy of their reunion.

"So, you are here at last. My little one, you're so thin! What have they been doing, starving you?"

"Well, you make up for me . . ." said Christobel.

"You get away with you."

"And, Carrie, how is it? Is all well?"

I detected a note of anxiety in her voice. She had certainly told me very little. That and last night's outburst seemed to have shown me a different side to her part of it all.

She remembered me then and said: "This is Mistress Kate Standish, my pupil."

"You with a pupil!" It was as though Carrie was so delighted to have Christobel with her that she could not spare a thought for anyone else, but she reluctantly turned from Christobel to me. "Oh yes indeed, Mistress Kate." Her dark brown eyes, still misty from greeting Christobel, swept over me rather pityingly, I imagined. I wondered whether she knew of my mother's death and the truth of my unusual parentage.

"So, you've come to stay at the Dower House and Mistress Chris has been teaching you . . . and is going on with it. Well, I never thought to see the day. Oh, here's May."

May, I discovered, was Carrie's niece who had come to help her and, as Carrie was very short of help in the house, her presence was necessary.

They talked for a while, not paying very much attention to me, which was natural enough. They were so pleased to have Christobel back.

Kirkwell came into the hall.

"Still down here?" he said. "I thought you'd be with our father."

"I had to see Carrie, and then May came . . ."

"Of course, of course. I'll go and tell him you are here. I think he is with Father Greville."

"With whom?" asked Christobel.

"Father Greville's a priest. He is visiting this part of the world. He's been staying in this house for some days now. He is moving round the district . . . visiting the faithful."

"So Father is still . . ."

"As fervent as ever," said Kirkwell. "I'll go up now and come back for you if it is all right."

He left us, and Christobel said to me: "Our father is very much involved with his religion. He always leaned towards it. We were constantly having priests to stay. In fact, he was far more interested in his faith than in running the estate. It was a passion with him."

I thought what an exciting morning it was. I was learning so

much that I did not know before. Christobel was like a new person
to me.

She was a very unusual woman and seemed to pass through
stages. She had come to me as a governess and I had known that,
like so many of her profession, she had been brought up to be a
lady and, finding herself in straitened circumstances, had had to
join one of the only professions open to her. There was nothing
particularly extraordinary about that; until she had been exposed
as the spy of Lord Rosslyn. Now I was being introduced to a
background of which I had been almost entirely ignorant, though
I had known that it was an impoverished one, as it was because
of financial shortcomings that she had been sent our way.

It was most intriguing.

Kirkwell returned. He said: "Father Greville has gone to his
room and our father awaits you."

"Then we'll come," said Christobel.

I followed them up the stairs. We went through a small chapel.
I noticed the lighted candles on the altar and the big statue of
the Virgin Mary. There was a small room leading from the chapel
and we went into this.

A man turned to us as we entered. He seemed old but I think
he would have been no more than fifty. He was wearing a dark
robe, rather like that of a priest. He gave the impression of not
being a part of this world—rather as a monk might have been.

His eyes were on Christobel.

"My dear child," he said, as she went to him and put her arms
about him, "you have come. I knew God would answer my prayers."

"Yes, I am here, Father, and I shall be here for a while, I
think."

"Bless you, my child."

"I must introduce you to Mistress Kate Standish, my pupil.
Kate, this is my father, Sir Harold Carew."

He took my hands in his and held them firmly while he looked
into my face. I immediately began to think of all the little sins I
might have committed, for I felt that, being so good, he would
be aware of them . . . even those which I might not know were
sins. Good people were always so very much more aware of sins
than people like myself.

"May God bless you, my child," he said.

"You are well, Father?" asked Christobel.

"God has been good to me."

Kirkwell came in. I was very pleased to see him. I was completely at a loss to know what was expected of me.

Christobel seemed a little uneasy too.

But Kirkwell said: "Is it not fortunate that we have Christobel back with us, Father?"

"God has seen fit to give her back to us."

"Well, we never really lost her," said Kirkwell.

"Indeed, God has been good."

It seemed that God must be everpresent for Christobel's father.

I was quite unprepared for this. I wished Christobel had told me what to expect. I wondered how I should address him if the need arose. I understood he was Sir Harold.

Kirkwell seemed to be aware of my uncertainty. He said: "Is this your first visit to this part of the country, Mistress Kate?"

I told him it was.

"Christobel must take you round the neighborhood. It is a very beautiful part of the country—but perhaps we think so because it is our native heath. However, Christobel should certainly show you some of our beauty spots. The Quantock Hills are a delight, and she should take you to Bridgwater and Taunton and most certainly to Sedgemoor. On Sedgemoor you can see for miles— the Quantocks to the south and the Bristol Channel to the north, and the Mendip Hills. There will be plenty for you to see."

"It sounds delightful," I replied. "I shall look forward to it."

"I have plans for her," said Christobel.

Sir Harold, who did not appear to have been listening to this conversation, said suddenly: "You must visit the church in Crantock close by here. It is a beautiful old place. It is sad that it is no longer used for the celebration of the true faith."

Kirkwell said that he had work to do and should get back to it. He had high hopes of restoring the barns and they were going to be very useful when they could be put to the use for which they were intended.

We left with him.

Christobel said to Kirkwell: "He has not changed."

"No, he becomes more and more immersed in his religion and,

of course, is becoming obsessed by one thing: the return to Rome.
I do not like it. I am a little afraid. Father Greville has spent a
great deal of time about here." He shrugged his shoulders. "If
only our father would have other interests. The estate, for instance."

Christobel sighed. By this time we had descended to the hall
and there laid out was a flask of wine with some oat cakes.

Carrie appeared.

"I thought you would like something to refresh yourselves with.
We do not want the young lady to think we do not know how to
look after our guests."

She smiled at me. I liked her. I had been a little depressed by
the old man and his constant references to God.

The wine was fruity and the cakes were good. I liked Kirkwell,
and I thought how different he and Christobel were from their
father.

I suppose it was because they regarded me as a child that they
talked freely before me.

"Is it improving?" asked Christobel earnestly.

Kirkwell smiled. "I think I may say it is. It is a great challenge,
Chris. But things are beginning to work out a little to our advantage. Crops were quite good this year on the home farm. I've
been able to take on a new man."

"Oh, that is good news."

"He is quite a good worker. He does all sorts of odd jobs, which
is what I need. He has firm religious beliefs."

"He should get on well with Father."

"Alas, his are on the opposite side. He is one of the old Puritans, I think. In any case, he is a firm Protestant. He is very
disturbed that the King might die and the Duke of York become
King, in which case he might bring back the Catholic rule. He
is quite fierce. I avoid getting into conversation with him. I saw
him give Father Greville quite a murderous look the other day.
He was passing outside the house when Father Greville had been
visiting."

"Oh, dear. I'll look out for him. What is his name?"

"Isaac Napp. He is quite a good worker. I think I was lucky
to find him."

"Kirk, I am so glad things are getting better. Do you think

you are going to save the old place so that we do not have to lose it?"

"I am determined to. But we are forgetting Mistress Kate," he said. He turned to me. "Christobel has probably told you about the troubles we are having here. In any case, it must be obvious. You see, everything here has been rather neglected. Our grandfather was a gambler and that was not good for the place. Our father is no gambler, but he never had any great interest in it. He ought to have gone into the Church. That is why we talk about it so much."

I said: "But you are going to put that right."

He laughed. "Mistress Kate, I like you. I like you very much. You believe in me, do you not? That is what I say: I am going to make it right. And I shall."

He smiled at me in such a friendly fashion that I felt very happy.

Soon after that we left and we rode back to the Dower House. I had been very interested to meet Christobel's family.

There was much to claim my attention during those first days at the Dower House. It was managed with the utmost efficiency by Isabel Longton, who kept her two maids, Daisy and Annie, in the same good order as she did the house. She gave no indication that this was not the most conventional of households.

My half-brother Luke was as interested in me as I was in him. He was intrigued by my theatrical background and wanted to hear more about my mother and Maggie and the house in London.

He told me his mother had been a companion to Lady Rosslyn. When Luke's existence was discovered, our father had set her up in a house in Bridgwater, where Luke had been born. He remembered her with sadness. She had been gentle and beautiful, according to him. When he was only five years old, he had come into the house and found her sitting in a chair, staring ahead of her. She did not speak to him. In fact, she never spoke to him again. She had had a heart attack and died a few hours after he found her.

He remembered that day as the blackest in his life.

He looked very sad, even as he told me, and I could picture that poor bewildered child who had lost the one he cared for most in the world. It was worse because he could not understand what had happened. Someone told him she had gone to stay with the angels and he had wanted to know why she had not taken him with her. She had always taken him everywhere before. And when would she come back? He was frightened and even angry with her for leaving him.

"For the next five years I lived on a farm. There were other children. I thought I was dead and had descended into Hell. And then I began to understand what had happened.

"I was a serious boy, I think. I suppose that, with that having happened, one might become serious. There were other children on the farm—the children of the farmer and his wife. It was not that they were unkind to me, but I knew I was not one of them. I was the outsider. While I was on the farm my father came to see me once or twice. I know now that he kept a watch on me, but he did not often come to see me. I did not know he was my father then. He seemed a very important gentleman, and when he came there was always a great deal of fuss on the farm. Everything was polished and the best they had brought out. I suppose the money for my keep was important to them.

"Then one day he came when I was nearly ten years old, so I must have been at the farm for five years or so. He said to me, 'You're not happy here, boy, are you?' He called me boy, never Luke. He was different from everyone I had ever known. He was so important, so grand. He did not speak as we spoke. I think it was my manner of speaking which made him act as he did. 'You must be educated, boy,' he said. 'You can't go through life like a farm laborer.' He was very thoughtful. He looked at me in an odd way, and I thought I had annoyed him. And then he laid his hand on my shoulder and reassured me. I was not sure what it meant, but I soon discovered. Shortly after that I was brought to the Dower House, and Roger came."

"You were happier then?" I said.

He smiled. "There was much to make me so. I was not the outsider any more. Life was very different and I began to learn something about myself. In time I discovered that Lord Rosslyn was actually my father. I learned to read and write with Roger, and it was like a new world opening for me. My father came now and then to see me. He was pleased with the change in me, I saw that, and I determined to improve myself. Oh yes, it was a change for the better, I can tell you. And when I saw Rosslyn Manor and I realized that the owner was my father, I was so proud. I loved the place. I became friendly with James Morton, the agent who looks after the estate. I was constantly trying to see him. He must have found me something of a nuisance. I used to get him to talk about the estate and all the things that had to be done. Now and then I would ride with him and I wished beyond everything that, instead of being born to my mother, I had been Lady Rosslyn's son—then that great estate would be mine. Then I thought of my mother and how dearly I loved her, and how my life was plunged into unhappiness after that time when I lost her forever. I can see her face now . . . and when I compare it with that of Lady Rosslyn . . ."

"You have met her, then?"

"I have seen her. She is proud and haughty and I could not imagine her loving the boy I was, and I felt disloyal and ashamed."

"It is natural, of course," I said. "But is it not an amazing thing suddenly to discover you have a sister? It is for me to find I have a brother."

"It's exciting, and I am glad you are my sister."

"And I am glad you are my brother."

"And all these years we did not know it. We could have met in the street and passed each other by."

And so we talked and in a few days it seemed as though we had always known each other. He introduced me to the countryside and used to ride out with Christobel and me, and we were almost always accompanied by Roger Camden.

Luke took us over to the Rosslyn estate. There was no rule that we were not to venture there. I supposed Lady Rosslyn would not be very pleased to see us there, but it was hardly likely that we should meet her. Nevertheless, I thought a great deal about her. She must be a very unhappy lady. It was not her fault that she had failed to provide the necessary heir; but the deficiency clearly lay with her, for here were Luke and myself to prove that her husband was quite capable of getting healthy children. How she must resent us!

I had been at the Dower House three days when my father came.

Christobel and I had been riding. We had had a very pleasant time. We had called at Featherston and had spent a merry hour with Kirkwell and the agent from Rosslyn Manor, who happened to have called.

Kirkwell told us that he had been consulting James Morton about some problems.

"He is the expert," said Kirkwell.

"More years of experience," explained James Morton modestly.

"But," added Kirkwell, "I am learning."

"And doubtless will surpass me one day."

I liked the agent. He was about twenty-eight years old, I suppose, a good ten years older than Kirkwell, but he was not in the least boastful of his superior knowledge.

"I am so glad he and Kirkwell have become such good friends," Christobel said as we rode away.

As soon as we arrived at the Dower House, Mistress Longton's manner told us that something had happened. She came hurrying out to tell us: "His lordship is in the sitting room. He has been waiting for ten minutes."

Christobel tried to look unconcerned, but did not manage it very well.

She said: "Well, if he had warned us that he was coming we should not have been out."

"It's Mistress Kate he'll want to see. Best get in there without delay, my dear."

He had been standing at the window, looking out, so he would have seen us arrive.

"Ah, Kate," he said. "Have you enjoyed your ride?"

"Yes, thank you."

"Come. Sit down. I would speak with you."

I sat down and he pulled up another chair so that he was close to me.

"You look well," he said. "I believe the country life suits you."

"Everyone has been very kind," I said.

"Mistress Longton assures me that you are happy here. And

you are continuing with your lessons under the guidance of Mistress Christobel?"

"Oh yes, indeed."

"That is well. You will be safer here. London is not a good place to be in at the moment."

"Have you seen Maggie?"

"I have. And I assured her that you have arrived safely and will write to her and tell her what you have found here. I hope you will give a good report of us."

"Oh yes."

"And thanks to Mistress Christobel, you can write a good hand." He looked at me earnestly. "I hope that you are going to be happy here. What think you of your brother?"

"I like Luke very much."

"A good boy. Ambitious . . . I like that. Perhaps it is good . . . but perhaps not. That remains to be seen. I gather you are exploring the countryside?"

"Yes."

"And you have been to Featherston?"

"Yes, we have just returned from there."

"And you have been meeting Mistress Christobel's family?"

"Yes, I met her brother and her father . . ."

"Ah," he said, frowning. "Her brother is an enterprising young man, making the best of a difficult job. How they have let that place go to ruin! But he's doing well. He will do it. The old man is not much use."

"You mean Sir Harold?"

"Yes, Sir Harold. If only he paid as much attention to looking after his home on earth as he does to concerning himself with his seat in Heaven, he might be able to offer his children some security. So you met him?"

"It was not for long."

"And what did he say to you?"

"He talked mostly about God."

That made him laugh. "Oh, these saints," he said. "How uncomfortable they make everyone else!"

"And Maggie is well? You said that London was not a pleasant place to be in at this time."

"You have heard of Titus Oates?"

"Yes, everyone was talking about him before I left."

"Well, it has become worse. He has produced this plot which the Catholics are said to have hatched and which is designed to bring England back to the Church of Rome after murdering all the Protestants. It is making life very uncomfortable for a number of people."

"And Maggie?"

"This would not touch Maggie. But there is something unpleasant about the whole business. That is why I said that at this time London is a place from which it is best to be away."

"So many things happen there. There was the plague and the fire."

"Before your time, my child. It is the capital city, and, as you say, such events are more likely to take place there than in small unimportant towns or villages. Well, I am glad to see you have settled in. Mistress Longton tells me you and she are good friends and that Mistress Christobel is a pleasure to have in the house. So everything seems satisfactory."

"And you, my lord, are well and happy?" I said.

He looked at me oddly, a strange smile on his lips.

"I thank you for your kind enquiries," he said. But he did not answer my question.

There were so many other questions I wanted to ask him. It is rather unsettling, suddenly to be confronted with a father and a brother whom one did not know one possessed not very long before.

But I could not say I was displeased by my new life. Much as I had hated leaving Maggie, I could not help being pleased that I was at the Dower House.

The Spy

IT WAS ONLY RARELY that I thought about the strangeness of our situation. I suppose it was accepted by the people around us more easily than it would have been in another age.

The King had several illegitimate children: they enjoyed high honors and included the Duke of Monmouth himself. In our community Lord Rosslyn was as the King, and if he pleased to house his children in his Dower House, that he might in a mild manner supervise their upbringing without any inconvenience to himself, it was not for his inferiors to question the matter. He could hardly have brought the children into his immediate circle. But what of Lady Rosslyn? How did she feel about having other women's children brought to live as her immediate neighbors? It could seem like an insult and a reproach.

However, it seemed that the situation was accepted by most people, including ourselves.

Luke, though, often cast envious glances at the big house. I think he had some secret dream that one day Lord Rosslyn would relent, depart from tradition and accept his son—though an illegitimate one—as his heir, since he had no other to take that place and become master of Rosslyn Manor.

As for me, I was enjoying life at the Dower House. I had Christobel with me and we saw a great deal of her brother, whom I was liking more and more. Then I had my own half-brother and he seemed to like me as I did him. Roger Camden was also interesting to be with. We were a happy little group and I had never before known so many young people, for, although they were all older than I, they were young in comparison with Maggie and Martha and Jane who had been my main companions after my mother had died.

All through those winter months I learned about the place I lived in, the people surrounding me. I saw my new father occasionally. I found it all interesting enough to prevent my brooding on the loss of my old life.

Then spring came, and with it tragedy.

It started with the arrival of strangers in the neighborhood.

In the village of Nether Green, which was nearest to the Dower House, two men came to stay. At first they were thought to be two travelers who would stay for a few days and then move on. Instead, they prolonged their stay and asked the innkeeper a great many questions, all concerning the priest Father Greville, who for some time had been living in the neighborhood. They wanted to know which of the local inhabitants had sheltered Father Greville and who were his friends. It was all very strange, and the innkeeper and his wife could not understand why these two men should be so interested in an old priest.

Christobel and I had made a habit of riding out each day and almost always called at Featherston Manor. We usually found Kirkwell working somewhere and we would stop and have a chat with him. I would often stop with him while Christobel went to see her father.

I had occasionally seen Isaac Napp about the place. Often he worked with Kirkwell, sometimes with another of the men. He had a faintly sanctimonious air and I imagined he was critical of those about him. I had heard him admonishing Jem Lee, one of the cottagers on the Rosslyn estate, on account of his irreligious ways. Kirkwell said he was a good worker, but he did not like that air of sanctity which he assumed.

On this particular morning I saw Isaac Napp walking some little distance from the house, and he was in the company of two men.

I said to Christobel: "Look. Is that not Isaac Napp?"

"Oh yes, it is," said Christobel.

"I do not know who those others are. Has Kirkwell been employing any more men?"

"No," replied Christobel. "Oh, I see. They are those men who are staying at the inn."

"I've heard of them," I said, and I watched them for a moment. They were deep in conversation.

"Perhaps Isaac is converting them," I added with a laugh.

"That is not unlikely," replied Christobel.

And we rode on towards Featherston Manor.

As we came into one of the fields, Christobel's horse broke into a gallop. I spurred up Lively Lady, expecting her to follow in her less than lively way. Then suddenly it happened. I was thrown forward. I felt the ground rising to meet me and I was down.

I lay there for a second, bewildered. Lively Lady meanwhile stood patiently beside me.

Christobel was bending over me. "Kate, what happened? Are you hurt?"

"She . . . she threw me . . ."

"I'd better get help. We're near the house, thank Heaven. Kate, don't move. I'll be back right away. We must get help."

In a very short time she was back, and Kirkwell was with her. He was kneeling beside me. There was deep concern on his face.

"Kate . . . are you in pain?"

"My foot hurts," I said.

"Let's see if you can stand."

He helped me to my feet. I tried to stand and cried out when my left foot touched the ground.

"It seems as if you have twisted your ankle," he said, as I tottered towards him, and he caught me, holding me against him.

"I'm going to get you to the house," he said. "We'll find out what is wrong. What happened to Lively Lady?"

"She stumbled over this root, I think," said Christobel.

It transpired that I was not badly hurt, though my ankle was sprained, which would necessitate my resting it for a while.

Christobel said that it would be best for me to remain at Featherston Manor for a few days and she would stay there with me.

This was how I came to be there right at the heart of the tragedy when it happened.

I had spent a happy day at Featherston. Kirkwell had carried me to the bedroom they had prepared for me on my first night there. I had had a very pleasant day lying on the sofa in the solarium, which still showed signs of its old grandeur. In spite of its shabbiness there was a very pleasant atmosphere about

Featherston Manor. Its lack of affluence seemed of little importance. Carrie made much of me and she and her niece May saw that I was comfortable: and my mishap, apart from the pain in my ankle, seemed to have been the means of giving everyone an exciting adventure.

There was no ceremony at Featherston Manor and Carrie and May sat with us while we discussed what had happened to make Lively Lady lose her footing.

Kirkwell said, "The poor creature is getting old. She may not see as well as she once did. Perhaps you should find a new mount, Kate. What do you think, Chris?"

"I think so. I have wondered for some time whether you should do that."

And so we talked.

It was later that day. I was still on my sofa. Christobel and I were reading aloud, taking it in turns to read a page before passing it on to the other. It was a pastime we often enjoyed.

Kirkwell came bursting into the room. I could see he was distraught.

"Father Greville has been arrested!" he said.

"Arrested!" cried Christobel. "For what reason?"

"For plotting against the King and the state."

We stared at him in amazement.

"I like it not," he said, sitting down and staring ahead of him and frowning.

"I don't understand," cried Christobel. "Father Greville is a feeble old man. How could he plot against the King?"

"He is a Catholic."

"Well, what of that?"

"You know what is happening in London, do you not? It started before you left. The Popish Plot has now become the main concern of the country, it seems."

"But what could Father Greville—an old man—here in the heart of the country have to do with that?"

"It seems that innocent people are being arrested. It only needs suspicion."

"Arrested," repeated Christobel. "I cannot believe anyone would arrest Father Greville. Who has done this?"

"It is those two strangers at the inn. They were not what they seemed. They are agents of Titus Oates."

"Surely not. There must be a mistake."

"Father Greville is their prisoner now."

"Where?"

"He is in jail at Bridgwater. They say that he will be taken to London."

"It can only be a rumor. You know how these stories start. Doubtless he has been seen with those men . . ."

"I wish it were so."

I said: "We saw those men from the inn. Do you remember, Christobel? They were talking to that new man of yours."

"Isaac?" said Kirkwell, and I saw a sudden fear in his eyes.

"They are spies, those men," said Christobel. "Spies for that man Titus Oates. Why should they talk to Isaac?"

"They will be finding out who were Father Greville's friends," said Kirkwell. "They will be asking questions of everyone."

"Do you think they were asking Isaac questions?"

Christobel and Kirkwell were looking at each other in the utmost apprehension.

"Oh, God help us," murmured Kirkwell.

"What will happen to Father Greville?" I asked.

They were both silent.

Gloom had fallen over the house. We were all very frightened. Titus Oates's spies were questioning people. They were going to take Father Greville to London. He was now waiting in the jail at Bridgwater until they were ready. I think we were expecting it when it came.

When we heard them knocking at the iron-studded door which opened into the great hall, it was like the toll of the funeral bell.

I lay on my sofa, my heart hammering.

I heard their voices, loud and hectoring, and Kirkwell's, protesting.

There was silence. Christobel and I stared at each other with wide frightened eyes.

Christobel whispered: "They are with my father. He will do nothing to save himself. I pray to God they do not take Kirkwell."

"How can they . . . ?"

"These men do what they will. They twist people's words. But my father will do nothing to save himself."

We sat in silence, waiting. Then we heard them descending the stairs.

They put Sir Harold on a horse and took him away.

There was nothing we could do.

It was with immense relief that we saw that Kirkwell was still with us.

My father came riding over to Featherston Manor. He was clearly worried.

"Is it true?" he demanded. "I heard they have taken Sir Harold to London."

"He is now in the jail at Bridgwater awaiting removal to London," said Kirkwell.

"This is a monstrous thing."

"The Popish Plot is a monstrous plot."

"Surely people are not such fools as to think your father—"

"People do not think. Titus Oates has them on leading strings."

"But Father Greville is an old man. He would not harm a fly. There is no justice."

"None with such as Titus Oates. Nevertheless, I shall go to London. I must do what I can to save our father."

"There is nothing you can do," said my father.

"It is just possible that I may be able to do something."

"It is well to keep away."

"I could not do that."

Christobel said: "If you go, I shall go with you."

"I will come too," I said.

My father looked at me in amazement.

I looked steadily at him and said: "I must be with Christobel and Kirkwell at such a time."

I thought he was going to forbid me to go, but he did not. He seemed rather pleased in a way. He said: "It is a grievous thing that has come upon us. Why does this man do it? It is to call attention to himself, I'll swear. He is the most talked-of man in England. He is given money for his pains."

"Why does not the King see that he is exposed for what he is?" cried Christobel.

"The King is cautious. He never forgets that his father lost not only his kingdom but his head. Our King Charles is determined that shall not happen to him. He knows the people's feeling. It could take little to bring about division in the kingdom such as we knew before. We have rid ourselves of the Puritans. We have had the Restoration of the monarchy and right glad the people were to have it back after years of Puritan rule. But the King is wise. Many times I have heard him say he will not go wandering again. He knows the people listen to Titus Oates. What do you think would happen if the fellow were put where he deserves to be? Riots, of a surety. It is the warring religions that are at the root of it. The majority of Englishmen and -women are determined never to have a Catholic monarch on the throne again, but the King has no legitimate heir. There is only the Duke of Monmouth, the firmest Protestant of all, and he is only the King's natural son. But the people are afraid of Catholic James, the heir to the throne. There is a protest against him at this very moment."

"And what of our father?" asked Kirkwell.

There was silence.

Then Kirkwell went on: "I must be near him. There may be something I can do. There may be someone who could help. Someone in court circles . . ."

He was looking at my father, who, after a moment's hesitation, said: "There is little I or anyone can do. I could speak to someone highly placed—Stafford, Arundel, Buckingham, perhaps even the King himself. But, as I say, this is not a matter of reason. The people at this time believe Titus Oates because they want to. They are afraid that when the King dies the Catholic Duke of York will be King. They want to keep the Catholics from the throne of England and they support this tale of Catholic plots."

"You make it sound as though there is little hope."

"Once a man is accused by Titus Oates there *is* little hope."

"Oh, our poor father. You see, he will do nothing to save himself. So I must do all I can."

"I will come to London with you," said my father. "If it is possible to do anything, that shall be done."

It was agreed that they would go to London, and as I desperately wanted to go with them, my father said that, if my ankle was well enough, I could go.

It was a somber journey.

We had seen Father Greville and Sir Harold leave Bridgwater as traitors, and we all knew that there was but the flimsiest hope of our being able to do anything to save them.

Christobel and I went to Maggie. It was certainly a pleasure to see her again, and for a moment I tried to forget the dismal reason for our coming. Maggie could not hide her pleasure in seeing me, but naturally she deplored the reason which had brought us. Kirkwell stayed at my father's lodgings and it seemed that it would not be long before the fate of Father Greville and Sir Harold would be decided.

Maggie wanted to hear how I was faring at Somerset, and I gave her an account of the Dower House and Mistress Longton; she nodded appreciatively, and talking of it made me stop brooding, if only briefly, on the fate of those poor old men who we now knew had been taken to the Tower and, like all the victims of Titus Oates, were being accused of treason.

Christobel and Kirkwell were seeing some friends they knew in London who they felt might have some influence, and I believed my father was doing all he could.

That left me with Maggie, and she talked to me just as she used to in the past. Alas, on this occasion the talk centered round Titus Oates, but that was because, as I quickly realized, that man seemed to have taken possession of the town and he was the most dominant figure in London.

"I believe him to be a wicked man," said Maggie, "and that is more than I dare say to anyone else. There are some who would call you Papist and have you in the Tower for saying as much. But how does a man sleep in his bed at night when through him wives have lost their husbands, husbands their wives and little children their parents? And all for the sake of religion. They do say that what he wants to be rid of is the Queen and that is one of the main reasons for his actions."

"But why?" I asked. "I thought she was a kind and gentle lady."

"Oh, she is, she is. But she is also a Catholic. They're looking at her household. Mark me, they'll be having some of her household brought up, but it is the Queen they are after."

"They could not harm her. The King would not allow that."

" 'Tis the old story. We need a Queen that can get boys. And when you think of the King's bastards . . . ! Why, I could name ten and I reckon there are more; yet she cannot get one. It is as though God is making a mock of kings, bringing home to them who is above them all. Oh, to see the airs and graces that man Oates gives himself! I have to seal up my lips or I'd not be able to stop the words coming from them."

"Why does he do it?" Martha asked.

"Why indeed? Look at him. He was nobody but a short while ago, and here he is, strutting round like the king of the realm. 'Tis dangerous. Oh, we live in dangerous days, I tell you. And that poor man . . ."

"I saw him, Maggie. He thought of nothing but his religion. And now these . . ."

"They say the King would stop it if he dared. But you see, there is his brother. He is one of them. The King wants to go on his easy way . . . and how can he with all this going on?"

"What is going to happen to Christobel's father?"

She was silent for a moment. Then she said: "He is of noble birth. It will be the axe for him."

"And poor Father Greville?"

"Pray let us not talk of it."

"Do you think my father can save them? He will try, I believe. He does not like this any more than you do."

"It will be a miracle if anyone can save them."

"Poor Christobel! Poor Kirkwell."

"Why do they do this? Why do they have to let everyone know? If they want to be on the side of the Pope, why not do it behind closed doors? I expect the Duke of York has at least one chapel. Why must they tell everyone?"

"I suppose they would think it was dishonest to pretend."

"So they let forth a bag of trouble and bring misery to thousands for the sake of being honest," cried Maggie. "I'd rather see a little dishonesty myself."

I agreed with her.

Then she changed the subject and wanted to know if I had met Lady Rosslyn, and what she thought of my being at the Dower House.

I could not say, but I imagined she would not be very happy about it.

"Like the poor Queen. There is another. And like the Queen, doubtless Lady Rosslyn must turn a blind eye to her husband's tricks."

"It is very sad for them both. I wonder how they can be so cruel . . . the King and my father."

"It is the nature of men. I doubt either of them could turn themselves into a faithful husband . . . no, not for a brood of sons."

"I should not care to be the wife of such a man."

"Then you must choose well. The handsome rake with the honeyed tongue is not for you. Your father must find you a good and honest man who knows the true values in life."

"Are there such?"

"Mayhap a few."

And so we talked while waiting for news.

It came. Among the last of those to be executed for treason were Father Greville and Sir Harold Carew.

There was very little delay in these matters. The streets were thronged with people come to see the deaths of those men condemned as traitors and discovered through the zealous work of their hero Titus Oates. We sat together, Christobel and I, with Maggie beside us. In our minds we were out there with the crowd. I could picture them so clearly, heads held high, perhaps clasping their crucifixes as they faced death, proud to die for their faith. I could picture the crafty face of Titus Oates, though I had never seen it. Wicked . . . he must be wicked . . . laughing to himself as the head of another victim fell.

And poor Father Greville . . . whose only crime was to be a Catholic priest.

Christobel's face was distorted by grief. This was her father.

He had been remote, more concerned with religion than with his family, but still her father, and innocent of any crime.

How long could this wickedness go on?

I knew that man Oates was evil. Why did so many people applaud him, almost make a god of him, calling him their savior because he had sent innocent men to their death?

So it was over. All our hopes of saving Sir Harold were gone. We sat silently in Maggie's parlor. Kirkwell was with us, and there was hatred in his eyes.

He said: "Our father was betrayed. And to think I brought that man into the house. I see it clearly now. Isaac Napp. He was a spy for that odious Oates. I wish I'd killed him . . . before he worked his mischief."

Poor, poor Kirkwell. I knew what he was suffering. He was blaming himself for having brought the man who betrayed his father to Featherston.

"I should have seen it," he said. "All that preaching, all that virtue. A spy for Titus Oates. I would have killed him if I'd known."

"You must not blame yourself," said Christobel. "How could we have known what that man was? Spies like that are everywhere."

And so we talked or fell into one of those brooding silences when we were all going over it in our minds.

"I must go back to Featherston with Kirkwell," said Christobel at last. "Kate, you may come with me."

So to Featherston Manor we went.

Carrie and her niece May greeted us somberly. It was a house of sorrow.

Carrie insisted that we eat, and we did, although we had little appetite. We sat for a long time in the solarium, and the tragedy seemed closer to us there than it had in London.

I am sure that that night the others were sleepless, as I was.

It was the morning of the day after our return to Featherston. Carrie had tried to tempt us with food, to which we could do little justice. We were in the room which overlooked the courtyard and suddenly we heard the clatter of horses' hooves and after a few moments James Morton appeared.

He came into the room in which we sat.

"I heard you were back," he said.

He did not mention Sir Harold, but his looks showed his deep sympathy.

"I suppose you will be getting down to work without delay," he said to Kirkwell.

"Yes," replied Kirkwell. "I must do that."

"I was wondering if you needed any help over that thatching job. The half-finished one, you know, at Downside Cottage."

Before Kirkwell could answer we heard voices outside, and two men came into the courtyard.

Kirkwell stared at them for a second and then he was on his feet, and to my horror I saw that the two men were Jem Lee, who did odd jobs on the estate, and Isaac Napp.

Kirkwell had risen, his face distorted with rage.

Before anyone could stop him, he was through the door. James went quickly after him and Christobel and I followed, but Kirkwell was there before us.

"You rogue! You spy!" he shouted at Isaac Napp. "How dare you come here?"

He had seized Isaac by the throat and was shaking him.

"You come here . . ." he was shouting. "You come here, getting our confidence with your talk of holiness, and you have murdered my father—an innocent man who never wronged anyone. I will kill you for that."

Christobel and I were staring in horror, terrified that Kirkwell would carry out his threat.

It was James Morton who took action.

He sprang forward and caught Kirkwell's arm. Kirkwell released Isaac Napp, who reeled back, his hands to his throat.

Kirkwell stammered: "He . . . he is responsible for my father's death."

"It is not for you to take the law into your own hands," said James quietly.

"He . . . he is a spy."

"Be off," said James to Isaac.

"I did my duty," said Isaac. "That's all I did. Traitors to the King . . . Papists . . ."

Kirkwell seemed to recover himself. He glanced down at his hands in horror. I think he was contemplating what he might have done if James had not stopped him in time.

It was a tense and dramatic moment as they all stood there, Kirkwell staring contemptuously at Isaac Napp, who returned his gaze truculently.

"Get off my land," said Kirkwell, "and never let me see you on it again."

"I've no wish to stay," retorted Isaac.

He turned and, still touching his throat where Kirkwell had grasped it, walked out of the courtyard. Jem Lee hesitated a second or so before following him.

"Thank you, James," said Kirkwell soberly. "Heaven knows what I might have done to him if you hadn't been here to stop me."

"He deserves it," replied James. "But it's for the law to punish him . . . not you."

"I lost my temper. It has been such a shock . . . my father."

"I know," said James. "I should have felt the same."

We were all terribly shaken by the incident—none more than Kirkwell himself. Naturally of easygoing temperament, it was rare that he lost his temper. But his father's death had so shaken him, and the sight of the man who had been instrumental in bringing it about on his land had so incensed him that he had completely lost his habitual self-control.

Sobered, we went into the house.

We were all trying to get back to normal. Christobel said that this sort of tragedy was happening all over the country. We had to take very special care of how we acted, and even what we said. People had been merrily rejoicing in the Restoration, and now they were getting a glimpse of the revival of intolerance. People were not to be allowed to worship God in their chosen manner. It was as though a blight had fallen over the country.

In London, we had had a glimpse of the state of affairs there, where the people's dread of a Catholic England had made them accept such a man as Titus Oates.

I stayed on at Featherston. My father had raised no objection. I missed Luke but Christobel wished to be at her home at such a time and she was eager for me to be with her.

I was becoming more and more fond of Christobel and her brother Kirkwell. I had always liked Christobel but I realized that I had not really known her until I had seen her in her own old home. I believe that when we had been in London she was so conscious of deceiving my mother and Maggie that she had not been quite herself. As for Kirkwell, he was more and more my friend. He seemed to find pleasure in my company, which was strange because I must have seemed quite a child to him. I was only eleven years old and he was about eighteen or nineteen, but I had been so much with older people all my life that I supposed I seemed older.

He talked to me quite frankly. He told me how ashamed he had been of his outburst with Isaac Napp.

"Do you know, Kate," he said, "I could have killed him. I do not know what got into me. I lost control of myself. I thought of my father . . . he was so meek and mild. He harmed no one. And to think of that happening to him and that poor old priest with him. And that I had brought that spy on to the scene. I think it was a kind of disgust with myself."

"It is understandable," I assured him. "Many people would have felt the same and acted in the same way."

"I thank God that James was at hand to stop me. I shall be eternally grateful to him."

"I know."

"What is so sad is that all the trouble should be in the name of religion. Intolerance. Why do people hate others because they do not share their views? But the source of the present trouble which is sending so many people to the block is the fact that the King cannot get a son, which makes the Catholic Duke of York heir to the throne."

"It all seems so trivial."

"Perhaps intolerance is."

Christobel and I tried to adjust ourselves to the old ways. We did lessons; we read with each other and we rode out often, though I had not ridden Lively Lady since my accident. I used another mare now who was much younger.

One day, when we were riding a little farther afield than usual, we passed a prosperous-looking place between the Rosslyn and Featherston estates.

As we rode past one of the fields we saw two people there. One was a young woman. She was carrying a tray on which was a tankard of ale which she was offering to a man who sat sprawling under a tree.

There was something familiar about him.

We came to an old inn from which hung a newly painted sign. It said "The King's Head," and there was a picture of the King, dark-eyed and heavy-featured, with a feathered hat and luxuriant curls.

"I have not been here for years," said Christobel. "I did not know they had opened again. There must be new people here. It was an old ruin when I was a child. Shall we go in and see what it is like? We could have a tankard of cider mayhap."

So we tethered our horses and went in. We took our seats and a young girl came up to serve us.

She brought us the tankards of cider and obviously expected to stop and talk to us as there was no one in the inn except ourselves. She tossed back her hair and smoothed her dress, as though to call attention to her charms. She was certainly rather pretty.

"You are new here, are you not?" said Christobel.

"I've been here two months," she told us. "The inn only opened three or four months ago. There's not much trade. I'm used to a place in town. I reckon I won't be staying here much longer."

"Where do you come from?" asked Christobel.

"Taunton. Now there's a bit of life there."

"Yes, I suppose so."

"Mind you, there was all that fuss over at Featherston, wasn't there?"

I saw Christobel stiffen.

"That was something," the girl went on. "They took them up to London. I knew that Isaac Napp. He came in here once or twice. He was the one who found out about them."

This was the last thing we wanted. Our great desire was to put it all behind us, to try to forget.

I looked at Christobel. Her glance said: Let's finish this drink and get out of here.

The girl was new and did not know who we were.

She went on: "One of those old families. Lots of them here. They have their chapels in their houses, so it's all set up for them. When Isaac Napp came in here once he talked to me. We were quite friendly, but now, of course . . ." She laughed significantly.

What did she mean? That he was still here? Much as we disliked this conversation, I felt there was something here we should know.

I said: "He left the neighborhood, I believe, after . . . I mean, this . . . er . . . Isaac Napp."

"Did he? It's the first I've heard of it. He's over at Fifty Acres now."

"Fifty Acres?"

"That farm that's only about a mile or so from here. He's working there."

"I thought you said he had gone away," I said.

"I said no such thing. He did not go away. He left Featherston. Well, he could hardly stay after getting the old man to the block, could he?"

"I . . . I thought he had gone a long way away after that."

"No, no. Only to Fifty Acres. You wouldn't think he would be . . . like he is . . . being so religious and all that."

"How is he?"

"Well, I could see that when he came in here. It is the way they look. You can see it at once. He talked to me all very sober, but beneath it . . . well, I'm no country girl. And now he's at Fifty Acres, and there's that Mistress Blake, is there not?"

"Is there? And what of Mistress Blake?"

"They came in here once. The farmer's wife with one of the farm workers. I could see how it was. You see, Mistress Blake is about twenty years younger than old Blake. It stands to reason she might look around. Well, there we are. He's now at Fifty Acres, is Isaac Napp. People are afraid of him, really. Nobody would say much whatever he did. They'd be afraid he'd say they were in the Plot."

We left the inn as soon as we could. I could see that the conversation had upset Christobel.

"Do you think it is really true?" she said. "Has he really gone to work so very close?"

"It is not so very close."

"It is in the neighborhood. I wish he had gone right away."

"Had you ever heard of Fifty Acres Farm?"

"No."

"Well, it is not very near, and people usually know their neighbors in the country. That girl did not know you. If it is not so far in miles, it is rather tucked away."

"Kate, do not mention before Kirkwell that Isaac Napp is living at Fifty Acres Farm."

Luke was glad to see us back at the Dower House, and so was Mistress Longton. There was a newcomer at Rosslyn Manor. He was Sebastian Adams. He came from the north, on the border between England and Scotland, and he was a distant relative of my father. James said that he had come down to train to look after the estate, which meant, of course, that Lord Rosslyn had despaired of ever having a legitimate son and in due course the estate would pass to Sebastian Adams's branch of the family.

"He is a very pleasant young man and eager to learn. I think, when the time comes, Rosslyn Manor will be safe in his hands."

James brought him to Featherston to have a look at the estate there and to meet Kirkwell. As Christobel and I were there frequently, we soon made his acquaintance.

Luke often accompanied us. After all, Sebastian Adams was a kinsman of his, as he was of mine, and we were all eager to know each other. Kirkwell, James, Luke and Sebastian were all interested in estate management.

Poor Luke was a little wistful. I believed he had secretly hoped there might be a chance of his inheriting Rosslyn Manor before Sebastian came. Since Lord Rosslyn seemed unlikely to have a legitimate son, why should his natural son not inherit, when he was surely more close than a distant cousin?

But it seemed this was not to be so and Luke's dream was over.

We talked a good deal about politics too, and speculated on what would happen when the King died. He was approaching fifty and although he had always seemed unusually healthy, there had been an illness, brief fortunately, but nevertheless a warning of what would have to come one day.

"I cannot believe that the Duke's reign would last long unless he changed a good deal," said James.

"He may well do so when he sees what is at stake," suggested Kirkwell.

"There are his daughters Mary and Anne, of course," put in Sebastian. "The King has made a point of seeing that they are brought up in the Protestant religion, in spite of their father's objections. James has many virtues. Mayhap he will change when the day comes."

"If he does not, there will be trouble."

"There is Monmouth, of course," suggested Luke. "The King could easily secure the throne for him by declaring that he had married Monmouth's mother."

"But apparently he did not," said Kirkwell, "and he has denied that many times. Though I believe there is a certain pressure to make him admit that there was a marriage . . . for the sake of peace."

"It seems to me," said Sebastian, "that it is not a very healthy situation. All we can do is pray for the King to continue in good health and to rule over us for another twenty years. By that time they may have sorted it out."

So they talked, and it was amazing how often that topic seemed to come up. Perhaps it was so in many houses in England.

The popularity of Titus Oates was increasing. He strutted through the streets of London, surrounded by his guards. He wore episcopal garments, silk gown and cassock and called himself—as many others called him—the savior of the nation.

"It seems," said Kirkwell, "that we shall soon not need a king; Titus Oates will be our ruler."

"His main target is the Queen," added James. "What next, I wonder? I heard today that they had arrested Her Majesty's physician, Sir George Wakeman. If he is found guilty, the next victim will surely be the Queen herself."

"But she is an innocent gentle lady," I broke in. "She loves the King. She would not plan to kill him."

Kirkwell said bitterly: "A man or woman does not have to be guilty to be found so by Titus Oates and his men."

There was a great deal of interest in the trial of Sir George Wakeman, and rumors of what the outcome would be were even reaching places as distant as Somerset. The local people were very interested. Indeed, had we not had our own little glimpse of what the tyranny of Titus Oates could mean?

Lord Chief Justice Scroggs was to try the Wakeman case. He was notorious for his hatred of Catholicism. He had recently declared in court that it was a religion that unhinged all piety and morality. Catholics ate their God, killed their King and made saints of murderers.

It seemed that Sir George Wakeman was doomed. James said that a great deal hung on the result of this trial. If Sir George was found guilty, the Queen would surely be condemned with him.

One morning when I went downstairs, I found Mistress Longton looking both shocked and exhilarated, as people are when they are about to impart something which excites them because they are the first to tell it, yet they know they should be horrified to do so.

I said: "Something has happened."

"It looks like murder."

"What?" I cried. "Who?"

"It does not surprise me. He being who he is."

"Who is it? Do tell me."

"It's that man who was here . . . spying."

I murmured: "Isaac Napp?"

"That's the one. He was found not far from Fifty Acres. That's just beyond the Rosslyn Estate. There's a little stream running along near the farm."

"Drowned?" I asked.

"Drowned! A child could stand up in that little stream and the water would come barely to its knees. No . . . that was just what finished him off. He was half dead before he was put in. Someone had strangled him."

"It sounds terrible."

"I doubt not he had his enemies, that one. Men such as he are certain to have. He'd been half-strangled and put face down to drown. There'll be a bit of noise about this, I shouldn't wonder. It looks like murder. Couldn't be anything else. And when you reckon he's that Titus Oates's man . . . Oh yes, there will be some bother about this, I'll swear."

I felt sick. I could not help thinking of Isaac Napp in the courtyard of Featherston Manor, and Kirkwell gripping his neck in his hands.

We waited in a state of near panic. Christobel's thoughts were similar to mine.

As soon as we heard the news, Christobel and I rode over to Featherston Manor. James, who was proving a good friend to Kirkwell, was already there.

Kirkwell was looking tense.

Christobel said: "Oh, James, you've heard the news. It is good of you to come."

"But of a surety I must come. I do not like this. I'm not surprised. The man must have had many enemies."

Kirkwell said: "I swear I did not do it. On everything that I hold sacred, I swear."

"We believe you," said James. "But what I fear is that, because of this man's work for Oates, this will be regarded as more than an ordinary case of murder."

"What shall we do?" asked Christobel.

James laid a hand on her arm. "You must not worry." Then he shrugged his shoulders. "What a foolish thing to say! Of course you cannot help worrying. We are all worried."

"I tell you, I have not seen the man since I ordered him out of the courtyard that day. I had no idea he was still in the neighborhood."

"I believe you," said James earnestly. "So do we all. But this is one of Oates's men. Oates will want to find someone to blame."

"But he will not be able to prove—"

"Oates does not need proof. He decides on his victim and he is so powerful that everyone bows to him. Once Sir George Wakeman is committed to the Tower and executed on a charge of treason, he will have the Queen in his grasp . . . and then we might as well say it is not King Charles who rules this country but Titus Oates."

"The King will surely save the Queen?"

"Mayhap he would be glad to be rid of her. Mayhap he is more enamored of his countless mistresses than of her," said Christobel. "There are some who say he would welcome the opportunity to be free and to marry again . . . a Protestant wife who would give him a son and settle this whole business of the succession."

"He is not a cruel man," said James. "I believe he is always markedly courteous to the Queen. He would not let this happen to her."

"Then why does he allow this man to behave as he does? He strikes terror into all the King's subjects. None can feel safe."

"The King is clever. He is afraid of trouble in the land and he realizes that to attempt to suppress Oates now could mean riots in the streets."

"How can he rule his kingdom if he is so much afraid of this man?"

"If the Queen were to be found guilty of treason and put to the axe . . . I tremble to think what would happen," said Kirkwell. "How could a man like Oates rise to such eminence?"

"Be careful what you say," warned James. "But let us think what we must do. Let us not blind ourselves to the truth. You are in danger, Kirkwell . . . unless the true murderer is found. You will be under suspicion, because of what happened to your father and mayhap because Jem Lee saw you threatening Napp. People like him tend to exaggerate. He heard you threaten to kill Napp."

"Where is Jem Lee now?"

"He is no longer working on my land. He was only a casual laborer. I did not have enough work to occupy him all the time and cannot afford to have a man with me if it is not profitable to do so."

"And he will not keep to himself what he saw in the courtyard that morning, I'll swear."

Christobel looked fearfully at James. "What then?"

"Perhaps Kirkwell should be called away on business and no one is sure where."

"Would that not look like guilt?"

"I fear it might. But on the other hand it would not be good to be here when Oates's men come to look for a culprit. Depend upon it, they will not allow all this to pass. One of their men murdered!"

We all looked at James. He was older than we were, more knowledgeable and wise.

"Perhaps we should not hurry into some action which might be unwise." He looked at Kirkwell, his brow puckered. "It would not do to go away immediately . . . but if Oates considers it worthwhile to send his men down here to look for a scapegoat, there will be no alternative."

"I do not want to run away and appear to be afraid of being accused of something I know nothing about."

"I understand that," said James. "But there are times when one must consider these matters carefully. It will not matter to these men whether you are guilty or not. They will come here to make an example of what happens to anyone who touches the servants of Titus Oates. You would be a good choice: You were seen to threaten Isaac Napp and you are the son of one of their victims. I fear that if they come they may settle on you. You would be the ideal choice from their point of view."

"You would have me run away? Leave my land?"

"I would have you save your life. But do nothing rash. Let us see what transpires. It may be that they will find the murderer here before Oates's men arrive. It may be that Oates will be too concerned with what is happening in London. Sir George Wakeman is more important than anyone here can possibly be. Mayhap Oates is too concerned with that to pay much attention to us at this time."

"What shall we do, then?' asked Christobel.

"For the moment . . . wait."

I could see that Christobel was very frightened, and I shared her fear.

Enquiries were made about the death of Isaac Napp but there was no sign of any men from London.

It was not discovered who had killed him. He had not been much liked; he was a newcomer, and the truth was no one cared very much that he had come to an untimely end. Informers were men to be feared and people felt more comfortable when they were not around.

Scraps of news from London reached us, and it seemed possible that what was happening there might be the reason why no one had been sent to Somerset to find a scapegoat for the murder of Isaac Napp.

To the amazement of all, Lord Chief Justice Scroggs, fiercely anti-Catholic that he was, had not acted in the manner expected of him.

Sir George Wakeman was a wise and clever man. He was a man of great dignity and integrity, highly respected at court. The Queen's physician was also a zealous Roman Catholic. He was able to defend himself with great skill. The witnesses against him were Titus Oates and his accomplice Bedlow, and men such as they were no match for the wit and wisdom of a man like Sir George Wakeman.

Sir George exposed the two schemers for what they were in a manner which could not be doubted. Oates declared that he had recognized Sir George's signature on a document which was a receipt for money he had received from the plotters, but when he was presented with a number of different examples of handwriting and was asked to pick out Sir George's he had chosen one which was quite different from that of Sir George and which could never have been mistaken for his by anyone who had seen it before.

Moreover, the other accuser, Oates's confederate Bedlow, claimed an acquaintance with Sir George and declared he had become on intimate terms with him in his duty to discover how base he was.

Sir George replied that he had not seen Bedlow before this trial began and appealed to the court, asking them if they really believed he could have been on intimate terms with such a man.

Such a friendship would certainly seem incongruous and the Lord Chief Justice, in his summing up, stressed this. It was clearly due to him that Sir George was released.

This was the biggest blow that Oates had received since he first brought the Plot to the notice of the people. He was furious and vowed vengeance on Scroggs, which he attempted to carry out, but when he had to face Scroggs in court he was completely outwitted by the Lord Chief Justice.

This was a major blow to Oates, and he must have known it. It was small wonder that, for the time being, he had no time to concern himself with what was happening in the remote country-side.

The Devil's Tower

OCCASIONALLY MY FATHER rode over to the Dower House. He liked to talk to Luke and to me. He was a strange man. Sometimes, when I was alone with him, I felt he was going to confide in me, tell me something about himself. Then he would become aloof and I would feel that I was merely a duty in his life, the result of an unfortunate mésalliance.

One day he visited the Dower House and I was alone there. He looked rather pleased to find me thus and I thought it would be one of those sessions when a certain intimacy seemed to creep into our relationship.

He looked at me rather searchingly as we sat together, and said: "You are growing up fast, Kate. You always seemed in advance of your years. When I am talking to you I feel I am not talking to a child but to a young woman."

I was pleased and showed it.

"You have not lived much with the young, Kate," he mused, and looked sad. "That might be a pity."

"I was very happy with my mother and Maggie . . ."

"I know. And now?"

"It is not easy to forget. But I think I have . . . a little."

"You are getting fond of the people here?"

"Oh, yes."

"Christobel has been a good friend, has she not?"

"Oh, yes."

"So I did well to procure her as your governess?"

"Yes. She has certainly taught me a great deal."

"And you are fond of your brother Luke and of Christobel's brother? I fancy you are fond of him too."

I felt myself flush a little.

My father noticed and smiled. "Yes, I am aware of it. Well, he is a good young man. He will work until he has brought Featherston back to what it should be. James Morton says so, and he would know . . . Kate, I think your friend Kirkwell may be in some danger. What think you of what happened to Isaac Napp?"

A terrible fear took possession of me then. My father realized it and he took my hand and pressed it.

"The man was an informer, a spy of that accursed Oates, who has caused much misery to many. We must do what we can to stop him doing his mischief here."

I did not speak.

"I have news," he said. "Oates is sending men this way."

"Here?" I asked.

"He cannot allow one of his men to be despatched just like that. He will want revenge for the death of Napp."

"But they could not find those who killed him."

My father looked at me sadly. "Napp was indeed a rogue . . . and a stranger here until that time. He is no great loss, and whoever sent him on his way doubtless had a good reason for doing so. But you see, Oates cannot allow that to happen to one of his men. It reflects on Oates himself, who considers himself the all-powerful avenger, and for his own sake he must protect his minions."

"So . . . they will come here. But they will not find the murderer of Isaac Napp."

"Mayhap not. But they will find someone whom they will accuse of the murder."

"Oh no!" I said. And I heard my voice tremble as I spoke.

"There is a place on the estate," he said, not looking at me. "It is called the Devil's Tower, though no one speaks of it now. I have not heard it mentioned for years. It is said to be haunted. It is more or less a ruin. There is a roof over part of it, so it is secure in some places from the elements. It would provide shelter and, providing a man were not afraid of ghosts, he could be as safe there as anywhere. It is on Rosslyn territory, some way from the house. There is some old story about the place. All old families have these skeletons in their cupboards. Most of them get lost in people's memories as the years go by. I think a wayward daughter of our house was walled up in the Tower by some of her zealous relations. She is the ghost. She would be kind, I am sure, to fellow sufferers from tyranny. No one goes to the Tower now. In fact, the place is so overgrown that one can scarce force a way through to it."

There was meaning in his words. I knew that Oates's men were coming. They must find a scapegoat, and that could well be Kirkwell, who was such a friend of mine. It was certain that Oates's men would look to Kirkwell as one who had reason for hating the man whom he would regard as his father's murderer.

"I would like to show you this place," said my father. "Shall we take a ride together now?"

I said: "Yes, I should like to see the Devil's Tower."

When I left my father I found Christobel and told her where I had been and what my father had said.

"We must not lose any time," she said. "I must talk to Kirk without delay. He is in great danger."

We found him in one of the fields and I told him that my father had news that Oates's men had set out from London and were on their way to us.

"There is only one thing to do," said Christobel. "You must go away, Kirkwell, at once. They will suspect you immediately."

"They'll suspect me if I go away."

"Not if you go now, before they arrive. They will not know that you were aware that they were coming, so they will not think you have left on that account. I think we ought to speak to James. He is very wise, and I am sure he will agree that you must go."

I was in terror lest the men should arrive before Kirkwell could make his arrangements to leave, but I was sure that Christobel was right. He must not be here when they came and he must not appear to have gone away because of them.

When James was with us and heard what we planned, he was in favor of it. He said: "We shall immediately tell everyone we know that Kirkwell has had to go away on urgent business. He has left for the North. He left in such a hurry that there was little time to explain everything. It is to some farmer in Yorkshire that he has gone."

"Will they not go searching for him?" I asked.

"They may, but they will not find him, for he will be in the Devil's Tower. It is ideal. People don't go near it. The undergrowth is so thick round it that it is forgotten except by those who know it is there."

"Then let us start immediately."

We told everyone we met that Kirkwell had been summoned up north on urgent business.

The Devil's Tower was indeed the ideal hiding place. It was in a remote part of the estate, and no one who had not heard of it would suspect it was there. Perhaps a century or so ago people might have talked of it and avoided going there, but the legend had become forgotten with time and it was only those who had an intimate knowledge of the land who were aware of its existence.

So to the Devil's Tower went Kirkwell. We took blankets and food for him and planned how one of us would visit him once a day, and when Oates's men had gone he would come back as though from his long journey north, and maybe we should not be troubled again by Titus Oates.

Three days after Kirkwell had settled into the Devil's Tower, Titus Oates's men arrived. They stayed at the inn, as they had before. The neighborhood was tense with anxiety. People cast down their eyes and hardly dared look at one another.

Many were questioned. The men came to the Dower House. They questioned Christobel and wanted to know when she had last seen her brother.

Carrie and I listened outside the door. We were in a state of terror.

Christobel was brave, but very frightened—not for herself, I knew, but for Kirkwell.

They also questioned Carrie. She did not know that we had been aware of the men's coming some days before they arrived; nor did she know where Kirkwell was hiding, so she could not be trapped into betrayal.

They questioned me as well.

"Do you know the man Kirkwell Carew?" they asked.

I said I did.

"When did you last see him?"

I told them it was the day before he left for the North.

"Did he go in a hurry?"

I looked puzzled. I did not think he went in a hurry, but he had told us only the day before that he had to go. He was not very pleased, because he was in the middle of restoring one of the houses on the estate, but he said he had better go and get it over with. The repairs would have to wait for his return.

"Did he say when he would return?"

"I think it was when his work up there was finished."

They did not pursue their questions. I had made myself look young and I behaved like a child. I think they accepted me as such.

It was a time of terrible anxiety. Kirkwell's whereabouts were a secret shared by Christobel, James, Luke and myself. Perhaps I should include my father, for, although he remained aloof from the matter, he was after all the one who had suggested that Kirkwell should go and where to.

I shall never forget that time. We took it in turns to visit Kirkwell, just in case one of us should by some remote chance be seen going to the same place too often.

I remember now the eeriness of the place and the fear I felt when approaching it, which was not all due to the danger of the mission.

I made my way through the undergrowth. It was not easy. Branches of shrubs caught at my cloak. I had the feeling that they were trying to hold me back and imprison me. It was quite uncanny. I suppose a kind of aura of horror grows about a place in which something terrible has happened. As I battled my way through the shrubs, I could not stop thinking of the young girl who had been "wayward"—I supposed that meant she had an illicit lover—and had had this dreadful punishment inflicted on her. What was it like, I wondered, to be put into a cavity and have the wall built up around you, leaving you shut in . . . alone, without air, without food, to await death?

And something equally terrible could happen to Kirkwell if he were discovered.

I shivered. The world was a fearful place when people could be walled up and left to die and men like Titus Oates could bring death and misery to thousands of people.

Kirkwell was waiting eagerly to greet me.

He put his arms round me and stroked my face, as though to assure himself that I was real.

"Oh, Kate, little Kate . . . they shouldn't have let you come."

"Of course I came. Christobel, Luke and James . . . they come when they can."

"You are only a little girl. Oh, Kate," he said, "can you believe this? Here I am, running away. Why did I not stop and face that devil?"

"Because it would be foolish of you to do so."

"I did not kill that man."

"That makes no difference if Titus Oates says you did, and he could. We have to face that, Kirkwell. He does not hesitate to lie. Oh, Kirkwell, you will be safe here. Nobody comes here."

He put out a rug over the broken tiles of the floor, and we sat on it, our backs to the brick wall, which was covered with lichen in places.

"I have good friends. My sister . . . you, and the others. What is happening?"

"The men are here, as you know."

"Yes, they are questioning people. They are asking where I am."

"It was good that you left before it was known that they were on the way. No one can say that you have left because of them."

"But they are asking about me. They have doubtless decided that they are taking me as their victim."

"We are not going to allow that."

"Oh, Kate, my stalwart protector! I cannot tell you what it means to me to see you here. It was due to you, was it not, that I am here?"

"It was due to my father."

"Yes, it seems to me that he too is my friend." He put his arm about me. "We have become very special friends, have we not, Kate?"

"Yes, we have."

"From the first time I saw you, there was something about you that made you different from other people."

"Was there? They say I am old for my years."

"That may be so. Kate, grow up quickly, will you?"

"I suppose I am subject to time, like everyone else."

He kissed me lightly on the tip of my nose.

"It is strange here, is it not? Do you know the story? Those of us whose families have always lived in the neighborhood are familiar with it. It happened in this tower. I have not thought of it for years, but I remember it now as I lie here, particularly at night, when I hear the sounds of all the wild creatures who live around here. I hear a fox now and then . . . creatures creeping through the undergrowth . . . the cries of birds. They sound strange in the night. One grows a little fanciful at night in such a place."

"Do you think of that poor girl who is said to have been walled up here?"

"Sometimes . . . and it makes me think of what would happen to me if Oates's men were to discover that I am here. Sometimes I think I hear them making their way through the undergrowth . . . but it is always some animal. I suppose I am expecting them to come."

"They will not! They will not! We are so careful; and they cannot say that you went away to escape them, because people here believe that you went before you knew they were coming."

"And you, little Kate, what if they knew you were visiting me . . . bringing me food?"

"They will not know."

"You are taking a risk. I shall never forget you took this risk for me, Kate."

"And so are James and Christobel and the others."

"I shall remember you more, Kate."

"Soon they will go away. Then you will return from the North, your business settled, and life will go back to what it was before all this started."

"Oh, Kate, will it ever be the same again? I lie here and think of my father, and I think of their coming here. They would find me guilty, not only because I hid myself, but because they were determined to. I shall never really be free while Titus Oates lives, Kate."

"Kirkwell, it is not like you to be so despairing."

"No. Blame this place. It seems so remote from the world."

"That is why it is such a good hiding place. They will never find you here."

"How long shall I be a prisoner here?"

"Until the men have gone."

"Kate, I want you to know that I love you dearly."

"Oh, Kirkwell, I love you too. I love you and Christobel. She has been like a sister to me."

"I am glad," he said. "If I come through this . . . and when you have grown up a little . . ."

"Yes, Kirkwell, what then?"

"Then you and I will talk more of this."

After I had left him I thought of what he had said. I believed he was telling me that he loved me. I might have been young, but, as they always said, I was advanced for my years. I knew that he was telling me that one day, if we continued to feel as we did now, we might be married.

I must have shown that I cared for him. My father had seen it.

Was it for this reason that he had mentioned the Devil's Tower? Was it done for me?

Tension was growing. More people were questioned and no one felt safe. I had a strong feeling that if Kirkwell had been here he would have been accused, however completely he could have proved his innocence. And if they had determined to make him their scapegoat and did not go, for how long could he stay in the tower?

Each day either Christobel, James or myself would go to the Devil's Tower with provisions: we grew increasingly afraid that someone would notice us.

Oates's men were becoming impatient, and with each passing day the danger grew closer. Everyone in the place lived in fear that in desperation they would select someone—anyone: it would not matter to them, as long as they had their culprit.

The matter was resolved in an unexpected manner.

Farmer Blake, of Fifty Acres Farm, was discovered by his ploughman in one of his barns. He had hanged himself from the rafters and people were talking of nothing else.

The night before he died, he had gone to the rector and made a confession. The rector was so startled by these revelations that he thought it his duty to write them down so that he could assure himself that he had heard them correctly and could then consider what action he should take.

Farmer Blake, it appeared, had, one year before, married Betty Drew, the daughter of one of his cowmen. Betty was a handsome, plump young woman and she had a merry way with her, whereas Farmer Blake's wife had been an invalid confined to her bed for the previous five years. Farmer Blake confessed that he had lusted after Betty while his wife still lived and had married her in indecent haste three months after his wife's death, which was doubtless why the Lord had seen fit to punish him.

One day, when he had had to be away on business at Nether Stowey, he had told Betty that he would be home at about six of the clock, and added: "You can never be sure, and I reckon I'll be lucky if I am back by seven."

However, Farmer Blake's business was concluded with far more speed than he had anticipated, with the result that by five o'clock he was on his way home to the farmhouse, thinking to give Betty a pleasant surprise. Passing along to the farmhouse, he had heard whispering voices coming from one of the barns. He thought it was some children playing there, and that was something he would not have. He opened the door and went in. He could not believe what he saw. There was Betty, and with her Isaac Napp, together caught in the act of adultery.

So lost in their sin were they that they were unaware that Farmer Blake had opened the door of the barn. He was amazed that his wife could behave so, and with this man who had professed to be in the service of the Lord, purging the world of Catholicism. Farmer Blake thought his legs would not carry him, but they did, out of the barn where he stood for a while, bewildered, unable to grasp the fact that his new wife was a wanton, and not what he had blindly supposed her to be.

He found himself back in the farmhouse. His anger was hot and he began to plan vengeance. It was not Betty he hated so much: she was a young girl, led astray, he convinced himself, by the Devil masquerading as a man of the Lord.

He was so distressed he did not know what to do, so he did nothing. He said nothing to anyone . . . not even to Betty who, when she found him at home, showed no sign of guilt and was just as usual.

The next day Farmer Blake went in pursuit of Isaac Napp. He told Betty he would be late back that evening. That he had to go out to see a builder in Bridgwater who would not be at his place until six of the clock, so he would be leaving at thirty minutes past five and could not say at what hour he would return, but he thought it would be eight before he got back to the house.

Then he lay in wait. He knew the way Isaac Napp would come. Bordering on the edge of the farm was a copse through which he must pass. He would lead his horse through to the other side on foot, as most people did, taking the way to the farm from there.

Farmer Blake was waiting in the copse and, creeping up behind Napp, he gave him a blow on the head which felled him.

"Adulterer!" shouted Farmer Blake.

The way in which Napp looked at Farmer Blake told him that he knew he had discovered the truth about him. He opened his mouth to protest. Isaac Napp would always find the words to explain that it was all a mistake or something similar. But the farmer had seen with his own eyes and, as he said, the picture of them caught in sin was something he would see for the rest of his life.

He put his hands about Napp's neck and pressed and pressed.

Isaac Napp was a comparatively young man, which Farmer Blake was not. The farmer was not sure that he had killed his victim, and he knew that it was very important that he should, so he dragged him to the stream and laid him face down in the water. And while Betty waited in the barn for her lover, her husband was watching him die.

Farmer Blake convinced himself for a while that it was no sin to kill such an evil man. It was his just reward for what he had done. And so life went on more or less as usual until he heard that Titus Oates's men had come to look for the killer.

Then his conscience began to worry him. Also, he gravely

feared that he might have betrayed himself in some way, and he did not want to hang for murder. For this was no ordinary murder. One of Titus Oates's men had been done to death. What would happen to the man who had been responsible for that?

Farmer Blake was then very much afraid, but he reckoned that he had had the right to kill a man who had sinned against him as Isaac Napp had, that the Lord would understand more easily than Titus Oates, and he was less afraid of his Maker than of that other. So, after some deliberation, he decided to take his own life.

All this he told the rector the night before he committed suicide. The rector had told him it was a sin to kill himself; his life was God's and it was for Him to give it or take it; and had offered to pray with him for guidance.

Meanwhile the men from London were asking a great many questions and some of those questioned knew Farmer Blake well. The investigation was getting nearer and nearer. Poor Farmer Blake was becoming more and more distraught.

Apparently he could bear no more. He did not want to listen to what the rector had to say: he did not want to pray for forgiveness and to give himself up, which was surely what he would be told to do. Life had lost its savor. It was not what he had believed it to be. He could not forget the sight of Betty in the barn with Isaac Napp.

So he went into the barn that night and hanged himself.

The case was solved. It had to be accepted by all that the murderer of Isaac Napp was Farmer Blake, and his reason for his action was clear to all.

There was nothing for Oates's men to do but close the case and go back to London.

And within a reasonable space of time, so as not to arouse suspicion, Kirkwell returned to Featherston Manor.

Time was passing, it seemed, at great speed. I was growing up fast and would soon be fifteen—no longer a child.

Life was pleasant and interesting. I had Christobel, my brother Luke, Kirkwell and James Morton and Sebastian Adams. We were all good friends and, in spite of my youth, I was one of them. We enjoyed being together, and one of the main topics of conversation was politics. The King had an illness which had sent a shiver of apprehension through the country, and the subject of the succession was discussed everywhere with more intensity than usual. Fortunately he recovered: he was seen sauntering in the park, enjoying the company of several women and making witty remarks in his old manner, and the country breathed a sigh of relief. The King would live a few more years and perhaps by then some solution would have been found.

We all took different sides in our discussions. Luke was in favor of the succession of the Duke of Monmouth. He was the King's son, Luke insisted, a little defiantly. Poor Luke! Just like the Duke, he longed to be accepted as his father's son. Monmouth yearned for a kingdom, Luke for Rosslyn Manor and recognition as Lord Rosslyn's son. It was little wonder that he stood for Monmouth. He said it was because the country would only accept a Protestant King, but I suspected he wanted to say it was the right of bastards to inherit if there were no legitimate sons to come before them.

Sebastian Adams was for law and order, and the law said that the Duke of York was heir. James Morton was inclined to agree.

Kirkwell believed that if the Duke of York came to the throne, there would be trouble, as there would be if Monmouth succeeded. He said we should have to wait and see. He wanted what was best for the country, but also that the country should not be involved in civil war.

And so we talked: and we were all convinced that it was a question for the future, for the King had many years to live, and while he did we could go along in our pleasant, easy way.

Now and then Christobel and I went to London. We would stay with Maggie, who was delighted to see us. She told me that she was glad I had gone to the Dower House. She missed me, of course, but it was better for me to be there, and when the time came my father, she believed, would do what was right and proper.

"What do you mean?" I asked. "Find a husband for me?"

"Whatever is right and proper," she insisted.

I was a little uneasy at the thought, but I put it from my mind. It was a long way off yet, I told myself.

She told me that Titus Oates was gradually losing his power.

There had been one or two cases from which he had emerged rather badly. Lord Chief Justice Scroggs had set the fashion. Others had discovered that they need not bow to Oates's wishes, for they could avoid doing so without fear of retaliation. He was still there, still struggling to continue in his evil ways, but the tide was turning against him and he was no longer the man of power he had been.

We always enjoyed those visits to London. It was well worth the uncomfortable journey to see Maggie and get all the news.

Francine

CHRISTOBEL AND I had always taken frequent rides. We both loved the countryside and one day, as we were riding through a narrow lane where it was necessary to fall into single file, we heard the sound of horses' hooves coming towards us in the opposite direction. Christobel was ahead and we both moved as close to the hedge as possible to allow whoever was coming to pass.

I saw a woman, very straight, rather angular, in an elegantly cut riding habit. Another woman rode behind her.

"Good morning, Lady Rosslyn," said Christobel in a very respectful voice. "Good morning, Mistress Galloway."

The woman who was in front returned Christobel's greeting with a curt nod. The other lady smiled rather hesitantly at her.

Then Lady Rosslyn was on a level with me. The look she gave me made me shiver, for it really seemed quite malevolent. Then she lowered her eyes, as though she did not wish to look at me, and passed on by. The other lady, who was quite a contrast, was plump and rosy-cheeked, rather subdued in manner. She also gave me a hesitant smile, having looked at me quickly and lowered her eyes as she passed.

When they were out of earshot, Christobel said: "Well, that was unfortunate."

"Why?"

"Meeting like that. She had to look at us."

"It was . . . my father's wife, was it not?"

"It was indeed. A very haughty lady, as you saw, and not very pleased to come face to face with a reminder of her husband's misdeeds.''

"You mean . . . me?"

"Don't look so unhappy. I wonder we haven't met before. It would have been better if we had not been quite so close. But meeting in the lane like that . . . well, it was like forcing ourselves upon her ladyship's notice, was it not?"

"She did not like me, I could see."

"You could scarcely expect her to welcome you with honeyed words, could you?"

"No, but . . ."

"I know. You're going to say it was no fault of yours. Nor was it. Whose fault, then? Hers? For not producing the desired offspring? I doubt not that my lord would have had his little adventures in any case. Well, don't let it disturb you, dear child. The lady does not like you. Is it because you remind her of her husband's irrepressible gallantries or of her own shortcomings? Who can say? So let us forget the matter."

"And the other lady?"

"Mistress Margaret Galloway—a connection of her ladyship who lives on her bounty, I believe, and is her constant companion. Now, don't fret, you're hardly likely to come into such close contact again with her ladyship, and that was only a brief encounter."

So Christobel dealt with the matter in her own lighthearted way.

Over the next year or so I did see Lady Rosslyn again on one or two occasions—not in a narrow lane, but on the road, and Christobel, who was invariably with me, would receive the brief nod of recognition while I was given a quick glance before being completely ignored.

One day when we rode over to Featherston, Carrie had news for us.

"What do you think?" she said. "Lady Rosslyn has been taken ill."

"Very ill?" asked Christobel.

Carrie nodded. "She's had a seizure. They didn't think she'd live . . . but she's come through. I met Mistress Hardy, who cooks in the kitchens at the Manor, and she told me all about it."

"And you are going to tell us," said Christobel.

"If you want to hear," retorted Carrie.

"You know we are all agog."

"Well, it seems she cannot walk. She was all seized down one side. They say she can't talk much either. That cousin of hers found her. She went in one morning and there her ladyship was. They've had the doctor up there. They say his lordship is sending for some doctor from London. He's on his way. The cousin will be there looking after her. They've been together for years . . . almost as soon as she came to the Manor, so she'll stay to look after her."

"Is she . . . ?" asked Christobel.

"Not yet. They say there's a chance she'll live. But, poor thing, what's life going to be like when you can't move and can't speak?"

I thought of that proud, arrogant woman whom I had met in the lane, unable to move . . . unable to speak . . . depending on others. In spite of everything, I felt an immense pity for her.

Later we heard that Lady Rosslyn was still alive and that the cousin, Mistress Margaret Galloway, was indeed looking after her.

There was one matter which was giving me cause for thought above all else, and that was the relationship between Christobel and James Morton. It was gradually brought to my notice that they preferred each other's company to that of any other. Christobel and I often met him when we were riding and then I had the distinct impression that, although he was always friendly towards me, he would have been happier if Christobel had been alone.

Therefore I was not altogether surprised when, one day, as Christobel and I sat reading in that little room in the Dower House which had been set aside for what were called my "lessons," she suddenly said to me: "James wants me to marry him."

"And are you going to?" I asked.

"Of course," she said.

So they were betrothed. There was no reason why the marriage should be delayed. James was manager of the Rosslyn estate and so had a good home to offer her. He was on excellent terms with Lord Rosslyn and mingled with the guests on occasions, as my mother had told me my grandfather had done all those years ago on the estate he had managed.

So plans for the wedding were discussed at great length.

I should not see so much of Christobel when she was married, of course, but she would be close at hand, so it was not as though we should have to face a sad farewell. We had become so much a part of each other's lives that that would have been a very great wrench, but why contemplate it when it was not to take place?

I had had occasional meetings with my father over the years I had been at the Dower House and one day he rode over to see Luke and me. Luke happened to be out, for my father had not announced his coming, and, as Christobel was with James, my father and I were alone together.

He said: "I wanted to talk to you alone, Kate. I will talk to Luke later, for this concerns him too. This coming marriage will mean that Christobel will no longer be here and you will be without your governess. You and she have been friends and I have seen how she has brought you along. But of course she will have other duties now."

I wondered if he were contemplating providing me with a new governess.

I said: "I am not a child any more. I shall be sixteen soon. Christobel has said that there is little more she can teach me."

He nodded. "Christobel has been a good companion for you . . . and will still be your friend. But I have been thinking a good deal about your future, yours and Luke's. I am going to bring you both to the Manor. I have wanted to do this for a long time."

I gasped.

"The idea does not please you?" he enquired.

"I . . . I don't know. It is so unexpected that I never thought . . ."

"I should have brought you there in the beginning, but there were difficulties."

I knew the one difficulty. The haughty lady whom I had met in the lane would be the chief obstacle, I supposed.

"Kate," he said, "I want you to understand . . ."

"I know you have done what you could for us . . ." I began.

"I want to tell you of this myself. You are my daughter, Kate. That means a great deal to me. And Luke is my son. I fancy you are a little fond of me."

"But of course. You have been kind to me."

"I mean as a father."

"Well, yes . . . a kind of father."

"A kind of father," he said rather sadly. "I wish I could have been more like a real one. You see, it would have been very difficult for me at the time."

"I know."

"I think you know a great deal about the situation, Kate."

"My mother told me when she knew she was dying. She thought I ought to know."

"I loved your mother dearly, you know that, Kate."

"Did you? And yet . . ."

"You know about my deceit, of course."

"Yes, she told me that too."

"You must have thought I was a very wicked man."

I was silent.

"Thoughtless . . ." he went on. "In the society in which I lived, it was something which men did. It was thought to be rather amusing, God forgive us. Your mother was different from others. Most of the ladies involved in such matters would have settled for a good endowment of some sort . . . but not your mother. She would have nothing. I was wrong. I was wicked. Please understand, Kate."

"I think I do."

"You are a wise girl. I would like you to look upon me as your father . . . not as a kind of father, but as a real one."

"Yes," I said.

"I was not happily married. There was no love between us, even in the beginning. My wife and I were chosen for each other. The basic idea of our families was for us to make a suitable marriage. My family had been in existence in this county since 1066 and we believed the family had to go on. It was our first duty to continue the unbroken line, and, of course, we failed in that. It was ironical . . . for it was the sole purpose of the marriage."

"It would have been better perhaps if you had married for love."

"Ah, who shall say? What I want you to understand is why I could not bring you to the Manor before, because . . ."

"Because of your wife?"

"You do understand? So, the next best thing was to install you and Luke in the Dower House."

"But she knew we were here."

"It was not like being under the same roof."

"She is still at the Manor."

"Kate, she is unaware. She does not know who she is or where she is. She is looked after by her cousin, who has always been with her, but she often does not recognize her. Christobel will be married soon. You are growing up. I want you to live as my daughter . . . which you are. You, my children, you and Luke, I want you to be near me, so I am arranging for you to come to the Manor after Christobel is married."

When Luke came in my father was still there. When my brother heard the news he was overcome with joy.

After my father had left, Luke said to me: "This means that we are really acknowledged."

I pointed out that we were before.

"This is different. I am my father's son, you are his daughter. Who knows?"

I hoped he was not going to be too ambitious, for I feared he would be disappointed. I knew his greatest desire was to own Rosslyn Manor. But he should remember that that matter was all settled, and that Sebastian was there because he had been chosen to inherit the estate.

Luke went around with brightly shining eyes. I was less euphoric. I thought of living in that house from which I had been excluded all these years because its mistress was that cold-eyed woman who had passed us in the lane. I was not entirely convinced that she would be unaware of the fact that her husband was bringing his illegitimate children into her home.

I could not feel elated in such circumstances.

Christobel was married at the beginning of the year and Luke and I went to live at Rosslyn Manor.

I was overawed as we passed over the old drawbridge, and I looked up at those gray towers. Gray-stoned, rounded arches, and those thick walls built to last for centuries—which they had.

I was to discover that a great deal of the Manor House had been restored over the years and it was possible here and there to detect touches of the more decorative Tudor style of linenfold paneling in some of the rooms.

The Dower House, of course, had been built much later and lacked that air of brooding antiquity which belonged to an earlier age.

I was given a room which was reached by way of a spiral staircase. It had a high vaulted ceiling and the size of the room dwarfed the four-poster bed, two chests and the carved wardrobe. The windows were long and narrow. Originally, of course, they would have been glassless, but fortunately that had now been rectified.

I had been given a maid called Amy. She must have guessed that I was unused to such grandeur and asked me if she could help me to dress. I told her I could manage very well, as I always had, and she said that if there was anything I needed I had only to call her. She was about my own age and, for that reason it was rather comforting to know that she was there.

That first night Luke and I dined with Sebastian and my father. The meal was served in what was called the small dining room, though it looked far from small to me. It was hung with tapestries depicting the Battle of Hastings which looked as if they might have been worked soon after that memorable event.

There were two other large tapestries in the room and I gathered that these represented scenes from a more recent conflict—the Wars of the Roses—and, seeing Luke regarding them in wonder, my father told him that he would see many such scenes throughout the house, usually depicting the part the family had played in these events.

"We were not always on the winning side," he explained, "but we keep quiet about those occasions. With the Wars of the Roses it was different. Although we were on the side of York, which did not bring us much glory when the Tudors came, we recovered, and Henry VII was too wise to remain unfriendly to a family like ours and we soon returned to favor. We retrieved those estates which we had lost, and, as the royal marriage of Henry to Elizabeth of York united the two houses, the tapestries were hung and have remained here ever since."

He went on to talk of the family. Sebastian joined in and said he would show us the interesting parts of the house. It would take us some time to become familiar with it. It certainly had in his case, though now he knew it almost as well as my father.

Luke listened, his eyes gleaming. I felt a twinge of uneasiness. I hoped he would remember that, although he belonged to this family, he could never be accepted as legitimate and this house could never be his.

When I returned to my room that night, Amy appeared to see if I wanted anything.

I rather liked her. Perhaps it was because I realized she could not have been much older than I, and she herself was a little uncertain, though she did her best to hide it. I wondered what it was like to come and work in a house like this. She must feel gratified because she was to look after me—who was as ignorant of the way life was lived in the house as she was herself.

I told her I was all right, and could look after myself.

She nodded. "Well, I hope you sleep well, Mistress. And if there is anything you need . . ."

"I will let you know," I said. "Good night."

I stood in the middle of that room and then thought that the silent house seemed to shut me in. I looked over my shoulder quickly, as though I expected to see someone standing there. I felt that eyes were watching me from every part of the room, so that if I turned to escape one pair I would be immediately in range of another.

It was foolish, fanciful. This was the effect such ancient houses had on people. The Dower House had been cozy, with Christobel in the next room, and Mistress Longton not far off. No ghost would ever intrude in her house, I was sure. And Featherston was cozy too—or it had been until that terrible time when Sir Harold had been taken away and never seen again.

I undressed and got into bed. I blew out my candle but sleep was impossible. There was a half moon which shone in through the window, and I remembered my first night at the Dower House. Christobel had been close to me there. Here I felt isolated. I wondered how Luke was faring. He was doubtless dreaming of the glories of the Rosslyns and of this mansion, which was theirs and which he coveted.

Oh, Luke, I thought, take care.

I was tired and longed for sleep. Alas, it remained elusive and my mind raced on. I was back in Maggie's house. My mother was there, dressing to go to the theater. I was sitting beside her, hearing her lines as she completed her toilette. It all seemed so long ago. And now I was here. Christobel was married and I had come with Luke to my father's house—this great mansion which was bigger and far more grand than anything I had ever imagined.

I must have dozed. I saw a woman's face as I lay in bed. She was coming towards me. She had a look of disdain on her hard, cold features which turned to anger as she bent closer to me.

I awoke with a start. I sat up in bed. Just a nightmare. Foolish, but natural, I suppose. Lady Rosslyn had made a deep impression on me, and now here I was . . . living under the same roof . . . because she was so ill that she was unable to protest.

I felt I should never sleep. I was not sure I wanted to. I was afraid of the nightmares. It had been horrifying to see her face so close to mine, and dreams are like reality while they last.

It was to be expected that my first night in a house like this would be restless. It would have been different if I had been born here and had lived the whole of my life here. It would be my home. But that was not so. I was here because my mother had gone through a mock marriage, a practice indulged in by degenerate young men whose main occupation seemed to be to think of outrageous adventures. If they involved others, that was just bad luck for them.

I thought suddenly of the Duke of Monmouth and his friends slitting Sir John Coventry's nose and killing a beadle. That was the way they amused themselves.

I felt a sudden longing for Maggie's simple household where everyone seemed good and kind and wanted to help each other. I thought of the Dower House and Mistress Longton, and Christobel, and Featherston and Kirkwell close by, and suddenly I wanted to go on like that. I did not want to live in a grand house where ghosts seemed to be lurking in every corner.

Luke might be delighted to be here . . . but was I?

I yawned. I would become accustomed to it, I supposed. It was interesting. Full of history, as I had heard. It was exciting. Oh yes, it was just that this was my first night in a new place.

I felt calmer after such consideration and in a short time I was asleep.

I awoke startled. The moonlight was streaming into the room. It was still night. Something had awakened me. What? I asked myself. Someone was in the room.

My heart was beating fast. I sat up in bed and said, rather hoarsely, "Who is there?"

There was silence in the room. I listened, but all I could hear was the heavy beating of my own heart.

I thought I heard a footstep. It was close.

I said again: "Who is it?"

There was no response. I got out of bed and looked around me. Then I noticed that the door was slightly ajar.

I knew I had shut it before I had got into the bed. I had made quite sure of it.

I went to it and looked out. I saw the spiral staircase at the other end of the corridor where there was another leading upwards. There was no sign of anyone.

But I knew someone had come into my room. The open door assured me of that.

Who? Why?

I thought immediately of Lady Rosslyn's cold, hard face, her look of contempt before she had forced it into one of indifference. Impossible. She was crippled . . . unable to walk.

I went back into my room and firmly shut the door. I stood for a moment leaning against it. It was strange . . . uncanny. Who had come into my room while I slept, and for what purpose?

I longed to be back in the Dower House. I wanted to talk to Christobel.

I went back to bed. I lay there, alert, listening for the sound of a step in the corridor, the slow cautious opening of the door.

No one came, and it was almost six of the clock before I fell at last into a doze.

Amy's tap at the door awoke me the next morning. I started up in panic. That experience last night was still with me.

"Good morning, Mistress," she said. "I trust you slept well."

I said: "Thank you, Amy." I could not tell her that I had scarcely slept at all.

She brought me hot water. I washed, put on a riding habit and went downstairs. One of the first things I would do would be to ride over to Christobel and tell her of my impressions and experience in the mansion.

Luke was already down in the dining room, sitting at the table eating.

"What a fantastic place!" he said, his eyes shining.

"Did you sleep well?" I asked.

"But of course. I had a wonderful room in one of the towers. Octagonal, an odd shape for a room, with slit-like windows. I suppose they used to pour down boiling oil from them on their enemies."

"That would surely have been from the battlements," I said.

I felt quite hungry, so I helped myself to bread and meat and a flagon of ale.

Sebastian came in. He told us that he was going to show us part of the house—the part we lived in. He could tell us quite a few facts about it.

"You cannot take it in all at once," he said. "It's vast, like a village, really. I do not yet know all those who serve us. There are so many. But I am learning much."

"It must be fascinating," said Luke enviously.

"I'll show you something of it this morning if you like. Had you plans?"

"I was hoping to go over to see Christobel, and perhaps go to Featherston."

"You can do those things this afternoon," said Sebastian.

"I am looking forward to getting to know the house," said Luke.

It was a long tour and very interesting. But I was thinking all the time of Lady Rosslyn, who was somewhere in this house, and wondering who it was who had come to my room last night.

I could not ask Sebastian. He would have no idea who it could have been. He would dismiss it as fancy, doubtless. I supposed many would. So I gave my attention to the house and learned of its history, how King Edward IV had stayed here with his mistress, Jane Shore, the goldsmith's wife, and other ladies at other times.

"He was a good king, but a little like our present Majesty, devoted to the ladies. Odd, is it not, how these kings live their rather—shall we say—dissolute lives, yet serve their country well. Whereas poor Henry VI was a real saint, and look where he led his country . . . into war. And the same with His Majesty's father . . . though perhaps we are too close to speak of these matters. Well, his present Majesty, for all that can be said, is hardly a virtuous man, as he would be the first to admit, yet he keeps us at peace, while his father, a faithful husband and a man bent on doing good, led us to war and lost his own head and brought to his family years of royal wandering in the wilderness—or rather on the Continent, living in exile, hoping to regain the throne."

And so we wandered through the house, up spiral staircases to the top of towers, looking right down to the ground, many feet below. We saw that spot where one lady of the noble house had thrown herself to her death because her husband no longer loved her, and looked across to the Devil's Tower, where another had been walled up because she had dallied with a lover.

In a house such as this, such legends lived on.

No wonder that the first night anyone spent in it was a restless one. The place was drenched in memories of past tragedies.

"That is the east wing of the house," Sebastian told me. "Lady Rosslyn has her apartments there. She always keeps to that part of the house. It is almost like separate households. And now she is there with her cousin, Mistress Galloway, who has been with her for years. I think she prefers to live apart from everyone. I dare say Lord Rosslyn visits her from time to time, but I have spoken with her only once or twice."

"It seems so strange. She is Lady Rosslyn, and yet there are two households."

Sebastian shrugged his shoulders.

"Perhaps it has been decided that it is better that way. Now Lady Rosslyn is confined to her couch. As I said, it is like a separate household, and, as you will have seen, this house is big enough to make that possible."

So we continued our tour of the house.

I thought: It is only the strangeness of it all that makes me feel uncertain.

Luke was different. There was no doubt that he was delighted to be here.

That afternoon I rode over to see Christobel.

She greeted me with delight. She had changed since her marriage. Her face had softened considerably and she was obviously pleased with life.

"Now tell me," she said, when we were settled in the charming room overlooking the garden, which she herself was tending with care. "How do you like living at the grand ancestral home?"

"I am not sure yet. I have really had so little experience of it."

"So it has not overwhelmed you yet?"

"No."

"You sound a little regretful."

"I was very happy at the Dower House, and of course also at Maggie's."

"And not at Rosslyn Manor?"

"It is early yet. Christobel, there is a rather eerie atmosphere about the place."

"It is always so, with old houses. So much has happened there, and the past clings and will not be dismissed. There will certainly have been tragedies over the years, and such things are remembered more than the happy times, I'll warrant. But you are happy . . . to be there, under your father's roof?"

"He is not like an ordinary father. All those years, I did not know him."

"I always thought you had a respect for him. And one good thing he did. He brought us together. I like him for that."

"Oh, so do I, Christobel. *We* shall be friends forever."

"If it is in my power, so be it. Has it occurred to you that he might have plans for you?"

"What plans?"

"Well, you are almost a young lady now. A few more months and you will be standing on the threshold of adventure."

"You mean . . . my father will find a husband for me? Christobel, I would rather find my own."

"Oh, but you are the daughter of Lord Rosslyn, and even if you did not become so by the most conventional of methods, you are still his daughter."

"Perhaps he will think of his own marriage. That was arranged for him, and it was not the most satisfactory of marriages."

"People always believe that the way they arrange things will be perfect."

"I shall be firm and strong. I shall be as you are, Christobel. After all, you more or less brought me up, did you not? I am a little like you, you know."

"But I was only the daughter of an impoverished gentleman."

"And I am only the natural daughter of Lord Rosslyn. No, I shall choose for myself."

"You speak with such conviction that I ask myself if you have already chosen?"

"Matrimony is not uppermost in my mind, and what I wanted to tell you about was a strange thing that happened during the night."

"Last night? Your first at Rosslyn Manor?"

"Yes. I couldn't sleep."

"Natural enough. Your first night in the grand old mansion. Creaking boards . . . dark alcoves . . . just the sort of house where ghosts would lurk. Was there not someone who threw herself from one of the towers, and wasn't there that unfortunate girl who was built into the walls?"

"That was in the Devil's Tower."

"Of course. Where Kirk hid when that obnoxious Oates man was prowling around. That was an alarming time, was it not? Well, ghosts have their uses when a place like the Devil's Tower can be used. But what about this nightly adventure?"

"As you've guessed, I could not sleep . . . but I dozed after a while, and then I was awake. Something had startled me. Christobel, someone had come into my room."

"You must have dreamed it."

"No. The door was open. I think someone was there, looking at me. I awoke and whoever it was slipped out by the door and did not close it. I thought I heard a step in the corridor, but when I looked out there was no one there."

"You must have forgotten to close the door completely. It moved and awakened you, and because you were a little over-excited to find yourself in such grand, antique surroundings, you thought someone was there."

"I do not believe that."

"But who would want to inspect you by night, when they would have a good chance of doing so by daylight?"

"I do not know. That is why it was rather mysterious . . . a little unsettling."

"Well, whoever it was scuttled off when there was a chance of being discovered. The easiest explanation is that the door was not closed properly. Many things in those old houses are a little faulty. Have they not been in place for many years? Forget it. Go to bed tonight and get some untroubled sleep. Life has become exciting for you. You are acknowledged. Maggie will be delighted, I am sure. You will often have exciting times, I'll swear, because your father will not want to keep you in the country. He will take you to London. I'll swear you will be presented to the King. My dear, dear Kate. You have become very grand. Soon you will not deign to visit my lord's estate manager's wife."

"That will never be so," I said indignantly. "It will always be one of my greatest pleasures."

"Bless you," said Christobel happily. "I know it will."

After I had left Christobel I rode over to Featherston Manor.

I was told that Kirkwell was working in his office, so I went there.

I said: "Kirk, you are busy. It is a difficult time."

"Never too busy to see you, Kate," he said. "Come in and tell me all about it."

"You mean first impressions and so on. Well, it is rather an awe-inspiring place."

"And you are regretting leaving the Dower House?"

"It wouldn't have been the same without Christobel. I have just left her."

"She is very happy," he said. "James is a fine fellow."

"It was wonderful that they met. I saw it coming for some time. Did you?"

"Oh yes, it was obvious. I am so glad." He looked at me a little wistfully. "But of course it has brought about this change for you, though I dare say you would have gone up to Rosslyn Manor at some time . . . even if not just yet."

"Yes, it was bound to mean change."

"Oh, Kate, I wish you were not there. It is going to change everything. If your father has plans for you . . . I mean, if he is going to take you into grand society . . . you will not see very much of your old friends."

"Of course I shall. You, Christobel and James . . . you will always be my best friends."

He looked a little sad.

"Don't forget us, will you, Kate?"

"What nonsense! As if I would!" I paused and, because I felt emotional, I went on quickly, "How is everything going here?"

"Do you know, I am beginning to feel gratified. My work has not been in vain. We are becoming . . . well, scarcely prosperous, but shall I say, showing signs of improvement."

"That's wonderful. You've worked so hard."

"It is very gratifying. It seems that everything is working according to plan. Then this happens, and you go to Rosslyn Manor, and I'm a little anxious about that."

I laid my hand on his arm, and he took it and kept it firmly in his.

"Don't be," I said. "What are you worried about?"

"That you will change. That you won't be our Kate any more, you'll be a grand lady. Your father will have plans for you."

I laughed.

"Nonsense," I said. "Whatever happens, I shall always be your Kate."

Amy and I were becoming good friends. She confessed to me that she had never been in such a grand place before, and she couldn't believe her ears when she was told she was going to be my maid.

"And when I saw you were only a girl . . . beg pardon, Mistress Kate, but you are young."

I laughed. "You thought you were going to have some haughty lady, and found it was someone of your own age who was as new to the house as you were. I had been living at the Dower House for a long time."

"Yes, I know that now, Miss. I did not know it when I was told. Mistress Clancy, the housekeeper, only told me I was to look after his lordship's daughter, and that sounded very grand."

"Well, now you see that there is nothing to be afraid of."

She had in a few days become my friend. She was determined to look after me in every possible way, and I was glad of her.

I felt lonely. My father had gone away; and Luke seemed different. He was obsessed by the house, learning all he could about it. He was often in Sebastian's company. I was a little alarmed, for there were times when I caught a slight resentment in him when his gaze fell on Sebastian. I hoped Sebastian was not aware of it.

From Amy I gleaned certain information about the household— quite different from the kind sought by Luke.

I learned about the people who inhabited the house.

There was an army of servants. It was inevitable with a place of that size. Many of them had been there for years, as their parents had before them. Sebastian had said that Rosslyn Manor was like a village, and I saw now how very right he had been.

Besides the grooms, who lived in the stables which were very extensive, there were the servants who lived in the tower and many others who had cottages on the estate, and most of those who worked in the grounds and gardens. There was also the home farm, which supplied most of the household's needs.

It was from Amy that I learned more about Lady Rosslyn.

I often wondered whether I talked too much of this, but the relationship between Amy and myself was not the usual one between mistress and maid, perhaps because of our ages and the fact that I was no more used to this way of life than she was. In any case, it removed any barrier between us that there might have been.

Everyone knew, of course, of the nature of the relationship between the master and mistress of the house. For years they had lived what was referred to as "separate lives." In such a house it was conveniently possible for there to be two separate households, and it had been thus for many years.

"There is talk about it in the kitchens," said Amy. "It has all come up again because you and Master Luke have come here."

"What do they say about that?" I asked.

"That the mistress don't like it and that she knows . . . even though she can't speak much, or if she does, it is only Mistress Galloway who knows what she is saying."

Amy was a little hesitant at first, wondering whether she ought to be talking to me thus, just as I asked myself whether, as my father's daughter, I should be having such conversations with a maid.

But, because we were both young and inexperienced in what should and should not be done, the conversations continued.

I was very eager to know about Lady Rosslyn. I felt she had played an important part in my life. It was simple enough to believe that her relations with her husband had led to my father's entanglement with my mother—and, of course, that concerned my very existence. Moreover, I wanted to know, and I did not care enough about the etiquette of behavior if it were going to bar my way to knowledge.

So I learned by degrees that there had always been this aloof relationship between my father and his wife. They each behaved as though the other did not exist, except on those occasions— traditional functions and so on—when they had to appear together. But that was in the past. There would be no more of those now.

For some years now Mistress Galloway had lived with Lady Rosslyn. She was a cousin. They had been brought up together and were like sisters.

It appeared that Mistress Galloway had become a widow and had been left in straitened circumstances. Lady Rosslyn had invited her to come and live at Rosslyn Manor with her, and this she had done. They were close as two peas in a pod, Amy told me, and always had been. Mistress Galloway made a goddess of Lady Rosslyn, thinking nothing but good of her, and she couldn't abide his lordship, because she blamed him for everything.

"For not having children?" I asked. "I thought that was the main trouble between them."

"Mistress Galloway believes that if he had been a good husband to my lady, it would have been different."

"Perhaps if she had been a good wife to him, he would have been," I defended him.

Amy said: "Mayhap neither of them were what they should be. And to get to this pass! And there his lordship was, leading the sort of life lords live in London . . . following His Majesty the King, that is." She stopped and hunched her shoulders.

I smiled. "Everyone knows how it stands with the King," I said.

"Well," said Amy, "it seems to be the way of the world. But Mistress Galloway does not like it and she says it is wrong, and so it seems does my lady. But it is a terrible thing that has happened to her, and it is a blessing, they say in the kitchens, that she has Mistress Galloway to look after her. Her ladyship has been good to Mistress Galloway, for they say it would go hard with her if she had no place to go, and then, of course, she has little Francine with her."

"Who is little Francine?" I wanted to know.

"Oh, Mistress Kate, there is much you don't know about this place. But I suppose it's you just coming here, and you being on his side, and little Francine being on hers."

"I should like to hear about little Francine," I said.

"She's Mistress Galloway's granddaughter. She's not been here long. It was good of Lady Rosslyn to let her come, but then I suppose she would, being fond of Mistress Galloway, and a relation too. Little Francine would be connected with Lady Rosslyn. So it is natural, like. So there she is, up in Lady Rosslyn's part, with her grandmother, you see."

"And you say she came here recently?"

"I don't know quite when, Mistress Kate, being new-come myself. Her mother died, you see, and she was left an orphan. And her being what she is . . ."

"What is she, Amy?"

"Strange little thing. Not quite natural. They say it was due to her being dropped when she was a little one."

"Dropped?"

"On her head. Some nursemaid, it was. She seemed all right at the time, but there is something about her . . ." Amy frowned and looked into the distance, puzzled.

"What is it about her, Amy?"

"I can't rightly say. It is just that she is not quite like other folk, if you get my meaning."

"I don't really, Amy. In what way is she so different from other folk?"

"I cannot rightly say. It is just the way she looks at you and smiles to herself . . . and the way she looks about her, as though she can see something you can't."

"Oh. It sounds rather uncomfortable."

"Yes," said Amy thoughtfully. "You might say that. She goes about quiet, like, and suddenly you find she's there, as though she's come from nowhere and is seeing something you can't see. It's creepy, like."

"I understand."

"Her grandmother thinks the world of her. I've seen them together . . . it's the way she looks at her."

I said: "I'll watch for Francine."

I did not have long to wait.

I had been a week at Rosslyn Manor but I had not seen my father since my arrival. I gathered that he was often away and that he spent a great deal of time in London. I guessed there was no need for him to stay in the country. James was the most efficient of managers and it certainly suited him to have no interference from the master so that he could do everything his way. I had long guessed that and Christobel had confirmed it.

I believed my father was giving us a chance to settle in before he let us know what he had planned for us.

Every day I rode over to Christobel's house, so I was seeing almost as much of her as I had done in the past.

One day I came back to Rosslyn Manor and, having left my horse in the stables, I made my way up to my room. As I mounted the spiral staircase, I had formed a habit of glancing over my shoulder. I had a feeling that I was being watched, as I often had when I was in the house alone. It was the vastness of the place, that air of brooding antiquity, the constant reminder of a long-past age.

I went into my room and pulled up sharply. A young girl was sitting by the window.

I said: "Hello. Who are you?"

She looked at me with those strange eyes which Amy had spoken of, and I knew before she spoke that this was Francine, Mistress Galloway's granddaughter.

"She said: "I'm Francine. I was waiting for you."

"How do you do," I said. "Did you want to see me about anything in particular?"

"I wanted to see *you*. I've seen you before," she said with a slow smile.

"When I was asleep," I said. "In this room, was it?"

She gave me a strange look and lifted her shoulders in a mirthful gesture.

"You were not asleep, were you?"

"I did not awake until you had gone. Wasn't it a strange time to come visiting?"

"Oh, it was the best time really. I could see you without your seeing me."

"I should have thought that might be a disadvantage to me."

She made the same gesture.

"I am glad you decided to come this time when I am awake," I added.

"Do you like it here?"

"Of course."

"It's not your home, is it?"

"It is my father's house, so therefore it seems my place might be here."

"They don't think so."

"Who?"

She waved her hand vaguely.

What an odd creature. There was a hint of madness about her, and Amy was right. One felt this because there was something strange about her eyes.

"I know you live in your grandmother's apartments," I said. She nodded.

"I like to be here," she said. "It frightens you."

"Does it?"

"Not you?" she asked.

"There is nothing to be afraid of, surely?" I said.

She looked at me with interest.

She said: "They don't want you to be here."

"Who?" I asked.

"Her, and my grandmother."

"*Her?*"

She nodded and pointed in the same direction she had before. I knew she was referring to Lady Rosslyn.

"No," she repeated, "they don't want you here, nor him."

I guessed the "him" referred to was Luke.

I thought: They would not tell her this. She must listen to their conversations. But then Lady Rosslyn could not speak. Her grandmother must talk to her. Perhaps she talked to Lady Rosslyn and the child listened. Lady Rosslyn could nod and so on, as often happened with people who had lost their voices.

In any case, this was a very strange child, and one to be wary of.

She went closer to the window, then turned and beckoned to me.

"Look out there."

She was pointing towards what looked like a pile of bricks just beyond the stables.

"It was a fire," she said. "Last year."

"Did you see it?"

She nodded. "The fire was making a roaring sound, as though it was angry . . . and you could feel the heat from it. The sky was red. It was a real fire. Fire kills you if you're in it. Some people can't get out of it. They want to but they can't. There were red flames and yellow flames . . . and it makes pictures, and you can watch them. They change and change. I saw it. You can smell it."

"So you saw this fire, did you?"

She nodded. "They left it all alone . . . after that. It was part of the stables. They were leading the horses out and they were very frightened. It was the biggest fire in the world, and it was all burned out. All that had been there wasn't there any more. That is what happens when there is a fire. Then the fire goes out and what's left is just like bones left on your platter when you've eaten your meat."

"It must have been very frightening."

She looked at me in astonishment.

"Frightening?" she said blankly. "It was the biggest, best fire in the world."

She rose suddenly and walked to the door.

"Goodbye," she said.

"Francine," I replied, "if you come to see me again, come when I am here, will you? Knock at the door and ask if you may come in. And please do not come at night when I am asleep."

She looked at me with that far-off, vacant smile, hunched her shoulders and went out.

A Question of Marriage

MY FATHER RETURNED to Rosslyn Manor.

After some little time he sent for me. I went to the room which was called his small sitting room and he smiled at me and asked me to sit down.

"Well, you are accustomed to the place a little now," he said.

"Yes," I replied.

"And you are finding it comfortable?"

"Yes, thank you."

"A little more congenial than it appeared at first?"

"It is such a large house to become acquainted with when one is unaccustomed to such surroundings."

"Do I detect a hankering after the Dower House or Maggie's neat little place in London?"

"My friends were there."

"And here?" He shrugged his shoulders. "But grieve not. You are going to London, and of course there you will be able to visit the admirable Maggie."

"Oh, that is wonderful."

"You will not have a lot of time with her. I have plans for you. Kate, I am going to show you London, and London you. You will be presented as my daughter and Luke as my son. Why not? It is the truth, is it not? You will see a different way of life."

"I have always known that there are many different ways of life. I did see a little of that in the theater, for instance."

"You will see more with me. Now, you will need clothes, both you and Luke. Those we shall find in London itself. No seamstress here would be adequate to provide what you will need."

"How long shall we stay?" I asked.

"A month or so. It depends. Don't be afraid. I shall be there to guide you."

"Where do we live while we are there? In your lodgings?"

He shook his head. "My lodgings were just an apartment for convenience. I have a house there in Chelsea. It is a pleasant old place with a garden which runs down to the river. It is within easy distance of Whitehall."

"When do we leave?"

"The day after tomorrow. You don't need to bring much. You will acquire everything you need in London. Your maid will see to that."

"Amy? She will not have any idea."

He looked puzzled. He clearly did not know Amy.

"She looks after me here," I said.

He laughed. "No, no. A country girl would be no use. There will be someone at the London house. No need for you to fret about that. It will all be attended to by Mistress Baxter."

"Mistress Baxter? Who is she?"

"She is in charge of the household there. A very efficient woman. She will know what will be required. Tell me, does the prospect please you?"

"It is always exciting to experience something entirely new," I said.

He surprised me in a rare affectionate gesture, when he took my hand in his and kissed me on the brow.

"Kate," he said, "I'm glad you are mine."

When I told Christobel that I was going to London her eyes sparkled.

"So you are to venture into the wicked world outside Somerset. Your father is doing the right thing at last and acknowledging you and Luke. Well, one might say it is time he did. I dare say he has grand plans for you both."

"What do you mean about plans?"

"Plans for girls of your age usually mean one thing. Mayhap he has someone in view. Some country squire. Some knight or baron, perhaps. You could hardly expect a dukedom, but I don't see why it should not be a man with prospects who has not yet attained the height of his ambition. But with the help of my lord as his father-in-law . . ."

"Oh, stop it. I shall refuse to marry any of them."

She looked at me a little wistfully.

"I wonder," she said. "Pressure may be great. Your father clearly has something in mind."

"You mean marriage. Well, in view of his own disastrous experience, I should have thought he would have been a little cautious on that matter."

"People always think their arrangements will succeed when those of others fail."

I did not wish to discuss the matter any further, and I told her about my encounter with Francine.

"So the strange little granddaughter turned out to be the nocturnal visitor," she was saying when Kirkwell came in.

"I was passing and saw your horse outside."

"Kate has news," said Christobel. "She is going to London."

"Oh, no," said Kirk under his breath.

"It is just for a visit . . . a month or so, my father said."

Kirkwell looked very downcast. I knew what he was thinking. His thoughts would be similar to those of Christobel. My father's interest in me was aroused because I was growing up, and parents such as he was were very devoted to their families and always had in mind the thought of the upcoming generations. Although, as some had said, I was only a bastard offspring. I was still a member of the Rosslyn family, and to be considered.

I wanted to go to Kirkwell and comfort him. I remembered the occasion when he had told me—or at least hinted—that he loved me. I also remembered how anxious I had been when he had had to hide in the Devil's Tower.

I loved Kirkwell. I would always feel a tenderness for him, but I felt so inexperienced, and was not sure that the feeling I had for him was that on which to build the foundations of a good marriage.

Kirkwell's obvious unhappiness cast a gloom over the excitement which the prospect of a visit to London had inspired in me.

When I returned to the house I found Luke in a state of ecstasy.

"This is part of it," he said to me. "Our father is acknowledging us. You know what that means. He will introduce us into the right society. There will be a grand marriage for both of us. Oh, Kate, life is wonderful."

The London house was built in attractive red-brick Tudor style and the garden was a delight. The river lapped at its edge and I enjoyed watching the boats going up and down the river, which was invariably crowded with craft of all kinds—from the most elaborate to the very humble. It made me feel that London life was passing along before my eyes.

Mistress Baxter took charge of me, much as Mistress Longton had at the Dower House. She was a tall woman, with an air of immense authority, and she commanded the house as a general might an army. All the servants jumped to attention when she gave her orders. She was, as my father had said, extremely efficient, rather formidable, but I liked her.

She produced Marie, who was said to be half-French, and she was to be my maid. She would dress my hair as it should be dressed, advise me about my clothes, for Marie had what Mistress Baxter called "the touch." It was the French blood in her, and although the French might so often be our enemies on the field of battle and were noted for their cunning ways, in the boudoir they were unsurpassable.

During my first day there was a great bustle about seamstresses and the almost impossible task of turning a gauche young girl from the country into a young lady fit for the court. My hair made Marie sigh in desperation and she was convinced that only time and her own artistic hands could remedy the disaster.

I did manage to get along to Maggie on that first day, because I knew that she would have been hurt if she learned that I had failed to call on her immediately on arriving back in London.

I was received with the usual delight, and I could see that she was excited because, as she saw it, my father was going to "do the right thing" by me.

I told her about the London house, Mistress Baxter and Marie, and all the bustle of preparations which were apparently so necessary.

There were tears in her eyes as she said: "Your mother would have been so pleased. It was what she always wanted for you."

Then we talked of Christobel's marriage with pleasure.

"He seems such a good young man by all accounts, and a clever one too. She'll be happy, the dear girl. We got fond of her, did we not, in spite of the sly way she came here."

Maggie shook with laughter, remembering.

I could see that she was very pleased about everything. My father's interest in his daughter was what she had been hoping for all this time. And that which excited Christobel delighted Maggie, and that which made Kirkwell apprehensive was about to happen.

That London visit was significant.

My father gave a banquet at his Chelsea house, and many of the noblest in the land were invited, among them the Duke of Buckingham. There were others whose names I had heard from time to time, and there were still others to whom I might not have paid great attention at the time but remembered afterwards—Sir Algernon Sidney, Lord Russell and the Earl of Essex.

After the meal the guests sauntered into the garden. It was a pleasant June evening and I thought how beautiful it was, with the willows trailing into the water, and the music which floated out from the ballroom.

I had never seen Luke in such a mood. This was clearly sheer happiness to him: to mingle with people who before had been but names to him, and to be accepted as one of them, was the materialization of his dreams, I was sure. I was beginning to understand Luke well; and while it gave me great pleasure to see him so contented, I felt a twinge of fear for him.

I saw William, Lord Russell, talking to him very earnestly and later they were joined by Sir Algernon Sidney and when the Earl of Essex strolled by, Sir Algernon called to him, and for a while he chatted with them all.

As for me, my father had presented me to many of the guests as his daughter.

There was dancing in the ballroom, in which I was delighted to discover I could join. Christobel and I had practiced a few steps, but of course we were not skilled in the new ones which were being danced at court. I fell into them quite easily and, if I was a little clumsy at first, I was forgiven on account of my youth, or perhaps because I was the now-acknowledged daughter of an important man.

There was one young man, Sir Anthony Warham, who paid particular attention to me. He told me I was born to dance, and I felt very happy. However, my father was soon beside me and I sensed he did not like Sir Anthony. He told me afterwards that Sir Anthony was one of those young men of whom young ladies should be wary.

During that visit to London I was to be given a glimpse of court life. On one very important occasion for me my father took me to Whitehall.

What preparations there had been! Marie had been in a state of great excitement. No single hair must be out of place. I must stand very straight or the fall of my skirt would be imperfect. She taught me how to make the correct curtsey when presented to the King. I should have to watch every moment. She wrung her hands in despair several times and then allowed her spirits to be revived; she lapsed into French to remind me that she came from that country which was noted for its elegance, attention to formality and innate awareness of good taste.

She made me quite nervous of the whole affair, but when I was face to face with the King and those dark somber eyes regarded me, it was all so different from that which Marie had hinted at that I told myself that she was not as knowledgeable as she made herself out to be.

I made my curtsey and when he looked at me, I was immediately aware of that famous charm which completely disarmed me.

My father murmured: "My daughter, Your Majesty."

And he said: "Welcome to my court. It pleases us to see you here."

"Your Majesty is gracious," I said.

"It is you, dear young lady, who are gracious to come."

It was all over in a very short time, but I should never forget

it. I was sure that no one else could be like him. He would have
stood out among them all even if he were not the King, and this
was not entirely due to his magnificent physique, though he
seemed to tower above all the other men near him.

I saw him again later, when he was completely absorbed in two
ladies who sat one on either side of him and who I learned were
Louise de Kerouaille and the play actress Nell Gwynne.

I was a little bemused to see these people, who had previously
been talked of so frequently that I had built up images of them
in my mind.

Several men talked to me and paid fulsome compliments, which
I did not take too seriously, for I had realized that this was the
fashion of the day. My father was never far away and I sensed his
watchfulness. I was delighted that he cared about me so much.
It occurred to me then that I was beginning to be quite fond of
him, although, having read my mother's own account of what he
had done to her, I could not forgive him entirely and believed I
never would.

It had been a wonderful time, and I returned to Rosslyn Manor
feeling that, having had this glimpse of another world, a remote,
fantastic world, I would never be quite the same again.

I was right. Life at Rosslyn Manor seemed very quiet after that
visit to London.

Amy was delighted to see me back. She said there had been a
lot of talk in the servants' hall about my going. She whispered
in confidence that Mistress Galloway was not very pleased about
it, for she thought it was an insult to her ladyship.

"But Lady Rosslyn is not aware of what is happening. I understood she could not speak."

"I don't know, Mistress Kate. What goes on in that part of the
house is a big mystery. Lady Rosslyn is ill, but some say that she
is not all that ill and there are times when she knows what is
going on. It's just that she can't speak . . . perhaps she can talk
in signs, as some deaf people do. Well, all I can say is that I
wouldn't like to be up there. It's a bit odd to me . . . with Lady
Rosslyn there, and that Francine."

"Oh, how is Francine?"

"She doesn't alter. She just goes round in her crazy way."

A few days later I had a visit from Francine.

This time she came to my room and knocked at the door. When I called "Come in," she came in, looking triumphant.

"It's what you said," she told me. "You said to knock."

"Hello, Francine," I said.

"You've been to London," she said.

"Yes, I saw the King."

She studied me with wide-eyed wonder.

I told her about it, the house, the gardens running down to the river, the boats which used the waterway, the carriages in the streets and the people going into the theaters.

She was fascinated by the theater and I told her about my mother and the days long ago when I used to listen to her saying her lines of the play in which she was to act.

Francine listened, her eyes losing that strange wild look.

I thought she seemed almost normal while she was so absorbed.

I wondered about her. She was living in that secluded part of this ancient house with her grandmother and an invalid. It was no life for a child, really.

She took to waylaying me and she obviously liked to listen to me talk.

Everyone was discussing the plot to kill the King.

I heard of it first when I rode over to see Christobel. James was rarely at home, as he was usually occupied with estate business, but he had heard the news and had mentioned it to Christobel.

"Let us thank God that it was foiled. Think of what would have happened if it had succeeded."

I was eager to know what it was all about and Christobel said: "Some traitors planned to kill the King and the Duke of York on their way home from the Newmarket races."

"How terrible!" I cried, thinking of those kindly, though worldly, eyes which had smiled at me in a moment I knew I should never forget. "Imagine if it had succeeded!"

"Well, if the Duke had been killed as well as the King, what then?" I asked Christobel.

"That was the idea. The throne would then have fallen by rights to the Duke's daughter Mary and, failing her, his second daughter Anne. But I am not sure that that was the idea in the minds of those who plotted this. The King certainly has the people's affection. They will demand someone's blood for this. Cold-blooded murder, that's what it would have been. There must have been several conspirators. The King had to pass along a stretch of road on his way to and from the races and there is a farm in a lonely spot which belongs to a maltster, they say. The farm is called Rye House. Everyone is talking about the Rye House Plot."

When I went back to Rosslyn Manor Luke was just coming in. He had been doing some business for James. Lately he had begun to busy himself considerably on the estate. It had worried me slightly.

"Have you had an interesting morning?" he asked.

"Well, I have been talking with Christobel about the plot."

"Plot?" he said. "What plot is this?"

"I believe nobody knows very much about it. It may be that it is only a rumor. You know how these things start. Apparently it was a plan to assassinate the King and the Duke of York near a farm called Rye House."

Luke had turned away slightly, but not before I saw the hot red color flood his neck.

When he turned to look at me his features were composed.

He said: "The what-house plot?"

"Rye," I said, looking at him in surprise, for I felt his voice was not quite natural.

I was silent for a moment and then told him what I had heard from Christobel. After a few moments he spoke, his voice sounding rather harsh as he said: "Is that all you know about it?"

"It was James who mentioned it to Christobel. He meets so many people and he had just heard that there had been this plot."

"Oh, it may well be just one of those stories which go round at times."

But this was not just one of the stories. It was proved to be true that a scheme had been planned.

It was the time of the Newmarket races, and everyone knew

of the King's fondness for the sport. He invariably traveled to Newmarket at this time; it was his custom to go on the day the races started and to return to London when they were over; therefore it was certain that at some time during these days he would be passing along that road.

It was a lonely road and what could be simpler for someone who planned mischief than to lie in wait for His Majesty and the Duke, and as there would be no resistance—or very little—the conspirators could achieve their aim with ease.

It might have succeeded but for a rare chance.

A fire had broken out in the house in which the King and his brother usually stayed when in Newmarket, and for this reason they had decided not to wait for the conclusion of the races but to return to London a day early.

The King and the Duke returned safely to London and on the day they arrived a letter which had been sent from one conspirator to another was discovered and the whole plot exposed.

Luck was certainly on the King's side on this occasion.

I was very frightened at that time, for I had come to know Luke very well and I could see by his demeanor that he was greatly disturbed.

I began to be even more afraid when I discovered the names of some of the conspirators—and the chief of them—Lord Russell, Algernon Sidney and Lord Essex.

My mind went immediately back to that Chelsea garden running down to the river at my father's London residence. No. It could not have been. They hardly knew him. But they had noticed him, they had talked to him, and now he was obviously afraid.

I wanted to talk to him, to ask him what he knew of this plot, but I could not bring myself to do so, and I tried to tell myself that I was imagining something which did not exist.

And then I heard another name mentioned in connection with the plot: the Duke of Monmouth. That added to my anxiety. I had heard Luke speak of the Duke and I had seen the burning fervor in his eyes. The Duke of Monmouth was not only an ardent Protestant but he was also the King's natural son; Luke shared with him that burning ambition to be recognized, not as his father's bastard but as a legitimate son. Monmouth might crave a crown, but Luke's desire to possess Rosslyn Manor was just as fervent.

What had happened on the night of the banquet? How deeply had Luke become involved?

My thoughts went back to that terrible time when Oates's men were close at hand and we were afraid for Kirkwell. Kirkwell had been innocent. There was no case against him, but that would have carried little weight against the followers of Titus Oates. This could be different.

If Luke had been guilty of plotting against the King in order to set on the throne that man who had become a kind of symbol to him . . . that would be considered treason, and treason was punishable by death.

By this time there was no topic of conversation other than the Rye House Plot.

The people, who loved their King and were very grateful to him for bringing merry England back to them after those years of Puritan rule, wanted the conspirators brought to justice.

The ringleaders were soon captured and were sent to the Tower.

Lord Russell seemed to be the chief of the conspirators. He was taken to Lincoln's Inn Fields and deprived of his head. Thousands were there to witness what they had decided was just punishment for a man who had plotted to kill the King.

Lord Essex, a man noted for his virtue and who could only have been persuaded to join such a conspiracy through his fear of a Catholic monarch coming to the throne, committed suicide by hanging himself in his cell in the Tower.

There was only one of those conspirators who escaped, and that was perhaps the one who hoped to profit most from its success. But the King was, after all, his father, and if, like my own father, he could not bring himself to legitimize his natural children, he could not suppress his affection.

The Duke of Monmouth, although it would seem that he had been as deeply involved as any, having more to gain—for the object of the plot was surely to set him on the throne—threw himself on the King's mercy and insisted that he had only listened to the plotters with the sole purpose of saving his father's life.

Did the King really believe that? I could imagine him shrugging his shoulders and telling himself that it was a good thing for a man to believe that which would give him the most comfort. So, with that cynical smile of his, he decided to give his son the benefit of the doubt . . . if doubt there could be said to be.

Monmouth was excused. He could hardly be pardoned, as so many had lost their lives for their part. He could not appear at court. That would be asking too much of those who had lost a dear one who was certainly no more guilty of treason than the Duke. So Monmouth was banished. He went to the Continent, the natural resort of those forced to leave the country. And I guessed from that distance he continued to view the crown of England with renewed and earnest longing.

As for Luke, as the matter of the Rye House Plot slipped into memory, I noticed the intense relief which came to him.

I knew then that he had not been deeply involved in the plot, for his name had not been mentioned, but I did believe that he had been toying with the idea. Clearly he must have betrayed his feelings to those conspirators, and his championing of the Duke of Monmouth's claim must have aroused the interest of those men, but by great good fortune he had not quite committed himself so far as to have become implicated in the actual plot.

All the same, he continued to regard Rosslyn Manor with a yearning desire and I feared that that would persist throughout his life.

But perhaps he had learned the folly of such thoughts. Who knew? This experience, which might have brought him to disaster, might have taught him a lesson.

I was aware of the reverberations of the Rye House Plot all through that year. Indeed, it was not until December that Algernon Sidney lost his head.

I was very anxious about Luke. I knew him well enough to realize that he was deeply disturbed, even anxious. The sight of a stranger would have an effect on him which was not lost on me.

One day I burst out: "Luke, were you in any way concerned in the Rye House Plot?"

He looked at me in such a startled way that I guessed my suspicions had had some foundation.

"No . . . no," he said.

"Look, Luke," I said. "You're my brother. I want to help if I can. I know something happened. I can see the change in you. You remember that time when our father took us to London. You remember the banquet and how we were all in the garden at Chelsea . . . I saw you with those men . . . Lord Russell, Algernon Sidney and the others."

He said nothing.

"Luke," I persisted, "I am very worried about you."

He drew a deep breath. "You need not be," he said. "I did not know that there was to be the Rye House Plot, only . . ."

"Only?" I queried.

Again that silence.

Then he said: "Well . . . I must have betrayed that I thought the crown should go to Monmouth."

I sighed.

He went on: "They did talk to me . . . Lord Russell and Algernon. They overheard my defense of the Duke's right to the throne and they agreed with me that it was necessary to keep out Catholic James. The country would never endure his rule, which would mean turning back to the Pope. There would be trouble. The best course for the country to take would be to rid itself of James right away. Don't look so scared, Kate. They did not tell me of the plot. Do you think they would have told someone they had just met? No. We just talked, and they were sympathetic. They did say that they thought I might be very helpful to the cause . . . when it came, and they would call me in then. That was all."

I sighed with relief.

"Do you swear it, Luke?"

"I swear it," he replied.

"So . . . they plotted this. They were going to kill the King and the Duke of York and set up the Duke of Monmouth, and then they would remember you. They would call on you as one of their supporters."

"I think it must have been something like that."

"And you have been wondering, of course, whether someone might have mentioned your name and then you would be questioned . . . even though you had no part in the plot. So that was the cause of your anxiety?"

"It is disturbing," he said, "when people one has known, however briefly, people one has talked to only a little while ago . . .

and then one hears that they have been beheaded for treason."
"Oh, Luke," I said. "Do take care. We live in dangerous times."

Christobel was going to have a baby. She was blissfully happy.
So was James. They at least were unconcerned about the Rye
House Plot and its aftermath.

James fussed around her, not allowing her to carry anything or
exert herself too much. Christobel reveled in it.

"I feel like a queen bee, with all my workers hovering around,
and just think what it means—a baby! A child of my own. I
cannot wait. I am so impatient. I am just longing for it. James
wants a boy, of course. I do not care. I tell him, just to be
obstinate, that *I* want a girl. Why do men always want boys? The
egoistic male. They think their sex is superior in some way. I
cannot think what gives them such an idea. I thought I had made
James understand by now that that is not the case."

It was wonderful to see her so contented.

She was told she must take regular rests for the sake of the
child, and she liked people to come and see her in the morning
when she could lie on her sofa and receive her guests.

I would go over whenever possible and Sebastian, Kirkwell and
Luke came often.

Luke was taking more and more of an interest in the estate and
was often with James learning about it. I believe that somewhere
within him was the belief that one day, in spite of everything,
Rosslyn Manor would be his. I was getting quite fond of Sebastian.
He was unlike any of the others. There was a certain nonchalance
about him. He was a good-natured man, content with things as
they were. Luke would say, why should he not be? Our father
had decreed that Rosslyn Manor should be his one day. Sebastian's
attitude to life was one of happy complacency. A distant connection of the family, he would one day be very wealthy and inherit
the title as well as the estate, and this he took as it came, without
it seemed any great excitement. He was relaxed. He was as courteous to a serving-maid as he would be to a lady of the court. He
was extremely popular. In fact, we all liked him.

He was often at Christobel's gatherings. He had the time. He was only mildly interested in the estate and left everything to James, which suited James. How different from Luke, who was deeply concerned about every little item concerning the place.

Kirkwell would often come in to see his sister.

One morning they were all there—Kirk, Luke, James and Sebastian—and the talk was, as very often, of that topic which seemed on everyone's mind since the discovery of the Rye House Plot. Oh no, it had been there before that. In fact, it was a perennial concern and I supposed it would be until some solution was found.

They were discussing it now.

"The King is well at the moment," pointed out James. "But he is no longer young and he lives rather strenuously," he added with a smile.

"While he lives," put in Luke, "all is well. But what would happen if he were to die suddenly?"

"Then we should have James," said Sebastian.

"James!" cried Luke. "You know what that means. Back to the domination of Rome!"

"They might work something out," suggested Sebastian. "Surely that would not be difficult?"

"There are some people in the court," said Kirk, "who would fight to bring back the Pope, and that is no good. What we need is peace. We want a country untroubled by conflict."

"But the Duke of York is a Catholic," declared Luke.

"So be it," said Sebastian. "That does not make me one."

"It might be necessary to be one. Remember what they did with the Inquisition."

"We would not have that here."

"Remember Bloody Mary."

"Nor would we allow a repetition of that."

"It's all very well for you, Sebastian. You'd go this way or that, whatever comfort dictated."

"It is not a bad approach, dear boy."

"I know it is your way," remarked Luke, who was looking at Sebastian and smiling.

Kirk said: "Suppose that plot had succeeded. Then we should have had a Protestant King."

"Monmouth!" said James. "That was impossible, because . . ." He did not finish.

"What difference does that make?" cried Luke angrily. "If the King and Duke of York had died and Monmouth had been set on the throne, the people would be rejoicing—"

There was a movement from behind.

Thomas Crabber, one of the men who worked on the estate, had come into the room.

He touched his forehead and fixed his eyes on James.

"Begging your pardons, ladies and gentlemen . . . I had to see Mr. Morton. 'Tis trouble, sir, over at Brewer's place. Old Brewer's in a fair way. Says he wants to see you and won't take no for an answer."

"It's that flooding, is it, Thomas?"

"Likely, sir."

"I'll be over right away."

He turned and grinned at the company.

"Take care of yourself, my dear," he said to Christobel. "And as for the rest, you go on fighting the battle for the succession."

Occasionally I saw Margaret Galloway in the gardens. She contrived not to see me but if there was no escape she would answer my greeting rather unwillingly. I had never had a conversation with her. Once or twice I had seen her with Francine, who would give me a mischievous look as she passed with her grandmother.

I had never seen Mistress Galloway exchange a word with the housekeeper or any of the servants, so I was surprised one day to come upon her in what appeared to be close conversation with Thomas Crabber.

I had often seen Thomas Crabber about the estate. There was something in his manner which I did not like. There was a perpetual smile on his face, but it was by no means a pleasant one. His small eyes were closely set under bushy brows and his was a face which made me feel rather uneasy. That was why I had been a little disturbed that he had come into the room when Luke had been talking rather rashly about his preference for the Duke of

Monmouth as the future King. It was a reckless remark at the
best of times, but in view of the present situation very dangerous.

Francine sought me out frequently and then there would be
periods when she seemed to forget all about me, though I never
knew why, for when she returned she talked to me as though
there had been no change in our relationship. It was just a part
of her generally erratic behavior.

It really did seem that the atmosphere had changed with the
Rye House Plot.

I was in the garden one day when Francine came up to me.

She said: "Hallo, Mistress Kate."

I returned her greeting.

She said: "Mistress Morton is going to have a baby soon."

"Oh, it is not for some time yet."

"They were talking about it. Someone might put the evil eye
on her. Then her baby might be a little frog or a goblin."

"Whoever said such a thing? That is absolute nonsense. Mistress Morton will have a lovely little boy or girl."

"How do you know?"

"I feel sure of it. So please do not let me hear you say such
things again."

"My grandmother says that Mistress Morton will not be a good
mother. She is too flighty. That is why she will only get a frog."

"I do not believe your grandmother said any such thing."

"She said she was flighty and hand-in-glove with you . . . and
that other."

"Who is that other?"

"Your brother . . . who shouldn't be here. Nor should you."

"Why not?"

"It's something about a blanket. You got on the wrong side of
it, did you not?"

"Your grandmother said this? To whom did she say it?"

"To her."

I began to understand. Lady Rosslyn resented us. I knew that
already. I could imagine what Margaret Galloway said of us to
Lady Rosslyn. Did she still do so? And what of Lady Rosslyn . . . lying in her bed, unable to move some parts of her body,
her speech affected?

It was a sad image. Poor woman lying thus, and still resentful that her husband was bringing other people's children into their house, reproaching her because she had not brought him his longed-for heir.

And they must talk in the presence of Francine, though I could imagine the child listening at doors, hearing the conversations, most likely misconstruing what was said. It was not a pleasant picture.

"She hates you . . . and him," Francine said. "She's going to . . ." She hesitated and then said: "Going to destroy him."

"Who?"

"Your brother. You too."

"Who said this?"

"They did."

"Your grandmother and Lady Rosslyn?"

"My grandmother. Her . . . she just grunts . . . but that means yes. They hate him because he's here. They're afraid . . . well, it's going to be the other . . . not him. Though *he* thinks it might be him."

"It's all so muddled," I said, "I don't know what you are talking about."

She shook her head. "It's not. She's going to tell some-one . . . about your brother. What he said. Then they'll come here. Some of them had their heads cut off. She said he should too."

I was beginning to understand. Thomas Crabber had noted what Luke had said. He had talked. It had come to Mistress Galloway's ears and she was Luke's enemy . . . and mine.

I felt sick with anxiety and concern. I could never forget the days when Titus Oates's men were here and how we had feared for Kirkwell. I remembered those trips to the Devil's Tower. We had lived in dangerous times then, and still did.

And now Luke and I had our own enemies . . . here in Rosslyn Manor. I had always known they resented us, but I had never thought that they could be very dangerous enemies. And in times such as these, Luke could be most unsafe.

I had to tell him. I had to make him see that he must always act with the utmost care.

Francine was looking at me steadily. She sensed the alarm her admissions had aroused in me. For a moment I saw a certain softness come into her eyes.

She said, and there was sincerity in her voice: "I like you, Mistress Kate."

"Thank you, Francine." I was gratified, but very much afraid. I did speak to Luke. I told him what Francine had said.

"Those two old women," he said. "One in her dotage and the other a wreck! How could they harm me?"

"They can talk. You see how it has come back to me, through Francine."

"That crazy child!"

"She is strange, I grant you, but they must have been talking of you. I have seen Margaret Galloway in conversation with Tom Crabber. There is a man I do not like. And you were talking very rashly when he overheard you."

Luke was thoughtful. He realized the truth of that. I said: "Think of those men. They were our father's guests. There they were, laughing, talking, being merry with us all, and now . . . what are they? Rotting corpses, their heads doubtless on London Bridge, a warning to all men. Luke, please take that warning."

"My dear sister, I love you dearly, and I believe you are very fond of me, but . . ."

"You are my brother. Let us not forget that. Promise me that you will heed this warning. We have enemies, Luke, here in this house. Those two women in that part of the house which they have made their own. Imagine them . . . resentful . . . unhappy. Blaming fate. What can it be like? Their only pleasure is in planning revenge on us."

"You take too much notice of that crazy child."

"I think I am rather grateful for the warning of that crazy child. I think we should remember the times we live in. They are dangerous indeed."

The new year would soon be with us. Christobel's baby was due in July, a month after my eighteenth birthday.

My father had not suggested that Luke and I should accompany him to London after that first visit, although he himself went frequently.

I was happy enough, although Luke would have liked to go.

Occasionally Sebastian went with my father. He was known everywhere, of course, as the heir of Rosslyn Manor. I wondered that
he had not married by this time, but perhaps he was too lazy to
bestir himself. He seemed very content with life as it was.

Kirkwell was working very hard and, Christobel told me, with
good results. James, who knew of such matters, said that Featherston had taken a new lease on life and was becoming as it had
been in its most prosperous days. Kirkwell had worked wonders
and many of the neighboring squires had said they found it hard
to believe. James declared he had not. He had known from the
start that Kirkwell's hard work would show results.

I often called at Featherston and when she was feeling well
enough Christobel accompanied me, but on this occasion I went
alone.

I found Kirkwell in his office, where he spent a great deal of
time. He now had several men working for him, which meant
that he had more free time to spare.

His face brightened when he saw me. It was always a pleasure
to see, for he showed so clearly how delighted he was to see me.

"Come along in, Kate," he said. "For so long I have wanted
to talk to you alone. It is not always easy to find you alone, and
when I do . . . I wonder . . . if it is time. But I can wait no longer.
You know I love you, that I always have. We've seen how happy
Christobel and James are. Well, I want that happiness for us.
Kate, I want you to marry me."

I was not really taken aback, but I seemed so. I knew that he
loved me. He had told me so a long time ago and it had always
been clear to me. And I loved him. But for some reason I was
dismayed. I did not want to change anything yet. It was foolish
of me, I suppose. It was not that I did not love him. I did. It
was just that I did not want change.

He was looking startled. He said: "Why, Kate . . . I thought
you cared for me."

"I do, Kirk, I really do. It is just that . . ." I stopped, for I
could not explain.

"You are not . . . surprised?"

"Well, not exactly. But I felt that . . . well, that is for later."

"You will soon be eighteen, Kate, not a child any longer."

"I know. But things have happened suddenly . . . coming

here . . . the change of it all. And then all this trouble about the Plot and all that.''

"That is not our concern, Kate."

"But it is the concern of us all."

"It makes no difference to our loving each other."

"I think that perhaps I am not ready yet, Kirk. I hadn't expected it yet. I think perhaps in a few months' time . . ."

He looked faintly relieved and I clung to this idea. I could not bear to see him look hurt. Surely that was a sign that I loved him?

"Yes," I said. "That is it. I just want time."

"But I thought you knew . . ."

"I did, and I love you, Kirk. I'm sure of that. It is just . . . Could we leave it for a little, just a little while? I just feel . . . not ready."

"Well, if that is what you wish."

"I wish I could make you understand."

"I think I do."

"Oh, Kirk, Kirk. Please do. It will be all right in the end, I'm sure. It's just that for the time being I just want things to go on as they are. Only for a little while. I want to think about it all."

"This place is going to grow prosperous, Kate. You won't be ashamed of it."

"Oh, Kirk, as if I should. As if it were important. If you had a little cottage it would make no difference."

"I wanted to make sure that I could get things right here before I asked you."

"That is of no moment."

"It is of the utmost importance."

"No, Kirk . . . Oh, Kirk, I do love you. I was thinking of that terrible time when you hid in the Devil's Tower. Do you remember? If you could know how I felt when I used to make my way there."

"I never forget that time."

"I shiver now at the thought."

"Your coming to me like that was wonderful."

"They all came, did they not? Christobel, James, Luke, all of them."

"And you came too. That was the best time. I remember your

little face so anxious, and I was almost glad to be there because of that. I thought you must love me. But now . . ."

"Of course I love you. It is just that I want to wait. Say on my eighteenth birthday. It is not long now, as you say. Suppose we announce it then."

"Do you mean that?"

"Yes . . . I think I do."

It must be, I told myself, because I was thinking of him now as he had been in the Devil's Tower and of my anguish at the time because I feared that he was in danger.

I had ridden over to Christobel. I did not tell her that her brother had proposed marriage to me. She would have been delighted, I knew, but I should never have been able to explain to her my feelings. She would have laughed them to scorn. But how can we explain our innermost thoughts? Well, more than thoughts, really: it was a kind of instinct, something which said no, no, wait.

When I returned to Rosslyn Manor, I left my horse in the stables and was walking into the house when I met my father.

"Is all well?" he said.

"Thank you, yes," I replied.

"I thought you looked a little . . . distrait."

"Oh, did you?"

"You have something on your mind, have you not?"

I hesitated too long, and he said: "So, you have."

As we crossed the hall, he took my arm and drew me into that little room which he used as his study.

"You shall tell me all about it," he said.

I was nonplussed. He was the last person to whom I could have explained my innermost thoughts. I was quite fond of him, but we were scarcely close.

He looked at me steadily, and then said: "Come . . . tell me."

I found myself saying: "I have had a proposal of marriage."

The change in his expression surprised me.

He said sharply: "Who?"

I said: "Kirk . . . Kirkwell Carew. We have known each other a long time and have always been good friends."

His face darkened, and he cut me short.

"You declined, I hope?"

"Well, no . . ."

"What?"

I said: "No . . . not exactly."

"Not exactly. And what does not exactly mean?"

"I have not said yes . . . yet."

"That would save some trouble."

"I don't understand."

"I have already decided on your husband."

I stared at him in astonishment.

"I was going to tell you very soon. Are we not approaching your eighteenth birthday?"

"Yes, but . . ."

"Now listen to me. I am very fond of you, Kate. In fact, I did not believe I could be so fond. I like your spirit, your outlook on life. You are a complete Rosslyn."

"Maggie says I am just like my mother."

"That may be. But you are a Rosslyn too, and that is what I like. Now listen. These are my plans. If you married Sebastian, this would be your home. My daughter would inherit Rosslyn Manor. You see what I mean? All this would not have to go outside the direct line. Oh, Sebastian also has Rosslyn blood, but it is a very distant connection."

I was hardly taking this in. Marry Sebastian! I could not believe I was hearing correctly.

"It would be quite in order. You are both of the family, of course, but the relationship between you is not close enough to give any cause for concern on that score. You are only remotely connected. As a matter of fact, first cousins have married in the family before now. My dear child, this has become the greatest wish of my life. If I could see you and Sebastian married, it would not matter so much that I had no son to follow me."

"But Sebastian!" I said. "I had never thought of marrying Sebastian."

"Of course you had not, but the idea has been brewing in my mind since we went to London. It came to me suddenly then, when I saw you in that setting. You were charming . . . so adaptable, so right in every way. Then I was afraid that you would become involved in some adventure with someone there. So I brought you back. You were very young then. And I have been waiting for the time to come . . ."

Even then I was too overcome by surprise to say much. I thought of Sebastian—charming, nonchalant Sebastian, who shrugged his shoulders at fate and accepted what came with that mild tolerance which in some way endeared him to one. I had often watched him while the others were fiercely expressing their views, but he sat back, smiling, unruffled.

"Well?" said my father.

"Have you . . . told Sebastian of your wishes?"

"He knows."

"And what does he say?"

"He is happy with the arrangement."

That told me nothing. Sebastian would accept any proposition with equanimity. Marry Kate? he would muse. Well, it would be a solution for Lord Rosslyn, who was so eager to see one of his offspring mistress, if not master, of Rosslyn Manor. He was quite fond of Kate in his easygoing way. He would marry some day, he would suppose, so why not Kate? In any case, it was a necessity to please his benefactor, for Lord Rosslyn could as easily decide after all not to make him his heir. There were probably other remote connections of the family who would serve his purpose . . . I could imagine Sebastian's reaction.

"The wedding could be on your eighteenth birthday," my father went on. "That would be rather a charming gesture. What do you say?"

"I have just told you how I feel about Kirkwell Carew."

"Oh, no, that is just a young girl's passing fancy. They have them now and then."

"I have known him for some little time. So it is hardly passing."

"At one time," said my father, "I thought it would be a fair enough match. There are now possibilities at Featherston Manor. James thinks so and he also thinks Kirkwell is the one to set it in good order. It's true that at one time I thought that he would be a fair match for you."

"Which was why you helped us hide him in the Devil's Tower."

He nodded reminiscently. "This will be a wonderful arrange-

ment. Kate, it is what I want more than anything. If I could see
your children playing in these gardens, I think I could die happy."

"Please . . . please, do not talk like that."

"It's a shock to you, is it, Kate?"

"I can't really believe it."

"Why not? It's the most logical outcome imaginable. Why
should you two not marry? Your children—my grandson—would
inherit the place."

"When you married," I said, "you thought your sons would
inherit the place. There were no sons. You have had an unhappy
marriage as a result."

"That was unfortunate."

"It is not rare. There must be many barren marriages. What
if this one you are proposing were too?"

"I cannot believe it would be."

"Nor could you believe yours would be."

"I was forced into marriage . . ."

"And is that what you would do to me?"

"Oh, come, I know you and Sebastian are the best of friends."

"We are good friends, but . . ."

"You are thinking of Kirkwell Carew."

"Yes, and that I had never thought of Sebastian as a husband,
nor do I suppose he thought of me as a wife until it was suggested
to him."

"I have surprised you," he said. "I have not chosen the right
moment. It should have come gently."

"It is not that . . . though I must say it is a surprise . . . and
a shock."

"You could not have cared so much for Kirkwell or there would
not be all this talk of waiting."

I considered that. He noticed and a triumphant smile crossed
his face.

"You are really very young as yet, Kate. Look . . . do not say
I will not do this or I will do that. We'll agree to wait a little. To
give you time to consider. You are right not to become involved
too deeply at the moment. You see, you were aware of that. You
had not thought of Sebastian in the light of a husband. But let
me tell you, he will be one of the best. He is good-natured, kindly,
affectionate and tolerant, and that last is a very good quality in
a husband. You may not be passionately in love with him, but

you are fond of him. He will always be your good friend and that is also a wonderful quality in a husband. See here, Kate, do not be rash. Remember how you have dealt with Kirkwell. You were unsure about him. You are unsure about Sebastian too. Leave it for a while. Just think of Sebastian. Think of being mistress of Rosslyn Manor, which will be rather different from Featherston Manor. Oh, I know you will thrust all that aside. You will not marry for position, but for love. Very charming and romantic—and pleasant too, I will admit—but think of it, Kate. This house, with years of history behind it. Your children will be heirs to Rosslyn. Kate, think of it. And think too of the pleasure you will give to a weary old man because his dearest wish is granted."

"I did not think you regarded yourself as a weary old man," I said.

He laughed and said: "Kate, please . . . because it means so much to me, will you think about it? Let us wait."

I could only say that I would.

Rebellion

I COULD NOT FEEL the same towards Sebastian after that. I found myself watching him, thinking of him as my husband, spending my life with him. And not far away would be Kirkwell, whom I had half promised to marry instead.

Of course I could not marry Sebastian. Of course it must be Kirkwell—serious Kirkwell, who had worked so hard to restore his family home, who cared deeply about the future of the country, who loved me with a devotion which had begun soon after our first meeting and would last throughout our lives.

But on the other hand there was Sebastian, who was a kindly, even-tempered, calm and contented man, seeking a comfortable life and letting all discomforts flow past him, because he refused to notice them. I liked him very much, and I often wondered whether, but for Kirkwell, I might have become accustomed to the idea of marrying him.

He seemed to be more often in my company and I thought that it was because my father had told him of his wishes. The role of Lord Rosslyn of Rosslyn Manor would suit Sebastian well. He did not often refer to his home before he came to Rosslyn Manor, but I imagined it was in some decaying mansion whose upkeep caused concern to his impoverished father. Then came this golden opportunity, to go to Rosslyn Manor as heir because of this distant family connection to the powerful Lord Rosslyn, who was childless apart from those he had acquired outside matrimony. Of course Sebastian seized what was offered with alacrity: it was just the sort of life to appeal to him. And now, to please his benefactor, he was to marry a girl who was not too distasteful to him and whom he liked well enough. It would be an ideal arrangement, especially when the much-desired offspring appeared and the satisfied benefactor could look through his window and say: It has worked, just as I planned.

Oh, yes, Sebastian would be very ready to go along with that.

Christmas had come and we were in the New Year. It was cold and blustery.

Life still seemed a little unreal to me. My father watched me closely and I was always afraid that he was going to tell me his patience was running out and that he wanted to announce my engagement to Sebastian without any more delay.

Sebastian said nothing to me of marriage. I believed that my father had told him to wait.

When I saw Kirkwell I felt uneasy. He noticed and thought my mood was due to the fact that I was unsure.

He was not very happy, I knew, and I was desperately sorry about that. But I felt bewildered by my father's revelation of his plans, and I could not bring myself to discuss the whole matter with anyone, not even Christobel.

I went for short rides alone. I missed riding with Christobel. The baby was not due for a long time yet, but she was taking extreme care.

One day, returning to the stables after my ride, I met Luke. He told me he had been with James. He was very absorbed in something on the estate. James was explaining it all to him.

Poor Luke, with his dreams of one day inheriting the estate. I wondered what he would say if he knew of my father's plans for Sebastian and me. That would surely be a death knell to all his hopes.

Was Luke doomed to be disappointed all his life? And my poor father, I feared he would be disappointed too.

What wild plans these ambitious men could make. How could Luke believe that he would ever inherit Rosslyn Manor? How could my father believe I would ever marry Sebastian when I was almost certain that my husband would be Kirkwell? Of course, my father might well give Luke a small estate of his own. Sebastian would marry and perhaps my father would see his children playing in the gardens, but they would not be as close to him as he had wanted. But it would not be Rosslyn Manor for Luke, and it would not be my father's grandchildren there either.

It was dusk, which came early on these wintry afternoons, and as we approached Rosslyn Manor I saw a faint red glow in the sky. And then I detected a whiff of burning . . . and I saw smoke coming from one of the windows in the tower.

"It's a fire!" I cried.

Luke murmured: "God in Heaven preserve us, so it is."

Then we were running towards the house with all speed.

The fire was in that part of the house which I had never visited, Lady Rosslyn's apartments.

"Give the alarm at once," cried Luke, and ran on ahead of me.

It seemed that the fire had already been detected, for several of the servants were assembled in passages, shouting to each other. They were carrying buckets of water which would surely not be very effective if the fire had got a hold as, from what we had seen outside, it seemed it had.

Luke had gone on ahead. This part of the Manor was very like that which I inhabited, built to the same pattern, so it was not as strange to me as it might have been.

I pushed my way forward. Then I saw Margaret Galloway. She was crying wildly.

"My lady . . . she is in there. I cannot lift her . . . I cannot get her out. She cannot move."

A door was open and, looking into the room, I saw a curtain of flames.

"She is in her bed . . . I cannot move her," sobbed Margaret.

It was unbelievably hot and I found breathing difficult.

Several of the men were trying to beat out the flames and there were others throwing water over them. Some were carrying tubs of water up to the room.

Then I saw Luke. His face was blackened, his hair singed, but in his arms he was carrying someone.

Margaret Galloway cried: "Oh, praise the Lord. He has brought her out."

Luke was a hero. He had acted with selfless bravery. Lady Rosslyn had been in her bed, unable to move. Her bedcurtains were aflame. A few more moments and she would have been past helping. But Luke had reached her in time. He had rushed into the room and through the burning curtains with such speed that he had emerged with Lady Rosslyn in his arms with only singed hair and a few burns on his hands.

I thought afterwards how ironical it was that the one person whose presence in the manor house she had so resented had saved her life.

Both she and Luke had suffered minor burns. Luke's hair and eyebrows were singed. He looked unlike himself and his hands were painful. However, there were several of the servants with worse burns. One of the women on the estate was very skillful with lotions and unguents and was able to give immediate attention to those who had been burned, which saved them from being as bad as they might have been.

The fire was quickly put out. It was not the first fire the house had suffered during the centuries and the thick stone walls were almost impervious even to fire. This one had been confined to Lady Rosslyn's quarters and would certainly have been fatal to her had not Luke been able to bring her out.

No one knew how the fire had been started. Candles would have been lighted. There was a blustering wind outside. Perhaps a draught from an open door had sent a curtain fluttering into the candle flame. Who could say?

It was about a week or so after the fire, when I came back from one of my rides over to Christobel, that I saw Margaret Galloway. I had the feeling that she had been waiting for me.

She seemed rather embarrassed, and she said quickly: "Lady Rosslyn is better today. It was a terrible experience for her. Imagine her . . . lying there . . . helpless, with the fire all around her."

"Poor lady. It must have been horrifying."

"She would like you and your brother to come to see her, if you will. She wants you to know how grateful she is."

I felt a glow of pleasure. I knew she had resented us bitterly and I could understand it. This was quite a change of attitude. Understandable, of course. One cannot go on hating someone who has saved one's life.

I said we should be glad to go and see Lady Rosslyn.

"It was a terrible shock for her," said Margaret Galloway. "It was not until it was burning fiercely that I knew what was happening. It was too late to stop it."

"Everyone seems to have acted promptly and so saved a real disaster."

"But our apartments are unusable. We have other ones now. The maid will show you if you and your brother will come."

I said: "Francine was all right, was she?"

Margaret said: "Oh yes."

"It must have been alarming for her."

"Was it not for us all? Her ladyship is usually at her best in the afternoons."

"When my brother comes in, I will tell him."

And so Luke and I went to Lady Rosslyn's apartment.

She was in her bed, propped up with pillows.

She looked at us appealingly. Luke went to her and took the hand which she held towards us. He kissed it gallantly and she smiled, and her lips moved.

Margaret, who was standing by the bed, said: "She is saying 'Thank you.' She is telling you she is grateful to you for saving her life."

"I am so pleased to have been able to do so," said Luke.

"She wants you to know that she is sorry . . ."

Luke said: "There is no need to be."

"She thinks that she may have offended you."

"I fear that I may have offended *her*."

"She wants to say that it was just that she was wrong to blame you, and your noble action has made her ashamed."

"Please," said Luke. "All that must be forgotten. That is how I feel and I know my sister does too."

"Yes, yes," I said.

Her lips lifted at one side and she nodded. She could hear what was said, Margaret Galloway told us, although she could not reply.

"I trust," said Luke, "that you have recovered from the shock?"

She nodded again. Her face, slightly distorted, yet had a softness which I was sure had not been there before when she had contemplated us.

I was deeply touched and thought what an extraordinary turn of fate it was that Luke, whom she had so bitterly resented—

even more than she did me, a mere girl—should have been the one to save her life.

However, I felt happier at Rosslyn Manor than I had for a long time and I knew it was the same with Luke.

It was February, cold and bleak, when the news came.

The King had had a seizure and a few days after it he had died.

That which we had all feared had come upon us.

We waited for what would happen. For so long we had anticipated this and now it had come it was something of an anticlimax. We had a new King, James, who, it had often been said, would never be accepted since the English could never allow a Catholic to occupy the throne again.

My father left for London and we had to rely on news from travelers arriving or when someone had heard something from someone else. It was mostly hearsay. It seemed that the fears we had had were unfounded, and although there was grieving for a much-loved King, his brother was accepted as the true heir to the throne in the usual manner. Wine was distributed in the streets, that the people might drink the health of King James, and the King had made a speech to the Council assuring them that he would follow his brother's example, especially in his clemency and—what was most significant—support the government in Church and State as by law established.

When they heard of this speech, the people's fears were slightly allayed.

Alas, James could not, it appeared, keep to this promise, and, a few days after his accession, he heard Mass openly in the Queen's Chapel.

We waited in trepidation, but this seemed to pass over and there were no more rumors of his misdemeanors.

My father came back from London and I expected him to mention the fact that my eighteenth birthday was not far away, and to remind me of his wishes concerning Sebastian.

However, he did not. I think he was really concerned about

the political situation. The trouble with these internal conflicts was that it involved people taking sides, and who was to know which side was going to be the winning one. The Civil War between the King and Parliament was too recent for anyone to contemplate such a conflict without some misgivings.

I was glad that the matter of Sebastian was not raised again.

I had been thinking quite a lot about him and seemed to find myself more frequently in his company. I reminded myself often that he would be seeing me in much the same way as I saw him—assessing me, thinking of me as a possible wife. Yet he gave no sign of this. He was just as calm and friendly as he had ever been.

There were great discussions when we all met, usually in Christobel's house because she liked to be with us and was growing a little unwieldy now.

I could not help being rather glad of the state of affairs and the anxiety which had made my matrimonial plans seem temporarily of secondary importance.

When the King and Queen were crowned according to the Protestant ritual, it was thought that James intended to accept the authorized religion of the country for the sake of a crown, and that he had abandoned his attempt to introduce Catholicism again.

It was early in June, my eighteenth birthday was approaching, and I was sure that my father was contemplating bringing up the subject of my marriage. However, at this point, news came which made everything else sink into insignificance.

The Duke of Monmouth had come out of exile. He had landed at Lyme in Dorsetshire, not very far from our home. He had brought with him only one hundred and fifty followers and arms for five thousand more. He immediately published a declaration against the King, charging him with attempting to introduce Popery to England and saying that he, Monmouth, had come to claim the throne and set a Protestant King upon it—himself.

Christobel was stretched out on her sofa while we all gathered in her sitting room. In a month's time her baby was due.

We were all talking about the arrival of the Duke of Monmouth in England. It could only mean a rebellion, and that must have its effect on us all.

Luke's eyes were gleaming.

"The King should have made him his heir. Then this would not have happened."

"He could scarcely do that when the King's heir was here waiting," said Kirkwell.

"Monmouth could have been the heir," insisted Luke.

"Ah, but he was not, though," said Sebastian.

"Charles had seen this coming. He might have married Monmouth's mother and settled the Monmouth claim, if he wished," said James.

"It might have been that they *were* married," said Luke. "There was talk of proof."

"You mean the little black box with the marriage certificate in it? Oh, you can't believe that. Lucy Walter, Queen of England. Come, Luke, be realistic."

Luke said: "I hope he succeeds."

"Treason," said Sebastian flippantly.

"This is a serious matter," cried Luke hotly.

Kirk said that he agreed. "It is a very serious matter. But I cannot believe the King married Lucy Walter."

"He was an exile at that time," insisted Luke. "He had no throne then."

"It's fortunate that he did not marry all the ladies in his life," said Sebastian, "or we should have too many to choose from now."

James said that, whatever there was to be said for a Protestant Monmouth against a Catholic James, James was his brother's legitimate heir and that was the law and that was how it stood with him, and any attempt to dethrone him was treason.

"But it is easy to see the way everything is going," said Kirk. "You can depend upon it. James will attempt to lead the country into the Catholic Faith. He will try to return us to Rome, and I do believe that that is something the English will never allow to happen."

"But he is the King, whatever his religion," said James.

"That is no reason why he should take this country where it does not wish to go," argued Kirkwell. "The will of the people is all-important."

Christobel sighed and said: "It is a pity it has to affect us when all we want to do is live in peace."

" 'Tis indeed a pity," replied her husband. "But there it is, my love. What should we do? Depend upon it, the people of this country will attempt to be rid of James if he tries to enforce his religion on us."

"Perhaps he will realize that," I suggested.

"If he did," said Kirk soberly, "he would not proclaim so openly his Catholicism in a country he hopes to rule."

"Perhaps he thinks it would be dishonest not to admit it."

"He has flaunted it. To go to Mass in the Queen's Chapel where anyone can see him. It is clear what will happen. There will be trouble. 'Tis better to be rid of it now before it gets greater."

"And you think to do that by supporting Monmouth?" I asked.

There was some hesitation. Kirk frowned and said: "We cannot have another such war as we did when the Parliament decided to rid the country of the King's father. Wars do no good to anyone."

"Then why have them?" asked Christobel.

"That's not an easy question to answer. Sometimes they are resorted to in order to prevent something worse."

"And now you think . . . ?"

"Monmouth for King," mused Kirk. "That is not ideal. He was a wild young man . . . but sometimes wild young men become wise ones. We have the true heir to the throne who threatens to turn an inherently Protestant nation into a Catholic one, which is certain to provoke bloodshed; and on the other hand we have an ambitious young man, who has not proved he has the necessary qualities for government, but who is a Protestant. He is young. He can learn. King James never would."

"What a pity," said Christobel lightly, "that the management of these things cannot be arranged around this table. I am sure you could solve the country's problems far more efficiently than those in whose hands they lie."

Sebastian said: "I'll swear that, wherever the news of Monmouth's arrival in England has been received, men and women will be sitting round tables such as this and discussing this very subject and all of them will think they are as wise as we are."

One of the workers on the estate came hurrying in. It was Tom Ricks, whom I knew slightly.

"Begging your pardon, sir," he said, looking at James. "But I thought you'd be wanting to know right away, like. It's news from London. Gentleman just come in from Bridgwater. He says Lord Monmouth has taken Taunton. He has five thousand men now, rising to seven thousand. He's come into Bridgwater and they've crowned him King."

Luke had risen, his eyes gleaming.

"It has come. I knew it would. Down with the Papists! Long live King Monmouth! I am going to join Monmouth's army. I shall leave today for Bridgwater."

"I'll be with 'ee," said Tom Ricks, and as he went out a silence fell on us all.

"So," said James at length, "it has come to this. This means . . . fighting."

"He is already proclaimed King," insisted Luke.

"That does not make him so," replied James quietly.

"We are going to make him so," said Luke earnestly. "It is wonderful. He has just arrived and already is called the King."

"Bridgwater is not the world," said James.

"We are going to make the whole of England follow Bridgwater."

"Luke, don't be too hasty. Have you thought of what this means?" James asked Luke.

"I am certain it is what I wish to do. While King James is on the throne there will be conflict throughout the country. Once we have a good Protestant King the people will settle down. They will no longer be afraid of Catholic customs. They will be happy and we shall all live our lives in peace. I shall go to Bridgwater at once. The new King will need all the men he can get."

Kirk was staring ahead of him, with a very serious expression on his face.

He said: "I am not sure of the Duke of Monmouth. He was very wild in his youth. Do you remember Sir John Coventry, whose nose he and his friends slit, and how they murdered the beadle who tried to keep order?"

"That was his wild youth," said Luke. "He is different now that he will have the responsibility of the crown."

"He has not acquired it yet," Sebastian pointed out. "A cheer and a hurrah in a little country town is not a loyal reception in London. Forget not, the King has a strong army at his command with men like John Churchill leading it. Unless they have rebelled against the crown, they will be for the King, and how do you think Monmouth and his little band will stand up to James's trained men?"

"Bridgwater calls him King," said Luke.

"Bridgwater, dear fellow, is a very small place in a very small county. Do not set too much store by Bridgwater."

"The question is, which is the right cause to join?" said Kirkwell. "Is it a choice between two evils? On the one hand there is a Protestant country cursed with a Catholic King: on the other a Protestant King as yet unfitted to rule. It is not a very good proposition."

"Do you think James is fit to rule?" demanded Luke.

"Alas, no. But I think England, being England, would be better with the Protestant. When are you leaving, Luke?"

"Tomorrow morning at dawn."

"I shall come with you," said Kirk.

It is known through the depth and breadth of the land what happened in the next few days, how the proud young Duke was humbled, how his arrogant belief in himself was not supported by his deeds. How he reveled in those few days of his glory and how quickly that glory melted away.

We were deeply concerned. We were very close to the fighting and the field on which in due course the fatal battle was fought.

Our arrogant, foolish Monmouth was like a boy with ambitions which he could not hope to fulfill. James had done some foolish things, but he was wiser than his would-be rival. He was a mature man; he was the hero of several naval battles: he had the Earl of Frensham and Sir John Churchill beside him, seasoned warriors, against the inexperienced Duke and, as the people were unkindly calling them, his pack of country yokels.

But for those days when he called himself King, Monmouth reveled in the glory for which he must have longed ever since he had discovered that he was the King's son. Leaving Bridgwater, he had marched to Bristol, expecting as easy a victory there as he had enjoyed in Taunton and Bridgwater. Alas for him, the King's men had heard of his approach and were ready to meet him in such force that he lost heart and hastily turned back to Bridgwater. Defiantly he issued a declaration, offering five thousand pounds for King James's head.

It was ludicrous.

Meanwhile we waited at home for news. It was of the utmost importance to us now. Luke, my brother, and Kirk were there.

James was grim. He said they had been rash to go. Even Sebastian showed concern. As for me, I was thinking constantly of Kirkwell. What if I never saw him again? I wished then that I had agreed to marry him. Perhaps, had we been betrothed, I might have persuaded him not to go. I longed for his return. It was because I loved him, far more than I had thought.

Christobel was no longer blissfully happy and was clearly distressed. James was worried. It was not good for the baby. He said that Luke was a good-hearted fellow, he knew, though he had this obsession about his birth which had made him side with Monmouth; but to rush in like that was rather foolish. What he could not understand was Kirk's going with Luke. He would have thought Kirk would have had the sense to wait a while . . . to see how things went before he rushed in to serve a cause which might be of short duration. And, if it were, that would not have done a great deal of good to those who had supported it.

The King's forces were gathering around Bridgwater. The army was formidable and the great generals had decided to support the King against Monmouth. They knew Monmouth for the reckless man he was. Many of them believed that the law must be obeyed. Monmouth was not the true heir. Many times King Charles had denied that he had married Lucy Walter. If he had, why should he not have admitted it? For then he could have produced his son and heir, which every king and every man of property desired to have.

But no, the King had said it many times. "I was never married to Lucy Walter. Let them bring forth a hundred black boxes, a thousand certificates to prove that I was . . . I will continue to assure you, I was never married to Jemmy's mother."

The country did not want a Catholic King, but the people insisted that the law must be adhered to. Only the true heir could ascend the throne of England.

And so came the terrible tragedy of Sedgemoor. Poor Monmouth! What chance had he and his band, untrained laborers

most of them? How were they to stand against an army trained
and equipped with experienced soldiers, under the command of
men such as Churchill and Frensham? Monmouth himself was
not the bravest of men. He had shown that during his reckless
days, when he had cringed before the King, begging his pardon
when he was suspected of complicity in the Rye House Plot.

Monmouth would quickly see how the battle was going and
he, so the story went, slipped away before the end. That might
have been slander from his enemies, but we did know that he
was found cowering in a ditch, covered in ferns when he was
captured, and that he was taken to London where he begged his
uncle to see him that he might crave his forgiveness.

He found his uncle less lenient than his father had always been.

Monmouth's dreams were over. Fourteen days after he had
arrived in England to claim the throne, he lost his head on Tower
Hill.

We were living in a nightmare. I was filled with dread. The Battle
of Sedgemoor was lost and men who had escaped from the battlefield were wandering around the country, seeking shelter—the
fugitives from the defeated army. They were not to be allowed to
shrug off their misdeeds, their treason, as the victorious side were
calling it. Men could not behave so and then act as though it
were of no moment. The country had to be shown that treasonable
acts were given the treatment they deserved.

Kirk and Luke were in my thoughts all the time. I dreamed
of them. Where were they? If they had escaped, they would come
to us, surely. But where were they?

A whole day and night had passed since the battle and there
was no sign of them. I greatly feared that I should never see them
again. My dear brother, who had had such ambitious dreams . . .
wild dreams that could never come true without a miracle. And
Kirk . . . Kirk. I had not known how much I loved him until
now.

I tried to imagine life without him. I thought of his tender
looks for me, his kindness, his tolerance. Why had he gone into
this wild adventure? I knew why Luke had. I could follow his

way of thinking completely. But Kirk? He was no ardent fanatic, no fervent supporter of the Protestant Faith or hater of Catholics. He believed in freedom of worship for all. But he had believed that England would never support a Catholic King, and that there would be trouble for the country—and that meant for us all—if Catholic James remained on the throne. He was right: James's reign would be an unhappy one. But Monmouth! He was nothing but a boy playing at being a great warrior throughout his entire career, who had shown his weakness.

It was dusk. I went to my room. I sat down and my thoughts were on the battlefield.

Kirk . . . Luke . . . where are you? I was thinking over and over again.

There was a knocking at my door.

It was Amy, wild-eyed and tearful.

"What is it?" I cried.

"Oh, Mistress Kate, he be down below. He's hiding out. Scared out of his wits, he be. Wants to see ye. He's out there by the shrubbery."

"Who? Who?"

"Tom Ricks, Mistress."

I was speeding across the grass to the shrubbery.

"Tom!" I cried.

" 'Tis I, Mistress. I have to see you. I was with him, Mistress. He said to tell you and give this to you . . . if I got away."

He put a ring into my hand. I knew it well. It was gold and Luke had treasured it. He had told me it was the ring our father had given his mother. He had always worn it.

"He was hurt bad, Mistress. In the chest, it was. He couldn't speak much, but he weren't in pain. Well, not much anyway. He knew he was going, and he spoke of you. He wanted me to bring this ring to you if I were able . . . so you'd know it was certain, like."

I heard myself murmuring: "Luke . . . brother Luke. Oh no, not like this!"

" 'Twere so, Mistress. I were right beside him. Might have had it myself. A miracle I didn't. When he gave me the ring, he just closed his eyes. I stayed with him for a bit . . . then I had to go. They say they're looking for us. I've got to hide myself, Mistress."

"Oh, Tom," I said. "Take care."

"Right sure I will, Mistress. They say terrible things will happen to them who fought on Sedgemoor for him that lost."

"Oh, Tom. Get away, then."

"This'll be the first place they'll come looking. There was more than one from these parts as was there. I'm going to my uncle's over Taunton way."

"Oh, Tom. Good luck . . . and thank you."

I watched him disappear in the darkness. I was too shocked and bewildered to do anything but go to my room. Heavy-hearted and desperately afraid, I sat through the night.

In the morning I heard that the supporters of Monmouth who had not been captured on the battlefield were being rounded up. Tom Ricks had been caught on the way to Taunton and was now lying in Bridgwater jail.

Luke was dead. My brother, so full of life one day and then no more. All his dreams of one day being Lord of Rosslyn Manor, gone forever. And all for the ambitions of a King's bastard son! How our lives were governed by the acts of others. But for Monmouth's ambitions, we all would have been congregating in Christobel's sitting room, talking, talking . . .

And Kirk . . . where was Kirk? I greatly feared that he was one of the thousand slaughtered on that fatal battlefield. I would never go near Sedgemoor again. Never, I told myself.

If only I knew! Was it better to know the worst, or go on in suspense, hoping, hoping? And as time passed those hopes became more unlikely of being fulfilled.

There was a gloom on us all. Luke's death had sobered us.

"How I wish we could have news of Kirk," said James. "This is dreadful for Christobel . . . and at such a time."

Sebastian was gentle and tender. He really seemed to care. He was more serious than I had ever seen him before.

My thoughts were for Kirk. I pictured him lying dead on that battlefield . . . perhaps so badly wounded as to be unrecognizable. Where was he? My mind went back to that time when we had hidden him in the Devil's Tower. He had been in acute danger then.

"Oh, God," I prayed. "Let me know where he is."

If he were dead I should never know the details. There were so many dead. It was just by chance that Tom Ricks had happened to be near Luke when he had died. But no one had any news of Kirk.

I wondered after whether my prayers were answered, or was it because Kirk and I were so close that there was some communication of the mind between us. But I could not stop the memories of that other occasion from returning to my mind. It seemed—or so I thought afterwards—that something, some secret force, was urging me to go to the Devil's Tower.

It was two days after the Battle of Sedgemoor that I went.

It was a hot afternoon. There was no wind and stillness was everywhere. I went through the trees and there it was . . . grim, forbidding, haunted.

I felt a certain excitement. I felt that Kirk was close and where could he be but in the Tower? He was a fugitive, as so many were, and where else would he think to hide himself but in the place he knew so well, because he had been there before?

It may sound ridiculous, but I *knew* I was going to find Kirk in this place.

I pushed open the heavy door. I went up the spiral staircase. I made my way to that room which I had visited so often during that other time, when Titus Oates's men were in the neighborhood.

I pushed open the heavy door.

Kirk was standing there, sword drawn, waiting.

"Kate!" he cried.

I heard the sword clatter on the stone floor, and I was in his arms.

"Oh, Kate," he said. "I hoped you'd come."

"It's a miracle. I knew I'd find you here. I knew it, I *knew*."

"I wanted it to be you so much . . . I heard the steps on the stairs, and I was afraid it was someone else."

"Kirk, Kirk. What has happened?"

"You know we lost?"

I nodded.

"We had no chance against them. It was all in vain."

"Tell me, please, quickly. How long have you been here?"

"Since the battle ended."

"That is two days. You're hungry."

"One doesn't notice it so much."

"I shall get some food for you. Oh, Kirk, it's wonderful that you are alive. I feared that you . . . like poor Luke . . ."

I told him about Luke and he was very somber.

"Tom Ricks came to tell me. They have captured him. He is now in jail."

"Poor Tom."

"Kirk, we've got to think. You will have to stay here until it is safe for you to leave. We shall look after you as we did before. I must get food for you quickly."

"Take care, Kate. The King's men will be vengeful."

"Oh, why did you do this?"

"I believe we shall never have a peaceful country under James."

"But it was all fruitless."

"I thought it might not be."

"This is not the time to discuss that. We have to think of what we shall do. Christobel and James will help, and Sebastian. We can trust them. No one else will know. We shall do it just as we did before. It was successful then, and will be so again. Oh, Kirk, Kirk. Thank God you are still alive. Now I will go. I shall ride over to Christobel. I'll get food from her and James. That is safest. I dare say James will come over without her."

I left him then. I went back to the stables and saddled up my horse, then rode over to Featherston. They were amazed to see me, and when they heard that Kirk was alive they were overjoyed. Of course James would take food over right away, then we must all plan very carefully.

"I think," said James, "that he is in as great danger as he ever was with Titus Oates."

He went over to the Devil's Tower immediately, while I stayed with Christobel.

She was very emotional. She loved her brother dearly, and the last days had been deeply unhappy ones for her.

"Oh, Kate," she said. "Why did he do it? It was bad enough for Luke. But Kirk! He is usually so reasonable."

"He thought that England would never be happy with James and a change of Kings was what we needed. I think he is probably right. I remember Father's saying that he had heard King Charles had remarked that James would not hold the crown for more than

four years at most. You see, Kirk had the idea that it was better
to change immediately . . . even for Monmouth."

"He made the wrong judgment, that was all. But he is alive
and we will look after him, won't we, Kate?"

"We will," I said fervently.

I sat with her until James returned. He said that Kirk would
have to stay in the Devil's Tower for a while, until the situation
cleared. They would not go on searching for the Monmouth rebels, as they called them, for long, James was sure. We would keep
Kirk safe until then.

Early next morning, Christobel's son was born.

Who has not heard of cruel Judge Jeffreys and his Bloody Assizes?
They were upon us. He came to Winchester, to Dorchester and
to Taunton, to pass sentence on those who had dared fight against
the King, and left a trail of misery behind him.

When we heard that Tom Ricks had been whipped through
the streets on his way to the hangman's noose we were stricken
with horror. This was a man we had known, a bright, laughter-
loving man who had enjoyed living. That he should come to such
an end filled me with an angry melancholy.

This man, who had been sent to judge what were called the
enemies of the King, was cruel in the extreme: he was also
dishonest, far more of a criminal than those whom he was
judging.

We heard, and we knew it was true for there was proof of his
actions, that it was possible, if one could offer a big enough bribe,
to save a loved one, and the evil judge was growing rich from his
assizes. One of the most shocking stories of his conduct was being
talked of, and from what I had heard of the man already I was
ready to believe it.

A young girl, whose father had been sentenced, went to the
judge and begged for her father's life. She was young and comely,
and the wicked man made a bargain with her that, in return for
her favors, he would spare her father's life. The girl was ready
to submit to anything that would save her beloved parent and
agreed. When she had made her sacrifice, the cruel man appar-

ently thought it rather amusing to lead her to his window, where he showed her her father hanging on a gibbet.

That was Judge Jeffreys, the wicked, notoriously cruel judge, who had been given the task of bringing men to justice.

All over the West Country men were being sent to the scaffold. They hung on gibbets throughout the country at many a cross-roads. The axemen were busy, heads adorned many a bridge and some men were quartered and parts of their bodies displayed in prominent places as a warning to others.

Men and women were given to people in favor at court to be sold into slavery; even more were transported to the plantations.

Sorrowing relatives were everywhere. There was smoldering hatred for Jeffreys and his Bloody Assizes.

And this was the man into whose hands Kirkwell would fall if he were captured.

Christobel, James and I were determined to do everything in our power to prevent that. Sebastian, too, no less. He was more serious than I had ever known him.

My father returned to Rosslyn Manor.

He talked to me about the situation.

"Monmouth was a fool," he said. "He had too big an idea of his importance. He could never see things as they were, but only as he wanted them to be. None knew that better than the King, his father. It may be that that was why he set himself firmly against making him his heir."

"But he was not the heir."

"Indeed no. I'm convinced there was no marriage between the King and Lucy Walter. There was no need. Lucy was free enough with her favors. But Charles might have found the way if he had thought the boy would have made a good King. Charles was a great manipulator, under all that charm of manner and outward easygoing tolerance. That was why, in spite of the life he led, he was a good King. And now . . . this trouble. Luke killed." A spasm crossed his face, and I had a glimpse of his true feelings. Luke was his son and I thought then that he would have been delighted if it had been possible to acknowledge him as his heir.

Poor Luke, who had chosen an impossible dream and in a way it had led him to his death, for I feared his allegiance to Monmouth was partly because they were both in a similar situation.

My father said: "The past is done. We have the future to think of. You are eighteen now, Kate. Is it not time that you considered marriage?"

"Marriage with . . . ?"

"Sebastian, of course. Oh come, my dear, we have to be practical. You had this romantic feeling for Kirkwell Carew. He has gone . . . depend upon it. He died on Sedgemoor. That might be lucky for him. I would not care to think of what would happen to him if he fell into the hands of Jeffreys."

I shivered and for a few moments could not hide the horror which came over me.

My father was watching me closely, and he said: "Poor misguided young fellow. The young do foolish things sometimes. Kate, I want you to be wise. I should be very happy if you told me that you and Sebastian were to be married."

"No . . . no . . . I could not."

"Listen, Kate. You like him. He is one of the pleasantest fellows in the world. He'd make you happy, I know he would. He has all the qualities it takes to make a good husband. I know you have this romantic feeling for Kirkwell Carew . . . but you'll forget all that. You cannot go on mourning the dead forever. You have to try and forget him . . . and Luke. It was a pity they acted so recklessly, but it is done. You can't stop living because of such sorrows. Say that you will accept Sebastian. Let us forget the miseries this rebellion has brought about. Let us try to make a little happiness."

"No," I said. "No."

"But why? You like Sebastian. Kirkwell is gone . . ."

"No," I said. "No!"

He fell silent.

He said after a while: "In time you will see that it is best."

It was my turn to take food to Kirkwell. This always came from Christobel's kitchen. To have taken it from Rosslyn Manor might have attracted attention and aroused suspicion. We knew we had to be very careful indeed.

Christobel had taken some time to recover from the birth of her child. The shock of Luke's death, and the anxieties we had suffered over Kirkwell had had some effect on her. James had been very worried, but now Christobel was much better and her delight in her son had done a great deal to help her recovery.

The child—they had called him Luke after my brother—was a delight to us all. We marveled at him on every occasion and Christobel could not resist the temptation to show him off and boast of his beauty and the marvelous signs of intelligence he was already displaying.

I always chose the mid-afternoon to go to Kirkwell. It was the time when the household was quiet and in any case no one ventured near the Devil's Tower at that time; but there was the possibility that someone might notice that one of us was in a certain spot at the same time every afternoon.

James had said that it was necessary to take the utmost care always.

I had seen Kirk and spent about half an hour with him. I told him the news I had gleaned. The assizes were still going on and were now in Taunton. There was grumbling everywhere about the inhuman actions of the cruel judge, but none had the courage—or the foolhardiness—to speak openly against him.

As I made my way back to Rosslyn Manor I met my father.

"You have been taking a walk?"

"Yes. It is a pleasant afternoon."

He looked over his shoulder.

"I see," he said thoughtfully.

We walked towards the house in silence for a few moments, then he said: "Have you thought any more about Sebastian?"

"No," I said.

"Was it because of Kirkwell Carew that you hesitated?"

He was looking at me steadily. I thought of Kirkwell in the Devil's Tower, his life in such danger. In the last days I had learned something. It was that I thought I should never be happy again if I lost him. I felt deeply the loss of my brother. I would say to myself, Luke would say that . . . and then I would realize that he would never be there again. To lose one who has been close to you haunts you forever. It was not so long ago that I had learned

I had a brother, but our very relationship had brought us close. I knew I should go on mourning Luke for a long time. But Kirkwell . . . that would be for the rest of my life.

I realized that I had not answered and that my father was looking at me intently.

We went into the house and still I had not answered.

I reached my room, sat down and stared ahead of me. Then it struck me suddenly.

I thought: he saw me coming from the Devil's Tower. He knows, I thought. He remembers that last time. If Kirk had escaped, where would he come? To me . . . to his sister. It had happened before.

He thinks that, if it were not for Kirkwell, I would marry Sebastian. His plan would succeed.

It suddenly occurred to me that Kirkwell was not only in danger from the King's men, but from my father.

My great fear was realized. The King's men were here. They had been to Featherston Manor but were searching the area.

They were in the great hall. I was frantic with anxiety. I went downstairs. I leaned over the banister and saw them with my father.

I heard them say: "We have reason to believe that he escaped alive after the battle. If he did, it is likely that he would come to this part which he knew so well."

My father saw me. He called: "Kate. These gentlemen are here searching for one of the rebels."

I went into the hall. My father was looking at me. He must have seen the abject fear in my face and he knew that I was aware where Kirkwell was hiding and there could only be the one place where that was.

"They are looking round the neighborhood and, of course, will look at the estate. I shall conduct them round myself."

The men greeted me with respect as Lord Rosslyn's daughter.

"Go to your room, Kate," he said. "I will see you when this is over."

I gave him an appealing glance, but he did not seem to notice it.

I went up to my room. I shut the door and sat, staring blankly at the window.

It was over. Any moment now, my father would betray him. They would take him away to face such horror that I could scarcely bear to contemplate it. I would lose Kirkwell as I had lost Luke . . . I just could not bear to think of it.

I was convinced that my father knew Kirkwell was in the Devil's Tower. At any moment now my father would take them to the Devil's Tower and they would find him. And my father would say that he was a fool, as Luke had been foolish. Men have to learn that, if they do foolish things, they must pay for them.

Sebastian would not act foolishly. He was the husband my father wanted for me and he believed that, if Kirkwell was removed from the scene, there would be no more hindrance to prevent my marrying Sebastian.

I think I had never in all my life endured such anguish as I did during that hour. I knew then how much Kirkwell's loss would mean to me, and I thought of the cruel and humiliating death which would be inflicted on him. I knew I should never be happy again and I would blame myself for my carelessness in being the one who had betrayed him.

For my father knew. Something in my manner had told him that Kirkwell was here, and where should he be but in the Devil's Tower?

I loved Kirkwell. I should have married him when he asked me. If I had been his wife, I should never have allowed him to leave me and go into battle. He would have listened to me. I should have made him do so.

I did not know how long it was before I heard the sound of voices below. I ran to the window and saw my father coming towards the house with the King's men.

Kirkwell was not with them.

I saw the men leave, and I dashed down to meet my father.

He looked at me with a rather sardonic smile.

"Well?" he said.

I stared at him.

"They did not find him."

Relief flooded over me. It was obvious, of course.

"He is still safe . . . temporarily . . . in the Devil's Tower."

"You knew?"

He nodded. "And you knew I knew. You thought I would betray him, did you not?"

I was silent.

"It would have been a solution."

"What are you going to do now?"

"He can't stay there. That's clear. It is not safe. Not completely so."

"But . . ."

"Titus Oates and his minions were not so dangerous. These men are going to get Kirkwell Carew if they can."

"You did not tell them?"

"Well, perhaps it was foolish of me. It would have settled matters, would it not?"

"Then why . . . ?"

He thought for a moment. "Weak, wasn't it? I thought, if I told them he was there, you would never forgive me."

Again he was smiling that sardonic smile.

"That was one reason. The main one. The other . . . well, he's not a bad young fellow, and Jeffreys is a devil."

I was crying weakly. I think it was happiness, if one could possibly be happy with so much danger all around. But he had done this for me although it did not help his plans. I suddenly felt that he was my father indeed.

I moved towards him and he put his arms round me.

I clung to him.

I said: "You love me . . . and I will always love you."

I think I babbled something else. He himself was a little incoherent.

Then he put me from him and said in a cool voice: "Now listen. We must be practical. He can't stay there. Those men are determined to find him. They are tired of country yokels. They want some of more standing. Those are the ones Jeffreys enjoys tormenting most. They may be coming back here. I kept them off the Devil's Tower. Knowing the land as well as I do, I could keep them away from it. I might not be so fortunate again. They might question people and hear something of the Tower. Their suspicions would be aroused and they would wonder why I did not show it to them. So, you see, I have myself to think of. We must act quickly."

"You mean you will help us?"

"And myself. Am I not involved now? We'll get him away. He will have to leave the country. I can get him to France. He shall go tonight."

"You mean you will do this . . . ?"

"It is necessary, daughter. I must do it for you . . . for him . . . and for myself."

I went to the Devil's Tower. Kirkwell rushed to me and embraced me, as he always did.

He had no idea then of the great danger he had been in.

"Kirkwell," I said, "I have to talk to you. This is very important. The King's men are looking for you. They have been here today. My father knows you are here. He has held them off. But he says that you are not safe here any longer and you must leave. He is arranging it. He is going to get you to France, where you will have to stay until it is safe for you to return to England."

Kirkwell was staring at me.

"Your father . . . But he would be on the side of the King."

"We have to forget all that, Kirkwell. You are his neighbor, whom he has known all your life. How could he let you fall into the hands of that cruel judge? He is right, Kirkwell. You must get out. He says these men may come back, and if they found you, on my father's land, he too would be in danger."

"He's right," said Kirkwell. "I must go."

"He is arranging it all. You will get to the coast, where he will have a boat waiting to take you to France. Oh, Kirk, it is terrible that you must go away, but it is for the best. It is the only thing that can be done."

He put his arms about me, and held me close to him.

"Not to see you, Kate. Though every time you come I am afraid for you. But not to see you . . ."

"You will be safe. It will be settled in time. You will be back. This terror cannot go on."

"I will be marked, though, as the King's enemy."

"That will surely be forgotten."

"You say they have come here, looking for me?"

"That was what my father said."

"It is noble of him to help . . . But of course there may be some risk to him if it were known that I was given shelter on his land."

"Kirk, you have to go. It is the only way."

"And leave you . . ."

I nodded. "It will not be long, I am sure."

"And when I come back?"

"I shall be waiting for you."

"And those doubts?"

"They are not there any more."

"So, it has taken this?"

"Yes, it has. Oh, I was foolish. I don't think I had grown up. Perhaps it takes a tragedy like this to make us understand ourselves. I have lost Luke. I know what it means now to have someone you love taken from you. If I lost you too, well, Kirk, I believe I should never be happy again."

"So," he said sadly, "there is something good in this. And now I am hearing it when I have to leave you."

"Let us look to the future," I said.

"Because the present is too sad to contemplate."

"Kirk, Kirk," I said. "You are coming back. Then we are going to be married. We shall be happy then, I know it, Kirk."

"You do mean this? You do believe it?"

"I must. I could never be happy if it were not so."

For a few moments we were silent and I knew that he was pushing aside everything that stood in our way—just as I was. We were letting our dream of future happiness envelop us and were forcing ourselves to believe in it. It was the only way to help us through the days ahead.

That night, as soon as darkness descended, my father, with Kirk and James, rode to the coast.

I waited for their return, which was not until the next morning. My father told me then that all had gone according to plan. Kirkwell had got away safely to France.

My father had given him letters to friends of his and what he would need until he could fend for himself.

He would be safe there until the Monmouth rebellion was forgotten and therefore his part in it would be of no more interest.

Two days later the King's men came to the house again. They then searched the grounds and discovered the Devil's Tower, but it was of no significance. Kirkwell was safe across the sea.

The Return

THE WEEKS PASSED into months. Winter came, and then it was summer. All that time I hoped for news of Kirkwell, but none came.

I was with Christobel almost every day. Frequently we talked of Kirkwell and he was always in our thoughts.

Life was uneasy in England, as Kirkwell had known it would be under Catholic James, who was showing clearly now his determination to take the country back to Rome, while the majority of the people were determined not to go.

Christobel's baby was the main source of delight to us all at that time. Christobel could not be entirely unhappy, however anxious she was about her brother, while she had her little son. And, of course, James was excessively proud of the boy.

Life at Rosslyn Manor had changed a good deal. My father was closer to me than he had ever been before, but he still persisted in his eagerness for me to marry Sebastian and so bring about the complete fulfillment of his plans.

I could never forget that it was his actions which had saved Kirkwell's life and that he had done that for me, although, if he had done nothing, no one could have blamed him. If he had not acted as he had, for me, and Kirkwell had fallen into the hands of the King's men, death would surely have been his fate, and in those circumstances I should surely be more likely to turn to Sebastian.

Sometimes I wondered if my father regretted his rash actions, for he was growing impatient.

"It is very probable that you will never see Kirkwell Carew again," he said. "It would be unsafe for him to return. Trouble could break out at any time, and then you would see prompt action taken against those who have shown themselves to be the King's enemies."

I knew that he was right, but this separation from Kirkwell was heartbreaking. I could have borne it better if I had known what was happening to him.

I wondered if he would try to get a message through to me.

"He would be rash to try that," my father pointed out. "If the letter went astray and passed into certain hands, you would be marked as the friend of a traitor."

"He was no traitor."

"Not to his country, perhaps, but he would be considered so to James. No, he would never involve you, for that is what it could mean."

Lady Rosslyn's attitude towards me had changed since Luke had saved her life during the fire.

Messages from her came to me by way of Margaret Galloway. I was invited to visit Lady Rosslyn, which I did quite often and we were becoming good friends. Although her voice had not fully returned and speaking was very difficult for her, she could hear well enough and understood perfectly, and we devised a means of communication by signs from her hands, which had not been impaired since her seizure.

I used to tell her about London life and the theater, which seemed to interest her.

Two years passed in this way. It was odd, for the days seemed endless, one very much like another, and the time seemed to slip by.

The King was having trouble with the bishops. There was talk of William of Orange having his eye on the throne. He was married to James's daughter Mary, who was heir to the throne until James had a son; and William was also in line to the throne, his mother having been the eldest daughter of Charles I. Intrigue was rife and my father told me that many powerful men were making their way to The Hague and were showing quite clearly their support for William, because they realized that there would never be harmony in the country while James was on the throne.

Francine still flitted in and out of my life. I thought of her as a will-o'-the-wisp. I would not see her for weeks and then suddenly she would seek me out. She would be waiting for me outside the stables or without warning she would come to my room. It was as though she suddenly remembered me and wanted to talk.

She said one day: "Lady Rosslyn likes you now. She used to hate you. And then your brother saved her from the fire and she couldn't hate him any more and, as you were his sister, she couldn't hate you either. She was lying in her bed and the curtains round it were all on fire. Fire runs up the curtain like a little animal and then suddenly it's all red and blue and it makes a crackling noise, as though it's laughing at you because you can't put it out."

She laughed, and I said: "It is not very funny. It would have been terrible if my brother had not been there in time to save her."

"But he was, and he picked her up and walked through the fire with her. It was a beautiful fire. If they hadn't stopped it it would have burned up the house, all of it."

"Let us be thankful that they did stop it," I said. "You've talked of fires before, as though you have a fancy for them."

She looked at me slyly and laughed. Then she was serious.

"They're beautiful. They're red and blue and you can see pictures in them. Your brother walked through it. I wish I'd seen him do that. It was brave of him . . . walking through the fire carrying Lady Rosslyn. She would have been dead if he hadn't. The fire would have eaten her all up. It does. I don't like her, so . . ."

"So what?" I said.

"So nothing," she said, and, laughing, ran off.

I thought again, as I had done so many times, that she had an unhealthy interest in fires.

And when the tragedy happened I told myself I should have seen it coming, and it should have held no surprise for me.

It happened so suddenly, when I was in the library one day. The library was a large room with its long narrow windows and its high vaulted ceiling similar to most of the big rooms in the house. At the windows hung long red velvet drapes. I was sitting there, browsing through a book and thinking, as I so often did, of Kirk, wondering where he was and whether he was thinking of me, when I was suddenly aware of the door being cautiously pushed open. I turned in astonishment and saw Francine.

She was creeping stealthily into the room and to my horror in her hands she clutched a lighted taper.

I stared at her in astonished silence, and yet, in an instant I knew what she was about to do . . . and that she had done the same thing before.

She tiptoed towards the curtains, holding the taper carefully, a beatific smile illuminating her features. It was as though she were about to perform some rite.

I stood up and the book which was on my lap crashed to the floor.

I cried: "Francine! Stop!"

She turned and, as she did so, the taper touched against her dress. I saw the flame catch it and run from the waist to the hem and then all over the top of her skirt.

I shouted something and ran to her, but by this time she was a mass of flames.

Panic seized me and I felt helpless.

I picked up one of the small rugs lying on the floor and tried to wrap it about her. It extinguished some of the flames but was not enough. I tried to beat them out. It seemed minutes before I succeeded. She was lying on the floor. Her hair was almost entirely burned away. I stood for a few seconds, staring at that poor burned figure which had been Francine.

Then I ran out of the room, calling for help.

Francine lived for only two days. It was merciful really, for she was so badly burned as to be almost unrecognizable, and life as she had become would have been intolerable.

She never spoke again and I was not sure whether she knew what had happened to her. That which had so fascinated her and with which she had so daringly played, had killed her.

Poor Margaret Galloway was shattered. She was blaming herself. She was in a dazed state of acute misery and every now and then I would see the tears falling down her cheeks.

Once she talked to me. She said: "You see, I knew. She had done it before."

I said: "In Lady Rosslyn's bedroom?"

She nodded. "I should have done something. I just did not know what. They would have sent her away. Where to? Who would have looked after her? They would never have let her stay here. There was nowhere for her to go. Fire . . . it fascinated her. Right from a baby. And there she was . . . no mother, no father. I was the only one. I had to keep her here. So . . ."

"You cannot be blamed for doing what you thought was best."

"She would have killed Lady Rosslyn . . . and then she killed herself."

I tried to comfort her, but she would not be comforted. Poor Margaret, frightened, relying on the favors of her cousin. But I believed Lady Rosslyn was genuinely fond of her; and it was true that she had softened considerably since she had come so close to death before being saved by the bravery of Luke. I think that had had a marked effect on her.

I could not believe that three years had passed since Kirkwell went away. I was no longer a young girl. I was twenty-one years old.

On my twenty-first birthday my father had said to me: "You cannot wait forever. Sebastian is impatient, and so am I."

"This is my life," I said. "I must live it my way."

"I want what is good for you. While King James is on the throne Kirkwell cannot return."

"I think he will."

"If he came back, he would live in perpetual uncertainty. He knows that, and it is something he would never allow you to share. Every rising, every sign of trouble and he would be a suspect."

"I think he might brave that."

"He might. But would he subject you to it? As his wife you would be suspect too. He knows that. If he loves you he will not subject you to that. But, depend upon it, he will not return, and the time is passing."

"I shall wait for him. I have promised."

"You will change your mind. You could be happy, you know. Sebastian will be the best of husbands. You are living in a romantic dream. Come out of it and face reality. And anyway, what is happening to Featherston now? It will revert to what it was before Kirkwell took it in hand. There is a manager, but that is not the same. Look at James Morton and Christobel, with their little Luke, and expecting another. Perfectly content. There is nothing so satisfying as family life."

It was something he had never experienced. He wanted to enjoy it vicariously through me. I felt very tender towards him at times. He desperately wanted this. He wanted those grandchildren, and that would compensate him for those sons and daughters of his own whom he had never seen playing in the grounds of Rosslyn Manor.

I wished I could please him. I was often in Sebastian's company. He did not speak to me of marriage. He was too tactful. I think he understood me better than my father did. I had a feeling that he would ask me if the moment ever came when I gave up hope of seeing Kirkwell again and chose to take the way my father had chosen for me. But it was not yet.

Nevertheless, I was getting more and more fond of Sebastian. I recognized the kindliness and understanding behind that non-chalant exterior of his. I could enjoy a peaceful, serene life with his calm acceptance of whatever life brought him.

Meanwhile the rumblings of discontent went on throughout the nation.

The King was in conflict with seven of the leading bishops and, to the horror of many of his subjects, they were imprisoned in the Tower.

When they were released there was rejoicing in the streets, which was an indication of James's growing unpopularity with the people, and it should have been a warning to him that the people were getting restive. More and more influential and am-bitious men were slipping out of England and arriving in Holland. When the Queen bore a son, there was some misgiving in high places. If this son lived, then there would be a Catholic heir.

There were rumors about the child. It was said that there had been something suspicious about his birth. He was not the King's son. They had tricked the nation. The King's wife had given birth to a stillborn child and a healthy one had been substituted in a warming pan. All over the country people were talking of the Warming-Pan Baby.

Rumors said that the shipyards of Holland were working at full strength, and William of Orange was one of the foremost Protestants in Europe. His wife was James's daughter, next in line to the throne, if one did not count this newborn child, the Warming-Pan Baby.

After some months of speculation, when it came it seemed inevitable.

On the fifteenth of November, just over three years since Kirkwell had left England, William of Orange landed at Brixham near Torbay. There was no opposition. Weary of the ineffectual rule of James, and his determination to ignore the will of the people, many were deserting him. The defection of Churchill, with the army, was the fatal blow.

There was little resistance. The inevitable had happened, and, as King Charles had prophesied, his brother James's rule had not lasted four years.

My hopes were high. My father said: "Mayhap he has made a new life over there."

There was a certain wistful look on his face. He did not want me to be unhappy, but he longed to see me married to Sebastian.

It was mid-November. I was in my room thinking: Will he come? Is it possible that he has indeed made a new life over there? Shall I ever see him again?

Then I heard Amy's voice calling me.

I ran down.

He was there beside her.

He looked older, rather gaunt. He had changed, but he was still Kirkwell.

He looked at me and he smiled.

Then he said: "Kate . . . you waited."

I was in his arms, touching his face to assure myself that he was real. I was exulting, overcome with emotion.

Then I said simply: "Yes, Kirk. I waited."